"N   ONE."

THE BEAUTY

An exquisite American heiress, Louise Vandermeer is beautiful, brilliant . . . and bored—which is why she has agreed to a daring adventure: to travel across the ocean to marry an aristocrat abroad. Rumor has it her intended is hideous—a grim prospect that propels her into a passionate, reckless relationship with a compelling stranger she never sees in the light of day.

THE BEAST

Though scarred by a childhood illness, Charles d'Harcourt has successfully wooed Europe's most sophisticated beauties. For a lark, he contrived to travel incognito on his own fiancée's ship—and seduce the young chit in utter darkness. But the rake's prank backfired. It was he who was smitten—while the hot-tempered Lulu, now his wife, loves only her shipboard lover, unaware it was d'Harcourt all the time! And Charles will never have her heart—unless he can open her eyes to the prince who hides within.

JUDITH IVORY

BEAST

An Avon Romantic Treasure

AVON BOOKS ◆ NEW YORK

AVON BOOKS
A division of
The Hearst Corporation
1350 Avenue of the Americas
New York, New York 10019

Copyright © 1997 by Judy Cuevas
Inside cover author photo by Bobi Dimond
Published by arrangement with the author
Visit our website at **http://AvonBooks.com**
Library of Congress Catalog Card Number: 96-94952
ISBN: 0-380-78644-3

First Avon Books Printing: April 1997

AVON TRADEMARK REG. U.S. PAT. OFF. AND IN OTHER COUNTRIES, MARCA REGISTRADA, HECHO EN U.S.A.

Printed in the U.S.A.

RA   10 9 8 7 6 5 4 3 2

Acknowledgments

My thanks to Holly, Richard, and Helen of Keeble Travel for books, videos, whole trip itineraries, and especially this time around for getting me on the *QE2* for an explore (with additional gratitude to Cunard). *Gros bisous* and fat thank-yous to Lisa Middag, who encouraged this story in its earliest stages and invited me to Nice in the first place. Cyber-thanks and <G>s to writer Michele Albert for her help in the later phases. And a giant hug to author and friend Barbara Parker for numerous discussions on this book as well as all my others.

I also would like to acknowledge people who were instrumental in previous work, who have been sorely neglected up to this point. They include: Dr. Carole Abbott, who has been willing to put many the character "on the couch" to help figure him or her out; friend and wise adult Ken Goode for arguments and insights into human motives, especially on *Dance;* sculptor Barbara Price for leading me into her knowledge and love of sculpture, a shared interest that became the book *Bliss;* sculptor Michael Flick for the details of repairing gesso. Also my heartfelt thanks to Harry Kramp for always being ready to consult on matters of science and how things work; to Jean Kramp for unflagging and very vocal belief in me—no matter how much I get wrong, she always sees the right. Gary, Mary, Chris, and Angela, thank you. I love you all dearly, everyone.

Last though far from least, a deep bow of appreciation to my agent, Steve Axelrod, and my editor, Carrie Feron, both of whom provide the miracle of enormous freedom combined with rock-solid support. Thank you both.

Come, my languid, sullen beast,
Come lie upon my heart . . .

Charles Baudelaire
33 of Les Fleurs du Mal
DuJauc translation
Pease Press, London, 1889

Part 1

The Joke

Your body bends and sways
Like a slender ship that plunges the waves,
Rolling from side to side till
The spray has soaked its spars in seawater

Like a flood swollen from
the melt of gnashing glaciers,
When the waters of your mouth
Rise to the edges of your teeth,

I taste a wanton wine,
My briny undoing
That liquefies the sky and
Stews my heart with stars!

Charles Baudelaire
29 of Les Fleurs du Mal
DuJauc translation
Pease Press, London, 1889

Chapter 1

"**Y**ou beast! Rotter, scum, swine!"
Charles Harcourt slid his pillow out
from under his head, using it to fend off slaps of open
palms, a thrashing of naked arms. When the blows
didn't stop, he rolled away through the dark, across
the bed and out of reach. "I was going to tell you," he
said as he swung his bare legs over the edge of the
mattress.

"When? As you handed me the wedding invitation?" Pia took up her litany again. "Cow's hide,
tripehead . . ."

Over this, the ship's engine—a compound steam
engine of a steel twin-screw Atlantic liner—droned
suddenly louder. Charles had to wait before he could
tell her, "You're making too much of this."

"There's a wedding party on board, and it turns out
you're the groom? And I'm not supposed to be
upset?"

He tried to stand, got partway to his feet, saying,
"Upset, yes. Hysterical, no—" The engine's reverber-
ation drowned him out. The dark room tipped and
lifted, a gyration that sat him suddenly back on the
edge of the bed.

Over the past hour, the noise of the ship's engine
had ebbed and flowed like this, giving audible rhythm
to the liner's lunge and dive over the water. The ship,

3

the *Concordia* out of New York, and its eleven hundred passengers were riding the high seas of an approaching storm.

"Sweet Mary," exclaimed Pia as the ship righted itself with a majestic roll—she complained about the roughness of the ocean, Charles thought. Then something hit him across the back of his shoulders—the neck pillow that had been under her belly just a moment ago, for he could feel the imprint of its lisle crochet.

"Stop it," he said, twisting his head and shoulders around.

He tried to find her across the bed, but the room, the bedchamber of his stateroom suite, was lit only by the glow of the ship's running lights peeking in and out of swaying curtains. He perceived her as an effluvium, a little miasma of rose geranium vapor (not his favorite perfume, but rather Roland's, her husband's) drifting along the far edge of the bed. He couldn't detect any more of her than this.

Charles grimaced. Locating his clothes, he thought, would be an easier matter to deal with.

He stood, successfully this time, the vibration of the ship's engine rumbling into his legs. Then a very different sensation: Something cold and wet flopped against the inside of his thigh. A sheath, still half on. His *capote anglaise,* his English hat. With an annoyed tug, he plucked it off. He hated wearing such devices, but Roland was as promiscuous as a tomcat. Charles was afraid of getting some dread disease. Thus, he put the bonnet up on his carriage, so to speak, whenever out with Pia for a pleasure ride.

Out the side of his eye, he caught a glimpse of movement, a flash of Pia's milk-white skin as she disappeared again up under the shadow of the bed's canopy. A faint clatter alerted him. Charles threw his arms and hands up just in time to deflect a barrage of hard, sharp-edged objects: his cuff links, studs, her jeweled hair combs, his passport, notecase, whatever else she was able to gather off the nightstand. He tried to catch the last, a flash of metal—his own pocket watch as it turned out—which he missed completely. (Even in broad daylight, he had absolutely no depth perception.) When he heard her scraping something more off the bedside table, he launched himself across the bed through the debris toward the cloud of galling perfume, where, in her dark corner, his hand found an ankle. Grabbing her foot, he yanked Pia toward him.

She weighed hardly anything. Pia Montebello was all of five feet tall—though the most voluptuous, curvaceous five feet of woman any man could ever hope to lay hands on. Charles took her into his arms, an easy matter for a man well over six feet and over two hundred solid-muscled pounds.

She squirmed and reverted to her native language, Italian, for what became a scatological catalog of name-calling: *"Traditore di merda, merdoso, merdonaccio, merda di madonna . . ."* Treacherous *merda*, reeking *merda*, prodigious *merda*, *merda* of the sainted mother. She kicked pillows, churned satin covers as he tried to open her hand; there was another would-be projectile clenched in it.

He tried to reason with her. "I was *going* to tell you," he explained, "in Nice, under better circumstances."

"Pile of stinking, steaming . . ." she continued in Italian.

"I only decided a week ago. And I certainly didn't expect the whole clan to get on the next ship over. They think I went back to France last month."

The problem specifically was this: Tonight at dinner, at a private table not far from Pia, there had been some heavy celebrating by a group murmured to be the Vandermeer portion of "the Harcourt/Vandermeer wedding party." Only after Pia had been making love with Charles for the better part of the evening and into the night did she mention this "amusing coincidence of names," never allowing for a moment that it was no coincidence: that it was the very Harcourt on top of her who had contracted himself, name, titles, properties, and money, just the week before to the Vandermeers in marriage.

Even as Charles had admitted to this fact, Pia had thought he was joking for a full minute: so sure she was of him.

Holding her in the quasi-straitjacket of his embrace now, he pried her fist open, finger at a time, releasing her own small but impressive choker of diamonds and black jade—the likes of which *he* was not allowed to give her.

"*You're* married," he complained.

"And my being married has done nothing but complicate our lives!"

"So get unmarried."

She made a sniff and tried to push away from him. "I knew you'd say that! You know I can't." She sketched again all the reasons she listed every time this subject came up. "My children . . . the scandal . . . the money . . . Roland's position. I have a family, you know."

"And I would *like* one." He tossed the necklace somewhere into the sheets and let her wiggle free.

She hopped off the bed, a petite, shapely silhouette against the light through the moving curtains. "You're just being spiteful," she said as she bent and picked up what looked to be her corset.

"I'm being practical. I'm not getting any younger—"

"Oh, Charles, you could marry anyone any time—in your dotage, if you chose to." She faced him and laid it on thick. "You're charming, clever, extraordinarily well-liked." The coup de grâce: "And in your sinister, grim way, you know, you're quite the dashing figure."

He made a wry face in the dark, yet this wry face warmed slightly. He hated that he was vulnerable to such flattery: for Charles was both sensitive and vain of his appearance. Though tall and well-built, he had a few drawbacks. For instance, he was blind in one eye. This eye bore a scar. He also had a limp that came and went, depending on the whims of arthritis that had settled into an old knee injury.

Pia, however, ruined the advantage her flattery had won her. "And besides, you're as rich as a czar and wear an absurdly impressive title. These don't hurt your appeal, *bello.*"

Charles made a snort and stood up.

He had never associated with any but monied women so as not to be overly prized for his wealth. As to his title, it was nothing more than an appendage to his name, a legal cipher by French code allowed for the sake of distinguishing him from all the other Harcourts—his siblings, cousins, nephews, aunts, and uncles. He said, "Is that your corset? I'll help you put it on, but don't leave, not angry."

Pia paid no attention, concluding, "So you see, you don't need to marry."

He expelled a quick breath. "Nonetheless, I intend to. Grim, hard, blind, whatever, if I can't marry you, then I shall marry the girl whose papa owns this ship."

"This ship?" she repeated. "What are you talking about? Why ever would you want this ship?"

"Not this ship. Ambergris. Vandermeer owns all sorts of ships. He has a whaling fleet large enough that it is always gathering in a certain amount of ambergris."

"Ambergris," her voice said blankly.

"It is a key and very, very expensive ingredient of certain perfumes."

"A-ah," she said, then made a little click of her tongue, a *tsk.*

Charles owned controlling interest in a consortium that manufactured luxury goods. Italian leathers, champagne, and—his own special interest—perfumes made from flowers grown in his own fields in Provence.

"So that's what this is all about?" Pia asked irritably. "Money and your damn toilette water."

Well, more than just toilette water; and the blending of perfumes meant more to Charles than money. But, yes, Vandermeer had offered to double his whaling fleet, then give over *all* its collection of ambergris to Charles as part of the marriage agreement, a stupefyingly generous—and enormously useful—arrangement. If Charles couldn't marry for love, he damn well could marry for *something* that mattered to him.

It was God's truth, though, when Charles said, "No, Pia, this is about my not being able to see you unless Roland is out of town or seasick. This is about my not being able to make love to you without a condom, of your smelling of his bourgeois tastes in perfume. This is about my not being able to give you or buy you anything he might notice, about my not being able to have dinner with you when I'd like or to ask you to go anywhere or do anything on the spur of the moment. This is about lying in bed at night, churning over the fact that your stinking, whoring husband is not only allowed to touch you whenever he wants, he may one day bring you a disease that will kill you. Roland is the swine, Pia. He's vile—"

"You are so jealous—"

"Yes, and I am so jealous that the vision in my *good* eye dims at just the thought of his having more right to you than I do."

There was a kind of tender pause before Pia said, "Oh, Charles, this should certainly tell you that you mustn't, *mustn't* marry."

"By God, it tells me I'd better if I'm to have any kind of life."

She drew in a long, broken breath in the dark. "You are being so selfish—" Her breath caught, a sob. He heard her catch back a few more as she tossed her corset at him, its tangle of laces snapping and bouncing against his bare arm as the thing fell into the shadows.

She padded off, a barefoot march from the bedroom into the sitting room punctuated by sniffles and wet catches of breath.

He trailed after her. *"Chérie,"* he offered, holding out his upturned palms. "It is not that I want to leave you. I want to balance my life with yours, try to make myself more content with what we have together."

The sitting room was darker still, the overhang of its private terrace blocking light. Charles might have put on the electric lamp, but the wall-to-wall curtains were open. He and Pia would have made a fine picture, standing there naked, arguing.

Into the darkness, he said, "You are hurt and angry out of proportion. I am simply getting married because I have at last accepted that you are not getting a divorce."

"I can't."

"Fine."

"No, it's *not* fine to you."

"No, it's not. But there is nothing I can do about it."

"So you do th-this." She punctuated her words with a soggy, hiccuping sound that made Charles feel like the miserable, selfish wretch she said he was. She let out another half-sob. "You pressure me to do what is so—s-so b-bad for me."

He followed the sound of her voice, trying to pinpoint her by her rose–geranium scent as she seemed to move toward a pitch-dark corner by the door. "No, Pia, I'm not . . ."

He found her flesh, a round shoulder, just as the ship did one of its slow, inexorable tilts. He would never know if what happened from here was on purpose or if she merely grabbed for the door handles for balance. In any regard, the double doors unlatched, keening out a loud creak as they swung widely into the room with the ship's angled ascent. The corridor's yellow light washed up the length of Charles, from bare feet to naked genitals to broad, hair-swirled chest. He grabbed for something, anything, to hold on to—missing the nearer door edge by inches through lack of spatial perception—so that when Pia jerked back from him, he was left balanced for one weightless, precarious moment, then the ship dove. His center of gravity shifted, and Charles was thrown forward, out into the hall, catching himself on the far wall.

Behind him, the doors likewise obeyed the pull of the earth. They eeked in reverse, to slam shut at his back.

At this point, Pia most certainly could have reopened them and let him in again. But, instead, he heard the privacy bolt click in place, the little window reading the verdict in three languages—DO NOT DISTURB. VEUILLEZ NE PAS DÉRANGER. PER FAVORE NON DISTURBARE.

It took him a moment to admit what had happened: The love of his life, through plan or opportunity, had locked him out his own room at well past midnight, without his wearing a scrap of clothing—not so much as a prophylactic. He arched, pivoting around, flinging his arms up to attack the doors, to break them down if he had to. Childish, idiot woman. Then he jerked his whole body to a stop just short of a good thumping on the carved panels. There were three other *cabines de grand luxe* on this deck, the inhabitants of each presently asleep. Suppose his noise woke them, and they popped their heads out into the hall to see what the commotion was about?

And there was the Prince d'Harcourt standing out in the corridor in his all-together, not a stitch on, locked out of his own stateroom by—you'll never guess—the wife of the chief American diplomat to France, whom apparently he had been . . .

Good God, everyone thought he was in France planning a wedding, a misconception he very much needed in order to appear wholesome and trustworthy in the eyes of his future in-laws, not to mention to protect him from the chief American diplomat, who had become downright suspicious of his wife and her "French friend." No, contemplating the possibly touchy outcomes made Charles come up with a much better plan. At the end of the corridor was a short companionway down to the first-class promenade deck. There, among the line of wicker deck chairs, he would find a blanket, then settle back under a chair's hood, where, comfortable and safely hidden, he would wait for Pia to dress and clear out of his rooms.

Chapter 2

And ambergris, this rare and beguiling substance, did Sinbad carry onto his ship, making room for it among the ivory, gold, diamonds, sandalwood, camphor, clove, and coral.

Yves DuJauc
"Selected Stories from the Arabian Nights"
Pease Porridge, *vol. 24, no. 6*
London, 1887

The letters and telegrams, beginning five months previously, including the one letter that went astray:

February 9, 1902

Miami

Your Highness,

It was a great pleasure for Isabel and myself to meet you this past month. (For better or worse, Americans are unavoidably impressed with European titles, and we are no exception.) It was very kind of you to invite my wife and myself to tour

12

your offices, fields, and factories; your undertakings in Grasse and Cannes are most formidable. It was fascinating to see the source of so much of Vandermeer Sea Transit International's cargo and, of course, to see what will become of the ambergris that our subsidiary has agreed to deliver to their newest customer. Of course, it was kinder still of you to invite us into your lovely home on the Mediterranean. We are still talking about the splendor and beauty of the house itself—the view, the sea, the grounds— Oh, we simply cannot stop raving to each other.

I would now like to suggest something that may be a little presumptuous. Isabel and I were so terribly impressed with your home, your graciousness, your cultured outlook, your enterprises, your friends, your princely hospitality—in short, you. It must be obvious to you, surely, that we had a wondrous time, quite the most splendid visit we have ever had in Europe. Which brings me to offering my bold idea. We have a daughter, Louise, who has just come out this season. She is young, but we are very, very proud of her. She is quite extraordinary—lovely and accomplished. Her French is fluent. She likes travel. I am suggesting baldly that you, being a single gentleman, consider uniting yourself with our family through marriage to our daughter. I should like to fill pages with her accomplishments, but, I think, these days young people like to meet and decide these things a little for themselves. I invite you to come visit us at your convenience. We return to our home in New York shortly. Perhaps you would consider coming this spring.

I do not doubt that a gentleman such as yourself has had many fathers propose such arrangements. What gives me such nerve, then? On such short acquaintance, no less? Well, I like to think you were as affected by our company as we were by yours. In truth, however, it is Louise herself who gives me courage, for I know I have a remarkable daughter. She has gathered many suitors here—she is greatly sought after—but Isabel and I agree that we like none so well for our dear Lulu as we do you. Please forgive this impertinence, if that is what it is, but I could not resist speaking my heart's desire. Let us hear from you on this matter as soon as is possible.

> *Yours most truly,*
> *Harold P. Vandermeer*

19 February 1902

Nice, France

My dear sir,

I am most flattered by the kind words and offer in your recent letter. My business concerns, however, devour all my time for the present. A trip to America for me is out of the question. I thank you for your generous compliments but must respectfully decline visiting you and meeting, I am sure, your very delightful daughter.

I look forward to our continuing, mutually rewarding business relationship.

> *Yours most truly,*
> *Charles Harcourt, Prince d'Harcourt*

March 2, 1902

Miami

Your Highness,

I, of course, respect your decision not to pursue my presumptuous (but enthusiastic and good-intentioned) offer.

Mitchell, in port in Nassau—with a remarkable seventy-eight pounds of ambergris—has mentioned to me you wish to purchase the entirety of this windfall. I am very glad you wish to expand our business association. (A son-in-law, you realize, could own the whole fishing fleet and have, at cost, all the whale bile he could gather—this is a little joke meant to tweak your nez.) Please understand that we have several other regular buyers whom we must keep minimally happy. I have told Mitchell, though, that you are to have the best price and the majority of the haul.

I write to you from Miami still. We remain at our "winter" home while I negotiate new docking space for my cargo line. Be assured that our invitation to visit remains open here or anywhere you may find us. You would love Miami, I think—small but very sophisticated and so full of strange, sweet-smelling flowers that, once you smelled them, you would be mad to add to your botanical garden.

> Sincerely yours,
> Harold Vandermeer

P.S. Please forgive a father's pride: I enclose a photograph of my own sweet flower, my daughter, Louise.

March 30, 1902

New York

Your Highness,

I thought I might have success where my husband has failed. Harold and I still talk incessantly of our trip to the Riviera. What a fine time! And the *high point was the time we spent as your house guests. We do so wish you would consider a trip to America. We would not mention the word "marriage" or even hint or say a word to Louise. You could come as a friend, discuss new shipping and supplying arrangements with Harold—and meet our Lulu and just see how the two of you got along.*

Meanwhile, your cousin, Gaspard, has introduced himself to us. He is such a polite young gentleman. We enjoy having him around. He seems quite taken with Louise (but, alas, we are holding out for a full-blooded prince—ha, ha!) He does look a bit like you, though, which makes Harold and I sigh and postulate, If only, if only our friend from Nice would bless us with a visit. . . .

> *All our best,*
> *Isabel Vandermeer*

The letter that never arrived:

11 April 1902

Grasse, France

Dear Mr. and Mrs. Vandermeer,

This may come as a surprise to you. On rather short notice, I discover I am leaving for America within about three weeks, just enough time for an exchange of information. I shall be in New York overnight, after which I head for, of all places, Miami. While in New York, I should be pleased to stop by or perhaps invite the two of you and your daughter one evening to dinner. Unfortunately, I shall not have a great deal of free time,

*but I would not forgive myself for being in your
city and not saying* bonjour.

> *Yours truly,*
> *Charles Harcourt, Prince d'Harcourt*

Telegram sent from Nice to New York, May 2,
1902:

mr. and mrs. vandermeer stop I leave tomorrow
for new york stop arrive may 9 then on to miami
may 10 through may 30 stop can only imagine
that my letter of several weeks ago was lost in
mail stop hope nothing is wrong stop will attempt to contact you in new york stop charles
harcourt

Telegram sent from New York to Nice, May 2,
1902:

we are thrilled and devastated stop yes yes
please contact us in new york then we should
like to take you to miami ourselves in our
private railway car stop we shall roll out red
carpet stop alas louise is on a kind of grand tour
stop will explain more later stop we are not sure
exactly where she is but shall leave word for her
at all possible contact points to come to us
immediately stop again we are delighted you are
coming stop harold and isabel vandermeer

Chapter 3

Ambergris is a highly aromatic, waxy, grayish solid often found floating on the surface of the sea.

Charles Harcourt, Prince d'Harcourt
On the Nature and Uses of Ambergris
*Les Monographies de la Societé
des Études Naturelles
Paris, 1897*

I t was damnably cold to be out on the foredeck, stark naked in the middle of the night. The sea was rolling; the wind was chilly and damp. The deck was wet, high sprays of seawater coming up regularly over the rail. Thanks to the weather, the chairs in which Charles had intended to find cover were pulled back and tied down, not fit for sitting, barely fit for climbing and digging through in search of blankets. Worse, the general area of these roped-together chairs—under the companionway and against the bulwark—was the only area that was truly dark. A row of the ship's running lights, right below this deck, cast a dim, lurid effulgence, which was abetted further by a glow down the way. The grand saloon at midship

18

was still bright, throwing a dazzling white haze into the night. Someone was having a late party.

Thus, in the unnerving ambiance of wet, rocking shadows and distant music, Charles dug out three blankets and donned them more or less toga-style. When he turned to survey for possibilities of comfortable shelter, however, he was met with another unwelcome surprise: Two glowing silhouettes materialized out of the midship white-brightness—a young woman approaching rapidly with a young man in pursuit.

Charles ducked under the companionway, then wedged himself under the steps, arms braced, in response to the ship ploughing up the side of a steep wave. The tilt of gravity took the girl's flight off-kilter. She veered straight into the railing. There she turned quickly, hanging on, laughing in the face of her pursuer, who followed her to the rail, where he dropped his hands on either side of her. The young man, a junior officer in whites, pinned her there for a moment. Charles watched, half annoyed by this sudden intrusion, half charmed by their pantomime, the eternal game played out not thirty feet from him. He heard the rise of sweet, sadistic feminine laughter, the teasing sound of a young girl happily torturing a young man. This carried on the wind for a moment, then was gone. The ocean rose into view over the rail—a high black swell covered with a vast reticulation of white foam, like endless yards of floating lace—then dropped, sending a spray up over the deck. The girl squealed as she and her beau took a pelting of water. Then they both ran. Straight toward Charles.

He drew back, alarmed and madly scrambling for a logical, polite explanation for his being outside on deck wearing nothing but blankets. He was sure the two lovebirds were about to join him right here under the companionway.

This most certainly was the young man's intention, for when the girl veered again, toward the top of the steps instead of the underside, he grabbed her hand and pulled her toward Charles's little patch of dark. Quick as lightning, however, a rather large fan came out. It rapped him on the knuckles loud enough that Charles heard the crack and saw the young officer jerk his hand away, clutching the back of it.

The young man exclaimed, "By heaven, Miss Vandermeer, you quite nearly broke my fingers!"

Free of him, she trotted around and climbed up the first half-dozen steps where she turned and sat— sending a voluminous, shushing billow of silk and ruffles to flop through the spaces between the foot treads, directly onto Charles's bare shoulder and arm. He caught his breath—holding in a deep, pleasing intake, floral-scented. Then he quickly had to remove his own hand from the step or she would have put her sweet little feet right down onto his fingers.

The smell of her settled like a little cloud at his shoulder. She wore a jasmine perfume with hints of acacia and clover, one of the more elegant jasmine blends, though a bit too clustered in the middle range of notes to be perfect. Belvienne's of Paris. All this registered in an instant without effort, then became complicated. There was something more, something separate. The scent of real jasmine. There was distinctly about the girl, her dress, her entire person, the faint smell of the fresh flower itself, not the attar or perfume but something light, layered, harmonic, the sort only nature could produce, reminiscent of late summer when the blossoms themselves were piled waist-high on the floor of Charles's factory, ready to be spread on cloth frames soaked in oil. Then she bent her head forward, and the sharp, unearthly light from below shot up the back of her to reveal the explanation: Tucked into the neat shadows of very fair hair were small white stars, fairer still, of *Jasminum simplicifolium.* This little constellation of flowers trailed down the back of a rolled chignon; it intertwined the knots of the gown's dropped shoulders.

The young man, meanwhile, had swung round the handrail and climbed a step or two. He placed one arm on the bulwark wall, cornering her this time on the stairway.

"You almost broke my fingers," he insisted.

She let out light laughter, a sound that up close had a cool nuance to it. "No, I didn't," she said. "I know precisely how hard I hit you. It wouldn't have broken a finger, though I'm sure it smarted."

The young officer was annoyed by this response. "Well," he said, "don't use that thing on me again."

She leaned her shoulders back against the step at Charles's ear. "Then don't grab me when I don't want you to. You keep your hands to yourself, Lieutenant Johnston, and you shall walk away tonight with your knuckles intact."

Heedless of this warning, the young lieutenant leaned forward, putting his knee into her copious skirts as he bent his elbows. He pressed forward, an attempt to kiss her. Then pulled suddenly back. Or more accurately was pushed back. Charles could just see past a round, bare shoulder to where the girl's extended arm, aided by the fan again—held straight out not unlike a bayonet—put the fellow at more than arm's length. The lieutenant looked down at the thing poking him in the chest.

His face rose to hers again as he murmured inscrutably, "Don't be a fool."

She only laughed.

He countered earnestly, "He's a devil."

"Yes, you have implied as much all evening."

The young officer made a kind of violent guffaw. "Ha. Well, I won't imply any longer. I'll speak plainly. Harcourt is an abominable fellow . . ."

Harcourt? Miss Vandermeer? Charles frowned,

twisting his head around to scowl past a lot of silk and
shadows in the general direction of the young man on
the other side of the stairway.

". . . a lame devil who's quick to anger . . ."

Like the creak from a dark dungeon door, Charles
sensed his vanity stir.

The young idiot went on. "Ask anyone who will be
frank. He's blind in one eye and eerie to look at in the
other. He walks with a limp. And he's aged. He's
twice your age at least."

*He most certainly was not aged. Nor was he twice
her age (though last year he would have been).* The
girl's age had been one of Charles's own reservations
to the marriage. He had never particularly liked
eighteen-year-old girls, not even when he was eighteen. Time, however, would fix this particular short-
coming on her part. Though how to fix a babbling
simpleton who wooed at another man's expense . . .

". . . and when he's angry, which is often, he bel-
lows like a banshee at everyone . . ."

*No, sometimes, he simply saw to it that young
lieutenants lost their commissions on luxury liners—
to be sent into Antarctica on a dredge.*

". . . he's vindictive and confrontational . . ."

*Of all the stupid . . . and from an impudent imbecile
who couldn't so much as get a kiss from a silly young
girl.*

When the silly young girl laughed at this tirade,
however, Charles caught a trace of something in her
mirth that the lieutenant didn't seem to suspect: a
savviness along with a possible note of disdain.

". . . he dresses like some fantastical peacock, as if
he were something to behold, which he is." The young
man made a sound of disgust. "He's hideous. . . ."

Charles gritted his teeth and enjoyed the image of
his own "hideous" hand reaching out from between
these steps to grab this fellow by his throat—when
Miss Vandermeer came up with her own kind of

strangle. She said, "And let me guess: You're my answer. You want to 'husband' me in his stead, at least for the night?"

The lieutenant made a sound, a sputter. He couldn't respond for a moment. "Well, of course, er, no—" He cleared his throat. "Well, yes, though I, ah, was truly offering marriage."

Her laughter this time—two abrupt syllables that sounded as if they came from someone far older than her years—mocked him openly. "You're proposing I run off with a ship's junior officer based on an evening's acquaintance?"

"Well, yes, I, ah, assumed . . ." For a moment, he was lost in this conversation, then reentered it with almost comic solemnness: "Miss Vandermeer: I saw you; I adored you. You've come out here with me. Don't you believe in love at first sight?"

"No, I don't believe in love at all," she said flatly.

This didn't stop him. He took a liberty. "Louise," he said, "look at yourself. You are lovely beyond imagining, more than lovely . . ." The nincompoop was literally without words for a second. Then he uttered with ridiculous reverence, "You are divine. A man like Harcourt, why the fiend—"

"Oh, stop," she said. "I know who Charles Harcourt is, and he will make a wonderful husband for me."

This gave both Charles and the young man pause.

The young ship's officer standing above in the light neither said nor did anything further; he was stymied.

While the man beneath the steps was merely disturbed. The girl's assertion, though vaguely pleasing, held an irony in its context—since she was saying it to a young man she had laughingly led out into the dark, where the two of them now sat alone. Or almost alone.

The three of them watched the rough sea for a moment as it commanded their attention, only

Charles aware of their odd togetherness: the way they each, two men and a woman, leaned and angled their bodies similarly to counter the ocean's careless tossing, up then down, of their bodies, of their separate concerns. He thought he heard wrong at first when he heard a tiny murmur.

Almost inaudibly, as if to no one in particular, her voice asked, "Is he really lame?"

"Yes," said the young man firmly.

No, Charles wanted to defend. *I limp sometimes, only sometimes, and when I do, I use a very elegant cane.* He realized at that moment—a humbling piece of timing—that his knee in fact had begun to hurt, that it was becoming stiff, due either to the dampness or a barometric drop. As the ship took its next plunge downward, he had to brace his hand on the nearest support—a lower step.

"That's funny," she murmured, "my parents didn't tell me this." She added, "Though they did mention that the Prince d'Harcourt was not classically handsome."

"He's ugly," said the lieutenant's low, vehement voice.

Charles grumbled inwardly and pressed his lips together.

As they ploughed into the next wave, the girl adjusted herself on her seat of steps. Something moved at Charles's fingers. Her dress was caught under his grip. In stabilizing himself, he had latched on to a piece of her hem.

She doubled over her own knees and jerked on the fabric.

He let go immediately.

"What's wrong?" asked the man above.

"Nothing. My dress caught on something."

The two of them bent down into their own shadows, heads together. They pulled at her now puzzlingly free skirts. From this position, the lieutenant must have pressed his face an inch closer, for a moment later—the reason for the mysterious catch of her dress left moot—he was kissing her.

She sighed softly and sat back, tipping her head up. This time she gave in to his advance, letting him knead her bare shoulders as he kissed her mouth.

The young man knew success for about ten seconds—ten chagrined seconds wherein Charles's irritation shifted from a meddling junior ship's officer to a callow, unimaginative girl whom, lame devil that he was, he seemed to have offended, sight unseen.

Charles's vanity whispered through the dark, its hot breath fanning this offense. *I am glorious,* it said. *Not to be judged by ordinary standards. I am fabulous to look upon, wonderful to see, unique.* His wrath grew hot. My God, here was his intended, the woman to whom he expected to give his name, properties, position, and all the respect attached, every consideration, and what was she doing? Why, emitting little throaty sounds all but into his ear as she kissed someone else, a total stranger she'd met on the ship on the way to her wedding. *The little tart. The floozy.*

Hang my own explanations! Charles thought. Let explanations fall where they may, starting with hers. She could damn well account for why and what exactly she was doing out here. (Where were her parents anyway?) He was about to step out from under the companionway.

Then the poor, bungling lieutenant arched back slightly, drew his arms forward, and grabbed all at once for the front of the young woman—presumably for her breasts—in an abrupt motion not unlike that which he might use to take hold of two steaming valves in the ship's engine room, wrenching them tight.

She drew back sharply, shoved him away, and the next moment, leapt down onto her feet. With a sniff, she faced him, which put her partway into the light.

Charles paused. The ship's lights from below shone up the side of her, making her dress, whatever color it truly was, a silvery mauve. Her fingers came up to play with beads at her throat. She wore multitudinous strands of black pearls—small, matched, round and glistening, like strung caviar lying in tiers down the white cream of her throat. She lifted her chin. Her face turned slightly to become visible, or partly visible.

And, good Lord, it seemed impossible, but Harold Vandermeer had been modest!

"Dear Lulu" was more than beautiful. Merely to list her attributes (blond hair, fair eyes, high cheek bones close to the surface of her skin, a full red mouth as plump and chiseled as a baby's) didn't do her justice. There was an aura to her . . . a glamour . . . a natural beauty polished to a high sheen by money. (The caviar analogy was apropos, the pearls being about the size and color of large, pale beluga. It occurred to Charles that, if he indeed married this girl, he could be acquiring something very expensive to maintain.) Louise Vandermeer was to the female sex what the Taj Mahal was to architecture: resplendent, elegant, extravagantly gorgeous. No hastily glanced-at black-and-white photograph could do her justice.

And something else her father's photo had not shown very clearly: She was also staggeringly young.

As Charles looked at her, he realized he hadn't truly understood what *eighteen* meant. Her pouty lower lip came out as she played with the necklace strand at her collarbone, making her look (accurately, he supposed) like a peevish adolescent—a very beautiful, jasmine-scented peevish adolescent. The hair on Charles's neck lifted.

This exotic young creature met the lieutenant's regard with a cool, unwavering poise, a seemingly ageless composure. She spoke only one more word:

"Clod"—that sang with such utter finality that even Charles felt a shiver of embarrassment for the sexually gauche young man.

Then she swayed around, turning her large skirts in an effortless, undulant sweep. As she walked back into the haze of light, her hips rolled leisurely from side to side, rather like the *Concordia* herself: listing, righting, impervious, cutting buoyantly full-throttle through the black, rocking night.

Chapter 4

The ancient Egyptians used ambergris as incense; the Turks carry it to Mecca.

Charles Harcourt, Prince d'Harcourt
On the Nature and Uses of Ambergris

Just before dawn, Charles, now fully dressed in his nightshirt and robe, walked out onto the terrace of his suite. The weather had drawn him out. The wind was high. The storm was nigh on top of them. The distant sound of rain on the ocean could be heard, a roaring hiss that seemed to advance from all sides. Charles stood there, the bracing, wet wind in his face, his robe—a huge Arabian gallibiya actually—flapping at him, billowing up and to the side like the colorful sails of some exotic ship. Oddly enough, in this atmosphere, he felt almost peaceful. Pia had called him twice already on the ship's telephone, each time whispering over Roland's snoring. *I'm breaking it off,* she'd said. *I just want you to know that I'm breaking it off. You are a cad and a traitor. I hate you.*

Charles knew, though, that one didn't call twice to break off an affair: One didn't call at all. He felt surer of Pia than he had in a long time; at last the upper hand.

He closed his eyes, letting the wind lick his face. He was feeling quite in harmony with the elements—the night lifting onto a livid, purple-gray dawn, the air shimmering with the promise of rain, alive with a sense of expectancy.

He had put last night, he assured himself, completely behind him. Pia was in hand. And as to the eavesdropped conversation on a companionway over his head, well, why make more of it than it was? Louise Vandermeer, like countless young girls before her, was no doubt experiencing the predictable panic that any girl might as she embarked on the solemn and life-changing decision of marriage. She was, he would grant, a little superficial to be so concerned about looks. But she was young and, lovely creature that she was, perhaps just a tiny bit inclined to place too much store in her own youthful beauty. What of it? She was forgivably inexperienced of the world. So she might indulge a bit more improvidently than most, but in what was only a tiny dalliance really, that she had, after all, aborted almost immediately.

Yes, all forgotten. All forgiven. Never mind that, sight unseen, she had been appalled by him, appalled enough that she had wandered off into the dark to cavort with an inane young man. When she *did* in fact set eyes on Charles, well . . .

He was an agreeable enough man to look upon, he assured himself, and he was more than agreeable with respect to charm and a winning manner. He had many friends; he was well-liked. And—he prided himself on this—he had had many lovers, among them the most beautiful, most sophisticated women on the Côte d'Azur. Moreover, he was classically educated, successful. There was no substantial reason why a woman should be anything other than pleased

to be his wife—a dozen or so women in Provence
would have been, in fact, delighted to oblige, women
of taste who valued uniqueness, substance, and style.

So why, he complained to himself, were all his
wonderful boatloads of precious ambergris, so pains-
takingly negotiated back and forth to America, dependent on his connection to a frivolous creature in
love with her own beauty? On a girl whose imagination was so easily engaged in a game of imaginable
horribles based on her fear of what might be a little bit
different?

Damn all pretty young girls, he thought, *with their
incessant primping and posing and naive understanding of life.* He didn't like them; he never had. (He
couldn't afford to, since it took a certain amount of
experience with the world to appreciate such an
elegant piece of work as himself.)

At this point, his temper and vanity drove him
inside. With a single, wide, backward swipe of his
arms, he marched between the open doors, through
the wall-to-wall draperies of his sitting room.

"And, worse," he said to the grand piano (he didn't
play; it was for parties, should he choose to have any),
"this child, this *naughty* child, is clearly willing and
capable of prowling the dark recesses of the ship—
looking as baby-fresh as a debutante while on her
jaded mission, out to defile herself as quickly as
possible." For here was the sharpest burr: All
Charles's worst fears came together in the possibility
that, though she wouldn't have the lieutenant, Louise
Vandermeer intended to experiment further. She
would find someone else, some regular-featured fellow, up to her banal standards.

She would make a fool of Charles.

You are leaping to conclusions, he told himself,
*leaping to offense. You must let this go. You must not
feast on this grievance.*

Still, he walked forcefully, slightly favoring one leg,

across a plush carpet, past a working fireplace, a
moiré settee and chairs, a genuine Singer Sargent oil
painting, around a large canapé table beside the piano
(a fairly large party would have been possible; sixty or
more people could have fit easily into the front sitting
room, side vestibule, and dining room), to the wall of
French doors, two of which opened into the master
bedroom. Inside this bedroom, on the dresser beside
the huge walnut-canopied bed, he found his medicine
chest. He dug through this, looking for his emulsion
of cod-liver oil and malt extract, a concoction made
palatable only by the addition of ether and a drop of
peppermint; his arthritis medication. Sometimes this
headed off an attack; sometimes it didn't. His knee
was aching like the blazes.

He took the cod-liver oil, then took his lapinin too,
for good measure, another supposed cure (though
nothing worked with any consistency). Then he found
his cane and hobbled back through the sitting room to
the side vestibule, where he dropped himself into one
chair, propped up his leg on another, then pulled open
his notebook into his lap.

The truth was, he had very little work. He had
already worked like a madman, anticipating the convenience of Roland's seasickness that should have
allowed Charles to plug away at Pia uninterruptedly
all the way back across the Atlantic.

With a deep sigh, he reviewed his notes, looking for
something to do, mentally fondling his favorite
project.

Charles was about to embark on a lifelong goal: to
create, blend, then sell his own special perfume.
Normally his perfume factory in Grasse manufactured only extractions, attars of rose, jasmine, lavender, mimosa, other flowers. He supplied a number of
the perfume houses in Paris with their essential oils.
He also sold small quantities of imitations of these
houses' products. With a little sniffing, Charles could

recognize and separate the components of almost any perfume; he could smell the pieces, distinguish the differences. With a little mixing and measuring, he could duplicate any perfume to near perfection. But Charles had no real interest in imitations, not of perfume nor of anything else, no matter how perfect. Charles wanted to create a peerlessly beautiful—unmatchable, unparalleled—scent, which, with an adequate supply of ambergris and one other ingredient, he was ready to do. Magically, both the ambergris and the ingredient had come together this trip.

Of course, Vandermeer would be supplying the ambergris. But it was the promise of the other more elusive ingredient that had brought Charles across an ocean.

Charles had been searching for several years for a beautiful—and relatively unidentifiable—component for his own perfume, something that any other perfumer would have difficulty identifying exactly, for there were other experts, or "noses" as they were called, such as himself, others who could imitate. Until now. Charles had found a way to confuse them. He had come to Miami to see, smell, and possibly obtain a rare jasmine, one he had thought only existed in legend, the *Jasminum nocturnum* or Wedding Night Jasmine. Letters back and forth between him and a Miami botanist had yielded the clues that, to Charles's surprise, left him now traveling home with the legend in hand and in good supply. Wedding Night Jasmine existed. Plants and clippings of it were at this moment sitting in the florist's cold hold for him.

Charles now knew the real plant to be a New World indigene, bred through a South American species. And, better still, he knew it to be one of the sweetest, most fragrant jasmines he had ever smelled (though something of a curiosity in that it was the only jasmine he knew that by day was a scraggily, tight little shrub to become by night a wide-open bouquet of sweet-smelling blossoms; its flowers only opened at night). Charles intended to quietly graft it onto his standard root stock in his most remote fields around Grasse and Cannes. By day it would look like a poor harvest, a bad year. By night he would gather the petals, then extract their scent to blend. He would make a new perfume based on this jasmine and fixed with ambergris, a carefully complex perfume that would smell divine while being a perfumer's conundrum to dissect or decipher.

The idea thrilled Charles—to make something of singular beauty. Scents, in general, thrilled him; perhaps because his vision was one-sided, his sense of smell had become fuller, more three-dimensional. His nose was certainly more discerning than most. He experienced the world a great deal through his olfactory organ. Smell overlaid everything. It intensified the moment; it could vividly trigger the past. He could call up memories by odor, like a scrapbook of sensory recollections. He could, for instance, close his eyes and be in Provence by just recalling the fragrance of his *Jasminum grandiflorum,* fields of lovely, floral-sweet clouds that sat above him on a stairway—

He opened his eyes with a start. That damn girl with the jasmine woven into her hair. Louise Vandermeer had smelled very much like his fields, a variation with seawater and rain mingled in. Damn girl. Silly creature. Somehow this line of thought left Charles staring at the telephone at his elbow.

It occurred to him suddenly that he could test his fears regarding the lovely Miss Louise Amelda-May Vandermeer. He picked up the earpiece and gave the phone's crank a few turns.

The ship's operator answered. "Yes? May I have your name and room number, please."

"This is the Rosemont suite." Charles had, as was the privilege of those traveling in the grand luxury apartments, kept his name off the register. (He had recognized the son of a deposed emir stepping out of the apartment next door; also not officially on the ship.) "Is Miss Louise Vandermeer in her own stateroom or does she share her parents'?"

There was a delay, a silent marker of how inappropriate this question was. Except the operator was dealing with the occupant of a suite who was theoretically beyond reproach, to whom she was to offer every courtesy. "She is in her own stateroom, sir," came the twangy reply.

"Can you tell me what number that would be?"

With no hesitation at all, she said, "No, sir, I can't. Under no circumstances do we give out ladies' stateroom numbers. May I suggest that you ask the lady herself."

Charles thought for a split second then said, "All right. Connect me with her room."

After a moment of clicking, a whirring came over the line. The line opened, and a staticky voice said, "Hello?"

Even with the tinny overlay of wiring, he knew the voice. Low-pitched, smooth. She had a distinctive tonality, deep-voiced for a woman, resonant; contradictorily not at all young.

He had not planned on saying anything, yet he heard the operator disconnect, then found himself speaking. "What you're doing is a little dangerous," he said.

"Who is this?"

"That young lieutenant was an idiot, every bit the clod you told him he was."

"What?" A small but discernable note of panic edged her sweet-low, melodious voice.

"Do you want to take your game a step farther?"

"What game?"

"If you do, I have something that might interest you." He hesitated, but the temptation was too great.

He risked offering this sweet-smelling creature something he knew would entice. "Some jasmine," he said.

"Jasmine?"

"You like jasmine, don't you?"

"Yes."

"Well, this is unusual jasmine. A bit like you." He found himself swimming for a moment in the magical, jasmine-scented vision of this child–woman to whom he was so strangely connected. He remembered the ship's lights shooting up the side of her dress, lighting up her face at angles. He knew again for a moment the white jasmine flowers, when she turned to go, tucked into the sauntering, gilded shadows of her hair. "Then listen to me," he said. "I am going to send you a rather unimpressive branch of jasmine. When you get it, put it in water, then after dinner tonight, say, about nine o'clock, go to where you have put it. The blossoms only open in the dark: They smell like heaven. If you like them and want to know more about them, meet me at midnight"—he paused; why not?—"at the starboard companionway, the first as you walk from midship to the forward part of the promenade deck."

"You're mad. I won't—"

"Good," he said. "Then you are beginning to understand why this game of yours is a dangerous notion. Don't meet me then. Or do."

"How did you—"

"The jasmine will arrive shortly." Charles depressed the hook and hung up the earpiece.

The second call took less than ten seconds. He arranged with the florist to send one of the Rosemont suite's jasmine branches to Miss Louise Vandermeer's stateroom, after which Charles sat back, amazed at himself.

He was always astounded when he did things like this. So much pride. So much vanity. Yet he felt exhilarated, and he couldn't say he was unhappy or exactly ashamed of himself. He felt his lips curving up into a faint smile. An idea was taking shape, dim, slightly nefarious, amusing, and above all gratifying. Yes. Yes, yes, there was one very interesting way to ascertain just how devious this young woman was, how determined she was to make a fool of her "ugly" French husband.

Charles himself would lure her into the dark, where he would make considerably more sophisticated overtures than he had witnessed last night—he would show her just how charming and creamy smooth "a little different" could be. That is to say, if she allowed it, he would seduce her. He would woo her at night among the shadows of the ship where she could not see him with any exactness. Then, if he succeeded, he would allow her to awaken by daylight to the sight of her "monster," that is, to the husband-to-be whose looks—his "aged" differentness—made her run for the shelter of a pretty young man.

What a fine joke, Charles thought. For he knew how to hold up a mirror to shallowness—he had been mocking it all his life; if it was there within her, he would find it. He leaned back, lifting his bad leg off the chair to stretch it out with the other. (Even his knee felt better; an omen.) His black mood had lifted, or at least permutated. The whole enterprise was a jest of the first order, the possible outcome appealing enormously to the darker side of his sense of humor.

Chapter 5

Louis XV used ambergris to flavor his favorite dishes; Queen Elizabeth to scent her gloves and capes.

Charles Harcourt, Prince d'Harcourt
On the Nature and Uses of Ambergris

Louise Vandermeer hung up the telephone's earpiece, staring at it, amazed. Someone was spying on her. Then more amazing: It occurred to her that this someone could be her parents. How strange to think of them as the enemy, yet this was actually possible since her discovered adventure to Montreal.

Annoyed—as much with herself as anyone—she stood, then felt her collar flop open at the back of her neck. Reaching up and back, she began again with the buttons she'd been fastening when the telephone had interrupted her. (She was dressing herself, having sent her maid to the ship's clinic to fetch some seasickness medicine for her parents.) She stood there buttoning, one hip braced against the bedstead for balance as the room tipped. The floor leveled, and she paused, straddle-legged, elbows pointing to the ceiling. A more likely explanation occurred to her.

No one was spying. The source of her unsettling telephone call was that stupid ninny of a junior ship's officer from last night. Lord, he hadn't turned out to be at all what she had expected. And now, big man, he was shooting his mouth off, getting even. This phone call had to be from him or from one of his friends having some fun with her.

She could find out. She buttoned the last button as she turned back toward the telephone, then picked up the black earpiece and rang for the switchboard.

"Operator, this is Miss Vandermeer in suite one-oh-three. You put a call through to me a few minutes ago. Can you tell me who the caller was?"

A twangy voice replied, "I connected the Rosemont suite, miss. The gentleman wouldn't give his name."

Louise puzzled a moment. "Thank you." She hung up, frowning.

Not likely one of the lieutenant's friends, given the price of the Rosemont suite. It was one of the four grand luxury suites on an upper deck at the front of the ship, any one of which costs more than five times that of the largest first-class stateroom. The Rosemont suite was an extravagant bid for complete and utter privacy. Then another fact rose to the surface of her awareness: The voice spoke English with a faintly British accent or, no—there was another accent, slight but sure, the sound of non-native syllables educated in the British speech pattern. How curious. A European. Louise could count all the Europeans she knew on one hand—two of her fingers taken up by the woman who had been her nanny and the man who was the family butler.

For another minute she lingered over the rhythms and intonations of the voice. There was something else . . . *You like jasmine, don't you?* (How would a stranger know this?) An emotion seemed to come across the wire, acknowledged and given reign in a way that was foreign to Louise's experience. She mulled this briefly, then stood up. No, she corrected, she had heard nothing else here beyond the gloating of a stupid prankster.

Her father, of course, could get the name of the fellow. She would speak to him about this. The question was, though, How could she get her father's help without the subject of the phone conversation coming to light? No, given her own behavior last night, she would prefer her father didn't know about this call just yet. She would find out who this was and deal with him herself.

Twenty minutes later, just as she was leaving her stateroom, a scrubby, green-budded branch arrived. She turned the ugly thing around in her hands a moment, then with a snort of disgust pitched it into her wastebasket on her way out to breakfast.

Louise stopped by her parents' stateroom to make sure they had gotten the medicine. They had, then Josette, her maid, had gone on to the servants' dining hall. Thus, Louise found herself alone with her mother and father, something she had not exactly planned. They lay side by side on their bed, both of them sea green, with ice packs on their foreheads. She bent over to kiss them each, then leave immediately, but alas as she raised up, finished with the last cheek, her mother took hold of her hand. The torment began.

Her mother started off with her usual admonishments that Louise was to behave like a lady, with reserve, regally aware of her position, while being "generously kind to those with lesser blessings."

"And you must make more friends," her mother added.

Louise's mother wanted her to be both aloof, with "upper-class bearing," yet warmly beloved by everyone, from her father's valet to her mother's Friends of the Opera Society. Louise was not inclined to form quick friendships with anyone, least of all with two parents who had grown tetchy and carping.

As if the earth turned upon how she ordered her eggs and whom she sat next to, they took turns giving her advice on how to comport herself at breakfast without them. Then her father from his supine position, just his nose and mouth visible, launched into his well-worn lecture, "Behaving other than like some directionless adolescent."

"You have a future," he said for what had to be the hundredth time since she'd arrived back home just a week ago. "Don't lose sight of your goals."

Louise muttered, "*Your* goals, you mean."

"And don't be disrespectful." Her father raised his head, lifting the ice pack, his bushy brows furrowing out from under it as he looked at her. "You are becoming quite impudent, Louise Amelda-May."

She said, a little irritably, "I'm not becoming anything. You taught me to think for myself, only now you would like to take all that back because you don't like what I think."

She had liked Montreal, for instance. She had spent a very nice day and a half there before her parents had located her. Suddenly this episode, of course, was exactly what they were speaking of. In the whirlwind of the prince's offer of marriage, the three of them had yet to find the appropriate moment to discuss Louise's flight from home at any length.

Her father, staring hard at her now, said, "What *were* you thinking?"

"About what?" Louise asked, one last pass at avoiding the inevitable.

This made her mother lift her ice pack too. Louise groaned inwardly as she faced both of them, both waiting for an answer.

She defended, "I wasn't thinking anything. There was a train for Montreal. You thought I was at Mary's for a few days. I believed I could get there and back, and no one would know."

Her father asked, "Why, for God's sake?"

"Because there is a music hall there where they play backgammon for money, and I thought I could win."

Her mother's face took on a distressed, bewildered expression that was painful for Louise to see, the look of a mother who couldn't get so much as a foothold on her daughter's motives or logic. She said helplessly, "But you could have done *that* in New York."

"I have. But now I wanted to do it in French, just to see if I could."

"You've gambled in New York?" her father interjected.

"A few times."

"And could you?" her mother asked.

"Could I what?"

"Gamble in French?"

"Yes."

Her father glanced at his wife and said, "Honestly, Isabel, as if it matters. . . . "

From here, the two of them engaged in a little entwining conversation, where they both talked at the same time and finished each other's sentences. "Well, I know it's scandalous, her running off . . . on tour indeed . . . we should have told the prince . . . yes, then he would have been as wary of everyone else, should they find out . . . and just think if anyone fully realized . . . yes, what she finally did once she got there . . . I still can't get over the fact . . . our beautiful, clever daughter . . . the most extolled, sought-after girl this season . . . why, dear Lord, why . . . what did we do to deserve this. . . . "

All right, Louise thought. *It wasn't smart.* Or at least her adventure wasn't worth all the aggravation it had caused. But her parents—and she had *known* that they would—were blowing it out of proportion. She interrupted with, "You know, I haven't taken up gambling as a life's vocation. I don't even care if I ever do it again. I just wanted to see—"

Her father turned on her. "See what?" he said. "If you could ruin the best prospects since Consuelo Vanderbilt married the Duke of Marlborough?"

"I didn't ruin anything. I am about to do better, in fact."

"Because of *our* intervention."

Louise bit back the sarcastic reply, that she had *known* she could fall back on their "intervention," if necessary. She hadn't done anything her father wasn't perfectly capable of fixing.

Her mother added, "What in the world do you think people would say if they found out—if your father wasn't able to pay off every soul who had seen you, from the train conductor to the bellhop to the hotel night-clerk?"

Louise took the offensive. She said, "*You* don't worry about others' opinions. You stayed in your cabin all yesterday morning, even before the ship had sailed. Don't you imagine everyone else out on the promenade thought *that* a little inappropriate?" The closeness between Louise's parents had always been an anchor, a dependable piece of her life. Yet somehow in the last months their union, the way they joined against her, made her feel forsaken. She continued, "And you hold hands in public, when you have been married for more than two dozen years. I mean, I would feel like a third wheel—" She corrected, "a fifth wheel, whatever—unnecessary—if you weren't so old that I can't think why I should be resentful and—"

"Louise!" Her father stopped her diatribe.

Both parents had sat bolt upright in bed to stare at her.

Her face infused with blood. She wasn't certain exactly what she had said that was wrong, but her parents looked horrified. They looked hurt. In perfect unison, they looked utterly dumbstruck.

Louise wanted to apologize but could not find the words. And, in all honesty, a part of her was happy to have had such a profound effect on these two people. A separate effect, her own effect; an adult effect. There were times, these days, when she wanted to slap them. Or slap herself. Or slap someone. . . .

The words came haltingly. She said, "Oh, I'm—" She looked away, embarrassed, feeling both ashamed and righteous, misused. She cast her regard about the room, looking from the drawn drapes to the steamer trunk standing on end, to the chair over which hung her father's frock coat and her mother's dress; looking, looking for something she couldn't name, for something that perhaps just wasn't here. She took a breath then let it out, a heave of frustration. "Oh, I'm just feeling lost"—she scrambled angrily—"I mean, cross. I've had a very bad morning." Her stupid slip of tongue made her irrationally furious. She wasn't lost or confused or anything else childish. She was angry with these two people, fully and justly angry that they clung together, did as they pleased, then upbraided her for clinging to herself.

Meanwhile her mother, who was shy of sexual references to anything, least of all to herself, pretended Louise's windy catalog of complaints had never been spoken. She said, "Never mind. Montreal is behind us. We must move forward."

Reluctantly her father fell in with this lead. He muttered, "Yes, chock it up to experience. You are young. Just remember, as you explore life, to be a little more cautious."

Yes, oh, yes, Louise thought. *To explore life. Let us drink a toast to that!* But she only picked up her day fan and fringed shawl, murmuring meekly, "I'm going to breakfast now. I hope you both feel better."

Louise realized as she left her parents' room that

she had become a trial. She could almost hear them consoling each other over her. She wanted to scream, to cry. Until recently, she had always thought of herself and her parents as getting along well. Now, though, they acted as if she didn't know what was expected of her, which she did; as if she hadn't always accepted it, which she had.

It was just that everything was happening so fast. At what was supposed to be the happiest time of a young woman's life, she often felt fidgety, impatient, at times even depressed. As if a hundred things she had intended to do were left undone—except she could think of nothing she wanted to do specifically that she wasn't doing. She could think of no plans for herself but those that were unfolding: a brilliant marriage, children, a respected place in society, a rich, beautiful life. So what could possibly be wrong? Nothing. She kept her discontent to herself, that is, she tried to until it occurred to her that she wished she were somewhere else, like Montreal. Or France.

In this, she supposed, she and her parents had achieved some of their old harmony: She knew they were only too glad to marry her off to a foreign title who would not have had a whisper yet of her less than sterling behavior. For them, her marriage to the Prince d'Harcourt made the most of her good qualities, attaching an envious moniker to the family while not paying a single tithe to her odd quirk for heading off to foreign cities.

While Louise herself was happy enough to be on the move again. No one knew her in France. She liked to take readings off strangers, off their first impressions of her. *Who are you?* people always asked in one way or another when she arrived at a new destination. Yes, she wanted to know this too: Who am I? Not this silly creature, surely, who says the right things, knows the right people, reads the right books, then shops and fixes herself all day so she can impress all night the same people she has been impressing since she was an infant.

Chapter 6

Rich Dutchmen and Englishmen have eaten ambergris on eggs for breakfast.

Charles Harcourt, Prince d'Harcourt
On the Nature and Uses of Ambergris

The walk wasn't long from her parents' state-room to the dining saloon, both being at mid-ship. Yet the going was slow. Louise held to the brass handrail, her shoulder occasionally brushing up against the mahogany paneling. At one point the tilt of the ship pulled her away from the rail to do a slow, inevitable stagger to the railing on the opposite wall. In this manner, she swayed and lurched her way through the short mazework of carved panel corridors to the grand staircase that led down into the first-class dining area.

From the top of these wide, sweeping stairs, Louise looked down into an opulent room. The dining saloon spread the full width of the ship, extending upward through three decks and lengthwise a hundred yards. White Ionic columns embellished with gold sup-ported a high ceiling of arching coffered panels. These rose into a central overhead dome painted with a

mural of the open sea, sunny and sparkling, with the
seven continents represented around its border. The
dining-room walls were carved Spanish mahogany,
inlaid with ivory. The vast space—with its ceiling
lights of oxidized silver set with cut-crystal bowls, its
mirrors and flowers, its long elaborately set white-
linen tables, these lined with armchairs upholstered in
blue, figured frieze velvet—looked more like the hall
of a palace than the steel enclosure of a ship. This hall
teetered, however. Most of the seats, on swivels and
bolted to the floor, were turned out, empty. Only
about a third of the passengers had apparently ventured out to breakfast today.

From among one little cluster of breakfast diners,
her cousin Mary waved and called out from the center
of the room, this greeting making several dozen faces
turn. As Louise began down the stairs, an increasing
number of people turned to gape at her.

She was accustomed to this. Stares followed her
pretty much everywhere, a common—and demo-
cratic—phenomenon. Everyone tended to look at
her, then gawk. Strangers, friends, servants; friends'
servants, servants' friends; magnates, children, postal
clerks, charwomen. Louise knew herself to be beautiful in this way. She halted traffic in the street. Her
entrance into a room made young men lose their
tongues in midsentence. When she was younger, this
had made her shy; she had felt like a circus freak. Now
she accepted her looks for what they were: both a kind
of power over people as well as an obstacle, to one
degree or another, to meeting, knowing, and being
liked by them.

Another woman with the party at the far end of the
room's central table motioned for her to join them—
she sat across from cousin Mary and next to Gaspard
de Barbot, a polite enough young man who treated
Louise perfectly civilly—as if she were a normal

human being. There were several others Louise didn't
know. The waving woman made Gaspard move over
so as to make a seat for Louise between them, a
friendly gesture that attracted, since Louise's presence
among other women didn't always engender warmth.

Louise headed toward these people, rather like a
pinball rolling through a tilting game surface, everything affixed to the floor but her and the dishes and
vases—these slid occasionally with people stopping
them, laughing with determined good cheer. There
was too much laughter in the room, nervous and
brave. The storm was beginning to tell on everyone.

"Here is a place for you right beside me," said the
friendly woman as Louise came up. The woman was
small and slender, with reddish gold hair and a wide,
mobile mouth—and circles under her eyes. She had a
piece of plain, dry toast on her plate. Catching the
direction of Louise's gaze, she said, "I'll be fine. I
filched some of my husband's seasickness medicine
this morning—he's *really* under the weather." She
rolled her eyes, eyes emphasized by a fine line of kohl
about them, their lashes blacked. Her cheeks were
artificially pinked; she penciled her brows. By
Louise's standards, a lot of face paint, though it was
artfully applied. The woman added, "I've never had
such a bad crossing, have you?"

"This is my first." Louise sat down just as the
steward came to remove the fruit course, bowls of
melon. She nodded, letting hers go.

"Well, they are much nicer than this usually." The
woman held out her hand. "I'm Pia Montebello,
Roland Montebello's wife, the American plenipotentiary minister to France. If we can be of any help, you
must say so—I understand, Miss Vandermeer, you
are taking up residence in the very nicest part of
France."

Louise stared blankly. "I shall live near Nice."
Before she could accept the offered hand, it was

withdrawn. Mrs. Montebello required both hands to catch her plate as it slid toward her lap.

The fish course arrived: raw oysters with drawn spicy butter. Mrs. Montebello refused these, shaking her head with a tiny groan, then turned away and covered her mouth with her napkin. She emitted a loud, rather unladylike belch. Laughing weakly, she said, "I may just need a dash more of Roland's medicine."

Louise liked oysters, though for the sake of the delicate stomach beside her, she quelled any obvious enthusiasm. She speared a little fellow, sliding him out of his pearly shell into the cup-bath of butter on her plate, then ate him whole, her mouth full when Mrs. Montebello said, "I understand you are soon to be married."

"Mm," was all that Louise could say at first. She nodded yes.

"How exciting for you."

Louise looked at her. The woman wanted something. Her friendliness had a purpose. "Yes," Louise said, then popped another oyster into her mouth.

Mary volunteered, "She's marrying a real prince. Isn't that romantic?"

Louise eyed her cousin, then asked, "Have you been to the kennels today, Mary?"

"No."

"I went early, and I can tell you, someone brought aboard fleas. I killed two on the Bear this morning." "The Bear" was the name Louise used for her new puppy, until a real name came along for the little bugger. (She had named him Bugger for a day, until her father found out.)

"Oh, no!" Mary all but leaped up from the table. "Poor Cayenne! She's so sensitive." Cayenne, Mary's cat, became scabby and bumpy if she was bit by a flea.

"Cayenne is fine. I tucked her under my coat and sneaked her into my room, where I bathed her and left

her asleep on my bed. You can see her after breakfast." Mary, in the same suite as her parents, wouldn't
dare bring her cat into the room.

Mary settled into her chair again, relieved. "Oh,
thank you, thank you . . ." Then looking about the
table, she broke into rhapsodic descriptions of the
antics of her cat—successfully diverted from talking
about Louise to overly friendly strangers.

This conversation segued into another as omelettes
and grills of tomato and Oxford sausage arrived, a
sumptuous breakfast over which even Mary was
something less than eager. Louise seemed to be the
only one at the table whose stomach blithely answered
to hunger. Mary, meanwhile, made up for her poor
appetite with a gluttony of chatter, from pets to school
friends to lip colors that could only be found in Paris.
Louise lost interest.

Less boring, she noticed Lieutenant Johnston down
the table. (The ship's officers were encouraged to
spend their free time in the public rooms among the
first-class passengers, since many first-class parties
were short of men, well-off fathers tending to stay
home to watch over their businesses while the mothers, aunts, and daughters scoured the Old World for
titled bachelors.) There he sat, her mistake from last
night, smiling and nodding in her direction. She had
felt such a nice little ping of interest yesterday evening.

For a brief time, Louise had felt alive, enjoying the
company of someone she had thought gallant, suave, a
soul mate—a feeling not unlike the hopeful thrill she
had felt on her way to Montreal—only to arrive, so to
speak, at the sad destination of a gushing, revering,
oafish dolt.

The entirely inappropriate lieutenant winked at
Louise, as if they shared something between them.
She made a pull of her mouth and shifted her atten-
tion to her grilled tomato collapsing around its

mound of stuffing. Lieutenant Johnston remained, without a doubt, one of the finest looking young men on the ship, yet his handsome exterior clearly bred disappointment—which in turn bred an inexplicable yet increasingly familiar anxiety, the hum of a small, unnamed panic that tightened Louise's chest.

The feeling compounded a sense of urgency. For there was another newly revealed disappointment waiting for her, with little she could do about it directly. It hadn't occurred to her for an instant that her parents would marry off their "beautiful treasure" to a man who was scarred, blind in one eye, and lame. Yet she had cornered her parents last night before they had gone to bed, and, after a month of calling him "unusual," even "wonderful" to look at, they had owned up somewhat indirectly. ("Limp? Does he walk with a limp, Harold? I don't remember. But, yes, dear, he has a bad eye, though that hardly makes him less attractive. He is quite interesting to look at." Interesting. Louise was sure that the hunchback of Notre Dame was *interesting*.) Perhaps it *shouldn't* matter that the gracious and well-connected Prince d'Harcourt was a less-than-whole physical specimen, but, to be purely honest, it did. Louise wasn't too fond of homely men; disfigurement she found repulsive.

Covertly she scanned the table now, looking at the men. The older ones didn't bother her, as long as they weren't too old. But the plain ones and funny-looking ones and the downright drab . . . She was pretty enough to have *any* man. Didn't she deserve a handsome one, at least once before she was married (and perhaps even now and then afterward, if Charles Harcourt was as unsightly as she thought he might be)?

Louise reasoned with straightforward logic. The Prince d'Harcourt was a very good match for her in many ways. She shared her parents' opinion that a hospitable, intelligent, generous man with a lofty title

and as much wealth behind him as she had was
nothing less than what she merited. But she also
valued beauty; who didn't? (If it wasn't worth *something,* her own worth as a human being certainly
dropped.) She wanted to meet, to flirt, to kiss, to
know a man who was handsome *and* kind, handsome
and intelligent, handsome *and* generous. Then, as she
looked at all the very ordinary men around her,
craning her neck, she realized she was having to
stretch to see around Mrs. Montebello.

The woman smiled and moved her head so as to
make eye contact. "So what did *you* study, my dear?"
She had apparently not been put off by Mary's
chitchat.

Louise had no idea what they were talking about.
"Where?" she asked.

"In school, of course." The woman coached, "Sew-
ing? Music?"

The interest was sincere, but the question somehow
wasn't. Louise speared a forkful of omelette.

When she offered nothing immediately, the woman
said with the cheerful tolerance one shows dull children, "Deportment?" She added, "You really have a
lovely way of moving, my dear."

Louise slid her eyes to the woman again, ate the
omelette, then said, "Mathematics."

"Mathematics?" This made Mrs. Montebello
giggle.

"And languages."

The woman's giggle became open laughter. "A
young man's education," she said. "You're having me
on, aren't you?"

"No."

Lightly, the woman asked, "Which languages
then?"

"French, Italian, German—"

"My, how busy you—"

"Flemish, Spanish, and Sanskrit."

The woman grew quiet. Then she asked in Italian (one of the languages Louise actually *did* speak— another little vice of Louise's was that, under the right circumstances, she enjoyed lying), "Are you always this much of a smart aleck?"

Mary cut in. "Oh, don't," she said. "She'll answer. She really does speak some other languages, though not *that* many." Mary rolled her eyes. "She can be such a show-off." This complaint was followed, however, by a beaming smile into Louise's face. "We always say Lulu is way ahead of herself."

The woman smiled thinly. "Lulu?"

"A nickname," Mary explained. "From when she was little."

Mrs. Montebello raised one brow. "Not so very long ago," she said. Frowning, she grabbed up a pale, plump English sausage with her fingers and bit into it.

By the time cakes and coffee arrived, Gaspard, the society matron next to him, and Mary were discussing, of all things, great passenger-ship disasters. It was an uneasy conversation, full of reassuring jokes and false laughter. From here, the topic turned to food, the abundance and magnificence of it on the ship, and the great shame that everyone's stomach wasn't up to enjoying it completely. Someone said the wine, drunk the night before, had settled her stomach, one of the properties, she'd discovered, of a truly good, old red.

A reflex, Louise corrected this misinformation. "It was a young one. The old ones are terrible sailors."

"Pardon?"

"There is no ocean-going vessel that offers a good Bordeaux," Louise informed the table.

There was a pause, in which she realized that Mrs. Montebello had been speaking. The woman glowered at Louise a moment, then said, "Well, aren't you just a fountain of information suddenly." She quickly and diplomatically pulled her smile back into her cheeks. "I'm sure you're right, though." She added, "Lulu."

Unsettled, Louise murmured, "Sorry." Though she wasn't precisely sure what her apology was for.

"No, no," the woman insisted, again with obvious insincerity. "Never apologize for being right." She laughed. "I don't." As her laughter died, it left behind in her smiling eyes a kind of penetrating scrutiny. She looked hard at Louise, then sat back, dropping her arms onto the armrests. Out of nowhere she said, "My, but you are so young." She laughed again, this time seeming quite to enjoy herself.

Louise couldn't understand the humor, though she understood that there was something unpleasant in it that went beyond mere rudeness. She turned her back on the woman, responding to something Gaspard said.

The most interesting part of breakfast, however, came when a private dining alcove at the back emptied out, releasing into the main saloon a rare sight, a loose assembly of Middle Easterners—residents of the Mediterranean region toward which the ship headed. Few from the countries of this area had the money or inclination to travel to, or among inhabitants of, the West. All of them men, these people moved quickly by Louise, flowing past and between two tables, a tightly moving wave of murmured Arabic conversation. Their flowing robes swept along behind them in one exotic stream of colorful wools crowned with gleaming coils of silk—though beneath their robes they all, to a one, wore western trousers.

Noticing Mrs. Montebello's regard to be following this procession as well, Louise risked asking, "Do you know them?"

"No." She turned back toward the table, shaking her head. "Though for a moment I thought the tall one was someone I knew." She laughed incongruously then began to gather up her fan and reticule.

Louise stood as well, turning to watch the departing procession of men. "Where have they been? Where did they eat last night? This is the first I have seen them. Who are they?"

Mrs. Montebello faced around as well, and the two women stood together in uneasy truce for the sake of mutual curiosity. "Some sheikh or pasha, I imagine, with his retinue," said the older woman. "He must be staying in one of the suites at the top of the ship, where dinner or whatever you ask for is brought to your door."

"Really?" Louise glanced down at her—the woman was a good five or six inches shorter. "One of the grand luxury suites?" Arabia, it occurred to her, was known for its costly jasmine perfumes. Louise's interest increased.

The woman didn't respond further, but continued to watch with Louise as the Arabian men disappeared up the staircase.

Behind Louise, others along the table were standing to go. Yet when Louise turned to pick up her own things left on the chair, she found herself to be once more the object of Mrs. Montebello's close inspection.

Caught staring again, the woman laughed—partly a nervous, self-conscious sound, partly the odd, gleeful cackle she was finding so difficult to contain. She shrugged slightly. "I just can't get over how very, very young you are."

Louise rolled her eyes, making a "youthful" pull of her face. She told her, "Older than last night's wine, at least."

Mrs. Montebello raised one brow at this, the look on her face turning purely mean for a second; no social niceties, no disguise. She said to Louise, "Well, aren't you clever. It must be so nice being you: always the smartest, youngest, most beautiful woman in the room." Her eyes glittered with a bright, venomous anger.

Louise was so taken aback to stare into the face of

such intense animosity, she answered honestly. "No. It is a lonely feeling. I hate it most of the time. I would never wish these things on my most cursed enemy."

From the walkway two balconies above, Charles looked down fifty feet into the dining saloon to where Pia and Louise Vandermeer stood, two purple-skinned women in purple dresses standing in a purple panorama—all but for the edges of the balcony from where he watched. With one finger, Charles pulled dark, purple-lensed spectacles down the bridge of his nose, looking over the top of them. After hearing the American girl's voice again this morning—the delicious edginess that had crept into her cool, upper-class tone—he had given in to the urge to see her in better light. And there she was: taller than he had realized (she had to be five and three-quarter feet standing there in her shoes), as unflappable as he remembered (with Pia giving her some sort of trouble), as elegant a creature as ever breathed air, and . . . something else. Charles tilted his head slightly, studying her.

The girl's face was all but expressionless. She was cool, all right. He realized, in the time he'd been watching her, every glimpse of expression he'd seen on her face had been the same: even, unexcited, distant—that is to say, without much enthusiasm or connection to anyone or anything around her. Perhaps he'd missed something; after all, quite a distance stretched between them. Yet even from this distance, there was something sad about her.

He shook off any sympathy for her. There was every possibility that she was a self-centered young thing out on a devilish, sexually precocious experiment—who fully deserved to be the butt of a little playfulness herself.

Just then the sweet young thing turned her head and raised her eyes, her lovely, long neck arching slightly

as her gaze scanned upward. It was as if she knew he
was there. She was off by twenty feet and a pillar, but
her gaze backtracked unerringly to fix on him. (He
hadn't thought about it, but of course his very choice
of cover made him stand out, should anyone choose
to look up.) Their eyes met across the vast distance of
the dining saloon and up three decks. Charles felt
goose bumps ripple down his spine. Eerie. He pushed
the dark glasses firmly against his brow, grabbed up
the sides of his gallibiya and kaffiyeh, and withdrew
immediately.

Louise watched the man overhead turn, an embod-
ied flow of color; he was leaving. His robes unfurled in
folds of purples, blues, and golden yellows, then
wafted out, a blood-red sail behind him.

It was the Arab shah or sheikh or sultan or whatever
he was, an emir, a pasha, the tall man from the
screened private dining alcove, the one from the
grand luxury suite. And he'd been watching her.

Louise leaped. "Excuse me," she said. "I will see
you all at—" By this time no further valediction was
necessary. She was beyond the hearing range of her
breakfast companions. She took the length of the
dining saloon at a brisk walk, pulling herself along for
stability here and there by a chair back. At the
staircase she was able to pick up speed. She gripped
and slid her hand up the banister as her feet tapped up
the curving steps. Then at the top, she threw caution
to the wind; she broke into a dead run.

Chapter 7

The use of ambergris in perfume blending came to Europe chiefly through contact with the Arabs during the Crusades.

Charles Harcourt, Prince d'Harcourt
On the Nature and Uses of Ambergris

Charles heard someone behind him calling, but did not imagine that the sound had anything to do with him. It didn't occur to him that Louise Vandermeer would give chase, not even when he heard the tap of footsteps running.

"You!" a voice said firmly, loudly.

He glanced back, just to see what the commotion was, then was stopped by a surprising and irresistible sight: the splendid Miss Vandermeer, breathless and running pell-mell, zig then zag, toward him down the narrow corridor of a rocking ship. He halted so abruptly that she all but ploughed into him. Charles had to set her back onto her feet. How astonishing to find her slender, sturdy arms suddenly warm in his hands. Then he pulled back, bending his head so the folds of his kaffiyeh fell forward. He touched his dark

58

glasses self-consciously, checking, and stepped back. He was about to turn.

"No, you stop where you are!" said the imperial young voice.

He felt the tip of a finger press into his chest. He pushed her finger away as he said, "Excuse me?" He bowed slightly, using this posture to hide his glance over the top of his glasses at her. *My, oh, my, was she something up close.*

She narrowed her eyes—eyes that were so blue they were violet—large, clear, with long, lush eyelashes. Her hair, thick and shining, was an exceptional color: a dark, ashen beige at the temple that quickly became densely streaked with blond, varying in paleness from a kind of ivory gilt to silvery white. Her skin, meanwhile, was as flawless as the surface of a plateful of cream, setting off a long-necked, high-boned, hollow-cheeked beauty—a perfect, patrician good-looks. From any distance, from any angle, this girl was impossibly gorgeous.

"You're the one," she said with utter conviction. "I know it." There was a moment, as the ship tilted again, wherein she had to make a decision: She chose to grab the far handrail, stepping away rather than closer.

Charles stepped back as well, pulling himself into the protection of whatever shadows he could find. Along the floor of the hallway were lines of small electric lights; not much illumination but it was everywhere. More sporadically, and more elegantly, sconces dotted the walls every twenty or so feet, small-bulbed electric "candles" of vaseline glass— only a soft radiance, though more visibility than Charles would have liked. He wanted to retreat from this too well-lit situation; he wanted to stare at Louise Vandermeer while he had her in the light.

"You may as well admit it," she said. She had

marvelous stability, her feet braced, her knees giving her a swaying balance. "I recognize your voice, your English, from just the two words you've spoken."

Charles rather doubted this. He was inclined to stonewall, deny everything. Yet somehow this confrontation here in the teeter-tottering hall was so unexpected, so interesting. He found himself saying, "I intend you no harm." He took several more steps backward, while she followed like a hound on a fox. He wanted to laugh. He was aghast and at the same time vastly entertained by his own scrambling bewilderment. How had she done this? How had she picked him out from among so many other people? How had she decided he was the one? "Also," he told her, "I must find us a new place to meet. Anywhere on the open deck has become too dangerous with the storm."

With his admission, she stopped. She put her fists on her waist. "I'm not meeting you anywhere."

He bowed again slightly and kept on backing. "As you wish. Perhaps you shall find what you are looking for another way. It was dangerous, the manner in which you were chasing whatever you are after."

"You just don't bother yourself with what I am 'after.' It—I am none of your concern."

He paused, marginally safe in the shadow of his half-bow, in a penumbra of the double illumination. "Actually," he said, "you are a puzzle, though a more and more engrossing one." Charles felt this keenly, all at once; he meant it. "What *do* you want, Louise?"

She frowned deeply. "How do you know my name? Who are you?"

"I am whoever, whatever you want me to be."

"Pardon?"

"Come tonight. I will get word to you where. Then, if you want an ear to listen, I shall lend you mine. If you want sympathy, I will give it. If you want advice, I shall find some. And if you want a mouth to kiss you,

I shall put my mouth to yours. I am yours to command, my dear."

"Why?"

"For the pleasure of pleasing you."

"Because I'm beautiful." She asked in that faintly amused, faintly condescending tone from last night, "Do you adore me?"

He laughed. "Hardly. And this is the first I have seen you in reasonably good light."

She thought about this, her slender, high-arched brows drawing together into a delicate furrow. "Why then? Why would you want to do anything for me?"

"Because you are so suspicious." He laughed again and kept backing; she kept following, though more cautiously now, at greater distance. "And tenacious." He shook his head with confounded wonder. "And because you are smart enough to know that coming tonight is a little risky, yet you are so curious—and a little full of yourself—that you will probably come, anyway. Oh, and because you smell like jasmine, only ever so much better."

She contradicted only one part of this: "I am *not* full of myself," she said.

There was something plaintive in her protest; a child's wretched outcry in the face of what she feared was true. Charles felt a twinge of pity—surely misplaced—for this lovely, resourceful, supremely confident human being; then, more concretely, he felt something stop his heel. A wall had come up against it, a bend in the corridor. "Oh, but you are," he told her. "My guess is, You can never quite get away from the fact of your beauty, that you live by it. But not tonight. Tonight, if you meet me, you will do so in the dark."

"No, I won't."

He turned swiftly, cloth sailing as he took the bend in the corridor.

He thought for a moment that she was going to pursue him again. But instead she simply rounded the turn and called after him, "I'll meet you, all right. And when I do, I'll bring my father. And the ship's captain. . . ."

Charles knew she wouldn't. He kept walking, laughing, immensely enjoying himself. She was surprising. He hadn't predicted her energy or anger or, yes, her astounding willingness and capacity for aggression. But he felt fairly safe in one prediction: Behind him stood a young lady who routinely circumvented the rules. Louise Vandermeer paid little homage to authority; she would not quickly resort to its protection.

There was no doubt about it, Louise Vandermeer was not the perfect little creature Charles had been given to believe—hardly Papa's little prize, more like Papa's little heartburn. Whichever, Charles wanted more information, and he knew where to get it. His mind was suddenly filled, delighted, with the young woman beside whom, he remembered, Pia had had breakfast.

Thus, he went up the aft staircase, then doubled back to begin navigating through the narrow corridors of the next deck, bracing himself on walls as he rolled with the movement of the ship. Pia would be somewhere through her midmorning change of clothes, her first of many.

He came across her just as she was backing out of her dressing cabin. She and Roland always booked two cabins when they crossed, one for themselves and one for Pia's steamer trunks; in this second cabin she lined up all her trunks and dressed out of them, a real convenience considering she changed her clothes four and five times a day. As she backed out now, bending down to lock the door, the drapes and sweepers of her silver-satin skirt billowed out to take up half the corridor.

Charles moved these aside as he leaned on the doorjamb.

She jumped, stood straight, then frowned. "Charles?" She put her palm to her chest. "It *is* you."

"Who else?" Smiling, he slipped the dark spectacles down his nose to look at her over them.

She asked, "Was that you at breakfast as well?"

"At breakfast?" He shook his head. "I ate breakfast alone." Then he realized the source of confusion. The kaffiyeh and agal he had talked off a man standing guard at the doors to the suite next to his, one of the bodyguards of the old emir's son. (It hadn't hurt that Charles had known the old emir, nor that he knew about the blessings and respect an Arab placed upon his head apparel.) These fellows had gone to breakfast while Charles had decked himself out. The rest, the glasses and gallibiya, his robe, belonged to him. All in all, a fairly neat disguise, and an attire that he was somewhat familiar with, having lived in clothes like these years ago in Tunisia. He was quite pleased with himself. He wiggled his eyebrows as he grinned over the glasses at Pia. "A regular Arab prince, eh?"

Her relief turned to chagrin. She gave him an aggrieved look. "A regular idiot," she whispered. "What are you doing here? Roland is just inside." She nodded toward the silent, closed door one cabin over, then bent down again, preparing to insert her key into the lock. Charles's shoulder, however, prevented her from fully closing the door. She stood up and turned around, scowling, about to speak.

Charles remembered that she was put out with him. He had completely forgotten their argument. His mind shifted gears. Or tried to. In truth, he mildly resented being put off track of all he wanted to ask her about the girl with whom she'd had breakfast. Dutifully, though, he put his index finger across her open mouth and leaned closer. He bit her ear gently then whispered, "You have calmed down, I trust?" She smelled nice, not like jasmine exactly, but good. And of course she was an adult, a full-grown woman, which had its advantages. He nibbled her ear more enthusiastically.

She shoved at him. "Stop." She glanced up at his face, then down the length of him. Frowning deeply, she said, "You're up to something. What?"

"Cuckolding Roland strikes me as a fine idea suddenly." He grinned and ran his finger along her bare shoulder.

She made a sour face and pushed him all the way back. "Charles," she said, "I sat with your little fiancée at breakfast, and, honestly, this marriage with the Vandermeer girl has to be a joke. She's a child, for God's sake." Pia crossed her arms, perversely refusing to hurry now.

This wasn't exactly the cooperative tone in which he'd hoped to launch this conversation. He decided to attack it obliquely. "How is Roland feeling?" he asked as the floor beneath his feet slowly angled forward. He had to stand up straight to balance himself.

"Terrible. The doctor has given him something." The boat's continuing list became severe enough that she had to catch herself on her palm to keep from falling into the wall. Something low in the boat creaked, a long crooning groan of steel. Pia grimaced, muttering under her breath, "This damned ship. I took a little of Roland's medicine myself." She looked at Charles. "You aren't the least bit queasy, are you?" He shook his head. She tilted hers. "And you're plotting something. What is it?"

"Nothing." He smiled.

"Not 'nothing,'" she insisted. "You have that wicked look about you." She made a leap: "Your bride." Satisfied, she chuckled voicelessly. "She has somehow displeased you." Her voice took on a sly note. "They call her 'Lulu.' Isn't that sweet?"

"No. It's insipid." Charles cocked a brow and threw her a teasing smile. "Though, happily, she doesn't look the least bit like her name."

Pia ignored this, her good humor blooming. "Did you know she has a puppy in the kennel here? And a cat in her stateroom? Children so love animals, don't they?"

He sniffed.

Pia laughed. "I mean, she is eighteen, *really* eighteen, Charles. The conversation at breakfast included Cayenne the cat, her puppy named Bear, her studies at school, oh, and a new French lip color one can only get in Paris. I mean, if you *like* eighteen-year-olds—"

She knew he didn't. But just to be perverse, he told her, "I intend to develop a taste for baby-smooth skin and puppylike eagerness. It shouldn't be too hard: She's quite fetching."

Pia's smile faded ever so slightly. "If she's so appealing, then what's wrong? What are you doing walking about the ship like this?" She indicated his clothing.

"You think I should stay in my rooms and just wait for you?"

"Well, that is what we planned, isn't it?"

"We planned being together most of the time, because Roland gets seasick."

"Well, he's *really* ill now—"

"So should I run to my room? Are you on your way up?"

"No." She let out an exhalation of wounded dignity. Then glanced at him again. "You're having fun. I can tell. You're involved in one of your little machinations. What are you doing, Charles?"

"Will you help?"

"Will you not marry her, if I do?"

"I don't know *what* I'm going to do yet." He contemplated the idea of Louise Vandermeer again.

"She's certainly a lot younger and wilder and"—he paused—"oh, a little sadder, somehow, than I was expecting."

"Sadder? God, Charles. She's a little snot, is what she is. A vile, smart-mouthed little thing who is far too big for her own britches."

He laughed. "What a marvelous display of jealousy. So you'll help?"

She leaned a hip on her fist, thinking about his question, then said, "Perhaps. If you tell me the problem."

"Well, it seems my betrothed is slightly appalled by the notion of a lame, one-eyed husband."

This brought forth a small, involuntary giggle. "Oh, Charles, that is such a silly—"

"Precisely."

Her laughter turned mean as she added, "But what you deserve for playing with children."

"She's not so young that she isn't responsible for her own words and actions, or for keeping her own promises."

"No." Pia's smile grew slowly wider. "So have you figured out something terribly mischievous?"

"Does she like any of the men in particular?"

She raised one eyebrow. "The men?"

"Whom does she fancy? Anyone?" He added what he knew already, "Not the young Lieutenant Johnston."

Pia gave him a peevish look. "How am I supposed to know?"

"Come now. You are brilliant at this sort of thing. At whom does she sneak glances? Who makes her blush?"

"She's not the blushing sort." She frowned at him. "Why do you need to know this?"

He shrugged. "I don't. What's her suite number?"

"What?"

"Which stateroom? It's a midship first-class suite,

but there seem to be about forty of those. Which one?"

"I don't know."

"Can you find out?"

She heaved another breath. "If I did, I'm not sure I'd want to tell you."

"Don't be difficult, *chérie.*" He took her key out of her hand, about to pull the door closed and lock it for her.

But she grabbed at his hand as he touched the doorknob, whispering, a hissing sound, "Not with Roland in the next room!"

He blinked, confused. Then realized: She apparently had thought he was about to *open* the door, lead her *into* the room, and lock the door from the *other* side. Such foolery honestly hadn't even occurred to Charles. So he was nonplussed to hear her remonstrations go a step farther.

Pia said, "I won't go in there with you, Charles. Not there, not anywhere, not till you rid yourself of that little idiot. You go tell little Lulu Vandermeer and her whole family that it was a foolish notion, contracting to marry someone you don't know just for a lot of whale vomit."

When his dubious look said he thought this a pretty terrible plan, she tightened her mouth. "Well, whatever," she said. "Just don't come near me until you've done something. I mean it, Charles. I won't see you, not for a minute, not alone, not until you break this off. I won't have it."

Chapter 8

The Far East has used ambergris for centuries for its presumed aphrodisiac properties.

Charles Harcourt, Prince d'Harcourt
On the Nature and Uses of Ambergris

By late afternoon, the *Concordia* had begun to creak, as if a huge bass fiddle somewhere low in the ship's bowels were bowing two notes slowly back—*gre-e-ek*—then forth—*gra-a-awk*. This plaintive two-note drone unnerved most of the passengers; all gay pretense abandoned, people clung to their rooms. Charles could have met the lovely Louise almost anywhere.

Almost, however, became the operative word. Charles found the main saloon and dining room unsuitable for his purposes; the staff was optimistically preparing for dinner and dancing tonight. The gentlemen's smoking parlor harbored four hard-drinking fellows. An elderly woman, fit as rain, had staked out the library. In the vast game room, one single table was occupied by a threesome who whiled away the storm by playing cards. The Turkish bath was empty of patrons and staff, the boiler cold, but it was ankle-deep in water. The Pompeiian-style swimming bath next door, enacting its own indoor version of a storm-tossed sea, sloshed water that flowed over the marble floors throughout the entire area. Down the way from this, the children's playroom was locked.

All the public rooms seemed to follow this rule: They were either closed, uninhabitable, or occupied by some of the few passengers who, like Charles, endured the storm with ready balance and an unblenching stomach.

It delighted him to realize that among these passengers he could count his lovely Louise. And, for better or worse, since her run and stagger down the corridor after him, she had become *his* Louise, for he could not get over how enchanting he had found her. From her pettish demands to the contradiction in her less-than-innocent blue eyes to her simple, callow arrogance he should have found her obnoxious. But this was simply not the case. It was more than her being the perfect butt for his joke (which she was, of course). It had nothing to do with anything sexual (though he was aware of a vaguely obscene curiosity he was developing for the youth-soft smoothness of her skin, a curiosity that sent a shiver through him whenever he dwelled on it).

No, he fancied aspects within her personality; her quickness, her confidence and stamina. He *liked* her, beyond the sexual, apart from it—his interest in her was much broader than merely a thirty-some-year-old man sniffing around the flounce of a young woman's skirts, looking for the missed opportunities of youth. (He had thought about the fact that he had never known a young woman, a really young woman, and for the first time this had made him puzzle over his younger self.)

Most importantly, though, he had immediate rapport and sympathy for one of her defining characteristics: He sensed her deep fond attachment, conjoined with an animosity—it was a kind of love–hate—for the way she looked.

Charles hummed out loud as he pursued his quest, to find a safe, dry, private, dark point of midnight rendezvous for himself and this fascinating, if somewhat abrasive and misguided, girl. He hunted for someplace where he could control circumstances as much as possible. Not the ladies' parlor or writing room or the veranda cafe; not the gymnasium or squash court. In the end, he owed his choice to Pia; he would not have known the ship had kennels were it not for her mention of them. He searched for these, finding them finally on the top deck, where the ship's reeling was a regular carnival ride of motion.

Not a soul was around, save some frightened, baying animals. Here was a place where few would spend much time in rough weather and, even in good weather, would hardly visit at midnight. Moreover, Miss Vandermeer knew where it was.

Better and better, the kennel was completely internal, not a window to the outside, that is to say, not a window to catch so much as a reflection of light or attention from elsewhere. Its only disadvantage was its smell of disinfectant, which was preferable to what it could have smelled like, given there were several dozen dogs and cats and a monkey on board. Charles walked down a corridor between rows and towers of metal cages, most of them empty, though his passing brought forth the occasional burst of barking. Overhead, individual lights were spaced down the length of the walkway; he counted eight of them. He discovered these to be hardwired to a wall switch. If he intended that she should not be able to see him, he would have to disable the switch or get up there and unscrew all the bulbs. The latter was more tedious but ultimately more appealing, given his ignorance of the ship's wiring and his aversion to electrical shock.

Midway down this corridor of cages, he stopped before a crate labeled VANDERMEER. Bending down slightly, he came nose to nose with a puppy that looked more like a tiny polar bear than any dog he knew, a pudgy, fluffy, dirty white little thing. The fellow was friendly and immediately keen to be out. Charles moved away rather than torment the dog with hope of the impossible.

He kept exploring. The floors were tile, with gutters and drains. Inconspicuously placed were taps and hoses, a sink. Some of the cages were still wet from having been recently doused. The far door at the end of the corridor gave out onto the open deck, the dog promenade. But, more interesting, between two middle stacks of crates was a passageway into a gated area that dropped down several feet to run behind the starboard row of cages. An indoor promenade of sorts. Or just an area to play with one's free-roaming pet—a kind of carpeted, comfy pen. The only furnishings of this area were three round sofas, each encircling the cast-brass, hand-chased Corinthian column of a lamp stand. Each lamp wore a rather silly green silk shade beneath which was a single bright bulb. These three bulbs were the only light other than whatever came over the crates from the other part of the room.

In the pen or indoor promenade or whatever it was, Charles went from lamp to lamp, removing all the lightbulbs, until the long, cozy space became a dark, shadowy pit. He stepped up out of this, coming back into the main area again, where he went to the far end of the corridor, climbed the open metalwork of the last tower of cages, then, hanging by one arm off the highest cage, he began removing lightbulbs from the gooseneck, green crimped-glass fixtures.

He was hanging off a cage, his hand in his sixth overhead fixture, when he realized there was a sound outside the kennel, out in the corridor. The general stirring of the animals should have alerted him, but his concentration was such that their shifting in their cages, a few stray barks, only served to drown the exterior sounds out until it was almost too late: Someone was right on the other side of the entrance to the kennel.

Charles scrambled up onto the top of the crate from which he was hanging, his knee objecting to the quick strain put on it. Almost immediately, the door swung open. The rising din of dogs barking and clattering on the metal floors of their confinement allowed Charles to crawl along the tops of the crates till he was far back in the darkness he himself had created. Below him, down the way, just at the edge of remaining light, a young woman bent down and peered into a cage. She didn't even have to open her mouth before he knew: They may as well have been traveling in a rowboat together for the way she kept turning up, right beside him.

Louise Vandermeer opened her puppy's crate, saying, "Come here, you," then, "*Oo-eee,* you stink!" She laughed as the little fellow lunged himself out at her, whining with eagerness. He licked her face as she tried to contain him in her arms. She drew him against her breast. "Eww, my, you smell like a barnyard." She continued to chatter away to the dog as she grabbed a rag and wiped out the cage, then carried the puppy himself over to the sink. "And what happened to the lights?" she asked as if he were perfectly capable of answering.

Charles eased himself up into a sitting position, one leg dangling over an empty cage as he leaned forward slightly to watch her. The dog was delighted to be where he was, his tail wagging so hard his whole body twitched. In the sink, he stood on his hind legs, paws on her bosom, trying to lick her chin. The two of them seemed to have a real camaraderie; certainly she seemed to have an easier accord with the dog than Charles had yet seen demonstrated with human beings. She kept scratching the puppy and laughing as she pushed him under the spigot.

She cleaned the dog up, without regard for her dress, letting him lather the front as he scooted and squirmed up against it. Meanwhile she behaved as if she and the canine were having a conversation.

"No, my afternoon wasn't much better than my morning," she said as if in answer to a question. "What? No, no, I'm just so tired of talking about the weather and smiling at people. I mean, someone today expressed delight at my coming marriage, then said I looked just like a real princess should. What does that mean, Bear?"

She bent down, found a towel under the sink, and wrapped it around the dog. "Honestly," she continued, "this man I'm marrying, he isn't even a real prince of anything, no country, nothing like that. So I look exactly like a real Princess of Nothing?" She paused in toweling the animal. "You know what I'd like?" she asked him. "For someone to tell me I'm"—she searched a moment—"wise." In a low, mocking voice she said, "Why, that Louise Vandermeer, she is so wi-i-i-se." She laughed. "Or capable. Or independent. Or compassionate. But no one would notice, I don't think, if I were the most insightful person on the face of the earth." She carried the squirming puppy over to where she tried to put on the lights at the end of the walkway by means of the switch.

The lights didn't go on, of course. "Hmm. That's odd," she said. She shifted her charge up onto her shoulder, then headed toward the gate that led down into the play area. As she disappeared completely, she said, "Oh, to top it all off, Lieutenant Johnston wrote me a note today. He said I was cruel." She laughed suddenly, a titter. "All right I was, but that is part of being insightful, you see: He deserved it. Do you know what else he said in his note?" From the dark below, her voice took on the bombast of ecstatic declamation. " 'Miss Vandermeer,' he wrote, 'I am appalled to have offended your fair sensibilities. Blame it on your beauty. I was drunk on the blue wine of your eyes.' " She could barely get the last of this out for laughing with wicked enjoyment. " 'Blue wine,' " she repeated. Then as if the dog had censured her, she argued, "All right, I'm being mean again, but, Lord, what does a woman say to such twaddle?"

From the dark room behind the crates, Charles heard the click of lamp switches, one then another, as she continued her discourse with a dog who seemed used to it, even quieted by it. "It's so funny, Bear. Men write me notes. People want to talk to me, yet they don't seem to say anything that I have the first inclination to answer. And then there's the ones like that diplomat's wife who downright dislike me. What is there about me? What's wrong? I try to be nice, and then I know perfectly well that I'm not, that I am behaving badly. Yet I can't seem to help myself."

Charles heard her come back up, saw her silhouette reenter the edge of faint illumination, her voice near again. "Well, this is all so peculiar," she said. "What's going on with the lights?"

This time, however, the little dog must have seen or smelled something. He suddenly became a tussling knot of towel and fur in her arms, barking furiously as he tried to leap in Charles's direction.

At first, she upbraided the dog. "Stop that, Bear!" He quieted only so far as a yappy growl. After which, she peered into the shadows and asked tentatively, "Is someone there?"

Charles could not hold it back. He laughed. "We have to stop meeting like this."

She was motionless, in a state of alarm, as she stood there clutching the yelping dog.

He tried to put her at ease. "It's good to know you can be pleasant," he teased, "even if it's just to a dog."

He heard her come to a conclusion—she made an irritable sound, tongue against teeth. "You, again. Where are you?" Her silhouette stepped closer, looking up into the darkness.

"I'm sitting up here on the crates."

"You did the lights?"

"Yes." He laughed again. "Though I wasn't finished. Don't you think this would be a nice place to meet tonight? I mean, it sways a lot and doesn't smell like jasmine—"

"I'm not meeting you, I told you."

"Yet here you are."

She fell silent. After a moment, she asked, "Can you make the lights work in the visiting area?"

"Visiting area?"

"Down there." Her shadow pointed toward the darkened pen.

"No light, remember?"

She made another little click with her tongue, more exasperation. "I want to play with my dog."

"He doesn't need the light, I assure you."

"Your games are stupid. They don't interest me." She let out a sniff of disdain. "So what have you done? Where are the lightbulbs?"

She had checked the sockets to know the bulbs were missing. He didn't answer. Instead he responded, "So why do *you* need the light?" Something occurred to him: "Imagine all those conversations today that so annoyed you. Suppose they had taken place in the dark, without anyone knowing what you looked like, leaving you to rely on your other virtues." He chuckled at her silence. "You do *have* other virtues, don't you? *Are* you wise, Louise?"

She snorted. "Wise enough to know what you're up to."

He laughed again. He didn't know why, but she so amused him.

She said, "Why don't *you* want to be seen? I never got a good look at you this morning for all your ducking and bowing."

"All in good time," he told her. "I would rather get to know you without the influence of"—he paused for a split second—"my handsome mien." He let his voice grow serious as he aligned himself, without conscience, to admissions given to her dog. "Like you, I wish I could talk to someone as myself, just myself. To let them know me for something other than how I look, something closer to the heart of me than the way my skin spreads over muscle and bone."

In the dim light, he could not be sure of her face, but something in her posture changed, a shift of her weight. He had her reluctant attention.

"Turn off the rest of the lights," he said quietly. Why not? he thought. She was here. He was here. This was where he'd been heading. He would make the most of this fortuitous meeting.

She just stood there, wooden, the dog more animated than she was.

"Go on," he said.

Then to his surprise, with no more encouragement than this, she did. As she turned her back on him to walk to the wall switch, she said, "I'm taking the Bear with me. You can come down into the visiting area if you want. I'm going to play with him there. If you bother me, he'll bite you. He's very protective."

Charles wasn't much intimidated. He had eight dogs at home, field dogs, house dogs. Hers didn't seem any too ferocious. And dogs, he'd found, were not so unlike young women. If one offered no threat and showed respect for their essential nature, it usually wasn't long before a man had what he wanted out of them.

The last of the lights blinked off. He heard her and the little dog, panting at her feet now, its nails clicking on the floor, as they came back up the corridor. She opened the gate. It had a slight creak.

Once she'd passed, Charles slid himself down along the front of the crates, then followed slowly, being careful to keep the sound of his pace even. His knee hurt, though not so badly that he couldn't overlook the pain by keeping his attention riveted elsewhere.

In the pit, or what she called the visiting area, he could identify exactly where she was by the smell of her. No flowers in her hair today, but she wore again the same scent of perfume as last night, and another smell—her unique and specific odor that Charles was coming to believe he could identify from a roomful of women, could walk right up to her blindfolded. Louise Vandermeer used some sort of soap that mixed with the scent of her body; clean, warm. If one could have distilled an oil from, say, sugar cane—sturdy, grassy, sweet, sunny, green and fluttering, with a sawtooth edge, this, with perhaps a dash of the smell of fresh milk, or, no, the sweet, wholesome smell of a baby's mouth having just drunk fresh milk . . . well, this began to approximate the initial notes of her body scent.

When he sat down on the carpet, not a foot from her, she startled. He heard her move back. The dog came over to sniff him, being not nearly so discreet as Charles in the use of his nose. Charles shielded his crotch till the puppy became satisfied with his palm, his fingers. He let the dog have a big, slurpy taste of his thumb before pushing him away.

"You are remarkably persistent," she said.

"Not really. Just decided and relatively confident." Charles stretched out, leaning back onto his elbows— and the dog was back, sniffing, sniffing his elbow, then forearm along the floor, then down the length of his leg.

"And what exactly have you decided?"

"That you are up to no good," he told her, "fairly clever about it, and somehow lonely in a way I don't understand. As I said before, a conundrum."

She thought about this for a few beats, then said, "I don't believe you when you say all you want is to please me. That's pure pigwash."

Charles laughed again as he lay back, an arm under his head. With his free hand, he gave in to playing with the puppy, who wouldn't leave him alone. "Not entirely," he said. He pulled the dog's ears, scratched his belly.

"But partly. Let's discuss that part."

"All right."

"What do you want for yourself?" she asked.

"You."

"More than my company, I take it?"

"Oh, yes."

"I'm promised elsewhere."

"Ooh, not forever, just for the duration of the crossing."

This brought forth from her a single, soft hoot of laughter. She said, "I'm supposed to fall into your arms, then?"

"Oh, no, that wouldn't be any fun. You ask what I wanted for myself. I told you. I didn't say how I intended to get it."

"I want to see your face—I'm sure I'm missing something: You sound so perfectly sure—"

"In that case, you *are* missing something," he said, "because only a fool is perfectly sure of anything. Besides," he added, "any good poker player can keep things off his face. You have four other senses. Use them."

He heard her shift. The dark filled for a few seconds

with the whispers of muslin and silk, her change of position wafting up another potent dose of grassy, cream-fresh, odoriferous sweetness. Meanwhile the room was so utterly lightless that not so much as a shadow or silhouette stirred. Charles himself rather liked this blind experiment. He could hear her breathing, smell the warm, verdant scent of her. It would have been splendid to feel her, taste her as well, in this black space where only the two of them, along with a rather pleasant little wet-nosed dog, existed.

Her voice came from a slightly different location, a few inches lower, a few inches farther away, as if she'd leaned back onto her arms. She asked, "Are you really Arab? You don't sound it."

"Oxford. Class of eighty-nine." Nearly true; Charles had learned his English at the Other British School. Moreover, wealthy North Africans and Mid-Easterners were often educated at European universities.

In French she asked, "And *are* you a good poker player?" Her French was unexpectedly clean, without a trace of the usual American accent.

But Charles surprised himself by replying pointedly in English. He said, "I don't speak French very well." He didn't know why he lied to her.

"I thought all educated Arabs spoke French."

"Reluctantly, I assure you. It is the language of our oppressors. Besides, there are parts of the Arab world where French is unnecessary."

"For instance?"

He had to think a moment. He came up with, "Egypt."

"Are you Egyptian?"

"No." Of course, it didn't matter what he told her, whether he lied or told the truth. He was up to his eyeballs in pretense already.

Yet this gratuitous tangle he had just put into the thread of their conversation made him frown deeply—

for this linguistic deception had come out of nowhere and had nothing to do with his original purpose. He pondered this a moment, mystified, then let it go.

His answers went down much better with the lovely Louise. A quiet settled between them that said: She had challenged; he had passed his first round of tests. His dead ends and blind alleys were accepted as part of the mystery of him, which she had decided tentatively to embrace.

She was uncommunicative for a time, attentive to the dog who had lain down somewhere beside her. Then out of the blue she said, "I don't want you to misunderstand something. A while ago, when I was complaining to the dog: Well, I like being who I am. I like being beautiful. I like it a lot."

"I know."

She asked suddenly, "Do you know what it's like—" She rephrased, "Do you think there is any hope for people who are vain of their own looks?"

"Well, I certainly hope so," he said, letting out a soft laugh.

She paused then asked, "Are you handsome?"

"You just can't get away from it, can you?"

"From what?"

"How people look."

"But you are. I could hear in your laughter: You know what it is like to be overly proud of your appearance."

He sighed then admitted, "I can be vain."

"Can you control it?"

"What?"

"Your vanity."

"No. But neither does it control me."

"Explain this."

In these two words, spoken abruptly, she nonetheless seemed to have come to something she earnestly wanted to talk about. There was a neediness in her demand—*Explain this*—to the point of impoverishment. A huge lack in her became obvious, crystal clear; it said she was not good at human connection, yet she longed for it as the poor hunger for bread. And more disturbing, Charles realized that he had somehow become a source of fulfillment. It was more than his simply capturing her trust; she was, awkwardly and peremptorily, venturing into friendship.

He tried to measure up (and *make* up perhaps for all his otherwise, past, present, and future, dishonesty). "Well," he began, "I don't control my feelings. No one can. But I control my responses to them. I—" He changed grammatical person to redirect attention where he wanted it. "You," he said, "can choose to behave badly, indulging your vanity for instance, if you think it is safe or fun or satisfying, whatever. Or you can deny yourself vain gratification when you know it is dangerous to your well being or perhaps unjust to someone else. You feel what you feel and more or less accept it. Then to the extent that you can, you act in accordance with what is healthy."

She seemed to think about this for a few moments, then she said, "My parents tell me I should be happy, *feel* happy, when sometimes I can't."

"Perhaps they are just asking that you *act* happy and not cause any trouble."

To this, the rustling, sweet-smelling creature uttered a snort as loud and derisive as any sailor could emit. Then she cursed emphatically. "Well, damnation," she said, "they may as well ask me to eat rocks."

"Well, yes, parents can be quite impossible," he agreed. "Mine certainly were."

"Really?" she asked, but there was no chance to reply. She descended into pure, delighted—delightful—laughter. It was the first genuine amusement he had ever heard out of her, a clear, ringing, rippling sound that came from deep inside her. It sent goose bumps down Charles's arms. It made the hair on his neck rise on end.

Meanwhile, by his innocent, random comment, he
seemed to have unleashed a torrent of conversational
confidences—she opened up like a mussel dropped
into a steam pot.

Her cousin Mary bored her to tears, while being still
the object of great, baffling affection. The wife of the
American minister to France was as soft and sharp, as
deceptive, as a cat's paw. (Charles laughed at this
dismissal of Pia.) Louise's future husband's emissary
in New York, now on the boat, was likeable, her only
new friend, which surprised her since he was as pretty
as a man could be without lapsing into the effeminate,
while being as stupid as a man could be without
crossing over into moron. (Charles had to stifle his roar
of humor, as he recognized his cousin Gaspard.)

The lovely Louise adored her parents though she
wouldn't admit it, for she was currently in a rage
against them. She believed in beauty not love, though
she admitted there might be something, a deep experience, that passed between two people—her parents
seemed to lose themselves into something like this at
the most inopportune moments. As to her own life, the
young Louise awaited a "defining moment" that would
make her more intelligible to herself. She was admit-
tedly confused as to who she was, where she was going,
and what she really wanted to do of any significance.

For longer than Charles could keep track of, she
talked his ear off—though never about anything so
childish as animals or school or lip color from Paris.
She thoroughly entertained him. Less charming, she
eventually talked of her impending marriage and—
this was the most difficult—the ugly stranger with
whom she now realized she was supposed to conceive
children. She was not naive at all of the sexual process.
She was precocious in fact. Charles suspected her
virginity to be a matter of history. Certainly, by her
candor, her innocence was.

He grew warm at this point. This bumptious, soul-stirring young creature seemed more accessible suddenly, more acceptable—and far more appealing than he had ever imagined—as a bedmate. He lay there in the comfortable dark, vaguely contemplating her sexuality, as he scratched her dog or brushed up against her sweet-smelling skirt or was knocked in the knee once (the bad knee) for sport because he laughed at her. He was so thoroughly enchanted, he hardly knew what to think. The time flew.

He had no idea what hour it was when she said suddenly, "Oh, Lord, I'm going to be late for dinner! Mother and Papa are going to wonder where I am!"

She stood. He stood. The two of them, with her puppy following, made their way through the dark.

Charles would have been doubly surprised to know how astutely Louise had taken his measure—a surprise first of the thrilled, then of the horrified variety.

The thrilling part would have been this: Louise had found their bizarre conversation in the blackest of the dark to be quite wonderful and somehow . . . significant. Her Arab, if that's what he was, seemed to be everything the lieutenant wasn't: suave, fearless, magnetic, and, she suspected, smoothly hot-blooded. For here was the less than thrilling part: Louise knew perfectly of Charles's sexual interest, having fended off such interest from far-too-young an age and—like someone with always a royal banquet of choices—occasionally not fended it off, or not completely.

And here was another man, she thought, worthy of sampling, an interesting and exotic morsel to be plucked from the lavish buffet of men who daily laid themselves at her feet. He was intelligent, wise; he was older. She judged him to be in his late twenties, and his age—a savoir-faire and confidence she felt was connected to it—intrigued her for the first time in her young life. She had always dallied with men of the lieutenant's age, men closer to her own span of years. She felt wonderfully worldly and adventurous contemplating an affair with this mature man of a different culture.

Moreover, as Louise stepped up into the corridor of crates, she seemed to recall a physical impression of him: great height, a wide sweep of shoulders, the flash of a smile that was brilliant to behold. She tried to remember as much as she could from their brief confrontation in the hallway after breakfast, before he'd become a billowing dervish of bows and retreats. She thought she could remember rugged features, handsome features. Dark complexion, dark eyes, yes, his eyes had been dark, hadn't they? Semitic good looks. Besides, he had the easiness about him of a man who drew women effortlessly. An extraordinarily handsome man, she decided, a man of wealth, position. An equal.

She was going to let him kiss her. He was going to try. She was going to allow it and, by all early signs, going to enjoy it.

She was aware of him following closely as she walked along the corridor of cages, as she measured out the approximate distance to the Bear's crate in cold metal bars. Ultimately she found a cage with its door open. "I think this is it," she said. Then added as blithely as possible, "I could use some light at this point. Why don't you find the switch?"

Her pasha or sultan or whoever he was could have used some light too apparently, for he walked right into her. Then he didn't back off. They stood like this, all but against each other. She felt, heard, sensed him bending toward her. Oh, yes, she thought. Yet for an eternity nothing happened. He just hovered above her.

She asked finally, "Are you going to kiss me?"

His voice, a murmur, was within inches of her face. "No," he said. "You have an interest, a curiosity for what it would be like to kiss a stranger in the dark, but that's not enough."

This reply left her baffled, annoyed. "Enough?"

"Enough interest, initiative, purpose. I'm not keen to kiss a woman until she is hoping I will, her heart thudding: afraid that I won't."

Louise laughed at his cockiness. She had never been afraid of someone *not* kissing her in her life. She turned away from him. The fool. Let him wait, then. She picked the puppy up and slid him into his kennel cage. The Bear lay down, an ungraceful drop of his little bones onto the metal-grid floor as she closed the door and clicked the latch in place. The crazy Arab remained beside her. She turned, leaning a shoulder onto the crate, refusing to back up or give way in this game of who could push whom the farthest.

"What do you look like?" she asked. When he didn't answer, she said, "I'm going to turn on the light. The switch is two steps away. I'm not playing your game any longer."

His arm dropped down, his hand settling at her waist. He pressed his palm into the curve between rib cage and hip, his hand wrapping around her nicely, a warm, natural fit. A pause followed that said he would discuss neither his looks nor light nor darkness, all issues he considered beyond dispute.

In counter, she refused to lay her hands against him, though it was almost awkward to avoid it. She picked up the strand of pearls at her collarbone, twisting it to slip round and round one finger, holding her elbow, holding herself.

Above her, he whispered, "Louise, here's what I think: You would like to get away from the constant, overpowering presence of your own physical attractiveness. In truth, your beauty scares you. It's occurred to you, What if nothing else about you is as magnificent? The very fact that you worry about being shallow, though, my dear, means you are well on your way to some substance. So stop harking back to the visual, stop thinking in terms of what everything looks like."

"No," she insisted. "I'm not blind, and I won't blind myself for you. I want the light."

"I'll leave if you reach for it."

She laughed. "You can't. I stand between you and the doorway."

"I'll disappear. I promise. As surely as if I were nothing more than a figment of your imagination."

Louise thought about this. The difficult beast. Yet she was a little afraid. The whole afternoon had been so intriguing, almost magical. Almost as if she *had* dreamed him up. Well, never mind, she thought. She would catch him later. She said, "Then admit it at least: You are as remarkable to look at as I am, aren't you?"

He laughed. A low, rumbling chuckle that alerted something in her, a stirring in her belly. "You are as tenacious as your puppy. Do you know that?"

"Yes. If you won't show me, tell me."

His laughter was deep, a beautiful bass sound; mellifluous, contagious. And she could hear in it an unmistakable note of regretful folly—admitted vanity—then reluctant capitulation. He said, "Yes, we are two most remarkable people to look at. An amazing couple in the light." He lowered his voice. "And an even more amazing couple in the dark." He leaned forward.

She felt the warmth of his broad chest press closer, the moist heat of his breath on her cheek.

Her heart indeed began to thump. It seemed to rise up and wait in her throat for the touch of him at her mouth. She could feel her own pulse at her neck. Her lips on their own parted, already a little "Oh" of anticipation.

He wet her lower lip, a delicious and surprisingly intimate touch of his tongue. He blew lightly, her lips both warm and cool with sensation. Then he murmured against her cheek, "Still not enough," and pulled back.

Louise's mouth, her face tingled with feeling; incomplete, strange. She felt the lack of further contact all the way down into the pit of her stomach, a flip-flop low in her abdomen. Her face grew all at once hot. She was rooted to the spot, unable to believe what seemed to be happening.

She wasn't in charge. She wasn't in control. A part of her rejoiced: A true equal, a friend to play with, who could play as hard as she did! A part of her complained vehemently: A despicable, unpredictable fellow who thought about his own wishes over her own!

He continued in a murmur. "Tonight at midnight. Put a sprig of my jasmine in your hair, then come to me here again with your sweet mouth open just like this"—he placed his finger over her lips, touching inside for a moment, fingertip to the edge of teeth—"then, if you want me to, really want me to, I will kiss you. Or, if you prefer, we can just talk." He made a soft sound of amusement. "Yes. Tell yourself that, that we are just going to talk."

She felt a flurry of fabric, a faint breath of movement up the front of her. With the exit behind her, she didn't imagine he was leaving. Then she realized he had moved away. She frowned. What was he doing? Louise rushed for the light, a pivoting, gamboling few steps behind her. She switched the electricity on. The two fixtures immediately overhead burst into brightness, opening up the front portion of the kennel, a tiled walk between two rows of cages that dimmed into darkness where more than half the fixtures didn't come on.

Louise caught only a glimpse, a flying, colorful sail of light wool and silk as her Arab disappeared into the black end of the corridor. Then a sudden and impossible cool breeze cut into the room. A strong, wet wind blew her dress against her legs. My God, he was going out through the dog promenade. She ran after him, down the corridor into the dark, yelling after him.

"So don't kiss me!" she said. "There are plenty who will!" She taunted, "You could be a monster to look at, for that matter. I can't even be sure. I don't *want* you to kiss me!"

She caught the door on the back swing, then shoved it, taking herself outside into gusts of drizzling rain. She walked out onto the deck, the ship beneath her feet lunging. She took rain full in the face one moment, down her back the next—and for her bother saw only more indistinctness, more poor visibility. The night sky seemed a close black ceiling. The dim glow of a moon, looking near enough to touch, swam in a halo behind layers of low purple-black clouds. On the deck, beneath this sky, there was no one. Nothing. Every direction disappeared into obscurity beneath the hulking, gigantic outline of ship stacks. Before her, she could see two of these, like looming phantoms, their funnels spewing their own blackishness. Behind the kennels, she knew, were two more. But for these, the whole, vast deck was open out to its railings.

Louise let the topple of the ship carry her forward to the nearest grip she could get on the handrail. Over the railing, she looked down at the deck below, a twenty foot drop. A dangerous fall. Then looking toward the bow of the ship, she realized, there at the front this distance would be half that—if one leaped the rail, dangled, then dropped down onto the private terrace of one of the grand luxury suites.

This is what she thought had happened. Her shah or sultan (it amused her to think of all the possible Middle Eastern titles he probably didn't possess) had run the length of the ship, then jumped home. To add insult to injury, she lost her balance on the next sudden lean of the ship. She slipped and grabbed for the railing.

Her necklace flipped up to become a rattle of pearls

clicking over the handrail, so that when she caught a grip, her hand wrapped around the string of pearls too. She felt a sharp tug on the back of her neck, then a release all at once as the strand broke. Black pearls popped and flew everywhere. They bounced well; they bounced high. They rolled magnificently across the deck in every direction, as well as off the deck and down onto the next—a quick, nacreous spill swallowed up into the wet night, the roll and clatter smothered almost instantly by the hiss of the ocean.

Louise was left with the wet string in her hand, her dress soaked, her hair a ruin, and her vaguely sore neck wearing a tiered necklace, completely missing its longest strand.

Chapter 9

Ambergris begins as indigestion, when the beak of a squid or the hard internal shell of a cuttlefish irritates the stomach lining of a sperm whale.

Charles Harcourt, Prince d'Harcourt
On the Nature and Uses of Ambergris

Charles had an extraordinary fondness for beautiful women. A fixation, some might even say. Whichever, if he analyzed this predilection (and despite efforts not to, little bolts of understanding had struck him from time to time in recent years), it probably had to do with his horror of being thought ugly: To parade a beautiful woman on his arm seemed to say he *had* to be pleasing to the eye himself; how else could a goddess descended from Olympus stand to be near him? Whatever the reasons, his attraction to fabulous-looking females was legendary—along with his inordinate success with them, a success that was both his curse and his glory.

Most everyone at home suspected, for instance, that Pia was his mistress. This connection to her gave Charles a kind of glow up and down the Côte d'Azur, where cavorting with sought-after beauties was considered a mark of taste, adventurousness, and reflected on one's own irresistibility. On the other hand, Pia was not a very considerate woman.

For instance, when she called that evening, he mentioned he was having his dinner and asked ever so politely if he could call her back in half an hour. Her response was to tell him she hoped he choked on his food and fell over dead onto the table, after which she hung up on him. He stood there in the antechamber off the drawing room of his suite, clutching the phone by its throat in one hand, its staticky earpiece in the other. After a moment, he sighed and dutifully called her back. If she were this upset, he reasoned . . .

The next little run of conversation, however, didn't go much better. Pia began it substantively with, "What I am saying is, *I* am allowed to be married and you are not."

Charles set his fork down onto his appointment book, then sat down into the desk chair. He said, "Pia, you may as well get used to it: I'm going to marry her. There are too many motivating reasons for me to do otherwise."

"Well, I won't be your piece on the side."

"Why not? I've been your piece on the side for more than two years."

"It's not the same thing and you know it."

He laughed. "No, I don't. It *is* the same."

"No, no, no, it isn't," Pia argued. "Men who scheme to have two women are horrible cads or worse."

He laughed again. "Worse?"

She had no reply.

He asked, "And what are women called who scheme to have two men?"

She harrumphed in response, then the line clicked dead again.

He rang her back after she had had a few minutes to calm herself. Quite reasonably, he thought, he asked, "Why aren't you at dinner with everyone else? How are you feeling?"

"Terrible," she said. "I threw up my lunch. I'm so nauseated I can't stand. I hate this ship."

He paused, then braved an indelicate question. "When were your last menses?"

"I'm bloody in them. I have cramps too."

"Ah. Well, that's good. I mean, I'm sorry." He navigated awkwardly. "That you have cramps, that is. Can I get you anything?"

"Yes. Louise Vandermeer's head, if you wouldn't mind."

He scowled down into the black transmitter, instantly annoyed. "I think she's using it. Use yours: Stop bludgeoning me with this, Pia. Stop your pouting and tantruming."

The phone line disconnected again.

Charles went back to the dining room, tried to eat, but ended up wandering aimlessly through the suite, uncertain what he was doing, disturbed though unsure just what disturbed him. The telephone rang again. This time he didn't answer it. It rang more than a dozen times, stopped, then began ringing again. When he went over to it finally, he noticed a black pearl lying against the spine of his appointment book. He had collected this after his meeting with Louise, after she had looked for him far and wide (when she should have looked near—he had been standing in the shadows of the open kennel door).

Charles was contemplating his booty, the single black pearl, when he sat down and picked up the receiver.

Without so much as saying hello, Pia's thin, petulant voice began, "But I don't even see how you had *time* to court this girl."

"I didn't. Her father courted me." He rolled the pearl in his fingers, held it up to the light. It was small as pearls went, but he remembered a pirate's ransom of them draped down the front of Louise Vandermeer, the curve of her bosom as solid as beaded armor.

His response on the phone was met with staticky silence. Then, "And you thought this was a good idea, marrying a girl you'd never met?"

He leaned back in his chair and set the pearl down, deciding he'd better keep his wits about him. "No," he said, "I thought it was silly. But they kept writing. I was afraid of offending them."

"You told me some of this. These are the people who wined and dined you from New York to Miami in their private railway car?"

"Yes."

Pia sniffed. "But when? How?" she asked. "When you and I were in New York together, you weren't"— she avoided the word as if by not pronouncing it she could keep it from being true—"*affiliated* with her then, were you?"

"No, not until Roland came back and you went off with him for three days to see the sights of New York." He waited for her to say something. Static. Air. He heaved a huge sigh. "Picture this," he said: "After being offered the world by the Vandermeers for almost two weeks—the world, all save you—and turning it down, then still being treated as if I were a king by these people, I arrive back in New York. You and I are all cozy for a few days, while Roland is in Washington. Then he comes back to New York early. For his sake, we've pretended to all our friends that I've gone back to France the week before, so I am suddenly stuck in a hotel without so much as my own name to keep me company, hoping no one recognizes me, while you are off for three 'surprise' days we didn't plan on—he even buys you a damn necklace at Tiffany's. While I sit in a hotel room, alone, bored, and angry—and with a pretty amazing alternative staring me in the face.

"So I tested my options. I wired home that I wished a telegram sent in my name, inviting the Vandermeers to visit me again and reinitiate negotiations. My response through Nice was another telegram that leaped to the question of my cousin Gaspard in New York being given proxy to sign a marriage contract in my name. The suggested contract itself, short and sweet, was also wired—twice, to Nice and back across. Vandermeer said he had been thinking of retiring and that as his son-in-law he would give me everything, that he would step down and be 'pensioned off,' so to speak, though he requires a pretty big 'pension.' Still, it was a marvelous offer. Gaspard signed the agreement two days ago. And there you have it."

After a long pause, her voice said quietly, "You spent a small fortune on telegrams and engaged in a lot of complicated posturing, so you could sell yourself into a marriage to a girl you had never seen?"

Charles grew quiet. "Not exactly." He admitted, "I saw a painting of her at their house that first night I went there." Defensively he added, "It was stupid, really. I assumed it was one of those paintings that rich parents have done to flatter their offspring. You know the sort: idealized, much more comely than the subject is in reality. Never for a moment did I think she would be *more* stunning, *more* beautiful."

"*More* beautiful? She's a child, Charles."

His fingers had absently found the pearl again. He said, "Louise Vandermeer will be beautiful when she's eighty. It's in her bones, the way her eyes are set into her skull, the texture of her hair."

"You really find her that appealing?"

"Aesthetically."

She huffed a little breath. "As a man, a mature man,

Charles, do you honestly find a smart-mouthed, eighteen-year-old brat physically appealing?"

Perhaps he should have lied. He might have, had he been speaking to Pia in person, been able to see her face. But sitting there at the desk in his anteroom, as he rolled a black pearl between his thumb and forefinger, the truth was such a revelation to Charles that the dishonest alternative didn't even occur to him. He said with simple wonder, "Yes. Absolutely."

When Pia hung up this time, it was so loud it made Charles startle and pull away from the earpiece.

A half hour later, Pia called again. She was crying when her voice burst through the receiver. With great howling sobs, she said, "We're through. If you don't give her up immediately, we're through forever."

"You're being absurd, Pia. You will regret this on dry land. You are sick and out of sorts."

"Yes." She was caught up for a few moments in a long concatenation of sobs and hiccuping. "I am sick of your philandering."

He laughed. "In two years, I have never strayed from your bed. I have loved you and honored you and offered to marry you a dozen times."

"Well, offer again."

Charles tensed, then asked, "Where is Roland?"

"Asleep beside me here."

He let out a guffaw—of relief, though he tried to disguise it.

Oblivious to everything but her own feelings, Pia returned to her original premise. "If you don't foreswear her right now and take care of this matter—you can send some more of your circuitous telegrams to her parents right here on the ship—we are through, Charles. Forever and always, finished."

Quite calmly, he heard himself say, "All right, Pia. Then we're finished forever and always."

It was as simple as that. Charles set the telephone down, receiver into its hook, astonished at himself. He tapped his fingers on the desk a moment, waiting to feel inconsolable, desolate. But he felt merely disencumbered, freer and better than he had felt in an eon. He and Pia were over. Done. Finished. Whereas he would have expected this to level him, he straightened up where he stood and stretched effortlessly, glancing about him.

On the desk lay a pearl. Idly, he rolled it a moment over the surface of his books, his notes and formulae, his schedules and appointments. Then, putting the pearl into his trouser pocket, he reached with his other hand and began to riffle through pages. Standing there in the dim light of this little room, running his eyes down columns, slanting his head sideways to read the addenda and marginalia of his future, Charles realized he was going to marry Louise Vandermeer because it was good business, but that he was going to enjoy being her husband for one very unpredicted reason: He wanted to hold her so badly his skin twitched; at the thought of her, his scrotum thumped like a butter churn with its paddle in action. And just admitting this profound insight to himself gave Charles an erection that could have lifted logs off a river.

He wanted this young girl to the point that his vision blurred. He could imagine her naked, as round of limb as a pearl, her skin iridescent. There *was* no other woman in the small mind of the only voting member of the Appealing Female Committee: the member in his pants, who stood at attention ready to make his vote count at the drop of a dress from pale shoulders . . . down a slender, young body into a pool of fabric on the floor. . . .

God in Heaven, could his imagination ever fantasize on this particular subject.

Why? Charles wondered. He suspected he was

experiencing a kind of belated adolescent lust, steamy, heady; especially piquant for all its delay. He could remember a girl, now that he thought of it, that he had eyed in his youth, a dunderhead next to Louise, but beautiful all the same. This girl—Ginette, as he recalled—had refused to sit beside him at mass. He had never spoken to her beyond one question. (Is this seat taken?)

She had never honored him with a word beyond her one brainless answer. (No, er, yes, it's taken; um, in a minute it'll be taken as soon as somebody else comes.) After this setdown, Charles had quickly, and fearfully he concluded now, determined that Ginette was "too young," "a baby, really." He required more mature company. And so he had in many ways. But he also had lacked the confidence at eighteen to go after the prettiest young girl in the province.

Something he seemed to be rectifying now. He was living that old satisfaction. For certainly the prettiest young woman he had seen in a long time liked him; he was sure of it. And fulfillment was guaranteed. Even if he didn't succeed here on the ship, there was France, a wedding, and a marriage bed. Hallelujah.

Pia? Charles quizzed himself one more time. For two years, so much angst and longing and hope. *Was* she mature? he wondered. Not especially. Yet she was worldly and experienced and knowledgeable of many things. So did he feel horrible to have lost her?

No, he felt . . . hungry. What had become of his dinner?

Charles went back to the dining room, where he sat down and devoured what he had only been picking at when the first rude phone call had come: a fat artichoke, a mound of wild rice, a pheasant in a sauce of cream and honey with green peppercorns, a salad, then a dessert of fresh pear, three different cheeses, and two glasses of sauterne. The meal was room temperature but perfectly delicious. Wonderful in fact. After it, he ordered himself a bottle of champagne.

He felt positively celebratory.

Chapter 10

*. . . whereas ambergris is never found ex-
cept upon the sea.*

> *Herman Melville*
> Moby Dick, *Chapter 20*
> *1851*

Of the nearly six hundred first-class passengers, roughly four dozen made it to dinner. Even Mary stayed in her room. Besides an elderly aunt down the table, Louise knew only one other person, Pia Montebello, who herself didn't arrive till the cheese and fruit course at the end of the meal. She looked, though, as if she too should have stayed in bed. She was sheet-white, her eyes puffy and red despite a good deal of makeup to disguise the face. Nonetheless, she joined Louise's far end of the group, which included a financier, a partner in Standard Oil (not Rockefeller but the other one who had something to do with railroads), and a society matron who had brought a little boy from across the hall to dinner, his parents having fallen victims to the storm's unrest.

Outside the long windows of the dining saloon, rain poured so hard upon the ocean, Louise had trouble hearing the man beside her (a young doctor and groom portion of newlyweds on their honeymoon). The weather pounded the decks. It beat against the windows. It turned the usual clink and chime of crystal, of silver on china into muffled clicks and clanks. The view itself was a running, watery blur of grays and purples. Inside, the evening's orchestra had been reduced to a quintet. Over the noise of rain, Brahms came through periodically in appropriate, weepy-bowed runs and sharp descents.

Meanwhile everyone sat at the captain's table, the captain, who often went absent, being present tonight for morale. He ordered champagne for all. It flowed. Except for this, with its attendant, slightly tipsy laughter, these survivors of the storm clung to decorum. The captain, in crisp whites, chatted magnanimously with men in full dinner dress: black tailcoats, stiff, starchy-white shirtfronts. The women were equally formal in satins and lace, their arms and necks jeweled, heavy with the trophies of lucrative unions with capitalist husbands—a boringly homogeneous group, not an Arab in sight.

For Louise, the dining saloon tonight—the whole ship—seemed a little bucket of artificial elegance, scooped up out of the glittering Upper East Side trough of New York, then set afloat on a reality of more fabulous proportion. She actually liked the storm. She liked the feel of it slinging her back into her chair, then allowing her forward. She liked its power to drown out conversation, to roar in crescendos louder than the music. The ride, the thrilling vitality of the elements battering away from outside, made life somehow more piquant.

"You know, we could all die," she said at one point. She meant to launch from here into a game of, What would you do if this night were your last on earth? An idea that filled her with romantic-morbid fascination.

It was nothing more than a parlor game to her as she sat here in well-lit, well-fed, dry, warm security.

Yet, game or not, conversation stopped so abruptly with her comment, she immediately herded herself back into conventional replies, polite disinterest. Dessert came. Coffee. This evening became like a thousand others, dismally the same as tea five hours ago, lunch before that, breakfast before that, dinner the night before, ad infinitum.

And of course there were more variations on Louise's leitmotif, as it were: All through dessert, the young doctor-groom struggled to say something to her, his hesitations and stammers partly from interference of the surroundings, partly from his own embarrassment at what he wanted to get out. Eventually, in one of the quieter moments of weather, he said, as if lifting a huge weight off his chest, "People must tell you this all the time . . . I mean, I adore my wife but . . . in a purely objective way, of course . . . the sight of you, well, you're, ah, amazingly beautiful—"

Louise said, "Thank you," and stirred cream into her coffee.

The little boy across the table—he must have been about six—who had stared at her fairly uninterruptedly all through dinner, added, "My tutor reads me stories. I was wondering, Are you a goddess?"

She smiled at him. "Yes," she said. "And I have brought the storm. So be good or I shall throw this ship to the bottom."

He nodded, wide-eyed, appreciative of her generous immortality.

They were all rising, preparing to adjourn to the ballroom and continue this charade, when Mrs. Montebello at last claimed Louise's attention. As others stood, she all but ran around the table. She had been forced to sit across and down four seats, just far enough that Louise could pretend she didn't exist.

Now, though, she took hold of Louise's arm.

"My dear," she said. "Charles Harcourt—"

Louise looked around at her.

"He is the prince whom you are going to marry, isn't he?"

"Yes."

"I know him."

Louise blinked, not certain how to react. "Well, for someone who was all questions this morning, you are certainly well-informed tonight."

"Yes," she said with a knowing, somewhat ghoulish smile. The woman looked positively dreadful. Sick, angry, fretful. She waited a moment before she said, "Someone told me. A prince. Then I thought, Well, how many French princes are there, anyway?"

Louise said blankly, "Several, if I'm not mistaken."

"So don't you want to know what he's like?"

"I already know what he's like. My parents have spent a good bit of time in his company."

"And so have I," the woman said meaningfully.

What was she saying? My goodness. It occurred to Louise: Her husband-to-be kept a mistress. Or had kept a mistress. Or was having trouble with one. This one. Mrs. Montebello of American diplomatic circles had slept with the Prince d'Harcourt, and she wanted Louise to know it.

"Wouldn't you like to hear what he *looks* like, perhaps?"

"I have a good idea what he looks like." But the woman was obviously going to tell her, anyway. Louise sighed, then said, "All right, what does he look like?"

"Well, he's magnificent."

Louise frowned, then blinked at this new interpretation.

Mrs. Montebello continued, "He's huge, muscular, imposing, and on the aggressive side when it comes to—" She laughed abruptly, as if this were a joke.

"Why, it never occurred to me before," she said, "but I suppose he could be quite terrifying, I mean, to a *young* girl—"

To a virgin, she meant. Louise was astounded—and mesmerized—by the woman's nerve, though she was unimpressed by the information itself. So her one-eyed husband-to-be was rich and powerful enough to have an attractive friend to play with, albeit a rather old friend—Mrs. Montebello had to be at least thirty. Good. Then this woman could take care of him in any area Louise herself found distasteful.

Mrs. Montebello seemed about to say something. But further mischief from this quarter was interrupted.

Everyone heard it at the same time: a loud, dull thud that came from the outside, the sea, and seemed to reverberate throughout the whole interior of the ship, above, below. Within the room, the wall panels themselves shuddered. The dining saloon tipped away from the sound, to the port side, and stayed tipped for the full length of a low, keening grind that started forward of the room, slowly sliding along and below to the aft.

All conversation, music, breathing itself, stopped for the duration of this—about five or six seconds. Then the noise quit as suddenly as it started, and the ship leveled.

Someone moaned. A woman still sitting at the far end of the table began to whimper. There was no doubt about it: The *Concordia* had hit something.

A second later the electricity in the room blinked out. Pandemonium. Louise just stood there as people began to scream. A man ran into her. Several people pushed her aside in their rush round the table, until she had been moved to the wall, pressed up against a mirror there. She heard the word *lifeboats,* then a man saying, "Women and children first. Let them by. Women and children to the lifeboats." There were perhaps two or three minutes of everyone trying to organize themselves. Then just as surprisingly, the lights at the far end of the room came back on, half the room still unlit—but enough light to leave everyone staring at each other, caught in the midst of what suddenly seemed a foolish panic.

The captain stepped forward. "Everyone be seated. I am going to the bridge. I shall send someone shortly with an advisement of what has occurred." He left.

Some sat. Louise remained at the wall, clutching the mirror's thick, deep-carved frame. Where she realized something: The idea of real death was not attractive at all, not the least bit gamelike. And she—*she*—was no goddess. She was mortal. If this ship disappeared into the foamy sea, she would die.

Louise, confident Louise, imperturbable Louise had a most unpredicted reaction. *Too young,* her mind cried. *There are so many things yet I want to do. Except for a few trips across town and one botched trip to Montreal, I have done nothing even remotely adult; I have done nothing to break myself out of this circumscribed life.* A kind of tantrum took hold. *I have not become anyone interesting. Anything more than pretty! Yet I am capable of it, I'm sure.* She revised, *No, it's not* interesting *that I want to become; I want to become myself, and I'm not even sure who that is! I want to experience the world, explore it, learn what part of it is me, what part is not. . . .*

Louise began to tremble, not a knee-banging shake but a jitter of muscles, a persistent shiver all the way through to her liver that wouldn't stop.

The captain didn't send anyone but rather came back himself to announce "the best possible news under the circumstances." All was well for the moment. Two bulkheads had been pierced, but the other fourteen appeared to be perfectly watertight. The *Concordia* would stay afloat. As near as anyone could understand, she had hit an iceberg that the search lights had missed, something very small. The chief engineers even thought it was possible to plug the two bulkheads and pump them out. Meanwhile the captain thought it best, given the storm, that they use what power they had to move full throttle forward. The sea was too rough to allow them a stationary repair. What this meant was that the forward part of the ship would have to be shut down of all nonessential power. Everyone was asked, please, to put up gracefully with the inconvenience of no electricity in those areas of the ship for a short time; a boiler was out, which affected the main generator. These too could be put back into service. No one was going to die. The ship would not sink. The *Concordia* was the safest, most modern vessel on the ocean, and she had just proven herself by taking a mighty swipe that would have sent lesser ships to the bottom of the sea.

The captain addressed a few questions. Yes, everything as usual, just a slight list to the starboard side till the repairs are made and limited electricity till the disabled generator is back in use. Yes, there are oil lamps for emergencies, but alas this, the first sailing, had set off without oil. An oversight. We are very sorry, but it should be of minimal inconvenience, just a short time. We will have full operation as soon as we can. Thus, the captain, this man in charge of the ship, their lives, assured them for a few more minutes, then said he had to return to the bridge. After which, he turned smartly on his heels and marched out.

Louise wandered back toward her room in a daze, alone, the shaking still with her. On the way, she stopped by Mary's room; Mary was well consoled in the bosom of her family. Then by her own parents' suite: Louise's mother and father welcomed her into their room. With the bump of the ship, her father had hit his head, badly enough that it bled and now rose in an egg. Though he and her mother invited Louise to stay with them, she wouldn't. Her father reveled in her mother's attendance. They were all right. And sufficient unto themselves, as usual. They noticed nothing out of the ordinary about their daughter, didn't ask or look beyond her nodding, *Yes, I'm all right.* Louise hugged them both. (They smelled vile, sick.) They patted her back. What a trip this would be to remember. Then, smiling and agreeing that all was fine, she left. A quaking zombie, she walked across the hallway to her own room.

Her maid was nowhere to be found when Louise entered. But another presence was: The heavy scent of jasmine assailed her, the like of which she had never smelled. The scent was sweet, strong, heady. It drew her over to her own wastebasket. There, she bent down into the dark, picked up the bundle of wilting, blooming flowers, then thought to try her light.

It blinked on. She found herself standing before a mirror, clutching the flowers, looking like her own ghost. Pale, hollow-eyed. Alone and quietly shaking. Cold with fright, though fright of what exactly she wasn't sure.

In the mirror, she caught a glimpse of something. Darkness. *I am the darkness, my own darkness. I know nothing about myself.* She turned her head. Beyond her iron-framed windows, the sea was black. A sea that would not swallow her up. Not tonight. She was alive; a reprieve.

The telephone rang.

When she picked it up, the voice said, "The phone works." His voice. The voice of her pasha, deep, gentle, self-assured. "Are you all right?" he asked. There seemed to be genuine concern in the question.

"No," she said. After a pause, she asked, "Who are you?"

"Why do you keep asking this? You know I'm not going to tell you." He waited, then said, laughing, "You know, we could meet anywhere in half the ship right now. From midship forward every deck is cave-like, not even the ship's running lights. A bat could sleep happily and sail with us."

She didn't smile; she couldn't. All she could say was, "I don't really like the dark."

There was a pause on the other end of the line. Then he answered, "No, I imagine you don't. But you should get on better terms with it. It's as natural as daylight."

"I hate it. It makes me feel stupid."

"You did fine with it this afternoon."

His arguments and encouragements, if that's what they were, made her want to weep, to scream at him. But instead, all she said was, angrily, idiotically, "If God had wanted us to live in darkness half the time, He wouldn't have given us electricity."

He chuckled, as if this were a good jest, then said, "Well, tonight He taketh away. Louise"—his smooth voice became understanding, patient—"light would mean nothing without darkness. They define each other." With hardly more than a pause, he continued. "I'm not too fond of the kennel anymore. It has electricity; you could actually put those lights on. So now, since God has provided me with this wonderful opportunity, what do you say to the ballroom or maybe the library. I frankly don't think anyone would intrude. Which do you think?"

She didn't answer. She couldn't; her throat felt too tight to speak.

"Do you hear me?" He asked again, "Are you all right?"

She stood there, holding the earpiece in one hand, the fragrant, blooming branches in the other. Then his question made her aware of something: Though she was hardly calm, neither was she shaking inside any longer as if she'd swallowed the tail of a rattlesnake.

"So where will it be?" he said. "I rather like the idea of the ballroom. Can you find your way there at midnight?"

In a voice that sounded distant even to her own ears, she said, "No. I'm not meeting you—"

"You've met me once already."

"I didn't—"

"What are you afraid of?"

"The obvious."

"Which is?"

Her argument, her words, she realized, were her mother's, all her mother would have told her to say: "You're a stranger. I don't know you. You could strangle me or worse."

He laughed his deep-chested laugh. "What could possibly be worse?" Then he softened his tone and said, "And I'm not a stranger. Not any longer. Besides, I could have hurt you already if I had wanted to. Think about it."

She did, unable to locate any of her own objections. A dry sob came up from her chest, like a tiny breath of air from deep beneath the sea, popping to the surface. "I don't even know what you look like," she offered feebly.

"I look like whatever you want me to look like. I've told you. I'll be what you want me to be. Come now, Louise, use your imagination."

Her name. It seemed natural that he would use it, soothe her with it. No, he didn't feel like a stranger. In this instant, he felt like her only friend. A decision settled over her. And with it there was release. Blood began to flow again, a warming.

Her decision. Her own choice. Not her mother's or father's or even this man's on the ship's telephone.

"No," she said, "I won't meet you in the ballroom or in the kennel or anywhere else like that."

Louise hung up quickly before she could change her mind.

She broke off a piece of jasmine, dumping the rest of the branches onto the bed (destroying Mary's cat's peace of mind—with a mew of indignity, it leapt to

the floor). Louise ignored this and every other piece of
her real life. She left her gloves and shawl and evening
bag behind as, tucking the jasmine sprig into her hair,
she hurried out her stateroom, then turned into a
darkened corridor.

Charles was still holding the telephone's earpiece,
staring at the mystifying thing that held the female
voice he had so grown used to, when the knock came
at his door. Barefoot and bare-chested, he thought to
pull on his gallibiya as he went to answer the sound.
He thought it must be the steward who had brought
the champagne—and the details a while ago of an
iceberg that had sideswiped the ship. He thought it
was more information in the wake of an extremely
generous tip.

When he opened his door, though, he was almost
glad for the small, submerged chunk of ice. No light
thankfully. No steward either.

Surprised was not the word for what Charles felt—
stunned, floored, blown away and lost on a sea of
astonishment—as a slim, jasmine-scented shadow
walked past him, into his suite of rooms.

He turned around, his full weight falling back
against the door, closing it literally with amazement.
While Louise Vandermeer, or the willowy movement
of her lightless intimation, asked, "So what shall I call
you? Do you have a name? Or shall I just refer to you
as 'my pasha' from here on?"

Part 2

The Petard

I want to tell you, soft enchantress,
Of the diverse graces that somehow
  circumvent your youth;
I want to paint for you your beauty,
Where your girlishness flips over inexplicably
  to womanhood.

Set upon your plump, round shoulders,
  atop the long curve of your neck,
Your head shows off its spectacle of wonders
As, with a placid air of triumph,
You go your own way, majestic child. . . .

Your breasts advance and strain the stretch
  of watered silk,
Triumphant breasts . . . like polished shields
  with rosy points
Behind which lie coffers brimming with
  sweet secrets, delectables . . .
Enough to make hearts and minds delirious!

Your noble legs, beneath the flutterings
  that they chase,
Torment the dark desires that they
  themselves evoke,
Like two sorcerers stirring up
A black love potion in the unseen depths
  of a crinoline-jar.

Charles Baudelaire
55 of Les Fleurs du Mal
DuJauc translation
Pease Press, London, 1889

Chapter 11

All the electric fixtures in Charles's rooms had blinked off almost at the moment of impact. His sitting room, like his bedroom beyond it, was lit by moonlight alone. Even this illumination came from the far side of the ship, through a filter of storm clouds and rain, then passed through drawn curtains, drawn to keep in the heat—the radiators were out. What small visibility existed in these two outside rooms was faint, to say the least. The inside rooms, of course—the dining room, the alcove study, the marble bath and water closet—were pitch black. Having roved his suite for the last forty-five minutes, looking for oil or candles or something, Charles could attest that, without electricity, nary a room, not a drawer or cupboard, contained anything that might shed light. Not so much as a match. Even the ship's search beams were out; he hadn't seen a glimmer of their sweep yet. The *Concordia* ploughed through a rugged sea blind. Or half-blind, since the stern of the ship seemed to have light. She listed slightly, enough that Charles could feel a degree or two in the slope of his floor. What irony. This great ship that carried all their fates upon her steel and rivets sailed like a compeer under him, half-blind with a limp.

Across from him now, in the dark, with the raucous rain and ocean at the terrace doors behind her, Louise

Vandermeer waited stoically. She'd asked for a name—more importantly, she expected an Arab name. Charles stood there, trying to come up with one.

"Rafi," he said. The first to penetrate his dumb-struck mind, that of a friend in Tunisia.

"Just Rafi?"

He frowned and folded his arms. Arab names should be long and involved, he thought; Rafi's went on forever. He added, "Hamid"—a form of Muham-mad, *If you have a hundred sons, name them all Muhammad*—"Abd-al-Rahman." This sounded like an appropriate mouthful. He could only pray the young Louise was as ignorant as he on the subject.

"Is this really your name?" she asked.

"No."

She dismissed his whole effort, as if dusting her palms of it. "Well then," she said, "I shall call you 'Charles.'"

He nearly choked. "P-pardon me?" *Sharl*, she said. The way every French friend or acquaintance said it.

"It's as good as any name, and I may as well. It will eliminate the possibility, once I'm married, of wrong names at inappropriate moments."

He stood, leaning against the door, speechless, watching her silhouette become more defined as she passed in front of his terrace curtains, a lithe, curving glimmer that gave off the exotic-sweet scent of his own flowers. This impossible jasmine phantasm walked across his sitting room, then around the bulky shadow of a chair.

She sat into this by the cold fireplace, then said to him, unbelievably, "Well, Charles, what shall we do with ourselves tonight?"

What he would like to have done was swat her once and throw her out. What was she doing, waltzing into a man's suite? (Did she do this often? Did she call all her lovers "Charles"?) Never mind that he was trying to get her into a situation more or less just like this one. He had barely started. This was too easy. It felt wrong.

When he didn't say anything for a time, she said from her dark chair by the fireplace, "Are you angry that I'm here?"

"A little. How did you find me?"

"The operator."

He grimaced, remembering the tinny voice who, over the telephone line, had been so remarkably uncooperative with him. A conspiracy of women. "You can't get to the private suites without a key."

"You can if you use the service exit out the ballroom, then the side companionway—from the top of which, if I am not mistaken, you watched me last night with Lieutenant Johnston."

Not exactly from the top, but close enough. All right, a stalemate, tit for tat.

She crossed her legs, a kick and churn of stiff satin that kept time in the dark, a *shush* of silk, to the beat of a nervy confidence within her; she kicked her leg. "So," she said, "here I am, arrived and in thrall to the question: Just what do you want of me?" *Kick-shush, kick-shush.* When he didn't say anything, she added, "I thought perhaps walking half the length of the ship in the dark to find you, in your own lair, so to speak, might put your insecurities to rest."

"Insecurities?"

"Yes, with regard to my not being interested or interesting, whatever 'enough' to kiss. I mean, a secure man wouldn't need a woman to fall on her knees if he wanted to kiss her, would he?" *Kick-shush.*

Charles laughed. "Maybe I didn't want to."

Her kicking stopped for a moment. Then resumed. Her voice from the shadows by the fireplace was dismissive, a shrug. "You know better than I," she said. She left a pause—*kick-shush*—then asked, "So would you like to kiss me now, Charles?"

The hair on his neck lifted every time she used his given name. Damn this girl. Oh, he was going to kiss her all right.

He heaved his weight up off the door, moving forward, toward the outline of two chairs by the fireplace, a piano-phantom hulking off to the side. He had the advantage, he knew, of no light behind him. As he came round the empty chair, he kicked the base of the occupied one with his foot and grabbed hold of the chair back. With his hand and foot, he gave it a solid push, sliding it around on the hearth tile, turning the chair with her in it as he bent and braced both hands on the stuffed armrests.

He heard her startle, then the rustle of her dress as she uncrossed her legs to square her stance. The kicking stopped. She pushed herself up and back from him in the chair. He bent low, his head down in her shadow. While muted, wavering, moonlight backlit the top of her head, a fairy-like array of curling individual hairs that haloed the faintly anxious sound of her breathing.

"Why the hell are you here?" he asked into her face. She smelled like the damnable jasmine—a sweet, compelling odor at the back of her hair, low, near the nape of neck.

Less sure of herself, she answered, "Because I—I was frightened and—"

"You were *what?*" he asked, incredulous.

"I was— Well, you talked to me." She struggled to stay cool, but he had scared her—thank God, she *could* be scared. He was beginning to wonder about this arrogant girl. Was she always this dauntless? She finished, "The ship hit, well, you know, and I was—" She choked back something, then grew brave again. She blurted, "I was looking for company, and I liked the way that we talked today."

He gripped the armrests so hard that the whole chair jerked. "My God," he told her, "you have a mother and father, aunts and uncles on board by the dozens, as I recall from your stories. Talk to *them.*"

"I can't." She said angrily, "My parents barely see me. My cousins either revere me or think I'm bizarre. My aunts and uncles are afraid of me; I'm considered difficult by most, if not bad outright."

Imagine that, Charles thought. He stood up.

He looked around. Everywhere darkness. Darkness other than his own choosing. He had the eeriest feeling, as if his joke had taken on a life of its own. He shoved his hands into his trouser pockets.

Where he found a smooth, hard, round little pearl.

He pulled it out then—an improvised moment that came from God knew where—reached down and touched it to her cheek.

She drew back. "What is—"

"Quiet. Close your eyes—your other senses, Louise—then you tell *me* what it is."

Letting his thumb and the tips of his fingers move it along, Charles rolled the pearl into the hollow of her cheek, down along the edge of her mouth, across her chin, up, around, into the philtrum of her lip. He held it there a moment. "What is it?" he said. He felt her relax a degree, settle slightly into the chair.

Her breath was warm on his palm. The pearl moved with her mouth when she spoke. "It's cool and hard and round." She paused. "I don't know." She guessed, "Candy?"

He laughed. "You *are* a child."

But he liked this, her pearl on her skin. He bent over the chair again, bracing his weight on one arm as his other hand held the pearl in the little indention between her nose and mouth. He intended to roll it down over her lips, maybe take it along her jaw, down her neck, across her collarbone, then into the valley between her breasts, possibly dropping it down into the darkness there. . . .

Louise flattened her top lip against her teeth, tipped

her head up slightly, and, by this, rolled the pearl down to catch it between her lips. She sucked it out of his fingers into her mouth. He heard it click on her teeth. "Come and get it," she said, then laughed, a low cackling giggle, slightly breathy. The sound of a young girl teasing, playing in water way over her head. Or the sound of a young siren—a hatchling just coming into her own—with him the one in danger of drowning. Charles couldn't decide.

With his one hand still poised in the air, he bent his weight forward onto the other, taking his face toward the sound of her seductive laughter, bending into a cloud of grassy-sweet jasmine. Such a fragrant girl. He revised his thinking. Though he must have always told himself that eighteen-year-olds were children, this one wasn't. He tilted his head, about to kiss her.

Then was nearly knocked in the face.

Apparently unaware of his movement, she sat forward abruptly. Warned by a waft of air, a shift of her odoriferous splendor, he ducked sideways. Her forehead hit his shoulder, narrowly missing his head. She bent into the darkness of the chair, presumably spitting the pearl out. "This is mine," she said, her speech clear of foreign objects. "It's my pearl! How did you get it?" With dawning discovery, she exclaimed, "You were there! Where were you?"

"Under the eve, on the other side of the door." Charles grimaced and rose up again. "Watching from around it as you got soaking wet."

"I thought that you'd come back here. You know, run to the end of the ship, then sort of vaulted the railing and dropped down."

"Hardly." Charles made a pull of his mouth at such romantic nonsense, then headed in the general direction of the champagne that he had yet to open. Less a celebration now, he needed a drink. "I would sooner wrestle snakes in a pit."

"What?"

He found the wine. The steward had put it across the room in a bucket of ice on the canapé table beside the piano. "Would you like some champagne?"

"Aren't you Muslim?"

The alcohol. A breach in the teachings of the prophet. *By Allah,* Charles thought, *this young woman had a frightening assortment of facts at her fingertips.* Trying to sound as sincere as possible, he said, "I am flattered that you should know so much about Islam. This is unusual in a Western woman."

"Oh, I didn't know much this morning. But I went to the library and read all day. I know a little more now."

Wonderful. She probably knew more than he did.

All the more reason to take hold of the neck of the bottle, pop the cork, and pronounce cynically what he had found to be true when he had lived among the believers: "The wealthier a Muslim, the more likely he is to misbehave, especially far away from home."

The cork released, shooting. Champagne gushed with the *whoosh* of a geyser. Charles found a glass, the only glass as it turned out, then wet his arm and the sleeve of his gallibiya trying, by feel, to catch a rain of bubbling wine as he maintained his balance on a teeter-tottering floor.

Behind him, he heard her say, "Well, then, 'To misbehavior.' Yes, I'll have some too. And what did you mean, you would rather wrestle snakes?"

"Pardon?"

She asked, "You hate heights?"

Absently, his thumb over the rim of the glass to measure the level, he said, "Oh. Yes." He poured till his thumb was wet.

"Yet you sleep at the top of a very high ship."

"Oh, I don't mind looking out over them. Leaping into them, though, is another matter. My father used to have to pull me off my pony, I mean, literally pry my fingers out of his mane and yank me off screaming. I loved to ride, but it took me years to get over simply swinging down off the animal. As to higher places, well, let's just say I take stairs one at a time and I don't leap over railings."

He took the full glass over to her. "We will have to share," he said as he offered it toward her shadow. "I hadn't planned on a guest."

Their hands found one another. Hers were cool and smooth; alas, as soft as a child's, though she had long, graceful fingers. These fingers slid under his as he relinquished the glass into them. Then he pulled over the piano bench and sat beside her. "So, Louise—" he began.

"You may as well call me Lulu. All my friends do." Something hit his elbow, her arm. "Would you like some?" she offered.

The champagne. He took it, another caress of fingers, another physical exchange in the dark. Her hands felt light, deft, as they passed their heavy object. The champagne glass was lead crystal, a mass of complicated cuts and edges.

It was also mostly empty.

She was a lulu all right. "So, Lulu—" Charles said, winced, then threw his head back to down the last swallow she'd left. "On a night like tonight, why would you come straight here? Why not hunt down a member of this family of yours that you so adore and hate at the same time?"

"I told you, I can't."

"You told me you wouldn't," he corrected. "You complained, yet all afternoon you backhandedly cherished them aloud."

"Did I?"

"Yes. Your parents, who pay no attention to you, except to take care of your every whim. Your cousin, who is silly but whom you love to the point of having taken the blame for her on occasion. Your aunt, who thinks you are a bad influence yet brags about you at dinner."

To hear this recounted annoyed Louise. She hadn't said this exactly, but of course he was right; she loved these people. She said, "Well. Ungrateful wretch that I am, then, I suppose."

Louise herself wished he would stop mentioning a family who would not approve of her decision to come here. They would not understand her willful step from the light, where she commanded attention, into a place where she wasn't sure what might happen next or whose rules governed.

She knew only that she had come to a man, the man from the kennel, who was comfortable in darkness. If anyone could feel at ease in a tilted ship with its lights out, here was the fellow. Her pasha, her misbehaving Arab in western trousers—she had glimpsed now and then the silhouette of his leg, the breadth of his shoulders; she had felt the furl of his robe when he moved. These hints, abetted by a few hours' reading, made funny things happen in her imagination.

In the shadows, she could almost see silk pillows on the floor, beside them a cold hookah full of Turkish tobacco, the room itself draped in fluttering, filmy curtains, a rolled prayer rug somewhere canted against a chest full of myrrh. For her, this forbidden room, from the second she'd entered it, held an exotic peace, a deep inner privacy, the sanctuary of a mosque. Or a seraglio . . . harem . . . zenana.

Words. The library's books today had been sprinkled with such impossible concepts, alongside random details and sweeping summaries, all interpreted through western prejudice. (Muslims didn't drink alcohol, yet were allowed to kill one another for honorable cause. They prayed five times a day, yet hid their women from guests and neighbors lest they be overcome by vice. The races were excitable and vengeful, Arabs, Bedouins, Berbers, and Moors, peoples older than time, their countries the cradle of civilization itself.) Most of her reading, she knew, gave superficial impressions, all probably wrong from over generalization. Yet these images were interesting, oh-so-interesting to her . . . symbolic of some profound difference she sensed between herself and this man, a cultural difference, she thought; a perspectival difference. She was enormously curious about him, no, titillated by him; no, both.

And oddly, rivetingly off balance without the ability to smile at him or otherwise dazzle his sight.

She held to her chair, almost shy to stand up.

Not her pasha. He rose and turned away from her, walking into the room's blackest shadows. She heard the clink of a bottle against crystal, the glug and fizz of wine.

"I wasn't criticizing," he said from across the room. "A moment ago. About your contradictory feelings toward your parents and aunts and uncles." When she didn't respond, he added, "Such feelings are not so unusual, though I found them to be uncommonly expressed. Articulate, perceptive. You are a complicated young woman in the rather engaging process of making sense of her own paradoxes. I salute you."

She laughed, lightly she hoped. "Flattery will get you everywhere," she said. Her voice, her laughter sounded more coy than she had intended. She frowned to herself. "Why don't you bring that champagne?"

She knew she was being too flirtatious; she was drinking more wine than she should. Yet the circumstance, or else this man, something—her own "paradoxes" perhaps—made her behave this way, more outrageous, more provocative. The room's blindness felt good one moment, then it turned around, leaving her vaguely apprehensive. While the man across the room moved in the dark—he breathed it, imbibed it—as if he were born to it.

She could feel his strength in the dark. He moved in it with more ease than she did. He seemed to sense her shifts and stances clearer, as if he could see her, in ways that had nothing to do with her sitting in his rooms, his territory. The darkness was his territory, as in the kennel; it was a place of power for him.

His voice stayed where it was, uncommandably on the far side of the room. He said, "It wasn't flattery. I am sincere: Your relationship to your family is fraught with the commotion that we"—he paused—"in my country call love."

Louise's face flushed. She shifted in the chair, feeling touchy, moody. He took too deep an interest in what she had only meant as passing diversion. She murmured, "I don't know what made me talk so much about myself."

"I enjoyed it." He laughed warmly. "Just as I am enjoying embarrassing you a little now. I don't know when a woman has been so"—his laughter grew softer, richer—"loquaciously open with me." He added, "Or so humorous while she was about it."

"Humorous?" She continued to frown down into her lap, at her own indistinct fingers as they felt their way along a fold of her gown, rolling a pearl in an indention of satin.

"Yes, you entertained me." He added, "And surprised me: As pretty as you are, you are more intelligent than you are pretty. You are more honest as well as, I suspect, more generous, more giving to those whom you love."

Louise scowled deeply and asked, "Could you bring that champagne?"

She had never thought of herself as generous or funny. Or even open.

She heard him pouring, but didn't know exactly

when he turned, when he walked back toward her. He apparently held to the edges of the room until he could approach from the darkest quarter, moving silently (on slippers, she imagined, red ones with curling toes, or bare feet). All she knew for certain was that he was suddenly near again.

She could feel his presence, was conscious of him, his closeness, in a peculiar way—through a heightened awareness of the sound of his breathing, the warmth, the humidity of his skin. He smelled of the ship's soap, a recent bath, his hair possibly damp. There was a faint odor of something else, something more personal, a man's toilette, bergamot perhaps.

Louise heard him sit again, take a drink of champagne, a quiet swallow. She leaned over the arm of her chair, toward him, reached. Through the dark, she found the glass, balanced heavily, relatively full, on his thigh. "May I?" she asked. She lifted it from his fingers. Then lost it; he lifted it higher and took it away.

She was stymied. Her poise disappeared into every vacant space where she wished she could read his reaction. Was he bent toward her or away? Was he teasing? Was he serious? What was he doing? Thinking? Conversely, she wanted to say, *Look at me. See me.* She wished she could light up her invisible beauty, distract, outshine any other judgment about her.

She leaned farther over the armrest, her whole weight onto her forearms, till her dangling fingers grazed his leg. "So," she said, "are you a holy man of sorts? Corrupted slightly by champagne? Is that why you can talk to me like this?"

"'Like this'?" he repeated.

"Like a priest? Is that what you are, a caliph or something?"

He let out a *ha* of surprise and sat back.

More wine, Charles thought. He drank up then

poured again—he'd had the presence of mind to tuck the bottle under his arm and bring it over. He topped off the glass, then licked his thumb as he set the bottle down behind him.

He no sooner settled forward again, though, than Louise bumped his arm. "Are you going to share or not?" she asked.

He let her take the glass, his fingers and all, keeping hold as she sipped.

She used both her hands to bring his and the glass to her mouth, tilting, taking a healthy slurp. Then he felt his fingers being pried off the glass. "Thank you," she said as she took it. She settled back, saying, "So are you celibate or what?" Her usually clear enunciation had taken on a kind of rounded tone. Nothing so crass as a slur, though she was indisputably tipsy. On a glass of champagne.

"Celibate?" he asked blankly.

"You know, do you not *want* to kiss me, because I was just wondering, since you haven't even tried."

He snorted then told her, "You're too used to young lieutenants, I'm afraid."

Charles had a vivid recollection suddenly from last night, of a girl who was not just pretty and sweet-smelling, but also tactile by contrasts: the hardness of all those tiny pearls covering the dewy smoothness of her throat, down over perfect breasts mounded above the neckline of her satin dress . . . strings of pearls waylaid by the hills of these breasts, detoured into their steep valley . . . then more strings, longer, falling, swinging down over her taut silky bosom, to dangle out precariously, far and wide from her slender waist, like an alpinist's lifeline gone wildly amok, pitons come unplanted . . .

Her shadow thought about his answer a moment, then apparently granted him leeway. She sank back into her chair, a hush of cushions and silk. Her ease was all the more engrossing in that he had just told her in so many words that he cared less about kissing her than about taking her measure, about judging where a kiss would lead them.

Through the dark, he reached over, touching her arm. He ran his hand down her forearm to the champagne. *God help him,* he thought; his fingers tingled. He felt a mild lift, the first pressure in the battle with the seam at his trousers, the buttons at his fly. He shifted forward on the piano bench, letting gravity reposition him as he smoothed his fingers around the back of her hand to find her palm. In this manner, he repossessed the glass, raising it away, his chest rising with it, then sinking. He closed his eyes. His breathing accelerated.

She was right. He was resisting, he realized. Why? Then this became a stupid question. He liked this Lulu Girl, cheeky, precocious thing that she was. He didn't relish hurting her or playing any sort of dark joke in which she was the laugh. Besides, her awakening to be possibly horrified by him didn't seem so funny anymore.

On the other hand, he wouldn't mind kissing her— having a little sample, as it were, of the bride-to-be. *God above, was she luscious.* Maybe even a very large sample, a full sample. Never mind his presumptuous idea of giving her a lesson in humility. New plan: Let her have her fling, quite safely, with him. There would be no embarrassment to his pride; no shame for either of them. Then he could send her on her way, off into marriage and fidelity—

Fidelity. Charles's brow drew down at the word, till the scar at his eye pulled the skin at his hairline. He couldn't help asking, as casually as possible, "Do you think you will be faithful once you are married?"

"To whom?"

"To your husband, for God's sake."

"I don't know." Louise didn't seem to be paying too much attention. "I hope to be faithful to someone someday, you know, faithful to something . . ." Her voice drifted off.

She reached over the arm of her chair, leaning toward Charles. Her hand found his thigh and the wine balanced there. She possessed the glass then didn't sit back, drinking another swill of champagne, an audible chug. She set the glass down on his thigh again, as if he were a table, leaving her arm draped there. "You know, this is much better than the champagne the captain was serving at dinner."

Ah, more than one glass. He wondered how drunk she was, while her sweet hand drooped perilously close to a quickening piece of evidence of how little any wonderings or ruminations were going to matter in a minute.

Charles leaned closer to her in the dark, closer toward a pretty young woman on a slightly sideways ship who sought the shelter of what must be a very secure part of her life—the attraction of the opposite sex. Which he felt in spades. The backs of his eyes were hot from it.

He was going to kiss her. He was going to. She wanted him to; he was going to. Yet he sat there, reluctant, inexplicably cautious—only God knew why—of what seemed to be happening, anyway.

She made a joke out of it. "Has the cat got your tongue? Or some other part of you?" She giggled nervously at her own bawdiness, then said, "I'm not drunk. I want you to know I'm not drunk. I swear it." She raised a hand high enough that the dim light from the curtains outlined a flat palm, a sworn oath. "Ask me anything." She was not squiffed exactly beyond reason, but she was ever so loose. "A question about Islam?" she suggested.

God forbid, he thought. He would kiss her just to shut her up.

Charles reached for her, finding the curving crown of her head, the back of her cool, silky hair, knowing,

as he slid into the sexual, he was making a mess of his
equilibrium somewhere. He felt upside down, frowning, smiling, drawn hopelessly . . . He found Louise
Vandermeer dear, surprising, puzzling; bright, funny,
sweet. His wild, misunderstood thing—he would
gnash his teeth at this naive assessment in only ten
minutes (and wish to shoot himself for it in a month's
time), but at this particular moment as he leaned
forward through the dark to find her mouth, he
thought the description not just apt but positively
inspiring.

While Louise herself was transfixed. With his hand
cupped at the nape of her neck, this man whom she
had never fully seen in the light pulled her through the
dark toward his mouth. Anything tentative about him
disappeared in the touch of his lips. He angled his
head and kissed her with openmouthed greed. Her
senses lit; they became the brightest point in the
room, blinding white heat. She turned her face into
the kiss as if it were the sun, as he took it deep into her
mouth; wet, lascivious, hot. She opened her lips
further, wallowing in the swift, steep pleasure of it.

There was an inciting, palpable ardor to his kiss, in
the press of his warm, slightly chapped lips, in the
deep, slippery-moist inquiry of his tongue. Each second her heart beat faster and harder than the second
before. As he kissed her, her hands of their own
accord lifted off the arm of the chair. They hung—
caught in erotic startlement—in midair. Until her
pasha took hold of her just above the elbows and
stood, taking her up with him into the drifting,
anchorless dark.

No chair, no support, just the rough ride of a
leaning, ploughing ship that brought her against a tall,
solidly built man. He was broad through the chest,
lean, more muscular through the arms than she had
expected; athletic somehow. Though nothing

matched his thighs. They were thick, hard, thewy and sinewed; a horseman's thighs, a strong horseman. (She imagined Arabian stallions ridden bareback in the desert.) She braced her weight against him, and he against hers; together they countered the movement of the ship. As he kissed her again, something dropped—the pearl. It bounced, *tap-tap-tap,* across the floor, with shorter and shorter distances between contacts until it *taddle-tapped* into a smooth roll across the tile and into the fireplace.

All modesty and control rolled away with it.

He brought her arms round his neck, and she clung, rising up on her toes, pressing herself to him. How strange this was. It was not that Louise had never felt the building sensations of willingness, but she had never felt them in such quick, sharp succession, as if all at once. As natural as gravity, his palms descended the underside of her arms into her armpits, the heels of his hands nestling against the edges of her breasts. His hands kneaded where the flesh first mounded at her ribs. It was a delicate titillation one moment, then his hands slid around them, encompassing. He took full possession of her breasts, and her breath caught. She let out a great, groaning burst of air into his mouth.

Charles swallowed up her groan in another fierce descent into her mouth. He wanted to live off the air in her lungs. His own breathing was ragged, coming in huffs like a steam engine. The only other sound he was capable of making was a grunt of satisfaction as he pushed her breasts together, letting them release back into his hands. Louise's breasts were full and high and warm to the touch—and smoother than the satin of her dress where her flesh pushed the neckline. He lifted these breasts, compressed them, weighed them, all the while stroking their tips with his thumbs. He mounded them above the neckline of her dress, then breathed down the deep channel there, a humid heat, before he kissed the place he'd made, mouth and tongue.

Louise bent her cheek to her shoulder and groaned. Her heart pounded in her chest, a hard, radiating beat that pulsed her throat, that throbbed down into her belly. She prayed for his hands and mouth to be everywhere, not to miss an inch of her. This man in the dark exceeded all imagination. Secure ... un-cowardly, un-celibate ... hot-mouthed, smooth-handed, warm-chested. In fact, bare-chested. She realized her hands had come to rest down into his robe at his shoulders, onto bare skin. He wore just trousers and a robe, half naked, her sheikh, her pasha of a primitive race. One sleeve of the robe was soaking cold where it brushed against her. Her fingers inside the edge caressed his neck. The hair at the base of his skull was damp. She touched his cheek. She wanted to kiss his face, his jaw, his nose, his eyes.

Her hands were caught by the wrists. He broke the embrace and stepped back.

They stood there in the dark, breaths hissing, him holding her wrists.

Louise wet her lips as she tried to control the intake and expulsion of air.

Charles let out softly, *"Ho-là—"* cutting off *ho-là-là,* an exclamation that was strictly French. Then, needing to exclaim something, he exhaled a nonsense phrase of Arabic that simply rose up from a decade ago, one of blasphemous wonder, *"La ilaha illa-llahu."* Half the creed of belief. *There is no God but Allah.* And Lulu-Louise, not Muhammad, was Heaven's messenger on earth. God above, she was unearthly in his arms, unlike anything else on the planet.

Where was the bedroom? Which way was the bedroom? He laced his fingers into hers, pulling her half a step in God knew which direction. He stopped, frowning at shadows. He was disoriented from having crawled all over and around her for five minutes in a slow spin through the dark. He stood there searching, frustration mounting, his breathing labored, holding the hand of a young woman who was more than compliant. She pressed up against the side of him, under his arm. He ended by turning, bending slightly to kiss her again. Another deep, lavish kiss.

More kissing. He couldn't quite get enough. Her mouth was soft, the smoothest, softest lips he could ever remember touching, and softer still on the inside. He shifted her around directly in front of him, stroked her with his tongue as his hands found her hips, pressing her closer, tighter, in rhythm to a slathering game of withdrawal and lingual penetration. The kiss became fervid, unruly. She followed, allowing it, contributing to it, taking hold of his robe in front, tight fistfuls. She rose up onto her toes, pressing her hips into him. He broke their embrace again a moment later, laughing, having difficulty speaking. "You know"—he drew a huge breath into his lungs, exhaling as he stroked her back—"we are going to end up right here somewhere between the hearth and piano"—another attempt to get air—"when the bed is so much more comfortable."

He was thinking of his knee that would not withstand too much of a pounding on the floor, not even on tight-woven oriental carpet.

He considered dragging her down onto the floor, anyway, here in the lost dark. It wouldn't take long, he was sure of that. Just a gentle descent, pulling her under him, another kiss like the last, and he would be on top of her, entering her with roughly the same drive and force as held the solar system in alignment.

As if his own concupiscence weren't enough, Louise lay her forehead against his chest. Softly panting, she said, "Oh—" She drew a heaving breath. "Oh—" A breath again. "I—oo—I didn't know this could—" A breath. "What a monstrous lust," she murmured, then laughed. "I feel as though it could break me in two."

"Yes, it's a little crazy," he said. Charles closed his eyes and listened to his own heartbeat thunder in his ears. He laughed raggedly. "Though very nice." It occurred to him to ask, "How much experience exactly do you have with this, by the way?" When she didn't answer, he said, "Because, dear heart, unless we are willing to stop periodically like this, I think I am going to lay you the moment I can find a comfortable place to put your back, and without too much preamble."

"All right," she murmured.

At least that was what he thought he heard. Her voice was small, her head still bent against him. "All right?" He laughed and pulled her shoulders up against him, into his armpit. He squeezed her tightly to him. "It's not all right. I want to make love to you properly. Which way is the bedroom? Do you know?"

He turned completely around one time, walking her with him, three hundred sixty degrees. The faint light through the terrace draperies materialized out from behind him, a landmark. Big, swooping hero that he was, he stooped, found the backs of her knees, and swung her legs up, cradling her back. Louise giggled and kicked lightly, nuzzling against him in a way that was perfectly worth a swollen knee in the morning. He walked with careful evenness, taking her toward his bed.

An hour ago, an eon ago, his mind had toyed with odd little tricks. Pearls fished out of necklines and passed between lips. Games, perversities in the dark. What he felt now was so simple and straightforward. No detours. No crooked turns. Just a bullet-quick shot straight up to the peak of arousal. From just kissing her mouth and touching her breasts. He could hardly wait to get her onto the mattress.

Once there, though, he wanted more. Sexual glut-tony. If it felt this good kissing with their clothes on, he reasoned, well . . . He wanted her undressed, un-done. He no sooner set her buttocks onto the counter-pane than he reached into her hair. She caught herself on her arms as he removed pins, at first delicately. One. Two. Three. But there were a lot of pins. Eventually he was slinging them like a madman, pins flying, some silently onto the carpet and some with faint ticks of steel against the nightstand.

Her hair fell in a mass, long and thick. It hung down to her hips, straight and heavy with a sliding weight to it that poured through his fingers like water—buckets and buckets of cool water, there was so much of it. Like all the rest of her physically, *too* much. Too beautiful . . . too smooth . . . too young . . . too willing . . . He took her shoulders and pushed her back, undoing clothing as he kissed her.

She wasn't as eager for this. Or rather was eager, but somehow bewildered by it. She didn't help. She even asked at one point, "What are you doing?"

"*Un*-doing," he answered. "The hooks at the back of your dress. There's a bloody lot of them."

"Oh." She giggled and rolled up onto an elbow, turning so he could get a better angle.

He got distracted halfway through the hooks, though. He had put his mouth into the crook of her shoulder, kissing his way up her neck, when she suddenly backed up into him, pressing her buttocks against his fully roused member. He was so surprised—and she had such a provocative knack for wiggling her backside with a kind of twist to her spine—he nearly expired of bliss on the spot.

"Oh, God, Louise," he groaned—as he fought another small, silent battle: He was having trouble holding to English. French invocations and magnif-icats kept rising to his lips, calls upon the sainted mother of God, the sacred blood of the saints.

Before Charles knew it, he was on top of her again, fumbling with the front of his trousers. An awful thought occurred: He was responsible for this young woman's health and reputation. And he possessed, in a drawer not ten feet from them, the means to guarantee both. A condom. He should get one. He fought himself over this issue for a split second, then kissed her mouth one quick time and heaved his weight up.

"Where are you going?"

"To get protection."

"To get what?" she asked.

"It's just over here," he assured her. "It will only take a second." He padded through the dark, his trousers open, an erection bobbing along as heavy as a log. His heart, his blood thundered for him to return to the bed and finish the deed off. God, he hated this, he thought. If he'd thought the marriage was as close as a month away, he wouldn't do it.

He found the drawer, bent, opened it.

From the bed, she called to him, "I should tell you something." She laughed lightly through breathy gasps.

He asked over his shoulder, "What?" He wasn't paying too much attention, his fingers fishing clumsily through the invisible interior of a drawer.

"Well—" A breathy pause. *"Technically* I'm a virgin."

Charles stopped, turned, and looked in the direction of her voice. *"Technically?"* He wet his lips. "What other kind is there?"

"You know. A pure one, I guess."

"You're not a pure virgin?"

"Oh, no," she said breezily. "I've kissed lots of men." As if this were sin of the first order.

"A virgin," he repeated dully. The notion rang miserably and instantly true.

She continued, "I mean, I have kissed a lot and,

well, you know, a little more than kissing, and I've *talked* a whole lot about what I might or might not do. Oh, but, Charles"—she groaned softly, sweetly—"there has been no one, nothing like you. If there had been, if I had known, why, I would be the biggest tart on earth!"

She meant this as sincere praise, of course. Yet her hyperbole could have been better chosen. Frowning, Charles had to remind himself that, if anything, he was the villain here. She was a virgin. Jesus Christ. An eighteen-year-old virgin who was slightly drunk and, even sober, besotted enough with this guise of his to come the length of the ship and make overtures of her own. She was *not* the biggest tart on earth. She was a young, inexperienced girl—with a precocious mouth—whom he was taking advantage of.

Charles stood up completely, rubbing his forehead. He squinted in her general direction, baffled, trying to take his bearings on this new twist to the situation. He asked, "Do you, ah, want to do this?"

"Oh, yes," she said quickly. "I just didn't want to surprise you."

"Well, I'm surprised," he said. He tried to make light of this comment. He laughed. "And, I'm afraid, I'm a virgin of sorts myself. I have never lain with a woman who was, ah—new to this."

She, her silence, didn't understand what he was saying at first. She rolled on the bed, her silhouette seeming to come to its elbows. She was trying to see him in the dark.

He said reassuringly, "Don't mistake me. If you want to, I'm sure I can handle the matter. I understand the concept, the biology of it, but I have just never come up against the idea in practice."

Understanding dawned and she fell back onto the mattress, laughing, peals of giggles. "Well, we shall explore this together then."

Perhaps it was funny, but Charles couldn't appreci-

ate it. He was halted by an odd feeling, that of
somehow cuckolding himself. He realized that, if
there was tender communion, a once-in-a-lifetime
act, he wanted it for himself, his *real* self. He wanted
something for them to share in memory, not something he could never speak aloud.

It occurred to him—with a mental clunk reserved
for moments when the obvious hit a man over the
head: He had separated himself in two. There was
Charles Harcourt who spoke French and would marry
this girl and love her, no doubt, for the rest of his life
(though he might worry a little about her propensity
to seek out affairs). And there was Charles of the
Arabian dark, who couldn't resist seducing this young
woman for his own ego, and whose English-speaking
games would get him into a great deal of trouble if she
ever found out what he'd been up to and why.

His blood cooled slightly for his game all the way
around.

"Perhaps," he suggested, "you want to stop? It's all
right. I would understand. A woman sometimes wants
to save this for her husband."

Her faintly tipsy giggles deteriorated into round,
ha-ing, belly laughter. She said in breaks and pauses,
"My who?"—chortle, chortle—"husband?"—soft,
laughing chokes from her delicate throat—"for my
hunchbacked husband?"

"Excuse me?"

She tried to calm herself. "It doesn't matter." She
sniffled. She had laughed herself to tears. "He's disfig-
ured," she reminded him. She added offhandedly, "I
don't look forward to this with him."

Charles gritted his teeth. "He's not hunchbacked."

"No, no. Of course not. It doesn't matter."

He pressed his lips together, a grimace that tried to
focus on an indistinct silhouette that seemed part
woman, part bedclothes. "You think of him as a
hunchback?"

"It doesn't matter," she repeated.

"No. Of course."

From the bed, Louise heard the drawer shut, then the shadow of her wonderful lover was suddenly standing over her again at the side of the bed. He said, "I hope you don't mind, but I don't seem to have a sheath."

"A what?"

"It doesn't matter," he said—her phrase and much her own intonation—as the mattress sank. He lay down onto her full-length.

He was heavy, warm. Louise's belly roiled. Her head grew light as he pressed himself along her body, his hands madly pulling at her clothes, opening, removing. This Arab certainly knew his way around the fastens of western women's clothing. She was in her chemise and petticoat in less than a minute. The chemise he merely loosened till it gaped. He rucked her petticoat up in bunches. It lay around her waist as he untied the drawstring of her knickers.

It all seemed a little fast. Fast. Yes. Like a race. Louise's mouth was dry from simply breathing. She breathed hard. Her heart pounded against the walls of her chest. She squirmed, a movement she couldn't seem to control. He backed up far enough to grasp her drawers with both hands, then pull them down her legs, yanking the fabric out from under her, taking it straight down her hips, her thighs, her calves, her ankles, and off, her knickers becoming so much refuse, tossed aside like the peel of a banana.

His hand came from nowhere down onto her bare belly, hot against skin newly exposed to cool air. She leaped. His touch was confident, adeptly aware. His palm slid over her stomach, then moved down to rub the rise of her mons; he rubbed her with slow, deliberate pressure. His fingers dug into the hair, combing, stroking closer, ever closer downward.

She knew what was happening, all that was going to

happen, yet as it unfolded, it was shocking. He cupped her between her legs. Nudging her knees farther apart, pressing her legs wide, exposing more of her to the night. Then he touched that part of her never felt by anyone . . . never looked upon or mentioned . . . her most intimate darkness, so forbidden . . . Then a surprise of even greater proportion, a delicious, horrible surprise. With his finger, he reached inside her. She had never imagined . . . It had never occurred to her . . .

Louise felt herself go liquid, her whole body in thrall to the slow slide of his finger entering her, inmost then out again; such a strange and remarkable breach of privacy. His hand moved on her, in her, unhampered by discretion or scruple or, as he explored, even her own unprecedented shyness. She wanted to close her legs; she wanted to spread them lasciviously, offer herself up, a remarkable urge to open herself to another. Contradictions. Paradoxes again. Louise felt sleek yet swollen . . . lax of muscle, of will, yet tight, coiling somewhere, rising, lifting toward . . . something, even as she felt herself sinking deep into the mattress.

He found other secret, sensitive parts of her, one place in particular awingly sensitive . . . *awwww,* that was what she said as he took this spot over, a coup d'état, an overthrow of any last trace of modesty, then fiddled with her—Oh, God, *fiddle,* the perfect word; he played her like a violin. Her body arched again, high.

He pressed her down again with his weight, his voice moving to her ear. "Louise," he said while she heaved for breath and wiggled and made sounds she would have never thought she'd utter in another's company. "I am going to take the hymen with my fingers. It ought to be possible, and it should save you the pain when I want your attention elsewhere," softly, "when I possess you fully."

She felt more than one finger; she didn't know how many. It felt like half his hand. She struggled briefly. "Sh-h-h," he said. His thumb found that place again, like a button he could push, a touch that made her weak with longing for something imprecise . . . inchoate . . . only God knew what, while making her insanely malleable to anything he wanted, anything he might suggest. "Sh-h-h," he repeated, crooning to her, *shh, shh.* "I will make it as painless as possible." He added a little coldly, "Though we both know I have to force a tear in your body."

His hand seemed to shove and pinch her at the same time, quite suddenly. She let out a yelp. Then his palm, gentle, settled over her belly again.

He murmured, "No longer a virgin." He laughed; brief, husky. "Except technically."

He rolled his weight on top of her, drew back his hips. She felt something much larger than his fingers, rounded, rigid, hot flesh. He didn't hesitate. He lunged, entering her. And he was wrong. It hurt again. "Ah!" she cried out. He was huge, thicker and longer than he could ever have duplicated with any other part of his body. Except maybe his whole arm, she thought.

She lay there stunned. So strange to contain something, someone, in so small a space.

Though not strange to him apparently. He waited a few seconds, as if to assess her willingness to proceed. Then without the least bit of self-consciousness, he pushed himself deeper into her—she hadn't thought it possible—till their pelvises bumped together. *Lord, what a sensation.*

He made a deep animal groan that seemed to say he liked where he had put himself. His head fell into the crook of her neck, his wet, open mouth at her jawline—as his hips pulled back.

His long, sliding withdrawal was something else again. *Lord.* The room, the world seemed to recede.

He immediately drove back in again. This entry faintly stung, while being mindlessly pleasurable. Her whole body shuddered, a quiver that spread through her from her core down to her toes, up her spine to her nipples all the way into her eyes. Her hands, her wrists, shook from it.

This man, this marvel atop her, set up a rhythm that worked somehow with a low, soft crooning in his throat, a vocalized drawing of breath in single, gravelly syllables. He sounded delirious. And Louise could sympathize. This bonding between a man and a woman, this copulation, was a fairly delirious experience.

She was wet at the source, a warm, messy wet that lubricated a pleasure that came in rising surges. Like nothing she knew or could even begin to compare it with. Like nothing conceivable. A faint, feminine grunt, she realized—gasps too punctuated to be called anything else—had begun to come from her own throat. Sensation shifted.

She took hold of his shoulders, tensing, lifting, as her head dropped back into the pillows. Oh, it was magnificent! Bizarre but incredible! He spread her, compacted her tightly with each swift filling of what she had never considered empty. Yet when he retreated, she longed only for the next drive into her.

He found her mouth, and she gave it over to him completely as she wrapped her legs around him, her heels digging into the naked, contracting muscles of his buttocks, heels and calves sliding for a moment with each thrust against the wool rumple of his trousers. Louise couldn't pull him close enough. Her hips couldn't encourage his to a hard enough, a deep enough plunge. As all the while she thought she would die of sensation itself.

Until what lay just beyond seemed like a kind of death. A daunting intensity, something that existed beyond the already ragged fierceness of their joining.

"Let go—" he whispered, the two words sounding swollen, coming from deep in his throat.

Yes. She wanted to, but didn't know how. And she was partly afraid to. Each entry into her body seemed to push farther, toward pleasure so far outside her knowledge and experience that it threatened a severity. She unclenched her fingers from his shoulders, yet held herself up, curled to him, thinking to steel herself for a blind run toward her own senses.

He murmured again, "Let go," his voice itself strange, low, deeper, the words harder to get to, as if borne from his chest. He took another ragged breath, then kissed her mouth wetly, ending the kiss with a sharp, hard thrust of his hips, burying himself. His head bent forward. She could feel his hair, soft against her cheek, her mouth, a rhythmic brush, light and silky. "Oh God," he groaned. Another thrust. Like the one before, hard, a kind of paroxysm of muscle, almost volitionless, followed immediately by another, then another. His last coherent words came out in a low, wrenching string: "Let—go— You almost can— I can—feel it— Come with— OhGodcomewithme- justfall—"

And she did. She let her arms fall out, away from her body into the pillows and sheets. She let every muscle go slack.

Her body took over on its own. It was like discovering she could fly. The mattress seemed to come up under her back and lift her. Her stomach rolled over, folding her into a series of exquisite, piercing spasms. Stars. Spasms that contracted muscles she didn't even know she had. Spasms that burned and twinkled in her veins, her pulse. Blood. Within the wetness there between her legs, the burning admitted that he slid in her blood.

Then her blood mingled with his seed: He cried out, a suppressed guttural of anguish, rapture. His chest came up off her, his shoulders seeming to levitate into the nothingness above. His arms on either side of her head straightened, rigid; they became pillars of thick muscle she grabbed hold of. While his hips shoved forward, driving fiercely into her, producing three, four more deep, quick rhapsodic convulsions.

The contractions continued and continued, shooting a quiver up through her. The skin of her arms, her neck, her spine rose in goose bumps. Her nipples shriveled. Pleasure rippled out from these tightly puckered tips, as if from a stone dropped into water, spreading, overflowing her veins, to meet a flood from the lower reaches of her body.

When her Charles collapsed, long-limbed and heavy onto her, his heart pounded so hard against her chest, she couldn't tell the beats of his heart from hers.

Meanwhile Charles's whole body throbbed with a sublime satisfaction that left his limbs too heavy to move. His body was joyous. But his spirit was ill at ease. *You have just taken a drunk virgin. Out of pique,* it told him. *A girl who trusted your counsel.*

And who had walked half the length of a blind, limping ship just for this, he argued with himself.

His conflict ended quickly, however, when the lovely Louise threw her arms and legs around him. She pulled him tightly to her and giggled, her breathy laughter sleek as silk against the skin of his neck.

"Charles," she said, "you are marvelous." She sighed a deep, contented sigh right in his ear, then asked, "Oh, can you do that again?"

Could he do it again? Well, maybe, given half an hour's recuperation. He was not as young as he used to be.

But, in light of this question, just how bad should a man feel?

Not very. He promptly kissed her, eventually shucking his trousers completely. They rolled around, hardly speaking at all, except with their hands and mouths, their bodies. After which, he "did that again."

Without a condom.

Now you idiot, Charles thought, *go get one.* He had a drawerful after all. Yet he himself had been careful. And Louise had come to him untried completely, as pristine as a new package he himself had just unwrapped. And, should the other misadventure befall them—a child between them—well, he was about to marry the girl, for God's sake: They would celebrate and push the wedding up.

The wedding, he thought. It couldn't come soon enough! No condom! Ever! Oh, the idea sang in his brain. For that was the point, wasn't it? A wife. A mate. A faithful companion. A life together. Tightly together. Skin to skin . . . oh, her skin was divine . . .

This was where he'd considered turning on the lights and ripping off the metaphorical mask, so to speak. This was where he'd meant to let her see whom she'd lain with and, if she was capable, see herself in all her shallow glory. Yet she was snuggled against him so sweetly. Her seduction had gone so well and happened so quickly. And there were still at least four more days aboard ship, a ship darkened by the loss of a generator. It just all seemed too perfect. Besides, here was a girl who had no place to turn, no better place to take her fear and concerns but here, to him. Any sort of trick or confrontation now seemed unfair.

There was time for that later, he thought, if he chose to follow through with his joke. At this point, though, he started to understand himself and his own small deviations that had begun this afternoon in the kennel. He was holding the softest, sweetest—most fearless—creature he had ever entered. She smelled like heaven. She felt like paradise. He wanted to draw this situation out, not bring it to a swift conclusion.

He would nuzzle her as long and as often as she would let him while they crossed the Atlantic. *Then* he might carry through and let her horrify herself, if she was so inclined. After all, a woman who lumped a man with a bad eye in with hunchbacks deserved the shock. Didn't she?

Yes. Of course.

No. He realized something else: He liked her and didn't want to make a fool of her. He didn't want to hurt this girl in any way. If her judgments weren't profound, well, whose were all the time, and didn't she have reason for a little superficiality? Her youth, for one. Her lack of experience with life. Parents who doted on her. Then there had to be a bevy of young men willing to tame tigers and level mountains for her. Charles frowned and drew the sleeping Louise closer. Her legs curled round his thigh as she nested against him. No, he was going to have to resolve any discontent with her some other way. He would think about it and figure something out.

He was clear about one thing, though. If he liked this young creature and wanted her affection, he was certain that teasing her all the way across an ocean was not the way to get it, nor did lying and pretense seem a very good introduction to her new husband.

She left just before the dawn's first light. He jiggled her awake, handed her her clothes, half dressed her himself, and with a kiss at the doorway booted her out into the hall.

Charles sighed as he closed the door. And secretly prayed that she would be back. He wanted this night all over again. And again tomorrow and the tomorrow after.

God bless this ship. It normally took six days to get across the Atlantic. But, with luck, it would take them more than a week at their present pace. He found himself hoping for another small leak, another minor setback, something to delay them and keep everyone else out of the way. How delightful, the slight uplift of his belly as the ship tottered. In the dark of his sitting room, he heard something rolling in the hearth of his fireplace—something tiny and hard that *tuppled,* grew silent for an instant, then spooled around slowly on the tile when the ship began to dip in the other direction. As the sound ticked back across the floor, Charles prayed for just this: seas rough enough to keep a pearl pitching along his floor all the way across the ocean and right into the port of Marseilles.

Chapter 12

❧〜◦◦〜❧

Ambergris is the most elegant of perfume fixatives, adding great lasting power while also imparting a subtle velvetiness to the overall scent.

Charles Harcourt, Prince d'Harcourt
On the Nature and Uses of Ambergris

Charles awoke at midday with a hazy sun streaming through his curtains. The sea was rough, but the rain had stopped. The sky had opened a little, though it remained cloudy. Beams of overcast light lit the room, spreading a ruddy, golden glow onto everything, from high ceilings to bolted-down furniture to his own belongings hanging or sliding a few inches this way then that with the ocean's toss.

He rolled over facedown into his sheets and took in a great, snorting smell of them. Louise. He put his nose against the pressed linen and traced her movements and outlines like a hound. Louise lying like a wanton, an arm above her head. Louise laughing, crawling on her hands and knees through the dark toward him. He wanted to lick the place that had pressed the small of her back. He wanted to have for

146

breakfast the pillow on which she'd rested her knee as she'd slept.

Charles groaned and collapsed, his cheek pressed into the pillow. He closed his eyes. He wanted to cover these sheets with perfumer's grease—colorless, odorless, purified fat—and spread Louise upon them like flower petals. *Enfleurage* . . . he wanted to impregnate a thick layer of this unguent with the exhalations of her body. Then he would melt off this sublime essence and strain it into a bottle: attar of Louise. He could rub it all over himself, take a bath in it. Have it to console him when she wasn't here.

By day, like now.

As he got up and dressed, his knee hurt a bit. But it held—a stiff, aching joint that remained relatively normal in appearance. Triumph. Charles felt immortal, manly, heroic. He'd made love to a delightful young creature, half a dozen times, half a dozen ways, as if he'd been seventeen. He'd carried her for goodnessake across an unstable floor, spent himself into a stupor of exhaustion, then risen in the morning like Lazarus, healed and alive, a new man, capable of superhuman endeavors—and eager to begin the whole enterprise again.

He rang her room as he buttoned his shirt, looking out the alcove across his bedroom to the wonderfully darkening rain clouds outside. He blessed the squalling weather.

She answered, "Hello."

"Louise."

"Charles?"

Much too easily, he said, "Yes. How are you this morning?"

Her voice laughed. "A little sore but in love."

He frowned and smiled into the transmitter. "In love?"

"I adore you," she said. "I hated to leave." She rushed into what almost sounded like a planned declaration. "I want to sleep with you all night. I want to fly away with you, stay with you night and day. In the dark forever, if need be; I will kill the sun. We will drown it, freeze it in ice. Or we can find a cave and never come out. Do you want me?" She added, "Do you have all four wives allowed by the Koran?" Her renewed laughter tried to sound carefree, rising in particular to the last question, as if it and everything before it were nothing more than flirtatious banter.

Charles said seriously, "You wouldn't like North Africa."

"Is that where you're from?"

He lied, "Yes." He told the truth: "You wouldn't like the restrictions placed upon you in a Muslim country. You wouldn't like my having the power of life and death over you."

She left a pause, then said, "I'm not sure you don't have that already."

"Louise. This is an affair, not forever."

She listened but said nothing; just the static immediacy of her unsettled breathing in and out over the wire.

He said, "You are going to France to marry and start a home and a family. That is as far from your own culture as you dare venture, and even France will be difficult for you at times."

She waited then said ever so meekly, "I know you're right." Softer still, she said, "I know you are wise." In a barely perceptible tone, she said, "I love you."

Charles stared at the phone, thrilled to hear this. He adored her. He wanted to tell her so. But he was, of course, distressed to believe her words under the circumstances. She was to love everlastingly Charles Harcourt, not Charles of the Dark Ship. "Louise," he said, "you are a young woman infatuated with your first lover. This is not the same thing as love. We have slept together one time"—he had to correct himself—"well, several times, but during one interval. We have known each other twenty-four hours."

There was a hiatus, a silence. Then she said, "You're right, of course." She released a breath into soft laughter. "Of course, you are. I'm sorry if I made you uncomfortable." Her laughter became more relaxed, more genuine. She said, "I will see you tonight. At the crack of dark."

Night arrived and so did she, on the dot. The sun had been down completely maybe sixty seconds. He suspected she had been waiting on the other side of the door to knock.

When he opened it, Louise literally flew over the threshold. She leaped, a dewy jasmine projectile through the shadows of a tilting, unlit evening upon the ocean. He caught her by her ribs as her legs wrapped around him, then he had to catch himself, them both, backward against the wall. He nearly fell from the impact.

Her mouth hit him with similar force. She kissed him; he easily returned her fervor. The kiss was fierce and eager and grateful, lips and tongues thankful to press and bite and touch and explore. Her hands alighted upon his face, a flutter of inquisitive movement up his cheek. He jerked his head back, clonking it solidly on the wall. Her hands followed. He turned his head abruptly. But her palms found him again, lightly surrounding his jaw.

Charles had to reach up and forcefully take her hands away. "Don't touch my face," he said. "You can't see me that way either."

"Why not?" she whispered and laughed into his mouth.

"I don't want you to."

She reared back in the dark, hanging off his shoulders. He had to brace her weight. "Why?" she said. "Do I know you?"

She was looking for a substantive answer to the questions, Why the dark now? Now that they were lovers already? Now that sight was so appealing?

She asked, "Am I *going* to know you? Do you visit Provence?" She continued to ask, then come up with answers to her own questions. "Oh. Oh dear. You *know* the Prince d'Harcourt. You can't be his friend, not sleeping with me." Then, "Oh, you are his enemy!"

This seemed like a solution. Charles even thought of a convenient mitigation. "His competitor," he told her. "We both make perfume. You're wearing jasmine in your hair that I'm going to sell him." Clever devil. This would allow Charles Harcourt to unload all the Wedding Night Jasmine off the ship into his own carts. He added, "Though this isn't the reason I want you, Louise. I want you for myself. For no other motive." It was true, so unconditionally true. "I want you, I want you, I want you, I want you," he said, spinning around from the wall and carrying her through the shadows of his rooms. "I have been mad these last hours without you."

He flopped her backward on the bed and joined her there, idiotically happy to slide up against the *shush*y silk of her dress and pull her to him. His glad mutterings turned into a chaining repetition of her name. *Louise, Louise, Louise . . .* A reiteration—did he speak this aloud?—that rang in his mind like a poem, a song, a mantra, an endless wonder. While he smelled his way through the dark to the soft place just under her chin where frontal jaw became throat, kissing her there as his fingers found the buttons of her stand-up collar. He must have uttered some of his inanely excessive pleasure aloud.

For she squirmed, giggled, and mimicked him: " 'Louise, Louise, Louise.' " Then she asked, "Why do you never call me *Lulu,* even though I have asked you to?"

He answered perhaps too quickly, too honestly. "Because I like *Louise* better. Much better. *Lulu* sounds like I am debauching a twelve-year-old."

She found this funny. After a startled pause, she erupted into rich, rippling laughter he could feel under his hand at her belly. He put his leg over her, his own belly against this vibration, then found her face in the dark and kissed this laughing young woman.

Less than a minute later, the two of them were so avid they ripped a button off his shirt then lost the drawstring of her drawers into its casing.

Afterward, lying beside him, her bare arm across his naked chest, she said into the dark, "Well, Louise, the mature and very old Louise, is perfectly capable of deceiving too, you know. I could see you in Provence and pretend I don't know you."

"No." Charles stared up into the blank, black canopy. He was having trouble making up reasons, making up more lies on top of lies. "I shall have a hard enough time pretending I don't know you." It was going to be awful pretending he wasn't her lover. He thought to add, "Should we meet, that is, which is unlikely. I rarely cross the Mediterranean." He sighed. He closed his eyes. "I like home. I doubt I shall ever roam far from it again. . . ."

Louise, however, only heard the part where he said no, then something more about their never seeing each other again. She preferred not to think about her future. She changed the subject. "What do you like about yourself?" she asked.

It took him a moment to respond, then he said, "What do *you* like?"

"Oh, your hands and that way you have of—"

He laughed and cut her off. "No, about yourself." His hand dropped out of the dark onto her mouth, covering her reply. "About yourself in the dark," he restricted. "What do you like about yourself best, here in this room, right now?" He lifted his hand.

The moment he uncovered her mouth, she said, "Oh, my senses," and giggled. "And wondering where your hand will alight next."

He *tsked* like a schoolmaster. (She loved teasing him, because his tone had become oh-so-responsible and instructive; he took their age difference far too seriously.) "All right, your second-favorite part." His hand settled to stroke her hip.

She snuggled against his motion, staring up, seeing nothing. She didn't know the answer to his question.

He coached toward a broader direction. "What seems important to you? What do you want to do with your life?"

"Nothing. That's my problem." She rolled up onto her knees, then on impulse stood all the way up onto her feet into a delicious, black instability. She could barely balance for the bounce of the mattress, the dark, and the sway of the ship. The springs gave noisily as she danced into compensation and adjustment in the middle of the bed. Charles's heavy body bounced with her movements, till he shifted—his weight left the mattress completely.

"Where are you going?" she asked.

"To the water closet. Keep talking. I can hear you from here."

To the sound of a heavy stream hitting the toilet, Louise declaimed in her mother's intonation, "'A lady should stand on a pedestal.'" In her own voice, she called, "My parents' bywords, you know, are, 'You must realize your potential.' My marriage potential, they mean; for them, I have no other."

"So what do you want for yourself?" he said as he came back round the doorway of the bathroom.

"I don't know." She thought as she swayed there on the bed to the rhythm of the ship. She said with some bewilderment, "Marriage, I suppose." She paused. "And something else. There must be something else besides." She laughed. She could hear Charles's breathing. She knew where he was in that uncanny way of the dark, when he stood suddenly nearby. He was at the bed, right in front of her. She said down toward him, "What do you think? Does this count as a pedestal?" She placed her hands on his shoulders and bounced twice on the bed, as if it were a circus trampoline.

"I think," he said, "that ladies—delicious ladies such as yourself—" He lay his hands on her hips as he redirected the pronoun, making it more specific. "I think that *you,* Louise, belong in the arms of a warm, loving man, right up against him. No pedestals. Just yourself as you are." He caught her on the next bounce.

In the pause as he held her in the air, her hair swung against her back and buttocks. The mass of it slid and brushed her like a cool, living thing as he threw her onto the mattress. She landed on her back, and her hair flew up. Louise had never realized how pleasant her own hair felt against her skin. Or how nice it might feel to fly naked through the dark. Every moment with her pasha seemed to bring more of this, new sensory awakenings. She closed her eyes and let herself bounce on the bed—until he stopped her with his own weight.

As he settled on top of her, she asked up into his face, "Do you know what my cousin Mary wants to do with her life?"

He petted her head, her face, saying, "You will find something to do with yourself, Louise. You are young yet." He kissed her forehead. "What I was saying a moment ago was that you must find yourself: know yourself, learn yourself. Then what you want to do becomes obvious."

She laughed at this. It sounded good, but she wasn't

sure what it meant. She asked, "Don't you want to know what Mary thinks is obvious?"

"All right. What does *Mary* want to do with her life?"

"Become a nun." Louise giggled.

"A nun."

"Do you know why?"

"You're going to tell me, aren't you?" He slid off her but stayed close, belly to hip.

"Yes. You see, there was this priest in New York. And Mary's parents made her go to confession. She went once, and it wasn't as bad as she thought, so she went back. Father Tata—that was his name. Isn't that a funny name? It's Italian. Anyway, Father Tata was kind to her." Louise couldn't keep from laughing again. She found this story so silly. "Mary just kept on going and going to confession. Everything the priest said to her seemed so beautiful and wise. So that, after a while, she just went to hear his voice on the other side of the cubicle. Sometimes she would come to my house afterward and swoon and fall back on my bed, talking about how deep his voice was, how intimately he understood her. Then she would get out her rosary and pray to the Holy Mother that he would give up the priesthood.

"We would both laugh at it. I mean, we knew him. He was big and bald, though we decided he had nice eyes. I can sympathize better now. I mean, there is a real seduction to having someone listen and know you, accept you just as you are." Louise paused. "You're not bald, are you?" Then she remembered the damp hair she'd felt last night when he'd let her fingers get close to his head. He had more hair than usual; it was long.

Mary's story, though, had lost some of its humor. She asked, "Do you suppose that's all this is, Charles? That I have fallen in love with my priest?"

He burst out laughing, though he dutifully tried to

calm himself so as to take her question as seriously as she'd meant it. "No," he said. He squeezed her, still grappling with how funny he found this. "Or perhaps we should shoot that Father Tata." He told her, "Louise, I am performing no holy service here. I am selfishly involved in the pleasure of your company, that is, in the delight of your sweet, open spirit, your frighteningly active mind, and in the voluptuousness of your body."

"But that's what I'm saying. I'm not always this open with people." She took this back. "I'm *never* this open. You're like that to me. My confessor." She rolled into his chest, put her arm about him, and kissed him extravagantly on the neck, with mouth and tongue along the warm, faintly salty, thick muscle that broadened out at the back of his shoulder. When she felt him shiver, she let out a soft cackle. "And maybe just a little bit more." She traced his shoulder with her hand. "Though, when I feel your body, I know you are finer, stronger than Father Tata." She pressed close and whispered, "My handsome priest." She murmured in his ear, "Give me, Father, something to regret."

"You are blasphemous," he said as he rolled himself up on top of her again.

She laughed. "I am impossible. My parents say so, and all my aunts and uncles agree. I am 'a handful.'"

"Yes," he said. "That you are. And I am never so happy as when my hands are full of you." He slid his arms under her, between the sheets and her skin to her buttocks, where his palms pressed two handfuls of her tightly against him.

She threw her arms around his neck and nestled her face in the crook there. He held her like this, in an embrace that was strangely less sexual, more the shared closeness of two people discovering, admitting, their friendship. Well, a little bit more than friendship. Better than friendship. Body to body, heart to heart, soul to soul in the dark; as close as two people can be without one of them being inside the other.

As they began the dance again that would broach this distance, Louise knew she had made a leap of faith when it came to her pasha: She trusted him with her private self.

He made her want to look not just *at* herself but *into* herself. He made her believe other aspects about her, beyond her looks, might be as wonderful or even *more* wonderful. He accepted and liked the whole of her; he believed in her. Strange paradox: With him, Louise felt herself begin to shine in the dark. This was what she grew to love best about her pasha—who she was in his presence.

Her entire family remained ill to one degree or another, save an elderly great aunt who was easy to dodge. By day, Louise checked on her parents and Mary, Mary's cat, the Bear, and a few others. Seasickness, however, generally meant people wanted to be left alone. Thus her missions of mercy took little of her time. Mostly she slept, trying to recover from her night's activities. Then she roamed the ship waiting for nightfall. When the sun began to set, she headed for the Rosemont suite, standing outside the door until the inner corridor became lightless, then she knocked.

Once inside, she became a different person. No, she became herself. She censored nothing, except perhaps questions that she knew were not welcome. If her pasha could accept her so completely, she reasoned, then she could accept the personal secretiveness he insisted upon. Beyond this, she proceeded with abandon. She made love in whatever way felt good and natural to her. She spoke of that which was on her mind at the moment.

The situation—an interested lover in the enveloping dark—invited confidences, Louise knew; it invited murmurs of things she might not speak of in the light. Yet she couldn't see how this mattered. Her Charles-of-the-Atlantic-Crossing was very clear about the ephemeral nature of their relationship. She would never see him again. *Fine.*

Perfect. That which burns quickly, burns brightest.

Chapter 13

The fragrance of ambergris itself in a perfume is referred to as amber notes or simply amber.

Charles Harcourt, Prince d'Harcourt
On the Nature and Uses of Ambergris

When a man—and not a young man, at that— is up two nights running, making love to a young woman of voracious energy with a seemingly insatiable interest in him and pretty much everything else in life, it is a fairly simple matter to get to nighttime again. One need only lie in bed until two in the afternoon, eat "breakfast," bathe, shave, dress, then read the paper as one waited for sunset.

On the fourth evening of their trip across the Atlantic, the third evening of their affair, Charles had barely got his newspaper open when a knock came at his door. He looked up, frowning. The sun was low. There was still enough light to read, if he stood by the window and strained his good eye. It was too early for Louise.

Nonetheless it was Louise's voice that whispered from the hallway. "Let me in, Charles."

He got up, irritated that she should not hold strictly to his rules. From his side of the door, he told her, "No. It's still light. Come back in half an hour."

Out in the hallway, Louise, all but giddy, only laughed then suggested, "Take the key out and look through the keyhole." She touched the blindfold she'd extemporized moments ago. It covered her eyes, from her brow to the tip of her nose. She couldn't see.

There was silence on the other side of the door, a hesitation. Then she heard the rattle of the key coming out. After a moment, though, Charles's voice merely repeated, "Come back, Louise. I want to see you, but not now. Not like this. Come back later."

She stood there, nonplussed. "No." Her high spirits was seized by an instant of surprisingly sharp disappointment. "You didn't look," she accused. Then it occurred to her: "The hallway—perhaps the hallway is too dim for you to tell that—"

"Go away."

"But did you see?"

"See what?" He sounded annoyed. He wasn't going to cooperate.

"Open the door a crack. Look at me." With growing desperation, "Or just let me in, Charles. It's all right. I swear." Pleading, promising—not at all how she'd imagined this game—then complaining: "You don't trust me."

He laughed, a distant sound; he'd moved away from the door. "No, I don't."

She pressed her lips together, then had to grab out into the sightless dark—her fingers hit the wall then found the doorjamb—as the ship lurched more steeply than she was ready for. Silence, except for this, the bowel-deep rumble of engines.

Finally, she gathered herself enough to ask, "Charles, are you still there?"

"Yes."

"Cover yourself. I don't know, wrap up in one of your robes or thingies. Just look, come on, look!"

She wasn't certain what made the difference but after a moment the door unlatched with a click. Relief. Reprieve. She *could* make him break from preconceived plan.

And, unexpectedly, her eyes knew light, a glow passing through the folds of the silk underdrawers she's wrapped round her head, through her closed eyelids themselves. A shadow crossed in front of her. She jerked before she realized—Charles had touched the blindfold, her eyes. He was assessing it.

"My God— By Allah." The soft light opened all the way out, darkly golden, while his deep, rich voice began to laugh. "I see," he said, "that the vogue for colorful undergarments has made it to New York."

Hers were a fiery saffron, a beautiful, unusual color, trimmed in rose lace and dark coral ribbons. "And you know so very much about Western undergarments?"

Still laughing, he said, "My dear, for better or worse, I am a walking catalog of erotic embellishments, from most any continent you can name." He pulled her into the room.

The door closed behind her, the key quietly tumbling the lock. And, oh, the glow, the lovely glow of light—an obscure, luminous amber—with his shadow passing in and out as he turned her around. He assessed the knot in back, turned her around again, then all the way around once more till she felt dizzy.

After which, he took her jaw between his hands and gently kissed her eyes through the shadowy silk. "Are the folds enough?" he murmured. "Can you really not see?" As if to answer his own questions, he touched her eyes again through the fabric.

Louise loved the feel of his fingers. She caught his hands and pressed his palms to her face. They smelled of soap or *eau de toilette,* the odor faintly oriental; the spiciness of dark incense, the coolness of earthy moss. Whatever he wore—and, though light, it was something more than merely clean skin—it was fragrant in the way of a sweet dark woods; redolent, she liked to think, of the lush, wet banks of the Nile.

She opened her mouth over his palm, biting, then murmured, "Half an hour ago, as I readied myself, the anticipation grew so keen that I began to shake." She laughed, lightly she hoped. "I got dressed all backward, my stockings on already before I'd even found fresh underthings. In the end, I dashed out with my knickers still in my hands. Just before I knocked, I tied them round my eyes. It seemed a better place for them, and I couldn't wait. I simply couldn't wait. Silly, no?"

His very serious voice said, "The effect is hardly silly."

Something leaped inside her. She reached out and found his chest. He had pulled back a step, either still caught in his reserve, his distrust, or simply looking at her; she couldn't tell which. While her own sense of touch was greedy for him. She dragged her fingertips down his broad pectoral muscles, downward over the smaller musculature that corrugated his abdomen.

Hers was an odd greed. Like she could store him up. She had touched him so much already that her hands, her body felt almost empty when he was absent from her. Even her spirit—

No. She forced herself to become silly once more. She turned her arms over, wrists up, wrist bones together. "Your slave, sire," she said dramatically. Then she folded down into the billow of her own skirts, bending over, kowtowing to the floor. "Without a shred of underdrawers on, except where you see them."

"You little idiot," he told her. "What a stunt."

"But it will work," she said into her muffling skirts. "I could stay with you night and day, if we merely put out my eyes." She resented all at once the ridiculousness of what she was doing, of what he demanded.

"Don't even say such a thing." He drew her up, touching the blindfold again, checking, pressing his hands gently over it, around its edges, tugging again at its knot.

"But it is what you are doing to us," she told him. "We both may as well be blind."

He stopped. Silence. He disapproved. Then his low, faintly dangerous-sounding voice said, "In North Africa women do what they are told without question or complaint. Turn around."

"What?"

"I said, turn around."

His hands dropped away. He apparently stepped back, for he was not within reach when she involuntarily grasped the air where he had been. She tried consciously to find him for a second more, arms waving in the air, searching. Nothing. At sea. In the dark again. While he had sight.

She couldn't tell if he was teasing, couldn't read his mood at all. She tried reminding herself that he looked at her. An advantage she had been trying to claim for three days. In the fading light, with her colorful blindfold, she would be something to behold. Yet he made no sound, no movement, no contact: no admission of her power. Till she had done as he asked. She turned around, away from where he'd stood.

And immediately he came up behind her, drawing her back into his body. He put his face into the curve of her neck, kissing her as he began to undress her.

"Oh, my," she got out. Then, "Oh, dear God—"

He removed her clothes quickly, taking her defenses—her looks—and turning them into something distinctly vulnerable: viewing her naked body from the back, only her eyes immodestly clothed. A strange sight indeed, she thought.

Though not so inappropriate. At his mercy. At his command. How she adored his touch, his gentle invasions of her privacy, herself unwillingly engrossed by this game of his inadvertently pushed further, to more compelling degree.

He stripped her, caressing her while he remained fully dressed. Then he made certain she understood he looked at her, murmuring words there in the last rays of daylight. Things about the lithe, shadowed curve of her back . . . the deep indention of her naked waist. He traced his finger down the bumps of her spine and called it elegant. He waxed rhapsodic of her legs, while running the backs of his fingers up the inside of her knee, her thigh. Her legs were the most amazing part of her—ungodly long, he said—strong and graceful enough that the entire troupe of the Moscow Ballet would have stopped in their tracks with envy had they seen them. Then where her legs stopped, between, below the soft, round curves of her buttocks, she was deep rose-pink and shining wet, inviting . . .

He made love to her with words and touches, with an imperative to please that was extravagant, ardent. Till she was pushed up against the door, breathing against it, fearful of her own sounds—they were so loud and unmistakable of origin. A woman overcome, possessed in every sense, deranged.

"I want you inside me," she said, stunned by her own explicitness. She tried to turn around.

He leaned, pinned her with his body. "No. Not yet."

Impossible, this. Impossible that she was pressed against a door, blindfolded, while his fingers performed the most intimate of pleasures. Impossible that he should be more familiar with her body than she, yet he was. He brought her to a fine pitch, without release, then stopped; once, twice. When finally, he let

her drop over the edge, every muscle spasmed; she let
her full weight collapse.

Dark and dizzy. She was on the floor, one leg
braced against the wall. When had the room become
dark? When had he pushed the blindfold up and off?
He'd been afraid that she could see before, she
thought, the reason he wouldn't let her face him. But
never mind. He kissed her closed eyes now, his lips
moist on the bare, thin, delicately folded skin of her
eyelids as he opened his trousers.

What had begun as the most thrilling experience of
her life was becoming, she knew, something else. For
when he entered her, their union became central to
her existence in that moment.

Inside, she kept thinking. Inside me. Not just
physically, but emotionally. She hadn't meant to let
him do this. But like the faint, exotic smell of him, she
had drawn him into her, inhaled him, drunk him
down. It was too late now. He'd crossed through,
seeped into her blood, from where he exerted a
mysterious force over her with—she feared—the
absolute authority of what could be nothing less than
love.

God help her. She didn't need a definition or a
lesson on the subject. This man *was* the subject. For
her, he was the avatar on earth of this emotion. She
didn't know where he came from, who he really was,
or even his true name. She only knew that she was in
love with him. Horribly, fully, and irreversibly. And
that her spirit needed him up against her, inside her,
as surely as her body needed water to survive.

That night, they talked until their comments, their
questions, and replies had become mutters. Charles
guarded against sleep—not so difficult, he thought,
with the infinitely engaging young Louise in his bed.
Even as she drifted off, her body falling limp against
him, he remained awake. He petted her, nesting

himself into the crooks of her warmth. He brushed his hands over her hip then her breast, loving the feel of her shift against him. He relished her movement as she entwined her limbs with his. The room grew quiet; the sea settled into a steady rock. Charles brought his leg up over Louise, pressing his genitals against her hip, feeling an intimate and unprecedented satiation, not just in his sexual parts but in his spirit. A blissfulness. He drew her against his chest, wrapping his arms around her. He thought he could wrap and rewrap himself around her, languishing in satisfaction all night, and never grow tired of this occupation. Yet he was more exhausted than he realized. For, in his comfort with Louise's body lying against him, Charles drifted off into a dark, rocking peace.

Only God knew how long he slept. When he awoke it was with a start, in a sweat of sudden, anxious awareness. He leaped awake, sat up, assailed by shadows, a thousand sleeping fears.

Daylight, he thought; she would wake in a moment and see him.

Yet it was pitch black outside.

He fretted she was gone; she had left him.

Yet she was right there beside him, one leg entangled in his, her arm lying limply over his waist.

Guilt. His deception was somewhere, somehow quietly unraveling. When it sank, it was going to take him to the bottom for the tangle he'd be caught in.

Yet all was well. Louise slept soundly, a sweet, faint whisper of breathing, in then out.

This sound made Charles realize what had changed, what had awakened him, and he let out a sigh of relief. All was well, better than well. All was quiet. Utterly quiet.

The ship was silent and still. No movement. Not forward. Not up and down nor side to side; no tossing. The *Concordia* was as motionless as if she were docked. The ocean was calm. There was no rain. Through his curtains there was even a twinkle of starlight.

Charles frowned. No, all wasn't quite well, come to think of it.

He slid out from under Louise's arm, then scooted from the bed. Standing naked, he pulled aside the bedroom curtains. Below, the ship's running lights were glowing. They cast a halo of light out into the water. The sea was as smooth as black glass. Low, deep in the ship, he heard a tap, a faint clanking.

They were repairing the boiler, getting the generator up and going again.

On the bed, Louise stirred. She reached for Charles in her sleep. Awakening groggily, she found only warm sheets, the spot where he had recently been. She opened her eyes. No suavely stretched-out man of Middle Eastern leanings; no Charles of the Atlantic Crossing. She noticed the new light where it cast itself across the covers. Rolling up onto her elbow, she looked toward the source.

And, there, at the window stood a man she had never seen, a naked man of magnificent proportion, his silhouette distinct. He was much taller than average. He was straight and square with wide, lean, thick-muscled shoulders that rolled tightly down and around into a broad, powerful back; this narrowed quickly into a neat waist, a taut, muscular haunch.

Louise smiled with wonder and surprise. She murmured, "You are beautiful."

He leaped, jerked. The curtains fell back. The room became slightly darker. Though not much. She could see his outline clearly, his head swung round, his arms out in surprise. Then he stepped to the side into the shadow of his own dresser.

"Charles—" she began.

"You have to leave."

"I don't want to leave."

"The lights are going to come back on. They are repairing the ship. I can't even think which ones I lit."

"Turn them all off."

"How? How many pulls of the chain? Which way of the switch?"

She sat up, able to see her own pale shimmer of flesh among the phantoms of light and shade that played upon the bedding.

"Go," he said firmly.

She was going to argue. But after a moment of pointless dispute with herself—over all that could be said and all he wouldn't listen to—she only sighed and scooted off the mattress.

Louise looked for her clothes, ravaging the covers before she admitted, "Oh, God, I can't even remember what I wore."

"Your green dress with the pearl buttons."

This information was useless; her mind was suddenly, stupidly blank. She stood there, feeling more and more naked in the faint light, witless for not being able to accommodate him in so easy a matter as finding her clothes and leaving.

When, out of nowhere, her underdrawers were suddenly laid into her arms, her throat tightened—as if indeed she were a child about to cry over the whereabouts of her favorite things. Where was this green dress? Which shoes had she worn with it? Only these thin knickers? Where were the rest? Had she had on her lavender corset with the elastic stocking suspenders? (She always wore her favorite dresses and ribbons and underclothing when she came to him.)

Her clothes were not on the bed nor on the floor anywhere around it. She didn't know where else to look.

"In the sitting room, by the front door," he reminded her.

Her disorientation evaporated with flabbergasting clarity. She remembered loosening each article with sudden and far too specific a recollection. She drew her knickers on—a ludicrous piece of modesty under the circumstances—then headed toward the sitting room.

There, she was lost in the new dim light. She passed a hulking shape that became a piano, a huge grand, either black varnished or dark wood. It looked like no landmark she had ever seen before. Even the door to her pasha's suite was larger and heavier than she recognized, one of a double set—which, yes, of course, she should have remembered, yet didn't. She had felt it, God knew, but she had never seen it from the inside.

She dressed quickly, then turned back. She knew Charles had followed, though he held to the wall, the shadows. Absurd, she thought again. This was all absurd. "You are beautiful," she repeated.

"Don't say that." He was angry.

"Handsome," she corrected, thinking this was the problem. Men who veiled their women and hid them away in seraglios must have clear-cut notions of gender.

"Get out of here."

Louise stood still, at a loss, waiting for him to say something sweet, something mitigating. When he didn't, because she didn't know what else to do, she did as he asked.

She gently latched the door behind her. In the corridor, though, as she proceeded toward her rooms, she found herself madly revising.

No, she didn't love him. Of course not. See how easily she had left when she needed to? What she felt for him was carnal: a physical joy. Pure, ecstatic. The feeling was too sharp for love. Too potent for anything that might be lasting. It had to be transient.

Yes, of course. They would get on with their nerve-thrilling affair tomorrow. He could climb up and take out all his own lightbulbs, she told herself. *Or I will wear a blindfold, whatever is necessary. I will see him again—no, no, of course, I will not see him. I will touch him again. I will hear, taste, smell, feel him again. I might even tell him again that I love him, just to see how this sounds to me.*

But she wouldn't. Because with the arrival of normalcy, something changed.

Chapter 14

The tenacity of ambergris is renowned. Applied to a paper and placed in a book, its fragrance will yet be strong when you open the book forty years later. When ambergris is handled, its smell clings to the fingers even days and many washings after.

Charles Harcourt, Prince d'Harcourt
On the Nature and Uses of Ambergris

With the dawn of the fifth day on the Atlantic, life on the *Concordia* became what it was meant to be: rich, generous, busy, social—not so much like everyday life as like an extended house party put on by an unstinting host. The dining room was bursting with people at breakfast. Every first-class passenger had a story of where he or she had been when the "disaster" had struck. The ship became epic in anecdotes for having survived the ordeal, while the "survivors" ate fried porgies with lemon, shirred eggs Aurore, grilled mushrooms, Irish bacon, and pecan waffles, after which they waddled out to promenade or play volleyball or tennis on her sun-drenched decks.

Louise dodged ladies in straw tennis hats who were swinging wildly at a ball lobbed back and forth over a loose net, the sea breeze ruffling their white skirts. Her parents walked a little ways in front of her, arm in arm. A stream of aunts and uncles and cousins followed noisily on all sides and behind Louise. "The Bride"—and Louise felt the title with a capital B this morning—had been joined by these people, thirty-one members of her family (minus three more still not feeling quite well), earlier on the veranda esplanade, where she and her father had collapsed on hooded chaises longues after a brisk dawn walk around the ship.

Alas, her father had called her room at five-thirty A.M. and, when she didn't answer, had gone across the hall to find her. He'd discovered Louise just coming in. Thus, she had had to come up with a reason for being outside her own door and looking windblown, to say the least. She had told him that she had taken to early morning hikes around the deck before breakfast. This lie had been met with the cheerful announcement that, feeling hale, he applauded her activity and would like to join her if she would just be kind enough to march off another lap with him. Louise had been so grateful for his unquestioning trust that she had led the way the full circumference of the large ship. Now, having just finished a large breakfast on top of almost no sleep at all last night, she was so tired she could barely stand up. Ironically, people kept saying things to her like, "Why, Louise, you look so content and happy." So like the radiant bride, they implied. They teased, "What *have* you been up to, while the rest of us were as sick as pickled sea dogs?"

She smiled. A permanent, fey smile had taken over her face, half sincere, half pasted on. A woman in possession of an amorous secret. She *had* been up to good things while the rest of her family was absent. But this family was back, and with a vengeance, and they were more fatiguing than three nights in the company of Pasha Charles of the Dark.

The Vandermeers and company promenaded all morning, visiting friends outside on the deck, then splitting up, men and women. The men went off to the gentlemen's smoking room to discuss their delayed schedules and the state of the ship and the world in general. The women meandered into the ladies' parlor, then onto the veranda café for a lemon squash, then into the writing room, where they wrote letters aloud to friends and relatives left in America. ("Louise, can we say this to Grandmama? 'You can be glad your broken hip wouldn't allow you come. The ship nearly sank.'?")

At lunch, corks began to fly. Good champagne came out at one o'clock and flowed the rest of the day. The captain of the *Concordia* was toasted. The chief engineer was brought into the dining saloon and feted. The mechanics, right down to the bilge boy, were bought lunch and made drunk. All got credit where credit was due, then got credit for what no one could control: calm seas. The Atlantic had turned blue and rolling. The sea wind settled into a sweet zephyr that made one think, This gorgeous, gentle ocean would never hurt a flying fish.

Louise stared over the rail just before afternoon tea, muttering down into the foam that lay so delicately upon the smooth water. *Oh, this wretched, miserably pacific Atlantic,* she thought.

At tea, her father declared his wish to dance with The Bride after dinner, because she'd been so "neglected and alone." Louise dreaded the evening—dinner, dancing, the full orchestra, with a play in the theater for those who preferred to take it easy another day. Louise's mother added to the burden, insisting

they find time to visit the flower stands and little
shops on the lower deck before dinner. There was a
lovely ruby broach in one of them that would match
Louise's magenta dress.

Now they took an interest. *Now* they mentioned
their daughter's complaints from five days ago and
said she was right; that they took great joy in her and
hadn't shown this lately with their attentions. *Now*
when Louise wished for nothing so much as their old
benign neglect, they lavished upon her their notice.
The guilt would wear off, she thought. They would all
settle in again. But possibly not in two days' time. The
ship was only fifty or so hours away from its French
port, and the sea seemed to stretch before them,
glassy and stable all the rest of the way across. Louise
wanted to throw up, in a kind of reverse seasickness,
for so much nauseating tranquillity.

Finally, between tea and shopping, she was able to
slip away to call the Rosemont suite. Charles picked
up the receiver immediately, but was odd and stand-
offish. He told her he was tired. Well, so was she, but
she still wished to see him. He was vague and condi-
tional about her visit to him tonight. Maybe she
shouldn't, he said. He wasn't sure he felt well enough.
He might be coming down with something. He all but
told her not to come. Louise hung up, not at all happy
with this development. *Well, we shall just see about
this, my difficult dervish, my puzzling pasha, my
moody eastern gentleman of the dark.* She tried to nap
before dinner, but couldn't sleep.

Sitting at the dining-room table of his suite that
morning, on one striped upholstered chair with his leg
propped up on one of the eleven others that matched
it, Charles stared down at his knee. It was the size of a
cantaloupe. He couldn't imagine what he had done to
deserve this—the stupid whimsy of his disease at-
tacking so suddenly and with such ferocity. Come to

think of it, he could imagine. The size of his knee probably had something to do with his spending three long nights mostly on his knees and elbows, shagging the sweet Louise to a fare-thee-well. Once married, he was going to have to teach her more about chairs and walls and less about the missionary position. But it had just felt so damned good, lying on top of her.

Of course, now the result felt like hell.

He had called down to the ship's kitchen and awaited their sending up ice. Sometimes cold helped. Sometimes heat helped. Sometimes nothing helped. Charles had already swallowed every serum and potion in his medicine kit and rubbed in every ointment that was supposed to ease the pain and bring down the swelling. He could only hope that by tonight his knee would be normal enough to the touch that Louise would not notice this oddity.

He knew, though, even under the best of circumstances, it would not be normal enough to place his weight on it for a week. The question became, How to have the spry and youthful Louise without her noticing his hobbling around after her? Charles closed his eyes and groaned into the bright morning sunlight as it poured through the dining-room archway.

Daylight. He longed for night. And dreaded it. If his leg didn't go down, he had no explanation, no solution but to keep Louise away.

Lunch came and went with his leg still on the chair looking as angry as ever. Tea arrived. He hadn't finished it, when Louise called. He hedged; he waited.

When, at six o'clock, his knee was as huge as it had been at noon, he called her back. She would be dressing, getting ready for aperitifs and dinner.

She answered expectantly. Then was clearly annoyed when he told her she mustn't come to his suite tonight. He said he was sick. Something he ate. "I don't know why, but I am heaving up my insides, darling. Leave me alone. There is always tomorrow night."

He hoped that, with rest, the swollen pressure on his knee would lessen by then.

Louise, however, felt only the pressure of time. *Tomorrow night, hah!*

That night, it took her till midnight to get away from her family, then twenty minutes to admit that Charles was not going to answer his door. She tried the handle; it was locked. She called. She whispered. She tapped, trying to keep from rallying everyone else from the neighboring suites, for surely everyone heard her. Including Charles, unless he was unconscious or suddenly deaf.

This was the excuse she used. She told herself she had to get to him, for he truly could be in distress, unable to get help. He was ill. He had sounded strange on the telephone.

She went straight to the ship's uppermost deck, the same deck as the kennels, passing by them tonight though to go in the other direction. She trotted around coiled ropes, past huge, dark funnels, making her way to the bow of the ship. Then, breathless, at the foremost starboard rail, she looked down. Sure enough, below, between decks, a shadowed terrace interceded: the moonlit marble tiles of what had to be the Rosemont suite.

Before logic could make her cautious, Louise quickly picked up a handful of skirts, then, lifting one leg, rotated herself belly-to-railtop over the safety railing. Her toes found an awkward footing—she had to reconnoiter to face around in the proper direction. When she had, however, all she could think was, Lord, but the drop looked suddenly a long distance. For an interminable moment, she hung there by her grip on a damp rail covered with salt, the ledge beneath her feet gritty, slick, too narrow for comfort. In the end, the wind whipped and tore at her hair, her clothing, and vanity got her. More than a few seconds and she would be a disaster, a wet, bedraggled mess.

She jumped, dropping into a swoop of evening satins that came up round her face, then landed hard with a terrible clamor. When she stood up, her hands were chafed, her knee scraped, and one stocking had a hole in it so large she could have put her hand through it.

But she was down. *Please, please, let this be the right room.*

Inside the suite, a sound stirred. Her heart lurched, then pounded into a thud that shook the walls of her chest. At the doors—two wide French doors of glass and dark wood, she tried to peer in. Nothing. Inside, the curtains were drawn, all lights out. The moon and stars reflected only themselves and her own image in a neat repetition of pieces in the panes of the terrace doors. She tried the smooth brass handle oh-so-softly. It gave! As quietly as well-oiled clockwork, the door ticked and swung. It opened, unlocked, unlatched.

As she walked through, a wedge of moonlight spread into a sitting room. She heard a faint sound, what might well be the tupple of a pearl, one that came loose from the carpet periodically to roll across the hearth. Louise smiled. Beyond, in the bedroom, she could hear—yes, it was Charles—the violent churn of his covers and bedsprings, his voice murmuring curses, expletives. He was alive.

And she was home.

His room was so familiar, his presence in it somehow palpable, affecting. Her muscles relaxed. Her veins themselves seemed to open, her blood coursing in a freer way. She felt looser; right.

Her pleasure, the strange relief she found each time she knew his presence, was marred, however, by his opening words to her. He said, "Jesus Christ, Louise.

What the hell are you doing here? I don't want you here. I'm sick. Go away."

"No." She felt her throat constrict as she came up to the side of his bed. He was a high-shouldered lump under a bundle of covers. Hesitantly, she asked, "Why, for goodness' sake, would you lock yourself away from me just because you feel badly? Are you really sick? Can I get you something? I want to help."

"You can't. Go away." His disembodied voice said, "I'm nauseous, for God's sake." He was turned away from her.

She caught an odd whiff, the odor of clove or menthol. "It smells ghastly in here." She sniffed the air. "Like liniment or something. What have you been taking?"

"Something the doctor sent. I'll be fine tomorrow. Now, get out."

She bit her bottom lip till it pinched, trying to distract herself from hurt feelings. So like a child, she thought. Yet her feelings were hurt to a new and indescribable degree, an emotional pain that made her pull back into herself. Defensively, she said, "I was worried." And this much was true. She said simply, "You should have answered the door."

"I couldn't."

"Why not?"

After a pause, "Because I was in the water closet throwing up my din—"

"Oh, shut up." She cut him off. Like a tantrum, the words welled, overflowed. "I don't want to hear any more reasons why you can't be with me, now or later. Just shut up." With a bounce of springs, she sat down on the bed beside him, then settled against his back.

After a moment and a small, fighting dig through the covers she found his hand. Taking it, she made him roll enough that she could bend it at the elbow and press it to her breast. She simply held it there.

The two of them sat like this, until the sound of

their breaths settled into a kind of labored harmony—two people worked up over something, a duet of sorts. Tentative. Watchful. Waiting.

For Louise, the guarded silence grew dense, filled with unspoken emotions. She knew what he would say, what he thought: that she was infatuated with him, nothing more. He would tell her this, if she so much as mentioned . . . other, stronger feelings. And he was wise. He was experienced, quite, quite smart in these matters. He was probably right.

So she wasn't in love, but what was he in? she wanted to know. He struck her as too sophisticated, too jaded, something, for infatuation. Yet *he* eventually pulled her hand to his mouth. *He* kissed her wrist then lay it against his chest, covering the back of her hand with his palm. He was angry she was here, angry at the lengths to which her willfulness could drive her, yet *he* forgave enough to relax and let her stay without another word.

Indeed, Charles lay wordless with inexpressible enchantment for her hand spread flat upon his chest. His knee throbbed, but it didn't matter. Louise stayed for an hour, her presence the sweetest consolation he had ever known.

She didn't say much. For a change. She merely said, as she stood to go, that her father expected her to be ready, bright and early, in the morning for a healthful walk about the deck. She had to get some sleep. She kissed Charles's fingers, one at a time, then put his hand back onto the sheets.

"Tell housekeeping," she said, "when they come tomorrow, to leave your door unlocked when they go. I will let myself in. I nearly broke my leg leaping over that railing. You're right—" She laughed, though a little despondently. "Heights are more interesting in romantic concept than in the reality of leaping over them." She added in words that began strongly— "What a fall"—then trailed off to hardly more than a hoarse whisper at the back of her throat—"what a very long fall."

Reality. They shot forward into it at twenty-six knots, the days seeming to slide beneath Louise's feet with the speed of the ocean rushing against the hull of the liner. The last evening, gulls appeared, chasing and diving in the kitchen refuse as it was dumped overboard. Louise watched for a long time from the taffrail as these land birds gulped up nautical miles while drafting in the tailwind of the ship.

Infatuation, romantic preoccupation, she thought, these things dragged like an anchor she needed to cut. Yet she knew where she would be tonight at the first opportunity: in Charles's lightless, curtained suite, inside the hollow of his arms. She would not give him up one minute sooner than she had to.

She watched the sun set into the water. It sank into a neat part of waves that spread out and out from the ship to become a gentle V of rolling wake. Farther out, these waves settled back into the vast, smooth sea that could swallow up even the sun. Behind the ship at the horizon was only this, an ocean as calm as if they had never sailed upon it, fading into night. Louise feared this was what was happening also to herself, that as wonderful as she felt on this ship recently, any change, the openness, the stirring maturity she had grasped for a moment was slipping through her fingers like water, as unclaimable as westward ocean disappearing behind a swift eastward bound ship.

Once again, she felt her old sense of everything happening too fast, events moving too swiftly for her to get a clear, defining perspective on them.

Fast. Full tilt. They were making good time; they made up for lost time. Everyone else was joyous. Out here in the open, Louise began to feel friendless and numb. It was an old familiar feeling; she hated it. But she needed it, if she wished to walk without reluctance straight off the gangplank and down the path she herself had always planned to follow.

That last night, Charles sat and waited for her. He had draped his bed's counterpane over the window, making the dark in his room fairly black again. He had mounded the rest of the covers over his leg so that the whole lower part of his body was impossible to find. He'd put his cane into the closet and literally hopped into bed to await Louise's arrival.

She came late, after one in the morning, in full evening dress. Satin and pearls and smelling divine. Her shadow was surprisingly tall as she sat beside him, until he realized her hair was piled high on her head, some sort of artful arrangement of feathers and a swept-up roll of curls. "Captain's table, high festivity," she explained to him. Charles tried to imagine traveling on this ship with her, sitting at the captain's table by her side in the light. Then this formal creature shushed and scooted and squirmed backward to settle into the crook of his arm, where she became his Louise again, sufficient unto herself, smelling grassy and nubile. She leaned her silky head onto his shoulder as the two of them rested back into the pillowed darkness, and he didn't care about anything else.

They argued briefly over his "stomach illness." But he would let her do nothing, say nothing to anyone— no doctor, no medicine, no home remedies—for a stomach that felt secretly fine. She gave up.

They wandered into conversational limbo, talking of nothing, everything, anything. She told him about her trip to Montreal and the money she'd won there. She gambled, with some success apparently. With amusement, Charles heard all about what she and her family were trying to keep from the ignorant groom. Her "tendency to roam" didn't bother him, since he believed his home would not provide the same motivations that sent her off from her own. The gambling, however, might be something to watch, at first at least, since Monte Carlo was the closest large neighboring town to the east.

Finally Charles said, "Tomorrow. You embark tomorrow on this adventure of marriage and France. Are you happy about it?"

"No," she said simply. Her head lay back on his shoulder, her cheek in the curve of his neck.

"Louise," he said, "this husband. I know you've been told he's ugly, but perhaps he's not as ugly as they say."

"I hate when you do this."

He sighed and grew still. "What am I doing?"

"Acting as if I were ten."

"Well, there are young women who would be affected by all the talk of a man's appearance, who might let that influence their first—"

"Oh, shut up. I'm not one of them." She lifted forward out of his arms, as if she could turn and face him. Her shadowy silhouette put the flat of her hand on his chest. "I'm not a ninny," she continued. "The only people who have said these things are those who have something to gain by slighting the Prince d'Harcourt. I'm sure he's fine."

What a relief to hear this.

"It's just—"

"What?"

"Well, he's not you."

Charles blinked, caught himself, then coughed— for fear of laughing. For fear of crying—how absurdly his ruse circled back on him at times. Its ironies were silly. They were funny. They were terrifying.

"Are you all right?" She patted his back.

"Yes, yes"—sputter—"I'm fine." When he could talk again without sounding giddy, he told her, "You must let go of what we've had here, get on with your life—"

"There you go again. I'm not a child, Charles. I know what I must do."

And there in the dark, he was stymied again, silenced by a combination of the masterful conviction in her voice and her use of his given name, always in the right inflection, now from a slightly condescending plane. She had a way about her, a confidence, a competence that was simply astounding for someone so young. After a few seconds, he murmured, "It's just that I am worried about you." More honestly, he admitted, "And a little bit about this fellow you are to marry. I feel as if I have done something horrible to him, when I didn't intend to."

"I know." She waited, then said, "I shall give him a fair chance. Don't worry. We'll be fine."

"Well, I can't tell you what a relief it is to hear how mature you're being about tomorrow." He added, "And the rest of your future."

She didn't respond. Nothing. Not a word. After a minute, he thought, despite her hauteur and bravado, he heard a catch in her breath. "Louise," he said, "you're not crying, are you?"

"No," she said instantly. "I never cry. What would be the point of it?"

Exactly. She was a strong, healthy young woman, capable of recovering from a preempted love affair. Moreover, he didn't plan on giving her any other choice.

Some joke, Charles thought.

It was supposed to have made him laugh, but it only made him wonder as he threw shirts and trousers into his suitcase the next morning. (He had already wrapped his gallibiya and kaffiyeh into a tight ball and thrown them into the ocean.) Who on God's earth would imagine that in five days he could have formed such an attachment to his own unfaithful soon-to-be-wife?

What a dilemma. He should shoot her. He should be furious. Yet he was in thrall. He adored this girl, his Louise, so much he grew lightheaded when he thought about it. And, poor beast, he longed for nothing so much as that his affection be returned.

Some joke indeed. He would have given all the ambergris in the ocean if only he had not begun it. Or if only he could imagine that this fierce and lovely creature would forgive him for it. No, the only solution was to start again. If she loved him now, which he thought she might, she could fall in love with him all over again in France. He would start clean, fresh. He would make every possible effort. He would woo her like no woman had been wooed before. They would recapture this. He was sure they could. Couldn't they? This wasn't a myth, a miracle. It was real. It would happen again because of the substance to it.

Chapter 15

Ambergris exists in not more than one whale among thousands.

Charles Harcourt, Prince d'Harcourt
On the Nature and Uses of Ambergris

Early the next morning, Louise was dressed and packed far ahead of the rest of her family, so she slipped away to pass by Charles's rooms. All she found though were the maids cleaning them out, bags and buckets standing in the hallway. From the door, Louise could tell by the breeze that every window was open. When she peeked in, every drapery was drawn back. The sitting room was streaming with sunlight. Louise stepped into the room, taking a good look for the first time at a place in which she had spent hours yet had never seen.

The suite was amazingly sterile. The expected art hung on the wall, predictably good without being wonderful. The furniture was solid, in a taste designed to impress without giving offense. The pieces, on the whole, were Western; no hookah, no silk pillows, no curtains or tents in the desert. Moreover, there was not, anywhere, a single personal belonging

184

or hint that a human had made the sitting room or the dining room or the little room off to the side a temporary home place. In the bedroom, a maid stared up at Louise when she walked in. The bed was stripped, a bare, satin-ticked mattress.

As Louise left, she happened to notice that the Arab men next door—her pasha's acolytes—were just leaving. When she spoke to them, they ignored her at first, then were clearly bothered, then alarmed, as if a fly had suddenly spoken to them.

Finally, patronizingly, the seeming head of these men answered her questions. His English had a sing-song rhythm her pasha's hadn't. No, he said, no friend nor—he laughed haughtily at the suggestion—ruler or master of theirs had stayed next door to them. No Arab stayed there. "I would have known," the man insisted. He smugly maintained he knew every Arab on board, all four of them.

He even went so far as to walk the few feet down the hall to Charles's doorway. "No"—the fellow cast a glance inside the suite—"no one," he said. "No one stayed here. One of the luxury suites was empty the whole way across. This one." He jabbed a finger toward the room as he turned and put it behind him. Over his shoulder, he said, "For the love of Allah, do you know how much these rooms cost, woman? Too much. And for such a horrible trip, the ship line should pay us the sum. It is a miracle that anyone sleeps up here at the top of the ship."

One of the advantages of the Rosemont suite was that, if its occupant wished, he could disembark with the first setting of the gangplank. Charles did just this. He had wired his uncle and sister and cousins that he was coming and what all he needed. Of course, Uncle Tino knew much already, since he was the one who had juggled telegrams all month. Then at the crack of

dawn, with morning just beginning to light up his
beloved Mediterranean, Charles Harcourt hobbled
off the ship with the aid of a sturdy cane. His uncle
had to help him up into the carriage. It had been years
since Charles's knee had been this bad.

The carriage took the groom-to-be to a nearby hotel
whose facade faced Marseilles's Vieux-Port, putting
the heart of the noisy, bustling city at his back.
Charles was not fond of Marseilles. Though the
second largest city in France and the country's chief
commercial port, it had none of the charm usually
found in a cosmopolitan city. It was crowded, con-
gested with traffic, and boisterous; no nice public
buildings or sights. Its diversity of humanity—and it
had this, for every culture in the world seemed
represented on its streets—had, to Charles's mind,
only one thing in common: an uncouth and aggressive
venality reminiscent of, say, a Turkish street market.
With one foot firmly in North Africa, this "gateway to
the Orient" seemed, to him, barely French. Arriving
in the city put him already on edge.

At the port hotel, after a bath (with new soap
because his old suddenly smelled too distinguishing
the scent of immediate detection), a shave (minus the
eau de toilette he had used for nine years), and a light
haircut (nothing that would look as though he had
primped too much), Charles fretted further: over
whether to wear a pleated shirt or a ruffled one
(settling on a safe, plain one, starched to boxboard,
with a high wing collar), over a new vest that buttoned
one button too high to suit him, then over every
necktie his uncle had brought him (eventually sending
out his valet to buy all that was available in dark
indigo).

Charles knew all this concern was disproportionate
to the decisions themselves, but he couldn't find his
balance. He was unaccustomed to feeling nervous.
Unaccustomed to his conflicted state. He felt happy,
elated, yet vulnerable almost beyond bearing. He

wanted everything to be perfect for Louise. *He* wanted to be perfect for her, which gave every excited moment a pinch of dread.

Charles soothed his anxieties with what had always been one of his strongest salves to soul: ironically, his looks. Or rather his substantial power to master them by means of clever distraction.

His entire wardrobe, for instance, was custom-styled vanity: trousers that conformed to his well-made legs, no crease, tailored in the supplest suedes (today, goat-antelope, the same hide that when dressed with fish oil elsewhere, was called chamois); boots with an unusually nice line, tall, with a high, stiff arch that slid neatly into a stirrup—practical, yet beyond practical. They were of butter-soft, glossy black leather that rose to buckle snugly over a muscular calf.

The most dramatic of all his sartorial distractions, though, were Charles's frock coats. His height allowed for more length than usual, just as his broad back and shoulders filled out a coat more tailored than average. His coats were high-vented for movement, with deep, slanting pockets for effect; they flapped, to a one, about his calves. He crowned today's, a midnight silk velvet that moved unusually well, with a dove-gray, beaver-felt top hat, banded in blue-black, with a tightly curved brim.

Charles was quite the figure in this part of France. From Marseilles to the Italian border, from the Mediterranean up into the Alps, the Prince d'Harcourt was singularly regarded, a darkly dandyish one of a kind. He usually felt quite in control in this regard—in dominion—of his outlandish appearance.

Yet as he picked up his cane and gloves, he recognized a refinement on his anxiety. Fear. Quiet, stark fear—of the whims and impressions of an eighteen-year-old girl.

He so looked forward to seeing Louise, to his own

sanctioned watching of her in the light. Yet what if she flinched at the sight of him in broad daylight? What if she couldn't meet his eyes—or eye, to be frankly accurate? Where would he hide his dismay?

Or, a new worry, what if she *did* find him pleasing, in some unspoken way: in exactly the same way she'd found him pleasing before. Would she recognize him immediately? Dear God.

Charles's thinking descended from here into a wretched spiral of logic, whereby he could not win no matter which way he turned.

If she liked him immediately, then recognition was a danger. He must explain his trick on her, in that case, and soon. But how? What would she do if she knew? Was his game on the ship really so terrible? He should have told her already. The longer he waited, the worse. Yes, yes, he would foreshorten his torture by coming clean immediately. *My dear, I am your Charles of the ship. I only* pretended *to go back to France and prepare for this wedding, because, well . . .*

No, no, he shouldn't dive into the subject of Pia and Roland. *I only* pretended *to be a man from elsewhere. Why? Well, to play a little joke of which you were the butt—*

No, no, no, he didn't have to be that honest, not yet. *Just to see if you could be seduced, which, of course, you could. By me, at least—*

This didn't seem like such a good explanation either. How to explain his motives, his actions in a favorable light?

He didn't know. And until he did, he'd best remain quiet.

When Charles made it down at last into the hotel lobby, the full retinue was assembled, everyone in their Sunday best. He was glad to see them: his uncle, an assortment of cousins and friends, a local monsignor, as well as some social and business connections here in the port. Most anticipated greeting the bride and her family, then traveling with the wedding party to Nice, where, joined by others, there would follow a long period of revelry. The Prince d'Harcourt was renowned for the entertainments that took place on his rather choice piece of property only a train ride east, a home with many and often-used guest rooms and space enough for a fairly spectacular celebration.

At the docks, the curious of Marseilles turned out as well. The *Concordia* was a novelty in this harbor—a rare American bid to compete with the successful German and English liners. Moreover, this novelty had brought a larger one: the bride of the only known prince this side of Monaco, of the only French prince this side of Paris. And, as archaic as prince-watching was, the French townsfolk appeared to be fascinated. And well informed.

A sketch of Louise had run in the morning's paper beside—more surprising still—the nuptial announcement. Charles had yet to speak to his uncle of how and why this had come about. Whatever the means, it brought the masses. Even people who were more or less strangers to Charles—the man from whom he bought his sausages when in town, the laundress who pressed his shirts when he was here on business, anyone who could claim an association showed up to shake his hand as he descended his carriage at the foot of the docks.

Charles walked into the crowd, leaning heavily on his cane and feeling consummately foolish—the groom, dapper, with flowers in his hand and an eight-piece oompah band behind him ready to strike up into American Sousa music. (What in God's name had Uncle Tino been thinking?) The second Charles saw the docks, the band, the crowd, he realized everything, simply everything, was too much. He himself felt over-washed, over-combed, over-dressed—not to mention over-watched as the crowd continued to build into a damn throng—and hopelessly over-concerned with more worry for Louise than his brain could possibly hold.

Would she mind all the people around? Would she prefer to rest? Had she realized that she would live so much in the center of attention? Would she be hungry? Thirsty? Overwhelmed?

Yes, probably this, but he couldn't think what to do about it. He turned and waved the little musical band away, sending them back to the hotel where they could play later. Uncle Tino had informed him on the way back to the docks that, between now and then, he'd arranged "a little welcome" in the hotel's garden. Their train didn't leave till late tonight.

Meanwhile, Charles's clothes, all the individual niceties that usually gave him so much pleasure and aplomb, felt radical one moment, then ineffectual the next in hiding the obvious. At all moments they felt notably outside the normal conceptions of chic. In addition to feeling suddenly less unique and more simply odd, he felt rumpled, despite countless checks that assured him he was well-pressed. For the dozenth time, he brushed a speck, a wrinkle from his dark frock coat. He removed his hat. He would carry it, as well as his gloves; his hands were making them damp. His entire body was in a sweat.

The ship began its regular disgorgement of first-class passengers, the wide gangplank slowly becoming crowded with women wearing flowers and flounce upon their heads, men in bowlers and top hats. Charles caught sight of Harold and Isabel Vandermeer first. *Where was she?* he thought. Louise wasn't in front or behind her parents. Then he caught sight of her, and his heart stopped.

The crowd itself on the dock hushed slightly, then rose in scattered exclamations. That's the one; it must be; *la voilà.* In Charles's ears, this chatter became a single voice that traveled along the dock and back around through the gathered people like a line of falling dominoes, *oohs* tumbling *aahs* tumbling deep sighs. As he watched her, he was so proud he could hardly breathe; he was terrified.

Louise Vandermeer appeared out of the shadow of the great liner into the sunlight, walking among many others down the gangplank. Yet she may as well have been walking alone for the way she stood out—magical, iridescent, a single human miracle upon the eyes.

She wore no hat, carrying hers instead upside down with a cream-colored puppy inside it who peeked over plumes. This hat and puppy pressed into her swinging skirts with charming nonchalance, while her bare head was on full display, her blond hair shining like silver shot with bullion. Her skin was radiant, translucent; it glowed in the sun. As she walked, her limber movement swayed in rhythm to a three-masted yacht that bobbed indolently behind her. Her dress, a dazzling deep violet put fields of Provençal lavender to shame. Its cloth shimmered; it shuddered in the sun, its thin layers of silk awobble on the mysteries of its slightly belled understructure.

It was in public that Charles came to full understanding for the first time, full knowledge of just how blindingly gorgeous she was. For all that he had recognized of her loveliness on the ship, he had hidden the degree of it from himself. Louise Vandermeer's looks were mythic. She was perfection, the epitome of flawless, youthful beauty, unaware of its own mortality, uncaring, as gloriously bright-burning as a shooting star. The moment Charles saw her he realized what he knew already, what the blood in his veins had been telling him: This young woman was the embodiment of his worst fears—a mixture of merciless beauty and exultant, self-centered youth—while being what he inexplicably desired more than anything he could name.

Among the masses, the Vandermeers found him,

Harold Vandermeer clapping him on the back and
babbling things at him in English that all at once
sounded like Greek. (Good, good, Charles thought.
He must remember to stick very strictly to French.
Louise would know the voice from the dark the
instant he spoke to her in his Cambridge accent.) He
couldn't swallow. He couldn't speak. He could only
follow Louise with his eyes. (What kind of an impression could he be making? It hardly mattered. She
didn't appear to see him.) The bride remained at the
distant rear of the party. Meanwhile Isabel Vandermeer threw her arms about Charles's neck, dragging
him down to plant a kiss on his cheek. There were
American uncles and aunts and friends and cousins,
legions of them. They all attempted French, even
those who didn't speak the language. (Bless them;
little did they know that they were going to have to
keep this up.)

Then at last she was there before him. Her eyes
settled on his face. He shivered. Her eyes, these eyes
he had seen so little of, were possibly the most
beautiful part about her. They were the blue he
remembered, but he dismissed their color quickly.
There was something more to their appeal. Their deep
lids folded in a continuous arch that echoed the thick
line of her lashes, emphasizing the largeness of her
eyes themselves. These generous lids didn't open
completely, even looking up at him. They made her
eyes look sleepy, smoky, innately sultry through no
effort of her own. She was Bo Peep come to provocative life, a nursery rhyme grown up, her sheep sold off
to pay for her new, cosmopolitan mien.

Charles melted on the spot, no more able to make
sense of what was going on around him than a puddle
of hot butter was able to talk. These fabulous eyes
focused on him. He held his breath.

It was not as if Charles couldn't be honest about the
particulars of his own appearance:

His coloring was dark. It spoke of the Spanish kings in his bloodline, a line invaded here and there with Arab blood; his hair was as black as a fakir's. This hair was fine and thick and so straight—and with so much a mind of its own—that it might have stuck out directly from his head had he worn it short. Thus he wore it long, a shaggy, wild shoulder-length of shiny black, baby-soft hair, the fineness of which made it flutter in the wind now like long strands of ostrich feathers. He had a broad jaw, a high cheek, the strong bones of the ancient, invading Franks, the thin, straight nose of the Romans. All in all, not an unattractive man.

Until—he admitted—one tried to look him in the eye.

Immediately this was difficult. He had a faintly off-center way of regarding people that came from his having to turn his head slightly so as to get a clear sight past the bridge of his nose. Then, once met, his good eye could stop a person cold—it was a deep, unearthly blue as vivid in color as the Mediterranean itself.

His blind eye became a kind of parody of this, a light, opaque blue faded to the paleness of verdigris, as if the iris had oxidized. There was no pupil, only the eerie blankness of a disease-scarred eye. The lid of this eye bore an additional disfigurement, a healed cut that drew a sharp line upward, leaving a bare swath through the end of his eyebrow and giving this side of his face a look of perpetual blank surprise—a look that Charles could furrow into a fiendishness, if he chose. When younger, he had worn a patch over his unfavored eye. Then he had thought of the patch as debonair, mysterious. Now he thought of it as cowardly; he no longer indulged in such hide-and-seek. The bad eye was his, part of what he looked like, part of what he was: half god, half devil. A fitting metaphor for the human condition, he thought. Besides, he'd

found there to be certain advantages to casting, with
just a frowning turn of his head, a glance that could
terrorize.

As to the rest of him, he was tall, well-proportioned,
and elegantly turned out. Charles thought of himself
as, if not handsome, at least something to behold: like
a sleek, stately piece of architecture with a few gar-
goylelike flourishes for decorative effect.

Louise gazed at his marred face a moment and
smiled vaguely. Not impressed; but neither was she
horrified. She seemed completely unaffected. She
looked away.

Charles didn't know quite what to think.

His cousin Henri, somewhere at his elbow, whispered something about "you crafty old dog" and "no
wonder you made us all tie ourselves into knots."

Someone else off to the side of them directed a
question toward the bride herself. Charles didn't hear
the particulars. He only knew that Louise responded
graciously, lifting her chin to look at those around her
and, by this, again took him aback.

She spoke startling French—a near-perfect, very
upper-class version of the language: no extra elisions,
every proper one made, every *R* rolled on the tongue
(unlike Charles's own fat *R*s in the throat); no slang,
no *tutoyer*ing familiarity, and no American accent. It
was Academy French, probably straight from a text-
book, but it nonetheless was a variety of the language
one seldom heard except in the company of the bluest
blood of Paris. Charles was mesmerized. The sound
of his language on her tongue filled him with both a
horrible pride and a galling, unfamiliar awkwardness.

"Your Highness, let me make formal introduc-
tions." It was Vandermeer, his hand on Charles's
back, speaking his anglicized version of the same
language, making hash of what his daughter made
into aria.

Charles glanced at him. "Don't do that," he said.

"Do what?"

"'Your Highness.' We don't use that. 'Monsieur' is fine." He had mentioned this before to the Americans, yet they were relentless. Now was the time to stop their royal fantasies, to remind them that France was a democracy with an aversion to such pretensions.

"Well, um, that is, ahem . . ." Vandermeer was going to argue.

Charles looked at him, narrowing his eyes into what he knew to be an unpleasant expression. When this left Vandermeer speechless, Charles let a smile steal back crookedly onto his face. He offered an appeasement. "'Charles,'" he said. "Please call me 'Charles.'"

Vandermeer looked unsettled, mollified yet bewildered and unhappy, no doubt feeling the loss of the princely form of address for his daughter.

Well, they would have to be satisfied with the rest, everything real and of substance that belonged to the Prince d'Harcourt.

Subdued, Vandermeer muttered, "May I present my daughter, Louise Amelda-May Vandermeer." He nodded toward Charles. "Charles Harcourt, the Prince d'Harcourt," then added, "and grandson to the late King Louis Philippe."

Charles didn't bother with more narrow looks and protests. The fact was true enough at least.

The lovely Louise glanced sideways, at someone or something else said. Comments, chatter flew. In response to it, she smiled almost shyly, prettily, then couched her face. As he stood nonplussed, Charles caught a bit of what was going through the crowd. People waited for him to do something, say something.

"Well, the prince is dumbstruck," someone said behind him.

Someone else called, "All he does is beam at her."

"Who wouldn't?"

Another quarter added, "I'd say, he likes his bride quite well."

He took his cue, bowing before Louise, a bow that was perhaps just a degree more sweeping than he'd intended. He rose, trying to recover; he found his tongue. He said in French loud enough for anyone nearby to hear, "If his bride is half so sweet as the sight of her, he shall be privileged to walk beside her till the last days of his life."

Her bland countenance swung around and up. Her demeanor changed. Louise's very lovely visage frowned deeply into his, her scrutiny affixing on him with an intensity that made his face run cold. She'd recognized his voice. She knew, he thought. Hell was going to crack the earth this instant and rise up between them, all his pathetic, over-lofty plans for their future together collapsing before they'd begun.

But she looked at him a moment, then apparently decided she recognized nothing. Staring at him, her expression faded to a faint melancholy, then went blank completely. Her eyes became remote, her thoughts elsewhere as her gaze shifted to settle on a boat coming into the harbor.

A huge relief spread through Charles, like the sun coming out. He warmed as she accepted the flowers he offered. The dog began to sniff and eat them where she set them into the hat. Then the lovely Louise put her hand innocently into the crook of Charles's arm, and he thought he would die there a happy man as she began slowly, to allow for his gait, so as to walk beside him toward the carriage.

Chapter 16

The ancient Chinese named ambergris "dragon's spittle perfume," because they believed it came from the mouths of dragons who, while sleeping upon rocks at the edge of the sea, drooled this fragrant substance down into the ocean.

Charles Harcourt, Prince d'Harcourt
On the Nature and Uses of Ambergris

Louise managed an amazing feat. She glided through her first eight or so hours in France without contemplating her future husband, barely looking at him in fact for more than a few seconds at a time. She was able to keep him—his tall, long-coated presence—at the periphery of her awareness. Which, considering, every moment of these eight hours had been by his arrangement, at the expense of his hospitality, and, like her future itself, dependent on his goodwill, was a fairly daring act of neglect on her part.

It was just that he seemed so bizarre, so unpredicted, she simply didn't have the energy to make sense of him; not yet.

And there was so much else going on. At the hotel,

she found herself dropped straight into a midday garden party of almost two hundred people, most of them strangers. Overwhelmed (and exhausted from lack of sleep), she barely saw any of these people, most of whom seemed content that she simply smile and look pretty—the easy trick she'd performed for most of her life.

Beyond this, when Louise's mind had any clarity or focus, it tended to drift into thoughts of her Pasha Charles, of how and where he had gone off to so quickly. Was he here in Marseilles? Or was he on another boat already, crossing the sea to his home?

Louise stole glimpses toward this sea over rooftops, between heads and shoulders, over trayfuls of local delicacies: wedges of chickpea pancakes, raw vegetables dipped in some sort of herb-fragrant, creamy-thick condiment, and fresh ripe olives that she thought at first were rolled in salt but, when she bit into one, discovered to be rolled instead in grain-fine garlic. *Manger sur le pouce,* her strange, black-haired host called it. To eat on the thumb. Snacks. Most of these novel tastes were strong to her palate.

Her Charles, again he'd been right: France was interesting but boggling on first acquaintance. She felt lost in among so much newness, even when it came to something so simple as getting her hunger satisfied. She couldn't imagine the bother of doing anything more complicated. Nothing was as it was back home.

In greeting, everyone kissed everyone else, including men kissing men sometimes on both cheeks. The carriages looked different. They seemed lighter, quicker. Automobiles, though only a few here, were faster and louder than the ones in New York; there were slightly more of them. French toilets were also louder; they flushed violently and were in their own room, separate from the bath. And the *new,* like motor-carriages and flushing toilets, lived side by side with an *old* Louise was unaccustomed to. From the coach on their way up the ridge to the hotel, she'd glimpsed steep, narrow streets that seemed of another century entirely. The hotel where they settled, in order to await their train, had stone sections built in 1607, a year the locals referred to as "recent." Marseilles, claiming to be France's oldest city, had a heritage that dated back to the Greeks.

In addition to coping with an unfamiliar ambiance, while smiling and nodding and trying to remember the names of a hundred strangers, the logistics of Louise's first hours in her new country were insane. Baggage was transferred, shifted about from carriage to hotel, then transferred again to the train station. When she wanted to change, she found that the trunk with her afternoon dresses hadn't made it to the hotel but had been sent straight along to the station. So had all her toiletries. There was a mix-up—an *emmerdement,* as the prince's uncle called it, which she suspected by its root word to be cruder than a mere mix-up and more annoying than the man acknowledged.

He was a rare bird, this Uncle Tino, a small, wiry man of forty or fifty or sixty, there was no telling. His age was as impossible to pinpoint as the age of a thin, adult monkey. His French was guttural and not always easy to understand. He liked to do everything himself, but then got so many things going he couldn't control it all. He was a self-professed expert on everything— baggage, train schedules, parties, music; he loved John Philip Sousa and imagined all Americans did too, since the music was—*eh bien, non?*—American.

What baggage of Louise's that did arrive at the hotel was a trunkful of evening gowns and a valise of clean underlinen. So at least she had clean underclothes. After the large, outdoor gathering, she changed and freshened what she could, then went

down to a late lunch in a private dining room of the
hotel, where she sat at table with more than fifty
people, all "family."

She chatted as graciously as possible for as long as
she could. Speaking French was a pleasure. She liked
the language, its sound and flow and the way it moved
her tongue and mouth. As in Montreal, it seemed
incredible that everyone spoke it. As if her tutor had
secretly been teaching the same lessons to an entire
country of people, the same books, the same dictio-
nary. When the Prince d'Harcourt asked if he could
get her anything (for the third time—he hovered
solicitously after this meal, closing in from the perimeter where she'd banished him), she said, "Yes. A
place where I can sleep for an hour before the train:
without a single, solitary soul within a hundred feet of
me, including yourself."

He blinked, a little taken aback. She might have
softened the request, had she had even an ounce of
stamina in reserve. But she did not. She merely let
him lead her away.

Finding what she'd asked for wasn't easy. It seemed
the prince knew everyone in the city, and every one of
these acquaintances had decided to come by personally so as to express his or her delight in the marriage
that was, as one man put it, "ending such a long and
successful bachelorhood."

Louise glanced at the prince then. Briefly. From the
back. At hair that was too long, at the slight indention
left in it by his hat. His shoulders were very broad, she
supposed. *Not so bad,* she told herself. Not so bad
really. Yet when he pivoted around toward her, no
matter how dexterous he used his cane to do so, she
felt her thoughts turn inward, her gaze become
unfocused.

She and he made it at last through the horde and up
the staircase, then in the room set up for the bride
they found more confusion. The prince's cousin's

children's nanny stood before a dresser, changing the diaper of his newest cousin once-removed. The bed was heaped with an overflow of coats and hats. Louise's misdelivered gown trunk lay in the center of the floor, her dog asleep on top of it. There was barely room enough to enter.

The prince declared himself "desolated" (the elaborate way he and his countrymen claimed sorrowful fault) by the inconvenience to Louise, then suggested the "only place" he knew. He walked her to one of the carriages that stood in a line of empty vehicles waiting to take them all to the train.

After helping her step up and into one, he stood there before the open door. His eyes—eye, actually—eerily scanned the dark interior. For a long moment, he stared like this, into every lightless corner of the carriage, his body tilted as he leaned upon his cane, the upper portion of him framed at this angle by the doorway.

And from her corner of darkness, Louise finally brought herself to look at him directly, to size him up. The Prince d'Harcourt was tall (taller than her Other Charles, she thought; too tall). Giant. He had a massive chest (though not nearly so lean muscled as the one she compared it to in her memory). And his face. Lord, his face. It was dominated by a blank bluish eye—unreal, inhuman—further twisted by a scar. The sight was so grotesque, it was almost fascinating: horrid.

It was an understatement to say the man was no beauty. Add to this a macabre taste in clothing—he dressed rather like the devil himself, if the devil were a dandy. Louise cast a glance at the cane on which he braced his weight. It was made of blued steel and ebony.

As if in response—he'd realized she was studying him—his cane swiveled up suddenly. The prince tucked it under his arm, shifting his weight onto one leg. He was like this, terrifically self-aware; every effect chosen. The man her parents so loved was a calculating one, though not necessarily in a bad way; he calculated to please. In this regard, the turn of his cane was a little trick he did—she had seen it elsewhere in the course of the day, she realized. He could negotiate the thing without disturbing a flap or vent of his coat, up and into his armpit from where he hung the weight of his hand off the end, making his cane into a kind of debonair accoutrement, Beelzebub's magic stick. Or he could hide it entirely among the flaps of his coat when he chose to. Or bring it out again with a twist of his wrist, with the dexterity of a swordsman.

Louise found his manner—his looks and size and demeanor—mesmerizing in the hair-lifting way of the outlandish, the unholy. In these first hours of their acquaintance, she realized, she had tried *not* to look at him, for he was a dazzling horror, this husband-to-be: a near-grisly sight made sharp and neat, meticulously turned-out, a perfect ruin to the left—the eye, the scar, the limp all to that side of his body.

His attitude, she reminded herself, was otherwise. He seemed normal; polite, considerate, a decent fellow. More than decent. She kept thinking, Stop being so nice to me. All his solicitude made her uncomfortable.

As Louise leaned forward to take hold of the door handle, she shivered once there in the dark—and immediately knew why she had avoided looking at him all day, why she let other preoccupations distract her. Though his physical mien was merely unsettling in a social context, it was more than unsettling in a private one: when she reminded herself what a husband and wife did together in the dark. Oh, she supposed she could get through it. She had once let a spider crawl on her when she was young—a large, furred creature with a surprisingly heavy, bulb-like body—just to prove that she could. And in Miami she had once touched an alligator, an ugly, huge, real-life dragon wrestled by the Indians for tourists, that had been both slothful and unexpectedly agile, faster—explicitly so—than a chicken or jack rabbit.

On this note, Louise closed the door quickly—and with an unexpected shot of gratitude toward, of all people, Pia Montebello (who had been present today, though keeping her distance). It was good to know that this man had found himself an appropriate mistress, being slightly demonic herself, who had an appreciation for his—what did one call it? Fiendish charm?

She told him through the window, "Thank you. I'll be fine now." Then pulled the curtain, obliterating the sight of him, while making the carriage interior as dim as a . . . as a tossed ship in the night. The vehicle jostled gently under the impact of the door's closing. With a sigh, Louise closed her eyes and settled back into this, the sweet comfort of indistinct, rocking shadows.

Why, anything could happen between here and a wedding. There was time for small changes, radical ones, intercessions, adjustments. Or even marriage to another entirely. She dozed into sleep, dreaming of the ocean . . .

The train was late in leaving. Everyone was tired, especially Charles. His knee was killing him. He was relieved when he could just sit down beside Louise and enjoy the simple pleasure of bumping against her as the train took a curve or went over a rough stretch of tracks. As they clattered along through black countryside, she alone seemed bright, rested. She'd slept for more than three hours. When the carriage had pulled away from the hotel, he'd let her fall against him; she'd sleep right through the ride to the train station tucked into the hollow of his arm.

What peace. How he had loved to feel her relaxed posture and movement, to hold her in such familiar circumstance while she slept. Then, as their carriage rolled into the bright station, how disconcerting to have to return to his new role, to slide away to a more gentlemanly distance as she startled awake.

Presently she read a book she'd brought with her, one in English on mathematical probabilities. *Egad,* he thought. No one else was up to talking. Their compartment—in a car with four such roomy compartments on a high-speed, entirely first-class express train—was quiet except for the rattle of the mind-boggling eighty-one kilometers per hour on the tracks. Across from Charles, Harold and Isabel Vandermeer slept, one against the other. Beside them, Uncle Tino sat wakeful but silent. He'd been signaling Charles since they had boarded the train that he wished to talk to him privately. Charles ignored him, closing his eyes and letting his knee drop against Louise's dress. His cousin Henri, stretched out on the other side of her, prevented her from moving too far off. She jerked her knee away effectively, however, when the "sleeping" Charles let the weight of his leg drop all the way up against hers. Like some degenerate on the Paris subway, he thought. God, this was going to be so difficult, pretending he didn't want—know—the feel of her. If they could only have been married immediately. They had gotten everything backward, having the honeymoon first—

"Charles."

Charles opened his eyes with a start and stared blearily into the face of his uncle not an inch away from his nose.

"Get up and come with me. I want to smoke my pipe, and Her Highness here won't let me do this in the same train compartment with her. We can step out into the corridor."

Charles shifted forward, a rote, half-asleep obedience to a relative who rarely made a to-do over anything. As he sat forward and found his feet, Charles realized he'd been sound asleep—and was coming to wakefulness with Louise and his uncle glowering at each other.

Louise twisted her head, tilting it at him, then said in her clear, flawless French, "It's a small compartment." It was a huge compartment, though Charles reminded himself that in America she and her family had their own private railway car all to themselves. She added, "If he smokes that thing in here, we will all arrive smelling as if we've been burned at the stake."

His uncle said nothing, but backed away so that Charles could stand and follow him. His expression, however, said that a burning stake was exactly where the young Louise belonged—and not as the martyr as she suggested, but as an American witch. The distaste in his uncle's face was surprising and dismaying.

Out in the corridor, with his back pressed against the cold, vibrating window, Charles asked, "So what is this all about? What is so important you will wake me up to tell me?"

"Well, I could have said something sooner, but you seemed nervous earlier. I didn't want to make you more nervous."

"More nervous? What's wrong?"

"Vandermeer was telegraphing us two and three times a day from the ship for the last three days."

Charles squinted at him. "He was what?"

"Sending us telegrams—instructions, questions, requests. It got to be too expensive and complicated to telegraph you back and forth, so I took it upon myself to respond."

Charles was amazed to hear this. "What did he want? What did the two of you have to say to each other?"

"What he wants amounts to a quick wedding. Something is very wrong. He wants to marry off M'moiselle High-Society here as fast as he can."

Charles laughed and leaned his head back, feeling the train *clackety-clack*ing against his skull, his shoulder blades in a rhythm of relief. He glanced past Tino's head through the partially open blind, at Louise sitting inside the compartment: a lovely young woman on a red velvet-tufted seat, with her nose in a book on mathematics. "Yes," he said, "I'm sure he does. Before she gambles him out of house and home. And sleeps with every fellow between here and Paris."

Uncle Tino's face blanched.

Charles touched his arm. "Only joking. She's a little wild, uncle."

His uncle frowned, then relaxed. "Well, good." He paused. "I suppose." He turned in the direction of Charles's gaze, staring at Louise himself. Then he said, with a note of deliverance in his voice, "I was worried you might have made her pregnant or something. You haven't, have you?"

"God, I don't think so."

It was a stupid answer. It admitted a great deal too much. And it was positively invalid in the way of information. Who knew if she were pregnant or not? A quick wedding, for a host of reasons, sounded damn fine to Charles.

When he looked at his uncle again, Tino's steady gaze was on him. The wiry, middle-aged man twisted his mouth sideways and sucked his teeth. Then he said, "Well, think about what you are doing, ambergris or no ambergris. You're letting the wrong head do your thinking. The girl is snappish and too pretty by half."

Charles frowned at him. "Come on, Tino. She is a bit of a priss—she's been bred to be aloof. But, believe it or not, I think she's lonely. But that is in public; in private, *o-ooh*—" He let out a low whistle of breath. "Never in my life—" was all he could get out in the way of words.

Uncle Tino snorted. "Well, think twice before you marry her, all the same. A man shouldn't wed a woman who is just a piece of cuckold bait waiting to happen."

A sore spot. Charles said nothing.

"You should take an ugly wife," his uncle advised, his voice sage and serious.

Charles laughed. This was not a slight to Charles's appearance, but rather honesty. Uncle Tino's wife, Heloise, was the ugliest woman Charles had ever met. On the other hand, Tino was enormously fond of her. Heloise and Constantine Dmetri Harcourt had, at present count, eight children between them, with another one due in January. Charles and Tino joked fairly mercilessly between themselves about their differing preferences and abilities to attract. He elbowed his uncle and said, "And have eight and a half ugly children like you do?" he asked. Tino's children were actually quite charming, and every one of them appealing in some way or other.

"You'll have ugly children, anyway," his uncle retorted, "if they look like you." A glimmer of a smile appeared as he bit down onto his pipe and began to hunt his pockets for matches.

"Only if they get an infection in their eye that the surgeon has to cut out." Charles grew earnest. He wanted no more remonstrations from someone he needed to count upon. "Tino," he said, "I really want to marry her. It has nothing to do with the ambergris"—he laughed—"though, of course, I want that too. By the way, was the jasmine unloaded all right?"

"Yes. It's on its way to the greenhouses at Grasse. Ernest and Maxime should be able to begin budding it in the next day or so." Tino took a moment to light his pipe with a puff, then shook his head. "Very bad," he said lugubriously, nodding back toward Louise. "You are a sure candidate for heartache. Women that pretty"—he jabbed the pipe toward the window once—"think they own the world."

"She's young. I'll teach her she doesn't."

His uncle made a glum face, the face of an accomplished pessimist. "You can't teach someone what they don't want to learn."

Tino puffed up a billow of smoke. Charles leaned on the window, his back absorbing the vibration again as he stared at a woman, the sight of whom he couldn't seem to get enough. After a few minutes of the two men standing there like this, Charles said, "I don't know if you will see this right away, Tino. Louise is socially adept, competent in a cool way, not in an endearing one. But in her heart—" He sighed. He believed what he was about to say, though a part of him prayed, after only five or six days' acquaintance, that his strong emotions for Louise Vandermeer could really be as clear and sure as they felt. "In her heart," he continued, "she is sweet and good-intentioned. She is funny and honest and dear." Watching her turn the page of her book, he added, "And bright." He poked his uncle in the chest. "She is smarter than *you* are."

"Which makes her *much* smarter than you, then." His uncle rolled his eyes, asking from within a puff of smoke, "So what do you want to do? Her father wants this wedding in two weeks, if he can get it. Is that what *you* want?"

Two weeks? Charles was stunned. "I don't know," he said. "I'll have to talk to her."

Tino rolled his eyes again, more elaborately this time, and groaned his disbelief. Then he turned and walked off down the corridor, trailing smoke as he shook his head and muttered in singsong lament, *"Ah làlàlàlàlàlà . . ."*

Chapter 17

⸎

When fresh, ambergris is tarry and foul smelling. Yet when exposed to sun, sea, and air it quickly oxidizes, fading to a hard, waxy gray with an appealing fragrance: earthy, cool, and sweet. Rather like the odor off the mossy floor of a dark forest recently pummeled by a hard rain.

Charles Harcourt, Prince d'Harcourt
On the Nature and Uses of Ambergris

L ate the next morning, Louise stood at the edge of the prince's front lawn, a wide, shady lawn that sloped gently down from the house to end in a neat shin-high border of carved white stone balusters. These ran along the front of the property, curving with the bend of the road just below it. Should she have stepped over the low balustrade or swung out on the tree branch that overhung it, she would have dropped down into the meandering two-lane carriageway that followed the coast. Just on the other side of this road, the land sloped further into a sunny beach, this descending into the Mediterranean itself, a sea so bright a blue it did not look possible. From beneath her shady tree, Louise looked out onto a bay of such vivid color it made the cloudless sky—a sky that would have seemed remarkably bright in New York— look powdery-pale by comparison.

It took no second guesses or long acquaintance to understand why the Côte d'Azur was becoming a very popular—and expensive—place to be. Nice and the prince's seafront house at the western edge of it were premium, part of a paradise on the shore of the prettiest piece of ocean she had ever seen, made finer still for being nestled into the steep, rising foothills of the Alps. Whole villages perched in the hillsides behind her.

She looked out over this sea now and tried to project her mind onto its far shore, onto the shore of North Africa, trying to envision there a tall, handsome man making his way to his family. She tried to imagine her Charles traveling home like this. And failed. She could not envision the man who'd talked to her so earnestly, spoken to her so softly, who'd called his darling, his dear, then uttered her name over and over in long, chaining repetitions, she could not envision *this* man simply packing his bags and sailing away.

Vanity perhaps. She hated to think of him as anything other than staggering around, lost without her. For she felt faintly lost herself. Moreover, she had sincerely felt—still did—that she had charmed him, captivated him. Not to put too fine a point on it, she believed that she had had him on his knees, at her feet, in thrall. It was a chief area of her expertise: Louise usually knew when a man was mad for her. Thus, she reasoned, wherever her pasha was, didn't his mind, his spirit and will, have to be as seized as hers by the memory of their trip across the dark ocean together? If so, then how could he leave? How could he stay away? Wouldn't he come back to her eventually? He knew where to find her.

No, no, of course not—she shook her head, frowning—this wasn't going to be the way things were going to work. She had had an affair, a memorable one, with a sophisticated adult, with a lover whose life was in a vastly different place, on a vastly different cultural plane, a disparity that left each of them with no claim upon the other. It had been a fabulous, perfect affair really: precisely as Louise had originally intended.

And now she would get on with her life—here in the present, not in the past or in some impossible future—just as she'd promised.

"Louise!"

She turned to see her delicate, pretty mother trotting down the green slope of lawn toward her, her mother's skirts held high enough to show her shoes.

"Darling," her mother said as she came up. She reached out and drew her daughter close, kissing her cheek. "Your father and I have just had the most lovely talk with the prince." Her expression was kind but solemn. "And I have been voted the one who must tell you something—nothing too bad now, don't worry, but something serious. Would you like to go for a walk on the beach?"

They went down the stone steps that led into the drive, then crossed the carriageway carefully, listening as well as looking up and down a road that bent and turned. Once on the other side of the road, balancing beside an iron bench, they took off their shoes and stockings, then tucked their skirts up. There was hardly anyone else on the beach. The season would not start for another two or three months. Leaving their shoes behind, she and her mother descended down toward the water.

There were no shells. The Mediterranean here had

little tide action to bring them up onto the shore—it was the calmest seashore she had ever walked upon. Her bare feet met smooth flat stones as large and round as fried eggs. These stones became smaller and darker toward the water. Eventually Louise crunched in step beside her mother on wet stones that felt like walking on millions of smooth, tiny gray buttons.

Her mother began, "Let me say first that the prince himself wanted to come and speak to you about this, but that I preempted him. Once you are married, he may have precedence." She smiled at Louise in a sideways glance. "But I am not ready to give you up until I have to." She walked maybe five or ten more steps then began, "So. May I say that your father and I have been pleased from the start with this marriage for you, and that now, well, we think it is magnificent"—she touched Louise's arm as they walked, then repeated the word emphatically— "*magnificent* for you." She took a breath, as if to steel herself, then launched into a subject that so surprised Louise. "You must realize that your father and I are honest people. We simply didn't know what to do when we first thought you might be behaving in a foolish manner—" Louise's mother held her hand up to stifle complaint.

Louise stopped, trying to rally a defense—a defense of only God knew what. She wasn't sure what she was being accused of. But there was accusation here somewhere.

Her mother turned and faced her. "Now hear me out before you say anything." She began again. "Your father and I were most uncomfortable marrying you to"—she paused then took audible pleasure in the name—"dear Charles without . . ."

Dear Charles? For one bewildering moment, Louise thought her mother was speaking of her Pasha Charles. Then her mind settled on the obvious. The one-eyed prince. Louise wanted to curl her lip, make a snide remark. As gracious as he was, the fancy, oddly self-conscious man hardly seemed worthy of endearment.

Her mother continued, ". . . without, well. Before he married you, we felt we had to be perfectly honest with him." She took a gulp of air, then let it out with, "Especially in light of the fact that we believe you were up to something on the ship as well."

Louise's face went cold. She had to consciously shut her mouth.

Her mother put both hands up now, like a New York policeman trying to hold back traffic. "Louise, stay calm," she said. "Don't fuss. We don't want any particulars, no denials, no explanations. We simply want you to know that we're not idiots, and we would rather die than have the prince believe our family is one of cheats. We are honest people. So we caught the prince as he was coming down the stairs this morning, pulled him into his own study, and told him everything, including our suspicions about, well—" She halted, let out a breath. "Louise, he is not a fool. He was very guarded when we spoke to him; he knew something. And his uncle was downright hostile yesterday. The rest of the world be hanged—" This was strong language for her mother. "But one simply cannot deal with good, intelligent people in any other manner than with decent behavior and straightforward talk."

Louise's mother seemed to have to gather her thoughts again, then said in a rush, "It was difficult. Please understand that your father and I love you very much, and that essentially we are proud of you. Nothing has changed. You are going to make a stupendous marriage, just as you deserve. But we want to play safe, darling, just as we always have with you. You are our treasure, and I don't want any bad talk or bad feelings, if you know what I mean."

Louise didn't exactly, though she was so disconcerted that her parents had even an inkling of what she had been about on the ship, she wasn't going to ask for clarification.

Her mother suddenly smiled through all this and said, "Anyway, I can't tell you how fabulously the prince took our revelations. These French." She laughed. "So incredibly broad-minded. He said he didn't mind a little spirit in a wife and that he was committed to you, to us, and would stand by you. Now listen to me."

Louise could hardly do anything else. Her face had gone from cold to hot. She looked away, humiliated to have so underestimated her parents. Honest. Yes. Her pasha had called *her* this. Yet she had not even given honesty a thought when it had come to this new beginning to her life. Here was one of the reasons perhaps that she was uncomfortable with the kindness the prince showed her at every opportunity. This notion—comfort through honesty—swam around in the muddle of her brain.

Her mother's voice continued. "Here is what we have devised, Louise. For form's sake, we will continue outwardly to prepare for a wedding, but the prince has agreed to take you off to Grasse in two weeks in an elopement. We didn't know what else to do, but marriage we think is the safest, surest refuge for a young girl who is, well, um, for you, that is." Her mother's voice caught. "I had so hoped for a big, beautiful wedding, but—" She stopped.

Louise didn't know what to say, where to look. Neither of them spoke for a full minute.

It was her mother who wanted the big wedding, of course. Louise didn't care. Yet she felt horrible to have deprived her mother of what had been a subject of conversation since Louise was old enough to understand what the words *huge society wedding* meant. A marriage "to some prince or other" had been a kind of joke when Louise was younger, an exaggeration of all her mother's hopes come oddly to fruition. Attending such a triumphant and happy event was something Isabel Vandermeer had spoken of with relish for as long as Louise could remember.

Her mother proceeded. "If you are willing, that is. If you agree. Do you?"

It seemed pointless not to. Louise nodded. She met her mother's eyes then and managed words finally: "Mama, I am sorry for any worry or pain I have caused you."

Her mother took her hand and began walking again. "I know, dear. Don't worry." She pulled Louise into a slow stroll across the wet, shifting stones. "Everything is going to be fine. Your father and I are going to take a house here for a while, just to be sure you settle in and are happy."

Louise bit her lip, then said, "Mama, I want to take care of myself."

Her mother only glanced at her sideways and kept going. "Of course, you do, darling."

Louise halted and pulled her mother around by the hand. "No, you don't understand. You and Papa can go back when you chose to. I'm sorry if I've hurt or disappointed you, but it's my life. I can manage it myself."

Her mother gazed directly into her face for a few seconds, smiling her cool, unflappable smile. Then, with this smile still intact, her eyes glassed. Tears. Two small drops materialized at the corners of her eyes, then overran to become two neat parallel trails flanking her nose down her cheeks. "Oh, my sweet darling," she said. "Let me be your mother for a while longer, please. I'm not ready to part with you." She sniffled once, then asked with rather poignant sincerity, "Do you so long to leave us as much as all this?"

"No," Louise said. She reached, embracing this woman who had held her more times than she could count. "No, of course not." She patted her mother's head. "I only want you to stop worrying or doing anything more." She felt a faint brush with sadness herself, a kind of nostalgia for what was not yet gone, if such a thing were possible. "Just let me be. I can take care of myself. And I don't think I shall make myself all that unhappy or make anyone too ashamed. I am not so stupid, you know."

As they came back up the stone steps and walked up the lawn again, Isabel Vandermeer grew bright once more. "Yours, darling," she said, "all yours." She indicated the new house before them, a wide rise of white stone, three stories, forty-five rooms, built only four years ago, with every modern convenience, on three seaside acres of what was becoming the most expensive property on the continent.

Yet Louise already owned things she liked. She didn't long materially for more. But there was something else here, she sensed, that she wanted: As she came up from the morass of emotion on the beach, she could smell freedom, as pungent and fragrant as the herbs growing in the hills, like the mingled whiff of thyme and rosemary and wild lavender. She felt her skin itself become prickly with knowledge, with the incipient freedom of a married woman who had an indulgent husband. And the prince would be indulgent. She had thought so within the first hours of meeting him. But now, with his knowing "everything" and still choosing to marry her, with hardly more than a graceful, flourishing nod toward her indiscretion, she was absolutely sure.

The next two weeks went by quickly. The prince was busy with his concerns in Grasse. He was gone for three days, then came back with more work. Yet he found time for a steady, public sort of courtship. They went sailing once. They went riding on the beach at Antibes. He took her to the gambling palace in Nice, then to Monte Carlo, where he introduced her to the big gaming tables—to test her attraction to them, she suspected. She was not much of a casino gambler, though. The games took little or no skill, and the odds, all stacked heavily in the house's favor, weren't interesting. She won a little money. He seemed quite content with this. They went to his sister's for dinner.

Louise and the prince, by all early evidence, appeared to get along well. He was most agreeable. He was, as her parents had assured her, intelligent and well educated. He seemed quite the perfect match, exactly as they had said. Every moment between them, in fact, went flawlessly in these weeks, except for one misstep during a carriage ride into the countryside.

Out in the surrounds of Nice, he pulled their little two-wheel calèche into an olive grove, where he attempted to kiss her—and where Louise nearly fell from the carriage in her mad haste to be back from him. After a particularly awkward moment, they laughed about it. Louise had been disappointed in herself, though, for she had been coaching herself for two weeks for just such a moment. Yet how to prepare for the sight of his lopsided face bearing down on her all at once? While his thick arm coiled round her back? She had managed till his mouth was right up to hers, then botched it, shying and bolting like a stupid horse missing a jump. It would be different once they were married, she assured him. Once she was used to the whole idea of physical intimacy. (Which was not the problem, of course, for she had swum in physical intimacy for an entire Atlantic Ocean crossing.) In any event, he was quite tolerant, most patient. Of course. He would wait, he said.

In truth, though, her bungle worried her more than she wished to admit. As to the prince's looks, she truly believed she would get used to them. But for one split second there in the carriage, as her future husband tried to kiss her, a far larger deterrent materialized than merely his looks.

Her pasha had loomed up quite suddenly, in smell and feel and substance somehow, and she had felt . . . odd, confused.

Unfaithful was the word. It had seemed a kind of betrayal, she supposed, of what she had had with him for another man to take hold of her so familiarly. It had seemed strange to see a man's face up against hers. Never mind what his face looked like; it was a face other than the one she imagined as her lover's. She had been angry to find the wrong one there, to breathe a breath that smelled of ripe olives instead of champagne. Her anger had been followed swiftly by a sense of revolt. Only God knew where exactly this feeling came from, whether from watching the prince's sightless eye squint in momentary offense, then turn away in timid retreat (oh, how unlike the forward, confident man she was used to). Or perhaps his eye didn't matter. Perhaps the most self-assured man in the world, any other than her midnight lover, would have been found lacking. She didn't know. She only knew that she was repelled. Then embarrassed by her entirely inappropriate response.

She had brought him a glass of brandy after dinner that night, out onto his back lawn where he was sitting dismally all by himself. He was tetchy about his looks, she realized. Oh, wonderful, she thought with a deep, inward groan. His ego had been dented. She tried to apologize, make amends, but he waved these away: *No, don't be silly. We have a lifetime, you know . . .*

This left the two of them to sit there silently together, the prince generous and mature, Louise feeling like a skittish, selfish shrew. She hated herself and her inability to explain her own behavior satisfactorily or make up for it—and she hated him for leaving her to languish in guilt.

For Louise knew when a man wanted sexual contact with her, the way a bee knows its way unerringly back to the hive. And, mistress or no mistress, it became clear over these two weeks that the prince was not entirely altruistic in his willingness to marry her. She had caught his eye, so to speak. In a very large way. There was something about him, suppressed, restrained, but obvious to her at least: He was just plain itching to get her into bed. Which made her a little annoyed with him. The nerve. She barely knew him.

Then it made her contrite: No, no, she tried to tell herself, he was reasonable in his thinking. He intended their marriage to be a perfectly normal one. Which of course it had to be, if there were to be children. Which of course Louise wanted.

She just wasn't sure how to get herself up and into bed with *him* without her stomach pitching. When she thought about this odd, limping fellow lying naked and panting on top of her—Lord, all she could do was cringe. She feared her own disgust. She had to find a way to contain the fact that, when she found herself looking at him, spellbound, her hypnotic stare had more to do with aversion than attraction.

How? She didn't know. And the question itself inevitably collapsed into a longing for her Ocean Charles. Was this what fidelity felt like? she wondered. Like a kind of tantrum one couldn't stop? A revolt at the thought of any but one and only one lover? How amazing. She had always imagined faithfulness had something to do with curtailing one's own pleasure for the sake of not hurting the feelings of a beloved. Yet this feeling was nothing of the sort. It was selfish, pigheaded. Like wanting strawberries, tasting only the pleasure in strawberries, and preferring to starve rather than have to choke down an apple while wondering, What on God's earth did this prince, this suspiciously magnanimous resident of Eden, expect of her?

* * *

What did Charles expect? Pretty much everything that had happened to date. The bride was shy of him. Most women were at first. The bride was smart enough, however, to know where her best interests lay.

The wedding took place in a tiny chapel in Grasse. In the end, Louise's parents couldn't stand the idea of not attending their daughter's nuptials, so it was they who sneaked away in a kind of clandestine manner. The bride and groom merely drove to Charles's house in Grasse, arriving late in the morning, then slipped over to the little church after lunch. Uncle Tino was there. Other than he and the Vandermeers, no one else was in attendance except for a priest and one of Tino's youngest, who served as an altar boy. Isabel Vandermeer sobbed quietly at the back of the chapel as the vows were exchanged. Her husband was stoic. Louise was predictably alert and breathtaking— prettier than pretty in a simple beige dress and a fine feathered hat with net that covered her face.

When Charles lifted this netting and kissed her at the altar—a direct hit of lips with no avoidance—he was beside himself with all that his future promised. Afterward, as a photographer exploded trayfuls of blinding magnesium, Charles smiled till his cheeks hurt. The six of them went to the magistrate's office, where they signed all the civil documents. *Fini.* Monsieur and Madame Charles Harcourt, the Prince and Princess d'Harcourt. Princess Lulu Louise.

His Louise. For better. For worse. Forever.

Chapter 18

*The sperm whale is found in temperate
and tropical waters throughout the world,
usually in herds of about fifteen to
twenty—though solitary males wander
into colder regions.*

Charles Harcourt, Prince d'Harcourt
On the Nature and Uses of Ambergris

Louise's parents parted from their newly married
daughter in a flurry of emotion, hugging her,
then patting her, then hugging her again. When
Charles bent and kissed them both on the cheeks,
calling them Mother and Father (it seemed a little
ludicrous, but it was what they asked for), "Mother"
burst into tears again, the tenor of her crying joyous,
yet somehow also sad to Charles's way of thinking. As
if she and her daughter would be separated for a long
time, when in fact they would be reunited five days
hence in Nice.

The Vandermeers had taken a house not far from
Charles's own in Nice. They went off in that direction.
Uncle Tino and his son departed just down the street;
they lived in Grasse. Charles and his new bride were

left standing in the town square, before the café where they had all toasted the bride and groom for an hour.

"Are you all right?" he asked when Louise stared off in the direction of her parents' carriage for a full minute after it disappeared.

She jumped slightly, then glanced at him. "Yes. Certainly."

"Would you like to walk for a while? There is a little daylight left."

The square in which they stood was fronted by a pretty, shady street, wider than most and dotted with gray-green aromatic hedges, rosemary, that gave off a lush scent when one crushed their spiky leaves. At the end of this street—what would have been a fragrant meander through a residential neighborhood—was a view between butter-yellow houses and over rose-colored rooftops to a surprising glimpse of the cobalt blue Mediterranean, twenty kilometers away.

Louise didn't seem much interested or aware of anything around her, though. She seemed dazed or perhaps tired.

He asked, "Would you prefer to go home?"

Her eyes met his again, as if startled to hear the word *home* used in this context. She stared at him a moment. He could never figure out just what she was thinking when she did this. She looked at him directly, then looked away, her eyes acquiring a kind of wistful lack of focus.

She said finally, distractedly, "Yes, I should prefer to go back to the house, if you wouldn't mind." This, in her perfect, formal French, which was becoming, to Charles's mind, a palpable obstacle between him and the young woman he had just made his wife.

In public, Louise carried off the high elegance of her brand of the language as if born to it, with all the grace of a *grande duchesse*. French jaws dropped when Louise spoke. Charles himself could not help but stare and blush and puff at the posh clarity in each sentence she uttered. In private, however, this same manner of speech—her inability in fact to speak any other way—chilled the very air that fueled his lungs. His brain frosted. Every warm overture Charles made had to proceed against a blizzard of politeness and protocol. Trying to speak with her in a friendly manner while, say, the two of them rode along in a carriage or, God forbid, as he tried to court her under the olive trees, left him feeling like some long-ago, foolish footman trying to have a chummy conversation with the queen.

English, of course, was out of the question. He had attempted to teach her some crude French. She had been bewildered then serenely appalled, shaking him off rather as she would her puppy, should the little fellow stand on his hind legs and latch on in an unseemly manner to her knee. Charles had tried several other approaches to narrow the emotional distance between them, from offering confidences of his own (of youthful pranks when he was only a year younger than she, pranks at which she smiled sweetly yet he somehow thought she found childish) to joining her when she played with her dog, hoping to get her Bear to break the ice for him, something that had worked so well in the ship's kennels.

As a result, Charles and the dog were getting along nicely. The dog adored him. Louise, on the other hand, hardly seemed to know Charles was alive.

He knew he was stumbling with her, their exchanges always stilted or else filled with awkward silence. He suspected he was coming across as inept and self-conscious. Yet he believed he would catch his stride eventually. If she would only give him half a chance, half a pleasant response—of which he knew her to be more than capable. He kept trying.

Charles escorted her across the square to their carriage, then helped her in.

Once inside, he opened all the curtains, partly

because it was a fine afternoon, partly out of qualms
for dark places, for possible detection in this charade
he'd become determined to carry out. Anything was
better than this high-toned creature realizing he'd
played her for a fool all the way across an ocean. So he
settled back. He watched dusk flit over her vague
expression as they circled the square, then jostled up
the hillside in the direction of their house in Grasse.

The house was simple. It was not a primary residence, but merely a place to live when Charles was
working in his laboratory or overseeing his factory.
Grasse was the figurative capital of perfume manufac-
ture in France (and thus the world, he might have
argued); it was home to his perfume enterprise, both
his and his French competitors. Though there was
nothing uncomfortable about his house here, it had
simply never been the object of much attention. It was
in fact quite lovely, though, in the way of old things
that had been lovely and functional for a hundred
years. It was unimposing. There was no room for
entertaining, barely room for a tea in the afternoon,
should Louise choose to invite some ladies from the
town. And tonight it would be particularly quiet,
since he had sent every servant, save the kitchen staff,
off so the newlyweds could be alone.

For here was Charles's next attempt: a private,
elaborate dinner out on the terrace overlooking the
descending countryside with the sea in the distance. A
gift of black pearls for the bride. He knew she was
fond of them; he knew hers were broken. Wine. Local
delicacies. Charming talk. She would surely *have* to
say something personal if they were sitting alone
across from each other for several hours. There was
wine with dinner and peach brandy for afterward. He
would loosen her up with alcohol if need be; all was
fair in love et cetera, he thought. Anything to get
beyond this damned Society Louise from New York,

with her courtly French that abetted the highest, most
impregnable wall of reserve Charles had ever encoun-
tered. Then up to bed, where he would suavely make
love to her in all the ways he knew she liked, which
happened also to be the means of his own entrance
into paradise. He had far too sharp a recollection of
Louise naked, Louise warm and liquid beneath him.
Just thinking about tonight made his mouth dry, his
eyes hot.

While it also made him ever so slightly anxious.

He'd made a mess of Charles Harcourt's first attempt to kiss the lovely Louise in the olive grove,
coming at her apparently out of the blue. That's what
he told himself. The surprise of his advance had taken
her unaware; she hadn't been expecting it. Or perhaps
he'd been clumsy; he certainly wasn't himself these
days in the face of her royal deportment and speech.
Whatever the reason, if he hadn't caught her arm,
she'd have fallen out of the carriage as a result of her
backward leap away from him.

He intended to be much more deliberate tonight.

At the front door to the house, she walked in ahead
of him. He closed the door. By the time he had turned
around, she was across the vestibule and halfway up
the staircase.

"Where are you going?" he called.

"To dress for dinner."

He blinked. She meant tiaras and tails. Her family,
as good-hearted as its members were, was full of
mannered behavior he found pretentious. "I thought
we might be a little less formal," he suggested.

She looked down at him over the stairwell balustrade. "We always dress for dinner. I *always* have."

"You look lovely as you are."

"It's a day dress," she said as if he were blind in
both eyes.

Charles made a pull of his mouth, depositing his

cane in the umbrella stand by the door—perhaps he
shouldn't have, but he wanted the damn thing out of
sight tonight, this emblem of his affliction. He hung
his hat, then limped as gamely as possibly to the foot
of the stairs, where, flustered but determined, he
confessed, "You are going to have trouble dressing for
dinnèr, Madame." Madame. No, he should have used
her name. Yet he went on quickly, "I sent your maid
away."

"You did what?" From the middle of the staircase,
she turned around then took a step down.

He found himself stepping back. "I sent all the
servants away except the kitchen help, who will leave
immediately after dessert. I want to be alone with
you."

This was apparently a very un-suave admission.
Her face in the shadows of the upstairs soffit looked as
if he had just said, *I want to stick my head under your
skirt.* She paled slightly and pressed her lips together.
As she came back down the stairs, her heavy-lidded
eyes passed a single glance at him—a stunning gaze in
every sense. He was rooted to the spot by the beauty
of these eyes, the dark, limpid blue of them, like deep
water off the North Pole, as sparkling and bright—
and as chilly and distant—as melting ice under an
arctic sun.

Her eyes looked briefly at him then right past him
as she walked by. She said, "Well, what is done is
done. Hereafter, I would like to dress for dinner, if
you do not mind."

Actually he was beginning to mind her dismissive
manner, and the hash he continually made of trying
to get around it, a great deal. Cool, snotty witch;
gorgeous brat.

She marched over to the mirror that hung above the
entry-room sideboard, ignoring his edgy silence. In
front of the mirror, she raised her arms and reached
back, her hands trying to find the hat pin in among

the plumes at her crown. Charles came up behind her, watching her both in the flesh and in the mirror, front and back, almost three hundred sixty degrees of Louise. He found the hat pin for her. She jumped when he moved her fingers to it, then she latched hold of the pin.

Her smallest movement captivated . . . her posture, her slim arms, elbows in the air as she withdrew the pin, then lifted netting, beige felt, and a concoction of white ostrich feathers backward off her neat hair, twisting, shaking her head slightly in a gesture as graceful as any prima ballerina. Charles couldn't resist reaching out, touching her where the bodice of her dress clung snugly to her ribs—

Louise bent immediately and automatically, so that his fingers barely grazed the taffeta of her dress. She curved away from his hand. "Charles. Please. I'm trying to put the pin through my hat. You'll make me stick myself."

"Sorry," he murmured.

He apologized. He stood there listening to himself. He'd just apologized for touching his own wife, his bride of two hours, a woman he had not touched or kissed in two long weeks, except today at the end of a wedding mass. He had to be insane.

She had to be a sadist. She could be making this so much easier for him.

By the time they actually moved out onto the terrace, Charles was up in arms, furious with himself, aggravated with Louise.

The table on the small balcony beyond the dining room was just large enough for two: two potted palms at the side, two chairs in the center at a table with two candles and a shallow bowl that held two floating roses; two china plates on top of two larger ones, two sets of sterling, and half a dozen wine glasses, in pairs of varying sizes, for aperitif, dinner, and after. On top of the china plates sat small bowls of caviar in ice surrounded by round little toasts browned and yellowed with saffron. Charles held Louise's chair.

She sat. "Oh, this is lovely," she said, almost grudgingly. Her head swiveled. She stared around her, then smiled up at him, one long, glowing look of surprise and pleasure. She added, "Really lovely."

He settled opposite her, instantly more content.

She dove in demurely, mounding dark gray caviar onto a toast, then closing her lips over it, crunching. She sighed and giggled with delight (perhaps just a little too enthusiastically—she was as nervous as he was, he decided, which was only natural and somewhat reassuring). "Ooh, beluga. My favorite," she said.

It would be, of course. It was expensive.

She added, "From the Caspian."

Trust her to know the specific geography of the taste. The most difficult to come by. It didn't matter. Charles smiled and stared at this wonder child of eighteen with the sophistication of a rich woman of forty.

In the candlelight, she looked ageless. Simply, ethereally as beautiful as an archangel. Charles ploughed some caviar onto a toast, then ended up handing it to her (with a mouth-watering brush of fingers). He couldn't eat. He wasn't even vaguely interested in food. Every slight from earlier, imagined and otherwise, he forgave in a blink. All he wanted to do was feast on the sight of her . . . the sound of her . . . the odor that was particularly Louise, mingling with the ambiance of his own back garden and an evening delicately gilded in scent . . . a whiff of herbs growing wild nearby . . . the immediacy of cultivated roses growing just beyond the terrace . . . Louise, like some species of flower all her own, tenacious and spiky like a weed, as sweet and heady as a mythic lotus.

"It's so nice here," she commented.

"Yes." If one looked over the terrace balcony, one would find a sunken garden that began with a small fountain, then became a long, tunneling arbor of climbing roses between parallel rows of cypress, leading the eye to rooftops and a hillside that descended all the way to the coast far, far in the distance.

With the invisible sun setting at the side of the house, this garden, fading into long slanting shadows, was picturesque, to say the least. Charles's favorite view from this house. Or he had thought so, at least, until he had sat across from Louise. He failed to look at it tonight; he failed even to point it out. He just sat there staring, smiling the faint, smug smile of a man who had everything he wanted sitting before him.

The woman across from him, on the other hand, felt like a creature coming to consciousness in a stew pot stirred by a cannibal: all but devoured. As if she were more a course of the meal than the soup that came next. The prince stared; he'd stared all day. He touched her in grazes and grasps of the elbow. He cornered her. Louise read clearly that she was sitting across from a man who had big honeymoon plans, the salaciousness of them written all over his ghastly face.

This face, its new proximity somehow, and the immediacy of what was going to occur tonight were suddenly so hair-raising that Louise found herself unable to look at the man across from her for longer than a few seconds.

"Would you like some wine?" he asked.

And it was this not-looking-at-him that suddenly riveted her attention: to the sound. *Would you like some champagne?* She looked up.

"Would you like some wine?" he repeated.

Staring, she jerked her head, a single movement. No.

His odd face registered disappointment. He set the bottle down.

Wine, not champagne, she told herself. No, it

wasn't at all the same. He'd said it quietly, in French. Yet something . . . his tone . . . something had stopped her heart. For Charles—*her* Charles—rose up before her, like the day in the olive grove, only stronger. This time, her soul turned upside down. As if a ghost murmured from somewhere beyond life.

Louise stared at a man so different from her handsome, wicked Arab, who could yet evoke him so intensely she didn't know how to speak. His husband's voice was similar, she realized. Deep. He and her lover had size in common. They both made perfume—they both used scented soap, or toilette water or something, not so common among men, but pleasant even though she liked the Arab version better.

It was uncanny, come to think of it, some of the things they had in common. And pathetic, some of the things that separated them.

Her pasha was confident, ridiculously so. This man was hesitant. She frightened him. She knew she bowled him over.

Her old tantrum of the olive grove welled up. *Charles, I want my Charles and only Charles; not this one.*

She missed the man who could scoop her up into his arms or, laughing, carry her on the front of him like a monkey to bed; her smooth, magnetic, impetuous lover of the ship. She had instead this circumspect, overly mindful husband, following her with his Mephisto's gait—a halting rhythm that by will alone he made fluid, like a musical phrase in a melodic minor with grace notes.

Her Charles was earthy. Unflinching. She missed his laughter. He laughed a lot. This man rarely smiled; he looked more often puzzled and on edge.

Her Charles was not afraid of her beauty or overly impressed with it. She suspected here in France, though—what with the drawbacks and contingencies that had come up to rush the marriage—she would not be wed to Charles Harcourt without it. The lame prince liked it. It proved something. He gloated over the idea of taking a stunning woman to wife.

Her Charles understood other ways to involve himself with her than this superficial one, turning her looks themselves into a kind of game. He knew how to play. He was not easily stymied. He was clever, kind. And handsome—

Louise picked up her soup spoon with a clank, then glanced over the top of it at the man in front of her. No, not handsome, not handsome at all. Though he was so peculiar to look at that a part of her wished she could narrow her eyes and glut on the sight, tilt her head and look and look to satisfy a kind of morbid fascination for his person that left her feeling ashamed, too curious for his disfigurement.

She couldn't do this, so she retreated back into the safety of glimpses, then realized: The really hateful difference between the two men was the difference she perceived in herself when in each man's presence. Tonight she felt unsure, unsettled, and her confusion itself made her behave badly, far beyond the word *shrewish*. She felt like a termagant, a she-wolf out of season, ready to bite and snap at any who came sniffing. She felt closed, defensive—when she wanted nothing so much as to be open again. She wished to be what her Charles had called her once: honest, open, intelligent, generous. Sweet.

She couldn't remember what he had found sweet about her, though she knew she aspired to a sweetness of sorts. A kind, compassionate spirit. No one ever before had been tempted to use that term *sweet* with regard to her, yet it had endeared her pasha to her for him to call her this.

Louise knew she was intelligent, perhaps to a fault. This left her with *honest, open* and *generous*. What did she *honestly* think was happening to her here?

Why was she so uncomfortable? So unlike the new self that had lived briefly in a suite on a tossing ship? Tonight, more than ever, she wished she could have talked to her naked priest of the dark, discussed her concerns, asked him what he thought. Her lover, her friend and confessor, maybe he could make her laugh about this: She was unnerved by the thought of giving herself to this man.

Giving herself. Even the phrase made her feel selfish. So much for *generous.* She didn't want to give anything. She wanted to take. She wanted to have. In the midst of all the prince's lavish attention, she felt needy and bereft. Alone again. No one who understood. . . . Which, in turn, made her feel miserly with herself; mean-spirited and small-minded.

Louise spooned soup and smiled as she tried to force herself to say something pleasant. "Nice weather," she murmured.

The prince looked at her, as if surprised to hear this topic come up, then nodded. "Yes. We get wonderful weather year-round, though autumn can bring a little rain, quick and heavy. Last year we had a flash flood that ruined a field of roses."

"Really?"

"Yes."

Her mind went blank.

Oh, yes, she thought. The weather on the Riviera. Good year-round, except for some rain. An earth-shattering discussion.

Louise tried to take appreciative pleasure in what she normally enjoyed—a fine meal in extraordinarily pleasant surroundings. The prince had gone to a great deal of trouble. "This is delicious," she said, lifting a spoonful of whatever-it-was soup. In her spoon bowl it was thick and pale pink. She swallowed it without knowing whether the flavor was vegetable, fruit, or meat.

He responded by naming fish, or what she thought

to be fish. Only the bass was recognizable, and translatable, as a fish she knew from the Hudson.

Why feel grateful? she thought suddenly. All this kindness had purpose. This genteel man wanted to take her to bed well-fed and happy; that's what this was all about. And the thought—*to bed*—brought instant panic. Louise tried to calm herself. The prince was sure to be just as considerate tonight. She could count on his sexual tact. Or she thought she could; she hoped she could. Besides, with the lights off, in the dark, wouldn't it all seem familiar, more appealing when it was more like—

This question made her stop as she broke off a piece of bread. The poor prince could never measure up. More importantly, she didn't want him to.

It was a relief to understand this. Oh, yes. Louise resumed, spreading her bread enthusiastically with French "rust," a condiment that went with the soup; there was no butter. She didn't want Charles Harcourt, not at all. And, with this admission, something became clear: Husband or not, the idea of giving her body over to someone else's use did not seem like something she ought to have to do. She thought herself far too valuable to give away in any sense, even for a night.

She didn't want him. And that was that; she wouldn't have him.

It wasn't a *sweet* decision, but it was honest. She dipped her bread in the soup and picked up her spoon again as she prepared now to be open.

She said, "I want to sleep alone tonight."

The prince stopped in midmotion as he brought his own soup spoon to his mouth. *"Vous dites?"* he said— the blunt French equivalent to *huh?* or *what?* that asked for a remark to be repeated.

She was sure he'd heard her, though. She continued, "By myself. It doesn't matter where, on the couch is fine."

"You want to sleep on a couch?"

"Yes."

"A couch where?"

"I saw one in your sitting room upstairs."

"You want to sleep in the sitting room by yourself tonight?"

"Yes."

He put his spoon down and sat back, his brow furrowing, half his face alarmed, half looking like an ogre with indigestion. "I hesitate to mention that it is customary for a married couple to sleep together, particularly on their wedding night."

She didn't care what was customary. It was her own private choice that unfortunately, she could see, rankled the man across from her. She wasn't happy to do this. But neither did she feel responsible for a grown man's ability to cope with the truth of a situation.

Truth. She struggled to find some more, looking for more comfort, more ease from the odd strain of emotion that bound her and held her back from being herself. "You have to understand," she said. "I'm trying to sort some things out. I didn't plan on being married to you two weeks after arriving. To say my life has changed too fast is an understatement." She scooped and blew on hot soup, staring into her spoon as if she might find propitiating words there. She added, "Mama and Papa believe you are very benevolent and broad-minded, so I hope you won't make a stink over this. I need time. I intend to—well, you know, have children eventually. I just didn't plan on being married so quickly and, to tell you the truth—" She glanced up and stopped.

Any charm on that strange face of his had fled completely. Without it, his expression, his whole posture took on a ferocious edge—a look of sullen disbelief made fierce by size and mass and facial anomaly. She had seen him cast a fearsome look at other people, but she had never been the recipient of such a countenance. One moment, she couldn't look away: his face, his mien so fascinatingly terrible to witness. The next, she couldn't bear the sight.

She dropped her gaze in order to finish what she had to say to him. "There is a great deal that I have to adjust to here"—more than she had imagined perhaps—"and I would rather take it a step at a time, so if you could give me a little grace."

There, she had gotten it all out, Louise thought. She set her spoon into the plate of her soup bowl. It clinked twice, ringing on the china. She looked down at the sound, rather than meet his eyes—or eye. Lord, he gave her the willies when he sat like this, still and quiet, scrutinizing, herself the converging point of his brutish discontent.

There was a long pause. "All right," he said at length.

She tried to suppress her sense of relief. "All right?"

"Certainly. How much time do you wish?" His voice was calm, smooth, but he was not happy. He kept his focus down on the table, where he began to tap the salt shaker with the tip of his finger.

"I don't know. I'll tell you when."

His regard lifted abruptly at this bid for total sexual autonomy, his one azure blue eye, alive, astute, macabre in its beauty, fixing on her, then narrowing. He had nothing further to say on the subject for the present. But she knew she had not gotten exactly what she wanted.

She had her reprieve, but it was not given innocently nor was this a charming understanding. He was angry and disappointed, and he made no attempt to hide the fact.

Louise was struck again by guilt, a feeling that he deserved better from her—though not so strong or brooding a guilt that she actually wished she could accommodate him.

The soup bowls were removed. The prince poured

himself more wine. An oppressive silence insinuated itself over the little table.

In an attempt to relieve this, she asked, "When do you pick up your first shipment of ambergris?" It seemed apropos to remind them both why he'd really married her.

He drank his wine, upending the glass instead of answering, then, as if this were just too laconic, muttered four words: "In about a week."

She had no clear idea where to go from here. "What is it?" she asked.

"What?"

"Ambergris."

"A perfume fixative."

She knew this already. "No, I mean, how does it end up in the sea. Where does it come from?"

"Squid beaks."

"Squid beaks?"

There was a long pause as if he meant not to speak further. Ultimately, though, he poured more wine and said, "In the whale's stomach. He can't digest these and some random shells of cuttlefish, so his body makes a bile that encases the indigestible pieces. This is squeezed into a bolus in his intestines. Then the whole is excreted in a black, viscous regurgitation. There it is"— *Voilà*—"ambergris." Gratuitously, he added, "It floats, of course: It's feces."

Louise blinked, looked up at him. He was turned from her, his best profile, which was sharp-featured, still not precisely good looking. He sat there in an angry slump, turning the wine glass by its stem— having put a pretty definitive end to this dinner conversation. She murmured, "How disgusting."

He glanced at her, his relatively perfect mouth sneering into a sarcastic pull. "Well, it improves under the right circumstances. It becomes quite elegant."

Indeed. It was boiled down and turned into something else entirely. If he were suggesting this as a metaphor for himself, she refused it.

Still, he didn't seem quite the same odd, timid fancy man she had first thought. His restrained manner did not seem to come out of weakness so much as out of a lack of interest in power for its own sake. He was strong, formidably so, she sensed. But like a vampire or incubus, mere obedience to his strength wasn't what he wanted. He wanted her will to bend toward him. This made her feel both safe, since she didn't honestly believe in vampires or incubuses, and on edge, since it seemed possible she had married the closest thing to them that walked the earth.

The main course arrived, something or other roasted, herbed, colorful, beautiful; a waste. With it, came a servant who lit the lamps at the cornerstones of the balcony railing, old, oil-burning glass and iron globes. Beyond the balcony, the towns and villages between Grasse and the coastline became nestled clusters of twinkling light, a plummeting progression that fanned and sloped toward the sea like a black velvet night brought out to show off a diamond spill of civilization. Far off, similar jewels, more closely arranged, showed the shape of the coast beyond which a tiny ship glided off-center through a watery ribbon of moonlight. Closer to hand, a glow from the dining room whiffed into existence. The terrace became awash in soft, romantic illumination, yet Louise and her husband avoided looking at each other. Neither ate much. Dinner was cleared. They were silent throughout.

When they did finally speak—at his strained but pacifying initiative—they held safely to the conversational surface. His schedule over the next five days. Her settling in. What she intended to do with herself while he had to work. Would she like to see what he did? The sort of exotic travel usually associated with a honeymoon was delayed for the same reason that

Charles Harcourt could not come to New York for a
wedding in the usual place, in the bride's hometown:
He had budded important plants onto rootstock. A
project he had been working on for some time in his
perfume laboratories was at a crucial point.

She realized, of all things, he was speaking of the
American jasmine he had picked up in Marseilles,
along with herself, both direct from the care of her
pasha. She had traveled just fine, better than fine in
fact. But the bud cuttings had apparently been worse
for the wear after their trip across the ocean. The
prince hoped that some would be willing to take. He
wanted to nurse the project personally through the
first months, and especially these first weeks, so he
knew all had been done that could be and exactly
what results he could count on.

Louise relaxed, listening. The promise she had won
from him left her more interested in hearing about his
work, his interests, his comings and goings, his movements that would ultimately circumscribe much of
her own life.

Dessert arrived. A platter of black grapes, local,
plumply fresh, the tiniest, sweetest she had ever put in
her mouth, with a bitter, tart seed if she happened to
catch it in her teeth. She actually began to enjoy
herself. Besides the grapes, there were bowls of this
summer's cherries, one dish of them marinated in
eau-de-vie, the other in vinegar and—he was quite
specific—lavender honey from his own fields. He
grew gracious again; stiff but decent. The fruit was
followed by a golden, homemade peach liqueur with
occasional leaf specks floating. When she didn't drink
this up, he asked if she liked it.

"Oh, yes." She looked up. She wasn't certain where
the next question came from. She wondered aloud,
"Don't you own champagne vineyards somewhere?"

"Yes. Near Reims. Though I wouldn't drink my
champagne. It's adequate, coming along but not

grand." He paused then asked, "Do you like champagne?"

"Yes."

He reached back, just inside the doorway, and pulled the bell cord. When a girl came from the kitchen, he said, "Marianne, run down to the cold room of the cellar and bring up a bottle of the Widow, not the brute. Oh, and some fresh glasses." The Widow was apparently the brand he preferred to his own.

The champagne arrived. He sent for fresh fruit and cheese, then popped the cork. The bottle smoked. He poured. Sec, despite its "dry" name, was faintly sweet, a champagne suited to dessert. It smelled familiar, reminiscent of bubbling wine shared in the dark, but more fruity. It was cold, delicious. Though not the same. Louise wistfully traced her finger along the curve of the bottle.

They talked a while more. He stood at one point, stretching as he looked out over the balcony into the night. The sky was strewn with stars. There was a three-quarter moon. He turned to lean on the ironwork of the balustrade, chatting randomly about nothing in particular.

Louise wasn't listening very closely, back inside her own head again, truth be known.

Then all at once he was right at her side, turning her chair around, taking hold of her hand. He tried to pull her up and out of the chair, into his arms.

There was no mistaking his intention. When she wouldn't stand, he bent down, one hand on the tabletop, the other braced on her chair back. It happened too quickly for her to be annoyed or defensive or have much of any considered reaction. He said, "Don't fall out of your chair. I'm going to kiss you."

His face came close.

She placed her fingers between their mouths.

She stared into his odd eyes inches away, his left as
opaque as marble, his right as fair—and as intense in
its radiance—as a clear, twilight sky. The flesh on her
arms prickled. She had to lower her gaze. She looked
him in the chin, then the mouth, then at the perfectly
chiseled philtrum of his upper lip.

She knew he watched this happen. He backed off
slightly and cocked his head to study her at this close
range. He said, "A kiss. May I please kiss my own
wife. It's not as if I'm trying to throw you down and
dive under your skirts."

It was almost reassuring to know the Prince d'Harcourt could be rude. But nonetheless Louise didn't
like the tenor of his thinking. And she was galled to be
in this position, after they had already come to terms
on the subject.

When he bent toward her again, she leaned back all
the way till her hair caught in the fronds of a potted
palm. She reached behind her, untangling herself, as
she put her prohibition into words. She said, "Please
don't." Louise remembered her pasha again and
thought to pass along what sounded like marvelous
advice all at once. "It would be better if you didn't try
to kiss a woman until she had enough interest, until
she is hoping you will: afraid that you won't."

He reared back to stare at her, as if she had just
spoken to him in tongues.

Then he stood up so abruptly that his thigh hit the
table. The dinner table shook, dishes, silver, glasses
jangling. The spoon in a dish of cherries looped
halfway around. Then, astoundingly, when everything
wobbled back, level, the politely controlled creature
she had married hooked his hand under the table edge
and flipped the whole thing over intentionally, in a
kind of fit.

Everything went. Round cherries leaped through a
stream of juice, their bowls following to the floor end
over end, crashing, splitting into pieces. Silverware

clanked into crystal. Splintered glass and roses slid into cheese. Louise herself scooted back so fast her chair went over backward in her hurry to get out of his way. At which point this husband became truly monstrous.

What a rage he flew into! With a swipe, he toppled the champagne stand. It went sloshing to the floor, a clunk and gurgle. He grabbed hold of palm fronds on his side of the terrace and yanked it. It tilted and rocked, almost righting itself, until, on the totter, he shoved it again. It toppled with a dull *clomph* to become a catawampus mass of leaves and stalks rooted in a spread of loose soil among shards of clay.

Louise had never seen anything like it—such an outward display of temper—except perhaps in a two-year-old. This done, a total disaster made of the dinner table, he turned to stare at her, breathing hard, his expression a one-eyed squint: a tortured visage if ever she saw one. Then he kicked the poor champagne bottle once to send it burbling and skidding through the archway into the dining room, after which the angry prince limped past the mess into the room himself, then out of sight.

Louise let her breath out, standing there with her mouth open for a full minute. She tried to think what would make a sane man do such a thing. Yet all she could think was, *It was just a kiss.* It wasn't as if he and she were in love or had even known each other for very long. She stood there speculating as to whether or not her parents knew the prince had such a temper, whether his temper was dangerous, and whether or not she had made an unforseen and horrible error in putting herself under his roof.

She looked at the floor, where the terrace gave into the dining room. Grapes and wine and cherries and cheese had scattered onto his—their, she supposed—Persian carpet. She shook her head. What an inscrutable and volatile creature to have done such a thing on purpose. Her own skirts were splotched with reddish eau-de-vie or vinegar and honey; she wasn't sure which. She smelled like a distillery.

Well, there wasn't anything else for it, she thought. She lifted her wet hems—it was pointless, but it felt civilized—and picked her way through the food and broken dishes on the floor. She would find her way to bed and deal with whatever else as it came.

What she didn't expect was to deal with Charles Harcourt again immediately. Once through the dining room she found him in the front salon. He had his weight, his hands, braced on the mantel of the large marble fireplace. He turned almost as soon as she entered, and there she was again, face-to-face with the lunatic.

"I'm so sorry," he said. He was "very, very, desolated" again in French, only this time he seemed to be so in some tangible and profound way: desolated, devastated, laid waste and inconsolable.

Looking at him, Louise felt quite sad for him all at once. He seemed such a mixture of uncanny strengths and vulnerabilities.

He pushed his hand through his hair, wincing his eyes closed. "I can be more patient," he told her.

She murmured, "God knows you have been patient."

He was taken aback for an instant. Then he shook his head, a wordless retraction. No, of course not; patience wasn't the problem. When he spoke next, it was with a frankness that seemed so brave she hardly knew where to look. He said, "I am sorry I appall you." He glanced at her. "This is the problem, is it not? You are offended by the sight of me. I horrify you." He sighed deeply, before he continued. "I had hoped I wouldn't. But since I do, there is nothing for it but to wait until I don't. I'm sure, in time—" He broke off.

His hand went, unaware, to fiddle with a gap in his

coat. His outburst had ripped the button there at his abdomen. He smoothed the front of his coat down once, saying, "Go on. Go up and get what you need from your trunks and bags. I need to stay down here, anyway, and gather my wits." He shook his head, his fingers going to his forehead. He rubbed a vein there. "Go upstairs and get ready for bed. I'll come up once I hear you're out of the bedroom."

Chapter 19

When basking on the surface of the ocean, sperm whales—notorious for their irritable digestion—are often heard before they are seen: great, lumbering hollows that barely break the surface yet rumble of whale-sized colic, emitting from time to time loud belches that are heard for miles across the open water.

Charles Harcourt, Prince d'Harcourt
On the Nature and Uses of Ambergris

Louise retrieved a few things from the prince's bedroom, a nightgown and robe and slippers, her toiletries, and a dress for the morning. She would have her trunk moved into the sitting room tomorrow, then figure out how to live with this arrangement. There had to be a guest room somewhere; she would ask. She washed and took her hair down, braiding it. She found sheets in the armoire at the end of the hall.

She was fastening the last buttons up the front of her nightgown when she heard Charles Harcourt come up the stairs. He entered his room from the hallway, making a ruckus, kicking and clonking around on the other side of the wall till light showed suddenly under the connecting door. All grew quiet. She thought she would see nothing more of him for the night. Then five minutes later, he opened the door between his bedroom and sitting room, just as she was laying a sheet out onto what was less couch, more divan, under the west window.

He didn't come in, but rather stared at the sheet, the divan, her activity, then leaned against the door-jamb. He folded his arms over his chest. He'd taken off the ripped coat. Likewise his vest. His shirt, collarless, cravatless, hung open. He was barefoot. He'd apparently been getting ready for bed himself when he'd suddenly found reason to open the door. He stood there brooding for several long seconds like some chimerical cross between a darkling Heathcliff and an angry cyclops.

Louise stopped, waiting to see what he wanted.

In just his shirt, he didn't look so . . . thick. . . . Is that what she'd thought? That his broad chest hid a slight corpulence? It didn't. He was muscular. Heavy-muscled and rather fierce-looking in the flesh. He looked extraordinarily hale, except for the limp, which she realized for some reason hadn't been as bad as usual tonight. He appeared to have left his cane downstairs.

At length he said, "There is an adjoining room on the other side of those curtains." He nodded to a set of heavy, drawn draperies Louise had thought hid a window to the south. "My mother used it. The room isn't aired out or clean, but we can see to that tomorrow." He offered this flat-voiced, without a smile, without a trace of the graciousness she had come to associate with him. Then, as if purposely holding to this tenor, he asked, "So I can't sleep with you, and I apparently can't kiss you. What exactly am I allowed to do as your husband?"

Louise stood up and faced him, annoyed that he wouldn't let the matter rest, at least for the night. "This matter was discussed and concluded downstairs, I thought. Closed."

"I want to reopen it."

"Well, I don't see any reason to. Unless you intend I provide sexual services that I wouldn't give freely for some benefit you otherwise intend to withhold. Which would amount to blackmail, to my mind." She said the last, intending to reap an immediate and gentlemanly retreat, a quick denial. "Or a form of prostitution."

He only shrugged, a lift of his shoulders without unfolding his arms. "Call it whatever you will. I'm not here to argue. I'm here to remind you that, if your whims should ever include children, I can't see myself providing my half of the service, as you call it, like some sort of hot and cold running tap, without having something to say in the matter myself."

Louise frowned, unsure how to answer this. She offered, "Your pride is wounded. That's all. You will get over it."

He looked at her with that sullen, magnetic glare he could command, ugly yet mesmerizing. Like the fixed stare of a serpent. He repeated, " 'That's all'?" then snorted. "If you knew the size of my pride, you would not dismiss it so easily." He shook his head, one quick, vehement negation. "I want to be understanding, but I'm telling you: This is not going to be easy for me to understand. I am wounded, yes. But I can't get over being furious as well. Quite frankly, sleeping with you *was* a pleasure I anticipated. And no small pleasure either. Not to put too fine a point on it, you are very beautiful."

Beautiful. She blinked. Perhaps if he had said *sweet* or at least acknowledged she'd been forthright . . .

He continued. "I can't watch you walk or your eyes glide over your surroundings, I can't notice the texture or color of your hair or the movement of your clothes that I am not aware of you as a woman. *My* woman." Or *my wife,* he said; the two were the identical word in French.

In either case, on top of everything else, the man was possessive, which Louise associated with *restrictive.* She said stiffly, "Yes, I gathered you were angry when you dumped everything from the table then attacked the potted palm."

He twisted his mouth and looked at her, as if his tongue reached for a back tooth. "So what do you propose?" he asked.

"We have already settled this."

"Yes, I thought we had too. But there was apparently a misunderstanding. I agreed you could sleep on a couch. I did not understand that to mean I could not so much as put my arm around you or my lips to your mouth."

Louise had played this game often and well, telling a man *no* and making it stick. One gave no quarter to a man who pushed. She said, "I won't discuss this. Just leave me alone for the time being."

"With your calling every shot?"

"It's my body we are discussing, I believe."

"How foolish of me. I thought we were discussing mine as well."

His display suddenly struck her. He'd come in here to show her. No coat, no vest, the open shirt. He was passably well-built.

No, that wasn't accurate. Louise slid her eyes down him. For a half-blind oaf, he bordered on the magnificent—in the way of those huge, Scottish draft horses. As if, with a good a harness on him, he could have pulled an eight-wheel wagon, wheels sucking and creaking, from the mud.

"Time," she said. "I am sure in time I shall be perfectly amenable to whatever you wish of me."

"What I wish is to be allowed to touch you. Now. Tonight. I don't necessarily want to sleep with you, if that is too much. But when I agreed to give you time, I wasn't agreeing to what you seem to be taking for granted. You have to come part of the distance, make an effort. I want to touch you, *give* pleasure as well as take it."

She pressed her lips together. He was not unattractive. This was a strange thing to realize. He wasn't handsome. There was even something quite horrid about him, if one stood at the right angle. But Charles Harcourt was so rivetingly peculiar to look at that, once the surprise of him wore off, one almost couldn't look away. And this translated into a draw of sorts. Attractive-repulsive. Then Louise felt strange for even acknowledging this, as if she were disloyal to think her husband interesting. Like a woman contemplating bigamy—with a man who happened to be handy and happened to remind her suddenly and profoundly of the man she wanted.

Her husband had her Charles's physique more than she'd imagined. Her own Charles had been lovely like this, his body vigorous and masculine. She missed him suddenly quite horribly, a strong lament for his gentle sureness, the way he listened, the way he accepted. His absence shot through her all at once with such emotional force she felt the room shift.

To Charles Harcourt, she said, "Well, you can't." She turned, agitated. "And don't mistake this for a negotiation. I won't bargain. You may not touch me unless I say you can, and for now I say you may not."

Silence.

He didn't leave, but at least he'd stopped arguing. Louise returned to straightening her sheet.

A moment later, a noise downstairs made them both turn their heads. It was a servant. No, several servants coming through the house. They had come home to sleep.

Without intending to, Louise cast an inquiring glance in the direction of the man in the doorway. The house staff was small, but large enough that sooner or later everyone in town would know that on the honeymoon night the bride and groom had gone their separate ways.

He watched her, narrowing the one eye he controlled completely, the other one more or less following suit. Then he said quietly, "I require your clothes."

She was momentarily nonplussed, then realized what he was suggesting. She joined him in unspoken conspiracy, gathering her dress and petticoats, her corset, underlinen and stockings from where she'd left them on the chair, a table, the floor. She took these over to him, then watched him run his hands through them, as if checking these were what he wanted. Then he tucked them in a bundle under his arm and walked back into his own room.

She followed the sight of him as far as the doorway, where she paused—her turn to stop, as if at a border to a hostile country.

His bedroom was spacious, not eye-catching so much as comfortable. Her bags sat at the edge still of a big feather bed, sunk down into its thick *eiderdown* beside a pile of pillows. Behind the pillows along the full length of the headboard ran a long, round bolster, a sleeping accoutrement to every French bed Louise had seen and what she could only imagine made every French neck awaken with a kink in it. The bed itself was uncanopied, just a solid old bedstead of dark wood with high endboards, graceful, simple, a heavy, old piece of furniture with a minimum of flutes and pediments. It was deep and boxy. Not so bad a bed, if there hadn't been an angry, lascivious man in it.

There was an armoire of similar dark wood, one side full of bronze pulls and knobs, the other a full-length mirror. Another large mirror on the opposite wall ran along a low, lengthy chest of drawers. Marble-topped nightstands. A matching washstand, its mar-

ble with a crack through it. On the wall beside the
washstand hung an odd piece: a sharp, curving blade
that ended in a gold and silver cross-handle, a scimitar. An Arab weapon. She looked at Charles Harcourt
again as he went to the washstand, turning his back to
her. She scanned the breadth of him, the length, from
his longish hair to his bare heels. In his bare feet, he
was about the same height as her pasha. He had the
right width of shoulders.

From the doorway, she asked in a language she
hadn't spoken in two weeks, "Do you speak English?"

In the small mirror over the washstand, his reflection came up to look at her. He paused, as if the
question itself were incomprehensible. Then he answered in two syllables that took a moment to recognize. "Nah tooell."

Louise frowned. She remembered reading his letters in English. They were short, but perfect. She
tilted her head, studying his dark crown in the
mirror—he'd bent over the washbowl again. She
supposed, there were people who could write in
French yet did not speak it. Or preferred not to.

Then he turned, and Louise drew back, alarmed:
He set a razor behind him onto the washstand, while
he held his thumb up. It was bleeding, sliced intentionally, deeply enough that a bright red bubble
oozed, then ran slowly down the inside of his wrist.

After which, gravity changed its course: He extended his hand over the bed. A bright red drop fell
onto a sheet as he pulled back the bedclothes. Louise
was transfixed by the sight as he dripped blood into
the sheets—four, five, then six dark droplets on
snowy white linen.

"We wouldn't want anyone to think you weren't a
virgin," he told her in throaty Southern French. The
sarcastic pull to his mouth said, in any language, he
thought she was not.

Staring at the sheets, Louise asked in a French murmur, "Is this what it looks like?"

"No," he said. "It is messier, lighter: mixed with the man's seed. Though I haven't the heart to do what it would take in order to fake that as well, I'm afraid."

Louise lowered her gaze to her own feet. "Have you known many virgins?"

"Oh, hundreds," he said. He noisily shook the covers.

Something in his voice, even in French, made her look at him and ask, "When you came back from the States, what ship did you come home on?"

"Pardon me?"

"Which ship?"

"The *Aubrignoise*. Why?"

She didn't know why. She shook her head as she looked down again, shaking off a brief, eerie disquiet. It made no sense, what she imagined.

So desperate, she thought: to turn the man she had ended up with into the man that she loved. And this was the problem, of course. Love. Never mind that she wasn't supposed to have loved her friend on the ship to begin with. Never mind he was gone. Love didn't seem to respond to permission. Or even absence. Never mind that adults played this way. Like a silly schoolgirl, she had lost her head and now couldn't find it again. She couldn't stop thinking of him.

Thus she made up unlikely scenarios, inventing similarities, mentally trying out nonsensical hypotheses, for no better reason than to make the Charles she'd married into the Charles she loved. Stupid, she thought. Don't be stupid; don't be childish.

The Charles she had ended up with said, "Such is life." *C'est la vie.* "My favorite shirt, lost to love." Louise frowned at this reiteration of her own thoughts, then watched him smear his cut thumb down his own shirttail.

Love, she thought. What did he know about it? This unsightly man who had married a conspicuously beautiful woman he hardly knew.

She found herself saying, "I'm sorry. For everything. It is not as if I don't understand your . . . your position."

He looked up from her chemise he had tossed to the floor. "You couldn't even begin to," he said.

"Well, I appreciate at least that there is no name-calling or bullying or threats," she added hopefully, "or silly retaliations. Thank you for being"—*What?* she wondered—"gracious, of sorts."

"I don't know where you got the idea that I'm going to be gracious." He stared humorlessly at her. While being as gracious as a man could be under the circumstances, all but heroic in fact, from cutting himself to draping her clothes around his room.

Louise said, "Well, thank you for your candor then. And your gentlemanly regard for my wishes."

He made an indignant grunt. "Listen, dear"— *écoute, chérie*—"don't thank me for what neither one of us is sure you're going to have. Now, get out of here, before my 'gentlemanly regard,' as you call it, is shown to be what it is: salvaged pride—that might insist at any moment on having something, anything to breathe a little life back into it."

Charles was up all night, finally settling out on his bedroom balcony, where he stared at the moonlit balcony across the courtyard, the balcony of the bedroom that would become his wife's tomorrow. The two rooms were at right angles, separated internally by the sitting room, externally by a courtyard with a white oak, a huge jasmine vine wedged into the niche at the bend in the building.

He sat outside in the September night air, wearing trousers and a long frock coat and nothing else, his chest cold, but he was too lazy or moody or something to get up and get enough clothes to make himself comfortable. With his bare heels balanced on the railing, he rocked back on two chair legs as he tossed small oblong acorns, windfall from an overhead branch: seeing how many he could get to hit the closed-up window boards of the room across the courtyard.

Grand, Charles, he told himself. *Thwap,* a hit. Married ten hours and separated already. God, even his parents had lasted longer than this. *Thwap, thwap.* And so clever of you to tell her advice more or less culled from the Kama Sutra. *Wait until a woman has enough interest. . . .* Not only, this way, did it become a neat, backhand slap of his face, but it also made his wife sound well-versed in quasi-intellectual erotica. Maybe next time a dirty verse or two of "Will You Come Up to Limerick?"

He glanced back into his dark bedroom again, toward the bed, and, as each time before, his chest constricted as if the blood in his heart were suddenly turning to lead. He was going to have to mess the bed linens up more than they were. But not yet. He couldn't imagine doing this in any way other than he'd intended, not now, not alone. Not a further ruse.

He was tired of games.

He felt estranged, not only from Louise, but from himself: Who was this man who apologized for touching a woman he adored, then threw her dinner on her? Who couldn't even use her name, a name he was so fond of, because—the coward—it sounded, he realized, exactly in French as it did in English. *Louise, Louise, Louise, Louise.* (If she didn't recognize who said it the first time she heard it, she would when he lost control of the beautiful sound and repeated it endlessly.) *Dear God,* he thought, *I even smell like someone else*—different soap, different *eau de cologne,* all for fear she would sniff out his duplicity. Different, different, different . . .

When all he wanted was for things to be the same.

Well, *merde de merde,* you stupid bastard. Tell her. Walk into the sitting room now, shake her awake, and tell her you're the one. *I am your lover from the ship.*

Except Charles couldn't. And it wasn't simply that he didn't want to tell a prideful young woman that he had deceived her, not anymore. A new—and more monstrous—fear had loomed up. The joke of having her awaken to find a monster in her bed had taken on the proportion of a nightmare. If she recoiled so dramatically—into another part of the house—when he only tried to kiss her, what appalled, shuddering reaction might he have to face if she realized . . . well, all the places he had already been, all the particular locales he had already kissed?

No. He had died a thousand deaths when she had begun to question him tonight about his English and the ship. For he simply could not have borne the sight of her disgust at knowing he had touched her, had already pressed his weight upon her and spent himself—relinquished body, mind, and possibly heart—into the sweet and scornful, soft and iron-willed, not-so-maidenly contradiction called Louise. . . .

Part 3

The Beast

Come, my languid, sullen beast,
Come lie upon my heart;
I want to plunge my trembling fingers
Into the thick tangle of your mane.
I want to bury my aching head
In the heavy perfume of your skirts . . .

I want to sleep in a drowsiness
*   as sweet as death.*
There I will spread my unrepentant kisses
Over your skin as smooth and lustrous
*   as copper.*
For nothing swallows my sobs
Like the gulping abyss of your bed:
Oblivion lives in your mouth

And rivers of forgetfulness flow
*   from between your lips. . . .*

Charles Baudelaire
33 of Les Fleurs du Mal
DuJauc translation
Pease Press, London, 1889

Chapter 20

Charles told himself, he had leapt off the starting block ahead of the gun. He knew Louise and was ready to begin where they'd left off, which sexually included rushing into the dark with her, stripping them both down, throwing her—flinging her literally through the air—onto the bed, then leaping on top of her. Yet to her, he was a stranger, a stranger rushing her like a randy adolescent. *Fool, fool, fool. Slow down. She is not entirely without grounds for her displeasure.*

He was a stranger, an ugly stranger—

And here his reasoning stumbled. His vanity hated to admit that he was anything other than fabulous to look upon. *Ugly. Repulsive. Horrifying.* He shuddered at these words. Yet he could not completely face his banishment from Louise's bed without them. Snarling, dragging his heels through the emotions these stirred, he owned up. In a limited way. In time she would see how handsome he was, once she developed some discernment for the finer attributes of men.

So. What he needed to do, he decided, was cultivate her a little. He would start from scratch and stop making unwarranted assumptions based on a history she didn't know they shared. He must behave as what he was to her: an odd looking man she didn't know very well. The point was, he knew *her.* He knew how to woo her. He knew how she thought, what she liked.

257

When Charles came downstairs that morning, he looked for the pearls he had failed to give Louise the night before. They weren't on the sideboard where he had left them. They had been cleaned up. He would have asked the housekeeper what had become of them, except at that particular moment he was too ashamed. She was there in the dining room with the maid, both women on their hands and knees, washing and clucking over the carpet.

Then the business of the day kicked in with all the grace of a motorcar backfiring, then shimmying to life—Tino came in with the dogs he had housed with his family overnight. Charles's own dogs, two French pointers, did laps about the front salon and dining room, then up the stairs to the bedrooms, while Louise's dog whined fearfully from all the excitement and peed on the floor. Chaos. Which Charles intended to leave behind him. He stole a baguette of bread from the breakfast table, biting the elbow off as he took it with him out the door. He wanted to arrive early at the greenhouse, so he could fuss with Maxime over the newly grafted jasmine.

In the driveway, however, he heard Louise calling her dog. She was outside on the west terrace. Charles immediately veered.

The dog had gone out the back door. Charles could hear him as he ducked under the arching passage through six feet of stone wall, then walked out into the sun. The dog immediately noticed him and changed course. He came running toward Charles, who bent onto one knee, holding his bread in the air. The puppy leapt into his arm, enthusiastically licking his fresh-shaven face. Louise, in the center of the open courtyard, stood up.

She angled her head, looking at the two of them, then frowned. "Well," she said. "He'll leave me and the bacon I brought him from breakfast just so as to get dog hair all over your trousers." She was in her dressing gown, a thick, nubby thing of purple with a raised collar and long lapel, the whole sealed up with buttons and sash. She lifted the lapels up, holding it and her arms against her, the gown covering her from jaw bone to knuckles to ankles. Her blond hair lay over this, still in a braid, though mussed from sleep.

Charles picked the puppy up and carried him over to her, sitting both himself and the dog at her feet. She folded herself down over her own knees as she nested into the thick layers of nightgown and wrap—her nightgown promised to be prettier, a froth of lavender lace that showed where the purple knit opened in front.

Charles offered her bread. She declined with a shake of her head. He pitched pieces to the dog, he and she petting the soft, fluffy fur. It was one of Charles's best ruses. The two of them sat there for a few minutes, their hands sliding together, his stroking hers, hers bumping his, as they conjointly pleased the puppy. The dog rolled over, offering his belly for a rub. *Oh, yes,* Charles thought, *clever fellow.* Louise accommodated him, scratching the spread between his ribs. Charles took the rise of his chest, the two territories colliding delightfully.

The west patio was nice this time of day. Cool, shaded by the house all the way out to the sundial in the middle. A quasi-garden of brambles and trees lined the perimeter, the foliage low to the south so as not to block the view to the sea. There were a few benches. It was a place for sunning or just sitting and staring across a few kilometers of France to the Mediterranean.

In the middle of this, at the edge of the sun, Louise smiled over the puppy's head and announced, "I've thought of a wonderful name for him."

"I thought he already had a name: the Bear."

"No, that is just what I call him. Doesn't he look more like a baby polar bear than a dog?"

"A little," Charles said. He liked the dog, its fuzzy, dirty-white fur, its floppy ears turning golden. He was funny, not at all like Charles's pair of pointers here or the hounds and mastiffs he had elsewhere. The Bear slept flat on his stomach, paws out, even his rear legs flat to the floor. In truth, he looked more like a bear rug than anything.

"He used to look more so," she said. "But he's growing up."

"How old is he?" He was starting to get leggy, rangy.

"Three or four months, I guess. And in need of a regular dog name."

"So what is it?"

"Charlemagne," Louise announced proudly.

Charles frowned. "Don't you think that will be confusing? I mean, you would probably call him Charle"—the same pronunciation as his name—"on occasion."

"Sometimes maybe."

"No." God, she would name the world after him, if she could, call everyone, everything *Charles*. "I would never know whether you were calling me or the dog." Except that she would say the dog's name perhaps more dearly.

She looked pensive, as if she hadn't thought about calling for *him,* about wanting Charles by name. Her brow creased. Then she shrugged. "Don't be silly. Families have members named the same all the time: Think of all the sons named after their fathers."

"Well, I'm not his father."

She frowned. She hadn't been making this connection.

Lord! he realized. It wasn't *him* she was naming the dog after. It was the goddamned man on the ship. Which was him, of course. In a circular way he could barely follow anymore.

He stood up, dusting his pants, aggravated again.

Oh, fine, Charles told himself. *You are so put out, so greedy for this woman, you are now jealous of yourself. And a dog.*

"No," he said adamantly. "You may not have my name for your dog." He thought to add as he straightened his coat, "Nor will we name any of our sons Charles." It was like one's wife trying to name a baby after her lover. "They shall all have their own particular names."

He huffed off, muttering to himself, "If we ever get to the particular process that makes them, that is."

Louise remembered, two weeks ago, her mother saying, "Isn't it charming?" By "it," meaning Nice, the Riviera, Provence, France. "Isn't it the most delightful spot on earth? Isn't he the warmest, most elegant man you've ever met? Isn't his uncle priceless?" Louise's parents fully expected her to be mad for Charles Harcourt and for France itself, both of which they granted a kind of grace through translation. Perfectly vapid things said in French her mother would wave away as being much deeper or more insightful or more poetic "if we only understood all the nuances." She accepted the idiosyncratic, often bizarre French way of managing as innovation, when the same thing in New York she would have dismissed as makeshift and inferior.

In fairness, of course, almost *nothing* conformed to what they were used to exactly. The house in Grasse, for instance, had a new bathroom that contained no toilet. The toilet was in a separate room down the hall called the W.C., the water closet, after the British nomenclature (which didn't seem very French at all). Louise could not figure out the use of the other thing next to the tub, something called a bidet.

In general, there was less gadgetry, though, not more. And what gadgetry there was had a wholly different face. The French seemed partial to buttons and gewgaws on things. There was a huge contraption in the basement of the house with dials and switches and coils of piping that led to another machine-ish looking gadget that connected to a boilerlike container with a lid bolted down by a dozen huge wing nuts. The whole display was nothing more than a water heater, as it turned out. One switched it on half an hour before a bath; one planned one's hot water— having it was not a given. Louise was warned by Uncle Tino of "waste" that morning as he showed her how to conserve hot water like everyone else, by operating the "simple" piece of basement machinery.

The word *simple* did not translate directly. He pointed and gesticulated as he explained, "You turn this dial here and push this button there, while you monitor this gauge, watching the needle to see how fast it goes up. If it gets to here, shut the whole thing down and stand back; call for help."

She suspected Uncle Tino of wanting to blow her up. "Is it dangerous?"

"But no," he said, "it is a fine thing." He meant, But yes. He accepted the dangers of his nephew's hot-water heater as normal concession to practicality.

Louise stared at the contraption, wondering how much she was going to like cold baths. "Is this a common piece of equipment?"

"Oh, yes, many neighbors have one just like it. A local man makes and installs them. They are quite good."

"Wouldn't it have been smarter to send for one from Paris."

Uncle Tino's eyes widened. "Paris? Do you know how much such a thing would cost? They take advantage"—milk you like a cow, he said—"in Paris."

"But doesn't it break a lot, with so many parts?"

"Of course, it breaks." Then he winked and said, as if it were an unconsidered advantage she had stupidly missed: "But the fellow is right here in town who can fix it." He added, "Not like some *Parisieng*"—he used a disgusted nasal—"who is too busy eating croissants to fix anything."

Lah-de-dah, she thought, a Frenchman who smugly hated the French.

Uncle Tino, who was not actually her husband's uncle but rather a cousin somewhere several times removed, did not stand on ceremony. He hated, equally and democratically, Parisians as much as he hated debutantes from New York who "stayed in their nightclothes till eight in the morning, then took an hour and a half to get dressed."

With total irreverence, he told her that he couldn't understand why a woman as pretty as she should spend an hour and a half arranging herself. He wasn't being mean. He wasn't angry. And he certainly wasn't attempting to flatter. It was merely an observation offered with gloomy resign, part of the sad state of the world, or that portion of it not run by Tino Harcourt himself.

With the prince attending to business, this glum relative was the man with whom Louise was to spend her first day of married life. He had been assigned the duty of guiding her through the house, of explaining its running and maintenance, and suggesting what part she might play in this. She could do as little or as much as she wished. Tino had also been given the task of opening up the south bedroom. With a lot of *là-là*ing and head-shaking disapproval, he set the maid and housekeeper to making it habitable.

After griping over her manner of naming her dog, Charles Harcourt had left. He apparently came through at lunch again, but she missed him when Tino took her to the house of a seamstress who made draperies. When she got back, Charles had "gone to the factory."

By late afternoon, when Tino gave her the choice of

his helping her to unpack or his taking her to the factory laboratory where Charles was working, Louise asked instantly, "Would you stay with me?"

"Only if you need me. Charles can bring you home."

"I don't need you," she said brightly, "and I'll be ready in five minutes."

The factory was plain and square and brown, a two-story edifice that covered more than a square block. It was a typical product of industry, dingy but practical. Louise stopped on her way to the front door to look through a dirty window. She spied women inside a long room seated at large tables, the surfaces piled with flowers—no, just the petals and some sort of frames. The women were sorting the flowers or cleaning them or something. Young men pushed wicker baskets of more petals, rose petals, she thought; they were pink. The boys dumped these into various mounds about the floor. At one place, the spartan room was waist-deep in pink petals. It was rather pretty and strange, the mechanized taking of fragrance from nature.

Charles was in a laboratory in back, a place of copper tubing and percolating vials. He was just putting on his frock coat as they came in. And here Louise was brought up short by a smell. Jasmine. The room reeked of it, in a generic sense, the way a small room—though this long, white room was by no means small—could be overpowered by a woman wearing too much perfume. It didn't matter what kind; too much was too much.

As he buttoned his coat, Charles said, "I was just leaving for the fields. Maxime says we have a fungus on the lavender on the west-most plat. I thought I should take a look before the sun goes down."

"I should like to go with you," Louise offered immediately.

"The carriage can't make it. I have to take a horse."

"I can ride."

"We have no side saddle."

"I can tuck up my skirt and ride astride. I have done it before."

Her husband glanced at Tino. He looked at her. "Are you good enough to keep up a canter or gallop? It's fairly straight across a plateau."

"I'm sure I can."

And she was free of Tino, the king of sentimental pessimism, at least for the rest of the afternoon.

It was unexpected to realize she preferred Charles Harcourt's company not just to Tino's, but to anyone else's she had so far met in France. Yet she did. She was comfortable with him. Even today, after his and her tangle last night. Even though they said nothing, just rode like the blazes. The wind blew in Louise's face, making her eyes tear. The pace, the horse knocked the breath out of her. Yet she loved their ride across the plane that spread out just below the south hills of Grasse.

Her husband flew on his horse like he was a part of it—a centaur intent on getting to where they were going before the light faded. Though she kept up, barely, he was by far a better rider than she. He rode, of course, with his good side to her. She wanted to laugh. Still, it was nice to admire him from a distance and at some speed. He looked almost . . . dashing with his wild hair caught in the wind, shining black, his long, dark coat flapping over his legs.

Louise was out of breath when they finally pulled up over a small rise and looked down into a valley of bright purple.

Lavender. In full, profuse bloom. It ran in rows, spreading in every direction out to the horizon.

They walked the horses down a steep bank, at the

bottom of which he dismounted. "Be careful," he said as he offered his hands up to help her from the saddle. "The hives are just over there."

Bees. Louise could hear a faint, irritable buzz as she swung her leg around. "Are they dangerous?"

"Not at all. Unless you swat at them or let them get in your clothes."

Then she placed her hands on Charles's shoulders and dropped into his grasp. He caught her up against him, letting her slide down his body—that had all the give of a mountainside—as nonchalant as you please. She pushed away when he released her, feeling maneuvered, annoyed, as if the bees buzzed in her stomach.

They tied the horses under a low tree and walked down into the lavender, with Charles Harcourt still steering her, necessarily, by the elbow. The last thirty yards were rocky and sloping. She had meant to help *him:* He was one who had retrieved a walking stick from under a strap in his saddle. Yet she was the one having trouble. He would whip the cane up under his arm or brace both of their weights against it as he offered assistance.

What became obvious was that he was used to handling a woman. By the elbow, by the waist, by her fingers, then letting go with a light stabilizing brush of her back as Louise traversed level ground for half a dozen paces. This simple, physical facility, the way he paired himself with her balance, did not jibe with her perceptions of him.

What was it he said last night? That he, his shirt, something had been ruined for love? Louise wondered what he could possibly know about the subject. Certainly, his taste in women was suspect, given that his last woman was roughly as easy to endure as stomach poisoning. Women. It occurred to Louise that there had been women. Despite her husband's drawbacks, it was not out of the realm of possibility that he frequently attracted the females he wanted. She glanced sideways at him, surreptitiously watching his gamboling, companionable progress.

She was surprised anew each time she realized how strangely appealing he was. *Beau-laid,* the French called it. Handsome-ugly, alluring in the way that charmed against one's will. In a way that played upon conflict, opposition, something that Charles Harcourt felt himself: He was proud; he was hostile to his own appearance. He dressed it up, calling it to notice, while he carried his massive frame—so restrained and overtly polite—in a state of tension, poised between a complex and developed gallantry and a self-aware rage against fate.

The result was a kind of energy, dark and edgy, held in check. Brutish. Broodish. The sort that could make women faint. Louise suddenly understood what Mrs. Montebello was all about, her barbs and jealousies. Louise didn't share her appetite but she could appreciate her taste.

At her side, this contradictory man told her, "The most abundant and prolific lavender grows near Nîmes, but I don't use much lavender, so this is fine for my purposes."

Louise raised her head. She had so been concentrating on the terrain of their progress, she had not realized where it had taken them. They had walked down into the lavender. And she could not imagine anything more abundant or flowering than the field that stood on all sides.

Symmetrical row upon row of gray-green shrub sprouted straight, bright purple stalks. Oh, it was wonderful, more wonderful than she could have ever imagined. The sun was low but bright, lighting up rolling rows of purple, knee high, like a sea of it. The lavender grew so uniform, it looked combed. Its stalks grew long-spiked, the spikes naked but for a dense growth of small purple flowers, delicate little blos-

soms that were a pale violet outside, a deep royal
purple within. The grayish-green foliage, long and
thin, curled where the new growth shot forth.

Louise walked into this, enrapt. Between bushy
plants, there was just enough room for a woman in a
narrow dress. She held this dress up somewhat
immodestly—the terrain was stony. Rocks moved
underfoot. She had to be mindful where she set her
feet or risk turning an ankle. Yet it was all so pretty:
bright, colorful. As she made her way deeply into the
rows, the air grew fragrant with clean, floral scent and,
everywhere, buzzed with the sound of insects turning
this to honey.

She watched Charles bend to uproot a weed from
their path—the occasional row was broken up by
weeds that had gotten the upper hand, bushes themselves here and there. Louise walked behind him, up
and down this breathlessly pretty flush of purple in
the midst of arid land the color of straw.

They finally paused at a plant that wasn't blooming
as much as the rest, and her husband squatted. He
pulled a piece of it off, looked at it, then pushed the
bushy branches back and dug at its base for a moment. "Damn it. We had this last year, and here it is
again with the damn rainy season coming."

"Your fungus?"

"Mine, yes. Unfortunately. Though I would like to
give someone else a turn. I'm sick of"—he said a
Latin name she missed.

They began moving again. Louise decided she had
married a kind of gentleman farmer, who cultivated
and harvested plant extract, which made him a chem-
ist of sorts, too, she supposed. Then he turned out to
be a botanist as well.

"Look," he said. He stripped a handful of lavender
off its stalk and offered it out on his palm. He looked
down, engrossed by his own flowers. "See?" He lowered his hand to her, then used the tip of his finger to

manipulate a small single blossom. "Here is the perfume of the plant. Every little flower, its top and its base, is covered in starlike hairs, and here—" He delicately dissected the flower with his nail. "See the shine? Oil glands are imbedded among these. This oil is what I distill."

He took her hand, crushing the flowers into it, against her open palm. "Smell," he commanded.

She did. It was divinely fresh and clear and sweet. He stroked her hand a minute longer, till she took it back. Her hand tingled where he had pressed the lavender. Rubbing it on her skirt, she looked at him, the ferocious-faced man with a love of flowers.

He continued. "English lavender commands a higher price, but I prefer this. The English stuff is sterile, propagated by slips and root division; no seeds. Mine"—he drew his loose fist lovingly up a whippy purple stalk— "is wild. It seeds itself in rocks. And I can smell the difference. It's less forced, more savage . . ." He said *sauvage,* which could have meant *wild-growing* again, but this didn't seem to be what he was saying. "More potent," he said and laughed. "In every sense."

An open smile. His face lit, bad eye and all. It was a fine smile, though crooked, displaying white, slightly uneven teeth. It was warm, direct, like the Provençal sun.

Louise was charmed by the sight, disturbed by the man. He liked her. He treated her well. And she wasn't sure why. He liked her even after last night, which seemed almost a brand of black magic itself, considering how impossible she had made it for him to have what he wanted.

Before they left, he pressed more lavender into her hand, saying, "The ancients used it for their baths. Some think the name comes from the old Latin, *lavare,* to wash. Here. We will have a handful for your bath tonight." Stooping, he plucked whole stalks, so fragrant, bright, pretty. He made a regular bouquet.

"Just use the flowers, though, for the sweetest scent. Pull them off, drop them into your tub of warm water, let them brew a minute, then climb in and brew with them." He handed these over, making another wry, slanting grin. "Think of me as they float around you."

This wasn't quite the way it worked. Instead, that evening, Charles heard the water run and thought of *her:* naked with tiny purple flowers bumping into her smooth, white body, a fragrant steam rising in his new and shiny bathroom, the dampness pulling down her hair. *Ooh là là.* He lay there down the hall from this, more aroused with each splash of water, and contemplated solitary sexual release. He decided, rather, to get up and go down the hall.

He knocked on the bathroom door. "May I come in?"

He heard her slosh of surprise. "Well— Well, no," she said.

"I want to come in, Lou—Lulu." A barrier surmounted. By God, he would use this name rather than have nothing, no handle, no way to take hold of familiarity.

More splashing. He thought he heard her get out. Rushing to lock the door, in all likelihood.

He opened it. She was pulling a wrap around her. He saw a snowy-white flash, the upward curve of breast, this fleeting glimpse covered immediately with a thick layer of woolly knit. Her purple dressing gown.

He said, "What I do is more beautiful than what I am. Beauty is necessary to our lives. It's not a luxury. You shouldn't hate being beautiful."

"Excuse me?"

"You bristled last night, I think, because I said you were beautiful. One of the reasons at least. But you are. You should enjoy it. The way you enjoyed the lavender today."

She laughed as she snugged the sash of the gown tight. "You came in here to talk to me about this?"

"No, I came in here to see you naked, but since you were quicker than I was, I'm willing to see if I can *talk* you out of that dressing gown."

She laughed again, slightly giddy this time, and tried to push past him. He moved and blocked her exit.

Then—instinct, frustration, he couldn't honestly say what made him do it, anger maybe: He bent, grabbing her round the buttocks. With a little *ooph* of surprise and a twisting kick of resistance, she folded over her shoulder. He carried her forward, wrap and all, breaking her fall just enough as she hit the water. His shirtsleeves got soaked, but it was worth it watching her go under, legs flailing, hands grasping at him, head and hair completely submerged for a moment. She came up with a sputter, her robe bleeding purple in his white claw-foot bathtub.

Spitting water, she shrieked, "Are you insane?" Her hair, which she had simply tied into a knot, leaned wetly, a dropping weight that unspiraled. It pooled around her purple shoulders.

Then sucked up against her as she got her legs under her. She might have leapt out, but as she rose her wrapper's laden weight began to pull it open. She sunk down into the water again and wrenched the soggy thing closed about her torso. One end secure, the other opened about her legs like the slow-motion parting of seaweed. A curtain coming up on a show. Charles stared at her streamline calves beneath ever-more darkening water—her robe ran fantastically, like some wet and sagging monster hemorrhaging violet blood. He stared through this water, at her slender ankles, her shapely feet with their high arch of bone, these white feet beneath lavender blossoms, bruised dark from the heat of her bath, afloat in water the transparent color of plums.

She was stammering at him. "You—you—" Her French vocabulary was deficient in rude expletives.

He tried to help, suggesting, "Cretin, troglodyte, bastard."

"Whore's son."

"Well!" he said by way of surprised celebration, *ouais!* "That's damned advanced. And so much better than your usual prissy discourse."

She made a tight mouth and managed to sit around, become stable. Lifting a soggy arm, she scowled and said, "You could have drowned me."

"Tu, tu. Use it," he said, encouraging the intimate verb construction. The language used between lovers and friends.

"I don't know those conjugations. My instructor thought they were too intimate."

"Learn them. They're spelled differently, but you pronounce them the same as the 'I' conjugations. That's what they mean: 'you' and 'I' are close, the same." He took a breath. "Lulu—" In French, her name meant *cute, darling,* as with a dimpled child or tiny, fluffy dog. He said it again, "Lulu," then, "look at me." It was spontaneous: He began to unfasten the buttons of his shirt.

"Charles—" Her lovely eyes widened as far as they were capable—an upward flap of heavy lashes as thick as the wings of a gold bird.

He braved her expression and kept unbuttoning.

His shirt gaped. He crossed his arms, grabbing two handfuls of shirttail, and lifted the damned shirt up and over his head, insisting, "Look."

She turned her face to the wall. "Put your shirt on."

"No." He brought his undershirt up over his head, dropped it onto the floor, then began on the buttons at the fly of his trousers. "Look at me. I am not such a poor specimen overall."

"Charles—" She brought her gaze around again, lifting those lashes once more in what seemed for the life of him to be a sly glimpse. Then her own behavior made her blush—an unusual occurrence. He had never seen her cheeks pink before.

He felt a surprising charge as Louise turned a deep, rosy red that vied in intensity with the water. Enough of a thrill that when he dropped his trousers, kicked them aside, and stood there in his underdrawers, the front of them lifted slightly. In so far as he could, he ignored the sensation, which she did not. Her eyes settled there, then glanced away. He said, "Look at me. Am I such a repulsive fellow as all that?"

She fixed her gaze down into her bathwater. "No," she murmured. She made a slight shiver; he couldn't decide if this was good or bad. She said, "You are a fine"—she hesitated—"mature man."

He frowned. "I am not old."

"No." She shook her downcast head. "You are—developed. Strapping."

"Then get out of that water and let me touch you, at least hold you."

"Charles, that's not it. I—I feel funny—"

"Funny how?"

"I can't explain it."

"Don't explain it, then. Get out of that tub or I'm coming in. One or the other."

Her eyes came up, open again, her mouth too, a little round pooch of lips, genuine prohibition. "No-o. No, no—"

He stepped in, one foot—she drew her legs together—then with a single *ga-lumff*ing splash, the other. He straddled her knees, then sat down, butt first, into the warm water at her feet. She drew her legs up to her chest and circled her arms around them.

Charles slid down to settle armpit deep—he'd displaced the water almost up to her shoulders—in a tubful of steamed lavender, purple water, and rattled woman, the scent of all three rising off the violet surface in visible rolls of vapor, mingling up his nostrils. His flowers . . . her soap . . . her soaking robe smelling faintly of the perfume she wore, jasmine . . . none of this as powerful for him as the sweet eddying perfume of Louise.

Who scooted back as far as she could, bringing her wet dressing gown, dripping and slogging-wet, up around her chin. Like this, wrapped in her own arms and her clutched wrap, Louise stared at the man at the other end of the bathtub.

A man with the build of Poseidon. And the face of— She groaned inwardly. The worst part of Charles Harcourt's face was the nice half. The alert, faintly defensive blue eye. The square jaw, bony, a muscle that tensed just in front of his ear. A thin, vaguely aquiline nose, not handsome exactly; bladed, sharp, stirring. Aggressive. He was that. Here he was in her tub.

Provoking a confrontation: He stretched his leg, hooking his foot between her ankles, trying to pull her leg out, to drag her knee out from under her chin. They had a small battle of feet. His wanted to unbend her. Louise held to a ball. The prince in her tub conceded the battle, then all but claimed the war. He pulled his feet back and, with a suck of water, lifted himself up on his arms, on the rim of the bathtub, to come up over her knees. Louise leaned back, broke hold of her legs, managed a shin on his chest. Lord, his chest. It was warm and hard and as furred as a beast's from the forest; it rippled outright with the muscle of a Hun.

With this chest, he pressed her bent leg forward till she made a face. "That pinches."

He didn't smile or apologize or back off. He said, "Move it."

Then he released the pressure an inch or so, took hold of her ankle, and pulled her leg from between them—to the other side of his body so that when he *ka-plosh*ed himself down, not only did his weight slosh water over the tub rim, it dropped right where he wanted: between her outstretched legs.

"Happy now?" Louise asked into his face. She pursed her lips.

"No," he said. "I'm miserable, to tell you the truth." Then with hardly more than taking a breath, he said, "Bear up, darling. I'm going to kiss you."

When she pursed her mouth tighter, he let out an exasperated breath, one she felt across her lips and cheek.

"Come on," he said. He mugged a face. "I'm strapping, remember? And your effing husband"— the French word began with *F;* she didn't know it, nor, she suspected, did she want to. "See if you can put up with my mouth on yours for thirty seconds, would you? It's only a kiss."

She made a disputing twist of her mouth. "In a tubful of water, lying on top of me in your wet underdrawers."

He actually smiled, a small curving line.

She turned her head the first time, the mistress of evasion. His mouth caught her cheek. He sighed, backed off. She didn't know what he was thinking, where he was getting the persistence when she could have listed a dozen other fellows she had stopped way short of anything like this.

The determined Charles Harcourt descended again, this time intentionally kissing her cheek in a path toward her ear, a damp trail of warm lips to where her jaw met her neck. It sent ghostlike prickles of gooseflesh up her arms, down her spine.

Oh, God, Charles, her Charles. He was suddenly there in the damned bathtub with them. How she missed him. *Will you be faithful once you're married?* Yes—who would have thought?—to you, my sweet pasha.

"Come on," said the real, robust Charles above her. He was massive. She couldn't see the ceiling or a good portion of the wall. He told her, "You're going to be as wrinkled as a prune before you get up from here. Kiss me, Lulu. Try it. Give me half a chance, will you?"

Lulu. When had he dropped the *madame* and *mademoiselle* and *my dear* that had been so serviceably formal for the last two and a half weeks?

He went after the kiss again, rather poised about the whole business. Not timid, not shy. His thumb found her lips, brushed across them, as he kissed the corner of her mouth. She shivered in the warm water, part melting pleasure, part anxiety—horrible, sharp, rising. He rolled her lower lip down with his thumb, opening her mouth. His nail ticked across her teeth, an intentional tap telling her to open them. He brought his mouth close, tongued the inside of her rolled lower lip.

What a sensation. It was like being wooed by something mythic. A titan. A dragon. His hand slid round the back of her head and pulled her face into his. Dry-mouthed, he pressed his lips to hers. Then he twisted his head, opened his jaw, pressing hers apart with it, and pushed his way past her teeth, his tongue deep inside her mouth.

The carnal promise of her husband, Charles Harcourt, the strange and ugly Prince of Nothing blew through her like a hot Goliathan breath.

He kissed her mouth, teeth, tongue, and lips. She felt her robe slacken, along with her fists that held it. It floated loosely away from her body, a small drift in the tepid bath. The shape of the tub, her position limited where he could put his breadth and length. She could feel him adjusting, struggling slightly, misplaced against the inside of her thigh, thick and rigid—it was a whole lot more than half a chance he wanted. Desire spun around and lifted her up into it. A languor took hold, the delicious, drugged feeling of sexual intention unfolding. As with Charles.

Charles and Charles.

The two men merged. Louise turned her head, emitting a soft groan—not entirely one of pleasure: of confusion, loss, frustration. The present Charles, her husband, slid his leg down hers as he repositioned himself more flatly on top of her.

Louise closed her eyes. Darkness. Her head swam in erotic vertigo, while her muscles grew lax, as heavy to move as if she were deep under water. The bath water lapped against the tub. And she was suddenly on a tilted ship. . . . She knew the feel, so precisely, of her Charles entering her body. His strength. The heavy substance of him as he pushed himself inside her. The rhythm of his breathing. Fantasy. He wasn't here. The man who was stroked his thumb across her lip again, the crevice of her closed mouth, encouraging her to open it, turn back toward him. *What a monstrous lust*—she remembered saying this, spinning in the dark, kissing her Charles of the Dark Ship deep within his mouth—*I feel as though it could break me in two.*

Her pasha and not her pasha . . . He was here; he was not. This all got tangled up in a fear of her own duality: one woman on the ship, another one here, cooler, more distant. . . . She had left a freer piece of herself back there on the ocean, one she couldn't find again yet she didn't dare lose. Louise felt broken in half indeed. Torn. Split. Drawn and quartered. Not enough anywhere. *Not enough.* Separated from a man, an experience, an impetus she wanted . . . fragmented . . .

She caught her breath, swallowing a sob before it broke the surface of expression. She didn't cry. She never cried.

"Louise . . ."

She was hallucinating. Now the voice above her even sounded like his, the mindless way he'd breathed her name sometimes into the dark. She opened her eyes dimly—and saw her husband, his ear as he kissed her neck. His mouth on her skin was warm, strong, sucking. So hungry he was going to leave marks. Had he said her name? Right name. Right place at the base of her jaw. Wrong man.

Fidelity, she thought. Yes, constancy. She hated affairs. She would never have another. She didn't want this one. "Charles—" She tried to push the man on top of her back.

After two or three good shoves, he said, "What? What is it?" His breath rasped. "What, for God's sake?"

She tensed her fists. She was going to cry. God, she was going to cry like a reprimanded child. She pinched her eyes closed.

Charles Harcourt grew still. After a moment, he said, "Look at me." His mantra tonight. *Look at me.*

She opened her eyes, slits. And what she saw on his strange face was surprising: She saw concern. There was frustration as well, even a note of anger. But the other was unmistakable: Charles Harcourt looked at her with a great and amazing kindness, mature, patient, the sort of goodness that didn't deny more selfish feelings but somehow transcended them. An extraordinary man, she thought. She bit her lips together. She could be kind too. She closed her eyes and murmured, "Go on." Let him. "Do what you want." She tried to relax.

He was still. He did nothing. He said, not meanly yet faintly exasperated, "Louise, if I had wanted to do this alone, I could have stayed in my bedroom and not had to deal with all your wet nonsense. What's wrong?"

She leaned her head back on the bathtub. It hit with a clonk. "Oh, Charles," she said. She let out a long, sighing groan. "There was this man. You remind me of him." Not the nicest position—under him in a bathtub—in which to tell a husband this. The connotations were obvious.

The miracle, however, was that this incredible soul rolled with it. He nuzzled her cheek. "That's all?"

"Yes."

"Well, he was a man you liked, I hope."

The amazing French, her mother had said. Yes, most tolerant. "Indeed," she answered. "I adored him." She needed to tell someone, and the man she had married—oh, how right her dear parents had been—was turning out to be one of the nicest human beings she had ever met. She told him, "He's dead."

Her husband raised up slightly, straightening his elbows. "Dead?"

"Yes, he, well—well, he sort of died. Suddenly."

Stillness. He didn't know what to say. Small wonder.

She added, "I think I am grieving for him. I think about him a lot." She ventured to open her eyes more fully.

His face looked stunned. He could barely speak. He whispered, as if truly aggrieved himself, "Oh, dear Lord." He shook his head as he stared into her face, a small back-and-forth no that seemed to wish he could explain away this profound absence she felt.

And all her husband's unbelievable empathy, sympathy, his patience and goodness and concern came crashing down on top of her.

The next sob wouldn't swallow. Louise half choked on it. Then she let out a big, blubbering wail and threw her arms about the neck of this very decent fellow. She cried for a long, horribly embarrassing time—a good ten or twelve seconds of throat-constricting, belly-buckling sorrow, then she turned in the water—he had backed off as if to assess and wonder at her sorrow. She tried to struggle to her feet. She slipped. Her legs were rubber. The robe fell open.

All at once she felt the tub, the floor itself lift away. Her stomach dropped from the swift scoop of arms that came up under her, one sturdy arm under her

knees, another under her back, hoisting her, then
rolling her up against a solid shoulder. High over the
tub, Louise turned her face into the wet hair of her
husband's chest, the sound of water, like a waterfall,
filling the bathroom, running, pouring, dripping. Her
robe pulled open under the weight of its own wetness.
It bent her ankles down, turning her feet awkwardly,
then this burden slid off. She was naked briefly, then a
towel hit her, nesting soft and dry against her belly.

There was movement, what she recognized after a
few moments as the slightly off-tempo rhythm of her
husband's walking; he carried her. He said nothing.
She couldn't speak and was glad.

For she would only have screamed out the rest:
Duality be hanged. Fidelity, indeed. She was being
faithful to a scoundrel with whom she had been
completely herself, from whom she had held nothing
back save the obstacle of her beauty. And what had he
done? He had left her. After five days. He wasn't
coming back. He wasn't coming to get her. He didn't
care where she was. He was gone. Without so much as
a good-bye or thank-you or backward glance.

Damn him anyway, the jackass deserved to be dead.

Charles took Louise to her bedroom where he lay
her down on her bed. She seemed small where she lay
upon it, not asleep, not crying, but not awake either;
moody and introverted.

Dead? He was dead? What did this mean?

How would she feel about a dead man crawling up
of his coffin to join her here? Should he tell her the
truth? Would she gasp with less revulsion now? Would
she be less angry? More welcoming? Surely, this pain
she felt was the disappointment of youth at the end of
its first love affair. *Come on, Louise,* he thought. *It
was only five days. And I didn't exactly drop dead or off
the face of the earth. We parted company. We parted*

company pleasantly, like adults. He'd left a dozen women under worse circumstances.

Yet not a one of them had been eighteen.

What had he done? What could he do to make amends? To comfort her?

Join her, Charles told himself. Comfort her like an adult. Oh, yes. And comfort yourself. He stepped back and out of his wet underdrawers, thinking this was what he was going to do. His action, however, was overly optimistic. As he kicked the wet wad of underlinen out of the way, he heard her sniffle once, a deep wet intake of breath through her nose. Then, young, healthy thing, after an equally lengthy, somewhat shaky sigh, her breathing settled into a deep and regular rhythm. She dropped off to sleep.

Charles stood there naked, bewildered.

Behind him through the sitting room and down the hall he heard the faint slap and slop of a wet dressing gown—or else his shirt or undershirt or trousers. The housekeeper had gone into the bathroom. She was *tsk*ing and wringing things out. The maid was with her, both of them cleaning up water. He and Louise had left pools on the floor.

At the next sound, though, Charles turned sharply and grimaced: whispering then giggling and tittering.

He skulked back into the sitting room, ducking into his own room via the connecting door. In his room, his consolation was a gawky yellow-white puppy. Louise's Bear greeted Charles with a mad race across the floor, then leaps of welcome up his leg. The dog's tail wagged so hard his rear feet slipped and slid on the polished wood. And, thus, Charles began to sleep other than alone: After the puppy made several pointless attempts to stretch and launch himself onto Charles's bed, Charles lifted him up. The dog went to sleep happily at Charles's shoulder, as if he were home, his fur smelling faintly of Louise's jasmine-acacia perfume.

Chapter 21

Ambergris has, over the ages, been worth as much as twice its weight in gold.

Charles Harcourt, Prince d'Harcourt
On the Nature and Uses of Ambergris

The next morning, Louise woke once, saw the day, then simply rolled over and slept until noon. Tino sent up a carping message at one point. She was supposed to be reviewing with him today the rest of the list entitled "The Princess d'Harcourt's Potential Responsibilities." As mistress of two different households, with a third somewhere in Paris, Louise was supposed to be finding her "most useful interests." With equal deference, or rather equal lack of it, she sent Tino a message back: Since he and everyone else were so blessed good at running everything, they could continue to do so. She had no desire to plan menus or meet neighbors or arrange for repairs or redecoration. At noon she got out her math books, in the margins of which she unraveled theorems till one.

She was just coming downstairs, dressed at last, as Charles, home for lunch, was about to leave again. On seeing her, he delayed in the entryway. "Lulu. Come with me. I will show you more flower fields."

Flexing her fingers over the large, round newel post, she tightened her mouth. "Why? So you can dump them and me backward into a bathtub?"

He smiled. She realized: This Charles, that Charles, she was angry at both of them.

He told her, "I wish I could say I regretted doing that last night." He shook his head, a slow, remembering back-and-forth movement; no regrets. His introspective smile drew up at its slightly crooked angle as he used his cane to brush her skirt down from where it had remained folded over on the last stair tread.

Louise stepped back from him. She was a little wary of what this fellow might think to do next. Upset tables. Women into tubs. Following them in in his underdrawers.

He drew his cane back and leaned onto it, one hand over the other atop the polished handgrip. He made a tutting sound, a French click of his tongue through rounded lips pushed forward. "Well, if you would rather spend what remains of the day with Tino—"

"Which fields are you going to?"

"Jasmine and roses, then I have to stop at the greenhouses."

Louise lifted a finger in warning. "I don't want you to think just because I'm going that I— Well, I intend to put a chair against the bathroom door next time."

He smiled politely. "That would be lovely. Your coming with me, that is. I much prefer having your company to going off by myself, and I think you will like what I show you. As to the rest, since we are giving fair notice, don't use a chair you like to hold me on the other side of any door anywhere, much less in my own house." More reasonably, he asked, "And why would you? Did I treat you badly last night?"

"No—"

"Did I do anything you didn't like?"

"Not exactly—"

"Then give me some credit, and stop roasting me on a spit."

His literal words, *roasting me on a spit*. Louise was taken aback. "I wasn't being—"

"No, of course you weren't, sweet thing. So, Your Highness, are you coming or not?"

He was being ironic. Louise didn't know what to say. No one had ever been sarcastic with her in quite his tone before. He continued to smile. He wasn't angry. He liked her fine, Miss High-and-Mighty-Not-So-Sweet-At-All.

She frowned, not sure whether to take offense or not; none seemed intended. Perhaps she was missing one of her mother's nuances here. "I'll get my wrap and a piece of cheese, if you'll wait. I haven't had, um, lunch." Or breakfast either, for that matter.

Charles Harcourt rode with a natural, loose movement, in a secure seat and with long reins. A mistral wind that took off rooftops could not have taken him out of the saddle. He was experienced, steady, seasoned, and not only as a rider. Louise, as she rode beside him, felt young in the worst sense, callow.

It was easy to blame her dissatisfaction today on a man who wasn't here to defend himself. Her caddish pasha. The bounder. "Be herself." Hah! *Be loose and let me have what I want* was more like it. She wouldn't think of him any longer. Proof: She had killed him off last night, hadn't she? She was better off without him.

Yet no amount of resolve or anger washed away her feeling of youthful foolishness. How she hated being young today; she wished she could skip right now to middle age.

She had no footing in her two-day marriage, could

find no place beside her new French husband. She couldn't see, even vaguely, a productive role for herself here. She felt like what she was: catered to, spoiled. As they rode in forced silence—hard and swift upon the plain—she nagged herself for doing nothing that anyone, including she, expected of her. Then railed inside, like the wind in her ears, for not knowing even what to expect.

Just not this. Not sleeping late and being cross and crying in the bathtub. Not this, please, God, not this.

She didn't recognize what they had come to when Charles first pulled his horse up. The land was merely green and even, the earth faintly brown where it showed in strips.

"Jasmine," he said, a little breathless, a little awed at his own huge field of bushes. There was no end to them except at the horses' feet, where the planted field began. "I own more jasmine than anything, more land planted with them, more blossoms produced, more than twice over than any other flowers." He owned seven enormous fields of jasmine by which he pieced together the largest jasmine holding in France, making him a prince of sorts, of jasmine oil. Louise's husband began to speak of an enterprise he clearly adored.

He grew and harvested other flowers for his perfumes—lavender for one, roses, as well as orange blossoms from the sour Seville orange, and acacia and mimosa. He grew six or seven of the ingredients of perfumes, while he used hundreds of different extracts in his attempts to make his own blends, including ambergris, one of the most expensive, now supplied by her father, who would retire at the end of the summer, giving the prince control over this important ingredient too. A few of Charles Harcourt's perfumes sold well enough, though he himself didn't consider any first-rate. His extracts, on the other hand, were used by the biggest perfume houses in Paris; they were premium. As far as his perfumer's enterprise went, he made his money here.

Jasmine was the most expensive essence to extract, though the fact that it grew "better between Cannes and Grasse than it grew anywhere else in the world" was of enormous help. There were too many kilometers of jasmine over too vast an area for him to take Louise down into them, to walk through them; too much to survey today. So they rode. And rode and rode. From horseback, jasmine looked dull compared with the lavender. It seemed scraggily. As with the lavender, the jasmine fields were planted in rows, but these dark, leafy bushes grew more helter-skelter. The plants were shorter than expected. The tail of Charles's horse in front of her brushed over tops of plants when he turned at the end of a row.

The roses were even more disappointing—droopy, short-stemmed, tangled, without a single open flower. What new blooms were on them were nice enough, but most every bush, roses and jasmine alike, was picked clean.

At the next jasmine field, as Charles rode through inspecting for disease, water, nutrition, he explained, "We take the flowers in the morning, when they are most fragrant. The lavender is harvested once a year: right now. You saw it at its finest. The roses bloom in cycles eight months out of the year; the jasmine only from July to October. Now, though, in August and September they are the most profuse and fragrant. These fields are full of flowers. Look." He pointed out unopen buds. "If you saw this field first thing in the morning, it would be more impressive. . . ." He grew animated and broad-gesturing as he spoke of his work, sweeping his arm out in one direction, standing up in the stirrups to point off in another. Louise envied him the absorption he found.

He told her, "This time of the year, we get very

aggressive, hire extra help, come out and scour the fields daily. We have every last flower by nine or ten in the morning." His speech branched off into Latin, *Jasminum grandiflorum . . . Jasminum officiale . . . Jasminum nocturnum* . . . the Wedding Night Jasmine.

"Where is this jasmine?" Louise asked.

"Which?"

"The new one, the Wedding Night Jasmine."

"In the greenhouses. We are trying to nurse and graft it back to life again."

"Could you buy more from, um, this same fellow?"

"I imagine."

"What's his name?"

"Who?"

"The fellow from whom you bought the *Jasminum nocturnum*. Where's he from?"

Charles stared out over his field of flowerless, dark green foliage as if he hadn't heard. When she repeated the question, he turned on his horse toward her. "Why, sweet thing?" *Mon sucre d'orge.* My barley sugar. Again, the soupçon of irony. He asked, "Is it that you want to buy your own plants and go into competition with me?"

"No, I was just—" She looked down, warm, feeling discovered, though this was patently impossible. Discovered in what? She'd only asked out of curiosity for a man to whom she wouldn't have deigned to speak on the street. The more she thought about him, the more angry she got. If she ever *did* see him, well, she had a few choice words.

The thought, if she ever did see him, dug up an insidious piece of information from this conversation: Her husband knew her pasha. He knew him well enough to do business with him, almost surely by face and name and place of contact.

As her husband led the way to his greenhouses, Louise behind him turned this knowledge over and over in her mind, testing and measuring its worth. Then, as they dismounted, dropped it.

She said instead, "Do you believe in love?"

Charles Harcourt offered his hands up to her and answered, "Yes, I think I do." His odd half-blank regard covered her for a moment. Then he smiled, as if this were a different sort of exchange than she'd intended. He asked, "Do you?"

"No." Only fools fell in love. She had always known this. From all the idiots who had made fools of themselves over her.

Her husband set her onto the ground, then cast his eyes—they moved together, his beautiful one and his strange one—down.

Louise added, "Though I believe in something. A close connection perhaps." For his sake, she added, "Mutual kindness and consideration." For her own, she couldn't resist, "Or on rare occasion: a person who lights you up, shows you something about yourself that you are eager to know."

The prince pulled his cane out of the saddle, nodding as if he were trying to figure out what she was saying to him. Then he walked off toward the glass houses in the distance, tapping the ground with the cane more than using it, playing with it. He called over his shoulder, "Are you coming?"

She caught up. They walked out toward an acre or more of small glass houses, twenty maybe thirty, each with an abundance of sashes at varying degrees of openness. Each greenhouse was attuned to particular experimental or delicate plants, held at controlled temperatures and humidities. The farthest was the propagation house, where they budded and grafted to rootstock. Here was a special project that he wanted her to see.

And here Louise stopped. As they entered, she faced tables and tables, trays and trays of something

far too familiar. A whole greenhouse full of tiny
Wedding Night Jasmine. A few here and there beginning to pop out from their sticks of understock. The
shape of the opposing leaves, the touch of them, the
color . . . exactly as she had pulled from her wastebasket on a ship. The sight made her faintly giddy.

A thousand questions sprouted, fecund, to mind.
Had Charles bought other plants and cuttings from
the man who had sold him these? Did the man live
far? How did her husband know him? How did they
contact each other? Where was this man now? Could
her husband get hold of him?

Instead of answers to these unvoiced questions,
though, she got a treatise on horticulture: the process
of "inarching," the best ways to bud via detached
leafbuds . . . the stages and frames of a greenhouse,
the flow and return pipes, the ventilators, the auto-
mated misters, and the importance of bottom heat on
occasion. Louise didn't know where to break in, how
to ask what she wanted to.

Charles continued, "You have come right at the
most interesting time of the year. I will show you at
the factory tomorrow, but back here, I have a little
experiment that is going particularly well." There was
an experimental laboratory attached, a little room at
the back toward which he led her as he spoke of
something called *enfleurage*. "We are trying several
processes, two with olive oil. It's plentiful and as
cheap as it gets right here among the olive trees, but
still more expensive than purified lard." She had no
idea what he was talking about. "Nonetheless, we are
seeing if we can get more extract with olive oil or if the
quality is better. We have been experimenting with
this a few months."

They entered the room. Louise halted then pulled
back.

The odor.

Charles smiled. "Isn't it something?"

Something? It was horrific. The air was heavy with the exact same smell she had stuck into her hair in sprigs, the odor that had followed her through dark corridors, then lingered in her hair the next day, drawing her toward catastrophe again night after night . . . *Such a fool,* she kept thinking. *You were played for a fool.*

"How— What—" was all she could say.

Louise began to understand that her husband had salvaged withering blooms off the plants he'd bought, that she was smelling experimentation with an essence that Charles Harcourt was keen to work with. While the small laboratory was filled with essence of *him.* The dark. The other. Her lover from the ship lay on glass trays framed with wood. His and her nights together lay half an inch deep in a pomade of purified fat spread in ridges. They lay on cotton cloth in wire frames. In vials. They floated—as if they were large white petals tinged red at their base—in bottles of oil.

As Louise's husband explained and explained and lovingly explained each process, her head grew light. She and her lover had been scraped off glass, melted at as low a temperature as possible, strained, and macerated . . .

A bottle was opened and offered under her nose, and Louise's skin went icy. It didn't matter if she'd killed him off. If she was angry. If she hated him for leaving her. He could rise from the dead to entwine around her. He was here. The phantom of the tilting dark—who offered a quick pretense of intimacy then left; a man who looked at her, closely, then found her wanting.

Her husband was saying, "It blooms only at night—"

Louise grabbed a table edge and blurted, "I want to go back to Nice."

He looked at her. "What?"

"Please, can we go back to Nice?"

The man before her said reasonably, "But I have just been explaining, I have work here."

"Please." How to implore, petition? She entreated, "I want to see my parents, my family, my friends."

She listened to herself, her tone desperate—surely compelling. She wanted out, away. No more flowers or perfume.

"Are you all right?"

"Homesick." She bit her lip. The smell . . . dear God, the smell. *Get me out of here.* "Nice," she murmured. "I want to return to Nice as soon as possible."

Her husband frowned deeply at her, then never had she been so glad for his uxorious attitude. He said, "All right. For the day. Then we return the day after. Will that do?"

She nodded, one quick, curt shake of her head. Oh, yes. "I want to go to the house now and pack."

Charles took Louise home, where she packed up everything she owned as if she were taking the next steamship back to America, then—without dinner, without her usual romp with her dog—she went to bed. Before dark. He'd never met a woman who slept so much.

After dinner, he packed his own satchel less dramatically—a brush, the odds and ends of shaving, a pair of trousers he liked. His house in Nice was stocked with more clothes, more of everything, so he needn't plan overmuch. He opened a drawer and came across a flat, velvet box. The pearls, the necklace he had meant to give Louise on their wedding night. He took the box out. It was large, square, as long and wide as his forearm. He opened it. Black pearls, big ones, small ones. It was a fine piece. More than a fine piece: It had cost an obscene amount—worth more than the damned house he was standing in. He'd sneaked off to Paris for it, then gotten carried away.

The biggest pearls made up a fashionable dog collar, six strands that would plate Louise's throat. Every third black pearl was alternated by a clear, perfect diamond—set in platinum and cut in the round, forty-eight faces—as large as the pearls themselves. The dog collar clasped with a catch in back that would dangle a string of smaller diamonds down several vertebrae of her back. She could attach or detach the rest of the necklace with this. The rest was a shimmering cascade of dark, lustrous pearls and bright diamonds, these diminishing in size as the strands lengthened to become swinging ropes of stones and beads the size of the pearls she'd broken.

On their wedding night, Charles hadn't given them to her for the obvious reason that the extravagance had become so goddamned inappropriate. But he hadn't tracked it down to give it to her since then either. He didn't wish to take it back. He wished for it to become a gift he *wanted* to give. It meant something. Trust. Love. Eternity. The extravagant happiness he felt could be theirs, if only . . . Meanwhile, to give such a present now felt asinine. It was too fond— a gift to a treasured lover.

He stared at the ridiculous pearls a moment, then set them into their ridiculous box, clapping the lid shut. He tossed the case into his satchel for no particular reason, perhaps just to get the thing out of the house.

Chapter 22

> Who would think, then, that such fine
> ladies and gentlemen should regale them-
> selves with an essence found in the inglori-
> ous bowels of a dyspeptic whale!

> Herman Melville
> Moby Dick, *Chapter 20*
> 1851

Marriage was easier for Louise in Nice. Even off-season, the city offered a luxury and ease more in keeping with what she was used to. With her family around her and the routine of social commitments, she became the Louise she knew, if not the Louise she liked. She felt in possession of herself again.

A week after arriving back in Nice (and after not having gone back to Grasse even once), she sat at her mother's writing desk addressing the last round of thank-you notes. Wedding gifts had begun to mount, most of them from people who had yet to realize the wedding had already taken place. She was alone. Everyone else (save Charles, who hadn't arrived from

Grasse yet, but was due any moment) was putting the finishing touches on a garden party to start in half an hour.

Louise blotted the wet ink on the day's final envelope. With her mother's help she had managed more than fifty brief notes today—her mother had ordered the cards, then organized a list; the gift, the name, the precise relationship, the address.

Her parents had also ordered formal announcements. These would arrive from the printer tomorrow, five hundred of them, all in need of addressing, many requiring more written contact, a few lines in Louise's hand. Louise was good at this sort of mindless nicety. *Dear Monsieur and Madame: As you can see from this announcement, Charles and I have already married. We were simply too, too keen to begin our life together, and though we cannot invite you to our wedding itself we hope you will help us celebrate our nuptials in December at the affair Maman and Papa are planning.*

Louise's parents were outlining the strategies for an ambitious ball. It was to be a grand affair, the first major event—and the best, if Harold and Isabel Vandermeer had their way—of the Côte d'Azur season. It would introduce the newly married couple while obliquely introducing the bride's parents as well, the host and hostess of the affair: a fine entrance to a social milieu they intended to frequent. "Our daughter lives here, after all. We want to be part of your life, be near our grandchildren."

Grandchildren, oh, Lord. Louise tapped the last sealed note neatly into the stack. No doubt, her parents were sincere in wanting to be close. No doubt, also, they enjoyed their new access to the prince's social circle. Louise was witnessing a phenomenon: Her parents, already among the society magnates of New York, were consolidating, incorporating, and going international.

As if in tribute to this feat, a *corbeille* had accumulated at their house, a French tradition of which Louise's mother swore she was envious (and of which she was also slightly possessive—if Louise took anything out or rearranged it, her mother grew annoyed). This French tradition amounted to a grand display of jewels given to the bride by friends and relatives: tiaras and brooches and necklaces, parures—one in platinum and white opals, one in pink gold and pale rubies—all laid out in a glass case in her parents' home and watched over by a plainclothes guard and Charles's coachman. Such was the social consequence of the prince and Louise's family that, if people knew there was to be no huge wedding, they seemed to be taking it in stride. Louise had been given a copious number of pieces, each displayed in the case with the name of the donor; a detailed list would be published in the newspaper. It was quite the tradition, with people vying to see who could give the bride the most important piece on show.

Yes, everything was going perfectly. She had married and thus entered into a social contract that was now functioning exactly as it should: Everyone benefitted. Her parents were happy. She was secure for the rest of her days, with the Prince d'Harcourt clearly committed, bonded solidly into union by the gain of business advantages.

And a few other advantages, of course. His friends couldn't have been more impressed with his wife's beauty, some with seeming good wishes, some with outright envy. Her husband, she knew, was aware of both sentiments and enjoyed both equally. Meanwhile, Pia Montebello, often present at gatherings, took raging jealousy to new heights; he didn't mind that either. Louise had married a man who *liked* to set people on their ears.

Certainly Charles Harcourt unsettled his wife. He wanted something from her, though *what* was not entirely clear. Something more complicated than a quick coupling in the bathtub, for he could have had that. So, if not sexual compliance, what? An eagerness? An emotional openness—an undefended nakedness, so to speak, in the dark?

Oh, no, Louise wasn't about to do *that* again.

Meanwhile, surprisingly, impossibly, when she had reneged on her promise to return to Grasse, he expressed only bewilderment and concern—then stayed with her, managing his business affairs anxiously from a distance. Another reprieve, more grace, yet more room: as much as she needed. He made his own life more difficult for the sake of making hers more bearable. And Louise couldn't even take this favor with perfect gratitude. She hated that she needed it, that it amounted to her running back to her parents.

If she had been a lark to her lover, to this man she was . . . something more. A great deal more in exchange for a great deal less. Why?

She didn't know. Charles Harcourt made no sense whatsoever. Except to note that, even when he was perfectly within his rights to be demanding and importunate, he instead met each new thing she threw at him with an attempt to see her view: a generosity of spirit.

Charles arrived almost two hours late to the afternoon garden party being given in his and Louise's honor—a tardiness he suspected that would not be popular with his new in-laws and wife—but there was nothing for it. The trip from Grasse was never an insignificant one. Then his horse had thrown a shoe ten minutes outside of Nice—ten minutes, that is, if he had been at a gallop. He'd had to get down from the damn horse and walk them both home. After a hasty toilette, he had then had another good half an hour by carriage to the outskirts of Éze where

Louise's parents had rented a house. He was lucky to have been only as late as he was.

An English butler took his hat at the door, then Charles proceeded through a residence he knew well. He'd helped arrange for the rental of this large, pleasant two-story home owned by a friend of his and perched into a cliffside like the nest of an eagle. He was directed outside to the terrace where the bride, her family, his, and more well-wishers were gathered.

The back terrace was huge, with the ubiquitous view to the Mediterranean. This particular sea view was made more dramatic by being set into breathtaking terrain. Over the back railing of the house, the cliffside fell steeply. The perspective from here was not only of sea but also of a wide, blue sky. This house was situated seemingly up in the air, in a kind of special limbo, like living on a cloud. If one reached over the terrace rail, one could literally touch treetops.

To get to the rail this afternoon, however, would have been difficult. As large as the terrace was, it was packed with people. As he moved into them, looking for Louise, several acquaintances greeted him, offering their congratulations. One friend he hadn't seen in weeks clapped him on the back, kissed him on both cheeks, then said, rolling his eyes, "*Ooh là là,* my friend: the bride."

"Yes, she is splendid, isn't she?"

Charles couldn't find her for the throng. Isabel Vandermeer found him, however, and chastised him as soon as she was close enough to do so.

"Charles," she said, sliding sideways between two people, "you are unforgivably late. I can hardly bring myself to speak to you." She half meant the chagrin that showed on her face.

He said, "But, Madame, I was out making your daughter rich. Richer," he corrected. He wiggled his eyebrows at her and smiled. "Oh, Isabel, I collected the first shipment of ambergris from Marseilles yesterday and, Lord—" He let out an appreciative breath. "Your husband is brilliant. It is the best I have ever laid hands on. It is almost"—he lifted his gaze—"as fabulous as that young woman you raised." In delayed greeting, he kissed Isabel Vandermeer on her fingertips, and she made a tiny sound, a literal squeal of delight. He asked, "Where is Louise? I don't see her."

"Oh, she is here somewhere, you charming man. Now, don't think you can flatter and beguile your way through every faux pas, but I'm letting it go this time, provided, of course, you introduce me to your cousin who arrived not ten minutes ago."

"My cousin?" He had a hundred of them. She turned him so he could see the gentleman in question. "Aah." Charles's considerably older first cousin, Robert d'Orleans, duc de Chartres, the man who, had there been a French king, would have been he. "Of course," Charles said.

As they headed toward this quasi-celebrity, she asked, "And how is it that you are a prince and he is a duc, yet he would be king, not you? Aren't princes higher than . . ." She continued.

Charles ignored her, only shaking his head and smiling. He had given up trying to explain what she and her husband didn't want to understand—that their son-in-law's parents were a younger daughter of an abdicated king and the son of a Napoleonic sovereign, the principality itself long ago ceded to the church. Nothing royal. Nor was Robert, for that matter.

Nonetheless, Charles introduced the excited Isabel to the duc, then left, wading his way back through more cousins, aunts, uncles, his, Louise's. Every soul Charles knew who was currently within a day's drive was here—friends, friends of Louise's parents, everyone's relatives, including and especially those who had come across an ocean to celebrate, then been "deprived" of, a wedding.

Charles tried to be agreeable, stopping when he had no polite choice, as he continued to look for his wife. Until he found himself unable to move: Someone tugged on his arm. He turned. Pia. This meant that Roland was sure to be around somewhere, for alas, Americans didn't have a large party without inviting the chief American diplomat and his wife. Charles wasn't certain how Pia had wormed her way through the crowd to get to him so quickly, but she straightaway had a death hold on his arm.

"Charles!" she said warmly. He let her chat him up with a bunch of nonsense, remaining civil as he scanned the terrace.

After a minute, he said, "Excuse me, Pia. That's so very nice for you." She was rattling away about her new "fancy man," her *beau gars,* she called him, while her old fancy man frowned and tried to ignore the diminishing term.

Pia gripped his arm a second longer, near to arguing about whether or not he had a right to take it with him. He finally looked at her and said, "Pia, get your fucking hand off me. I want to go say hello to my wife."

She released him with a quick, nervous glance around her. Two people wedged between them, and he was free.

Hardly three feet away, he was accosted again, this time by two gentlemen he didn't know, one already drunk. "We were wondering, old man, if you knew who that delectable creature over there is," a short British fellow said in English.

Accommodatingly, Charles hunted between heads and shoulders in the direction the man's finger suggested. He saw Louise's cousin, Mary, standing beside her parents.

"No, no, not that one, old fellow."

A lady in a very large-skirted dress moved, and Charles spotted the "delectable creature": Louise herself sitting in a chair at the east edge of the terrace. Charles's chest expanded. She was draped and tucked and ribboned into a concoction of silver-blue taffeta, her ivory-blond hair piled high on her head. He watched her talk to a mother and son down from Paris (met in the marketplace, and scooped up by Louise's mother "because they have such a glorious knowledge and love of flower gardening," and because the son was the new tenor at the Paris Opera—Isabel Vandermeer had a knack for sniffing out then collecting the renowned and elite).

Louise sat, gloved hands in her lap—voile gloves that came to her elbows and left her fingertips bare; he could see her skin through the cream-colored voile. God bless, he thought. She was so lovely. She nodded at the opera singer's mother, smiling at the son. While Charles stood there, stunned silly, as he was every time his regard happened to come across his own wife afresh.

"So do you know her?"

"Yes."

The drunken fellow said, "She looks rich."

"She is." All three men stared.

Charles realized the taller of the two men beside him was Pia's "new fancy man," whom she'd pointed out, a sculptor of some prominence with a long French aristocratic name he didn't remember. He glanced at him. The new fellow was lean, with clean, sharp planes to his good-looking face and two perfect eyes set beneath a dramatically deep brow; he was about thirty and drunk as a coot. He smelled peculiar, as if he'd been drinking something other than the sherry and whiskey circulating on trays. Something vaguely undrinkable. After-shaving lotion, perhaps.

Staring at Louise, this man said, "She looks like—off a Botticelli canvas. Only more gorgeous." He spoke clearly for a drunk, the sure sign of a lot of practice. His opinion seemed to come from an esthetic perspective without a trace of lust.

"I agree," Charles said. The British bloke did, too.

"She looks tight-arsed," said the sculptor. Charles frowned and turned to look at the fellow, who rephrased: "Difficult, hard to get along with."

"Aah." Charles nodded. The man was too ploughed to get really angry at him.

"I like easy women myself." With that he took himself off in Pia's direction.

The British fellow remained. He was possibly, if Charles remembered correctly, a graduate student skipping school for a week to play on the Riviera, a friend of Gaspard, Tino's oldest. The truant scholar nudged Charles's ribs with his elbow. "Difficult or not, I say *that* is a bit of all right. Can you tell me her name, and do you know if she likes fast motorcars?"

Charles responded, "Her name is Louise Harcourt. I'm sure she likes fast motor cars. But she finds young men like you tedious." He hoped the last was still true.

The young man looked around sharply. "And do you know her so well as this?"

"I could know her better. I've only been married to her a week."

The scholar with the fast motorcar visibly blanched, then after a humble, muttered congratulations slunk off.

Charles and Louise, actually, had been married a week and three days. Louise's one day in Nice had become two, which in turn had become more. He pushed her to return to Grasse with him, but she wouldn't. He'd finally gone there alone yesterday to take the ambergris home.

Now was the very worst time of the year for him to go missing in his fields and laboratories. He fretted over his experiments sitting unattended in his greenhouse. He worried for his new jasmine. Moreover, September—of which there remained only four days—concluded the most important time of the year for gathering and extracting the attar from several varieties of flowers. The volume of his success this month would determine his overall success for a year.

Meanwhile, he lingered in Nice too much and too long. It had been a hell of a trip to go to Marseilles, Grasse, and back in twenty-four hours. But Charles found himself reluctant to force Louise to return, reluctant to leave her behind.

He eyed the young scholar, who was skulking in her direction even knowing her husband watched. The young fool would become part of the entourage, he supposed.

Charles's wife had developed a little following, mostly of young men—or at least it was the younger ones who were willing to declare themselves. The tenor. The young race car driver. An English boy—hardly more than a boy—on grand tour who had decided to stay suddenly in the south of France "indefinitely." This boy-child (who was still probably a year or two older than Louise) wrangled and bribed his way to every event Louise attended. God knew, it wasn't that she looked approachable. And Charles himself did his best to look as formidable as a Foo dog guarding the entrance to a temple of Buddha.

He couldn't fault these fellows for the blind stupor in which they followed Louise, since he himself was under her spell. But he could damn well punch any of them in the nose if they followed too closely or did anything more forward than drool—Charles rather enjoyed their drooling, to be honest.

Still, he hated this aspect of Louise as much as he loved it. And he feared it as much as he loathed his own face. In a week, he'd determined that he had a problem in public with her: He grew jealous too quickly. He felt far too possessive. He knew that he touched her more often than she liked—and with something of an unattractive greed. Yet he seemed powerless to stop himself.

He went toward her now, twisting sideways through people, facing as he watched Louise, his old belly-churning worry: that he had married a woman who would make a fool of him. He kept remembering how easily she had been seduced on the ship. He wanted to believe this ease had been for his own sake. She had succumbed to the old Harcourt charm that he exuded by the liter. Yet liters and liters of the same charm, all he could muster, were having a devil of a time seducing her now. He hadn't kissed her since the bathtub, not squarely on the mouth, try as he might. Thus, as he shouldered his way through people, he was arguing himself into circles, into knots, making bets with himself as to which fellow had the best chance, the sculptor, the tenor, the twit with the car, or—oh, God, Roland Montebello materialized about four people nearer Louise than Charles himself. Montebello waved at her.

Charles held his breath, then laughed: Louise turned conversationally in her chair, without so much as an arctic lift of an eyelash in the roué's direction, no acknowledgment whatsoever. The dear girl could be miraculously aloof. So far, Louise herself held back any and all suitors for her affections (including, alas, Charles)—with as much interest and as effortlessly as a mare batting flies with her tail.

He watched her as he moved toward her. She had her mother's social skills. She was a gracious and elegant guest of honor. She talked pleasantly with friends and strangers alike. And there were so many of both! God, the people. *Get out of my way!* he wanted to yell.

Charles pushed through an entire family from New York who lived the winter in Cannes, then between an Italian couple Louise's parents had met through mutual friends in Miami. Then, just as he was within a meter of Louise, he spotted Pia again. She was ahead of him, taking Roland's arm, the two of them stepping in front of Charles, demanding Louise's attention.

Pia said something to her. There was an exchange.

Charles nearly knocked a woman down sideways in his haste to get to his wife. He came up to Louise, bending over her chair. "Hello, darling. I'm sorry I'm late." He kissed her cheek.

He won an immediate flustered look. "What happened to you?" she asked "We had started to worry." Her cheeks pinked slightly, he noted, as he stood up.

Charles promised details later, then stepped beside her. He touched her arm, ran his hand to her shoulder—more voile—up to her bare neck where he left it, his palm curved into the crook. He kissed the top of her head.

Louise reached for his hand, taking it into hers, effectively pulling it away. "Charles—" She was discomposed for an instant.

Embarrassed. *What must people think?* she asked herself.

But, of course, she knew what people thought. And the way her husband intentionally oiled the wheels, so to speak, of intimate speculation regarding the bride and groom brought heat into her face every time.

A strange sensation. Louise never blushed, or never had until lately. It was inappropriate, unsophisticated, and she was, if anything, a sophisticated young woman. In the last week, however, her sophistication had come under siege. She had learned, for the first time, the second time, the dozenth, what it felt like for a flush of heat to spread into her face, down her neck, and across her shoulders, a rampant, rubescent blush that answered to Charles's whims, not hers. There was no stopping it.

Moreover, he knew it happened. Anyone who

wasn't colorblind knew. He liked it. No, more than
liked; he watched it happen, waiting for it lately, with
undisguised fascination on his face.

Louise met his regard briefly up and over her
shoulder. His face smiled its peculiarly lopsided smile
as he squeezed her gloved hand, encompassing it with
his own. Just this, and she blushed faintly again, as if
some mechanism in her body—like Tino's dangerous
water heater—had run amok, gauges jumping.

Mrs. Montebello interjected into this, "Charles.
Louise is under the impression you were not on the
Concordia."

"I wasn't," he said, his voice flat. Louise had gained
the impression that he and his mistress had parted
company, permanently and unpleasantly, a surprise
she found gratifying for a host of mean, small-minded
reasons.

The woman laughed. "No, of course, you weren't.
But I have just done the funniest thing. I confused our
last trip across with our one before, when you were."
Her mouth drew into a wide smile.

Mr. Montebello took over, saying, "We wanted to
tell you both how happy we are for you." The diplomat smiled his best debonair leer.

Roland Montebello was an outwardly engaging
man, moderately good-looking. For a "young" man
(Louise's mother's assessment) he was "a great success for his age." Though not a full ambassador, he
held a high appointment—plenipotentiary minister
to a country with which his own did not have the full
diplomatic relations of an embassy. This was a credit
to his true diplomacy, Louise supposed, since he was
stricken by a case of skirt-chasing so outrageous it
would have sent a less savvy American to the bottom
of the diplomatic corps.

This man, the male half of a predatory, promiscuous pair, touched one finger to a curl at the front of his

hair, worn otherwise slicked back with pomade till it looked wet and black. His eyes were dark and lively, actively assessing Louise.

He said to her, "Your husband has been quite the heartthrob in these parts," then had to add, "strange as that may seem." He shrugged, a good-natured salute to incomprehensible fact. "There are many ladies weeping over this marriage. And quite a few gentlemen, I dare say, breathing a sigh of relief." He smiled, then made a meaningful, and perhaps suave, lift of one eyebrow. "You have harnessed a legend, my dear." He put his arm around his wife, patting her shoulder, smiling, confident. He said, "Yes, indeed, a legend. And not one that every man would be as happy to tell you about as I am."

The man was an ass. An ignorant ass. Whose judgment Louise was no more likely to trust than she was likely to fly.

The "legend" murmured to Louise, "Darling, I would love to speak to you privately a moment." To the Montebellos and the rest, her husband offered, "Excuse us." And Louise felt herself lifted up by the hand and pulled out of her chair.

"What's wrong?" she murmured at Charles's back as he pushed their way through the crowd. "Where have you been?" She flapped her fan against his shoulder blade, put out with him, though less so for the reason she pretended. She wished he would stop playing with her hand. "You are two hours late," she scolded. "I should skin you alive."

He glanced over his shoulder. "In a moment, precious."

She pursed her lips.

This made him laugh. "Your Highness. Dearest." He enjoyed teasing her; she couldn't figure out how to stop this either.

He drew her arm under his as he moved through the crowd, pulling her up against him.

"Charles—" She resisted, her hand at the small of his back. Her resistance went unheeded.

He dragged her the full length of the terrace like this, two waddling companions, back to belly like penguins in a line. At the far corner of the railing, he wedged his way through then pulled Louise in front of him and around by the elbow, placing her beside him. They came to rest, arm against arm, almost shoulder to shoulder, himself between her and the crowd.

He finally let go of her.

Louise breathed in a deep, clear breath, even smiling faintly—partly at herself, for fearing something so innocuous as his holding her hand. She asked, "Where have you been? You were supposed to be here ages ago."

He recounted a saga of thrown horseshoes, delays, frustration. When she became sympathetic, he added, "I have to talk to you about all this. I can't stay here; I can't keep going back and forth; and I can't leave you. I want you with me."

They had had this discussion before. She looked past his shoulder. The view was fairly stunning. Sky and sea. But for a near, jutting treetop, she stared out into blue that spread above, below, and out all the way to the horizon. "I'm happier here," she murmured. "It's safer."

"Whatever that means." After a pause he said, "*Safe* isn't everything. *Safe* is usually boring, in fact. You're bored to tears here, Lulu. I was thinking: My accountant in Grasse is retiring at the end of the season. You are good with numbers. You hate the running of a household, and I have plenty of people who can do that. So why not come with me to the factory and learn the books—"

She glanced at him. "Bookkeeping?" He may as well have said, *Wouldn't you like to eat dust?*

He frowned. "Well, even if it doesn't amuse you, it could keep you busy, and it would be of help to me."

"Oh," she said. A relief. She didn't have to plan or commit to anything for herself. "I'll help you, Charles, if that's all you're asking. Can you bring your books here?"

"No, I can't."

She dropped the subject, lifting her arm to point. "Over there. What exactly is out there?"

He looked, didn't understand at first. "More water," he said.

"No, on the other side of the water."

He turned around self-consciously, his bad side to her. When he understood she meant North Africa, he listed countries: "Morocco, Algeria, Tunisia, Tripoli, Egypt. The dark continent." He sighed.

For Charles knew all at once what—who—they were talking about, whether she knew overtly or not. Arab Charles. More his competition, he was coming to believe lately, than all the pretty young men out here on the terrace. Here in Nice, most mornings, Louise walked to the sea, where she stayed sometimes for hours just staring out over the water.

"I used to live in Tunisia," he said. "It's horrible. Crowded, dirty. Dangerous," he added. "A bunch of lunatics."

She must have heard the bias in his voice. *This* interested her. She glanced at him, then her regard fixed on his face, his bad eye. She reached out. Her hand came close, then backed off without touching. "Did that happen in Tunisia? You have a scimitar in your bedroom in Grasse. This looks like a cut." She tried to touch it once more, then couldn't.

Self-conscious again, Charles shook his head no. "It *is*. Though a doctor made it. My eye has been blind since birth. An injury from a difficult delivery. I came out the wrong way, I'm told. The doctor used an instrument that saved me and probably my mother, but ruined my eye. The infection that followed, lanced, really put the finishing touches to it, don't you think?"

She didn't comment on this unsightly piece of him, but asked instead, "Does it cause you trouble? Does it hurt?"

"No." Since they were discussing all his fiendish features, he said, "My knee does, though. The scimitar, from my days in Tunisia, belonged to the fellow who bashed my knee. I do owe my wonderfully graceful gait to that country."

She turned more toward him, leaning an elbow onto the railing. "Why? Why would anyone hit your knee?"

"I was young, a green attaché to the resident-general. The locals were unhappy with all Frenchmen. We had just taken over their country, a protectorate. One day, as I stepped out of a carriage, *voilà*, a Muslim fanatic decided Allah wanted me dead. He was wrong, though. Allah only wanted my knee shattered. He wanted the fanatic with the scimitar to bleed for two days then die of wounds I inflicted. I didn't take kindly to being attacked."

"Oh, dear. I'm— I'm sorry," she said, "that you went through these things. But I'm glad you survived them."

"I am too."

"You must hate the Arabs for that."

He shrugged. "Oh, Arabs, Moors, Frenchmen"— he laughed—"Americans. We're all about the same, good ones, bad ones." He sighed, turned around again, offering his good profile. "It's hard to like any place, though, better than this." He looked across the terrace, beyond heads to the steep cliff sides that rose behind them, while Louise at his side looked out toward the sea.

After a few moments of people bumping against them—a little crowd speaking excitedly that moved away after a minute—she said, "What about a tutor?"

"A tutor?"

"I don't much care for columns and figures, but I'm

good at higher mathematics. Suppose we hired a tutor in chemistry."

"Chemistry?"

"If you want me to go with you, I think I could if I were allowed to take apart your perfume."

"Take it apart?"

"Break it down, dissect it, understand it, examine it. It—it makes me feel—I don't know. Feel things." She looked up at him with a hopeful smile. "But it is just chemicals, no?"

"Well, no. Perfume is supposed to make you feel things. And it's more than chemicals."

She shook her head, frowning in dispute. "Well, if I took it apart, analyzed it, then I could derive the chemical formulas and build other scents, if you liked."

He gave her a distasteful look. "You want to make synthetic perfumes?"

"It's the coming thing, isn't it?"

"It's not natural."

"It's modern."

"They stink."

"Then they aren't mathematically perfect. I can figure them out, I'm sure."

Charles scowled. Blast youth and its fascination with the new and the "modern." He said, "All right. Tutors it is. But in Grasse, yes?"

"Yes. And I will need some of your perfume. That new one and some of the attar of the new jasmine as well. And some books and a slide rule and some space in a laboratory with lab equipment."

He was a little bewildered, but relieved. Whatever it took, he was happy to have Louise agree to come with him.

He stared back into the crowd—the men tried to hide their glances at her, though they looked, even leaning to steal glances around trays and shoulders.

Charles guarded her, taking her hand again. He stood there playing with it for several moments before he realized Louise was studying him, from the top of his head to, well, down as far as the crowd would let her eyes travel, which was about crotch level if his frock coat had been open—a curious sort of range of which she availed herself.

She scanned him up then down, with people bumping into them. It didn't matter. He loved the feel of her looking at him. He brought her hand to his mouth, kissed a knuckle.

While Louise herself wasn't sure what she thought. She watched, transfixed, drawn, repelled, hypnotic to the sight of his mouth—his face—kissing the bend of her thumb.

She was coming to think of Charles Harcourt as . . . interesting to look upon. She watched him, studying the way he brushed his lips against her thumb, her sheer glove, the way he tilted his head to do this as he held his shoulders slightly forward, his spine straight yet his body relaxed. He was a graceful man, square, elegant, and precise of gesture. Courtly. Courteous to a fault. Courteous, sometimes, to the point of her believing he made fun of her.

He kissed the rest of her knuckles between words. "And perfume is—more—than—chemicals—" He bit her littlest finger before he offered with a smiling, wicked wiggle of brows, "It's magic."

She stared at him, wide-eyed for a moment, at the antics of his face. Then she felt her mouth begin to curve into a smile. The smile grew. It was the reaction he wanted—he laughed as her lips parted. She laughed too.

And this sound was so welcome to Charles he all but let out a shout of rejoicing. Oh, the girl's laughter, too long absent, here now: bubbly, infectious. The old Louise he knew.

She bowed her head, appealingly shy all at once. She murmured, "It's true what Monsieur Montebello says, isn't it? You are a womanizer."

He made a wounded breath. *"Paah.* No, absolutely not."

Charles curved his free hand round Louise's elbow and pulled her closer, up against the side of him. He lay her hand out in his own, opening her fingers up, tracing the underside of each as he bent it out along her voile glove and past to bare fingertip pads, then around the pink oval of fingernail. Her hands were smooth, perfectly soft, not roughened or hardened anywhere through hard work or age. He said, more honestly, "There have been, women though. But not now. I don't want anyone else. There never will be anyone else again. Only you, my Lulu. Do you believe me?"

Face still bowed, she shook her head no.

He blew air through his lips, vocalized. *Prrhh.* Insulted. Then she raised her face to him, smiling broadly. What a smile this girl had. She was returning the favor of his teasing, playing, and, *ooh là là,* he liked it so much.

"Yes," she said. "I believe you." More seriously, she added, "Though I don't know why it should be true."

Satisfied, more than satisfied, he brought the palm of her hand to his mouth, kissed it, then rubbed the kissed spot, slightly damp, with his thumb. As if he could rub the kiss in. It was a nice moment. A really nice moment. Louise looked at him, her face and neck and shoulders suffusing with that furious red they could take on. He was willing to bet he could make her entire body flush like this, a real sight by the light of day.

For Louise, however, it was a real comeuppance, an unwelcome surprise to find herself so affected—and to discover the reason this time to be so much less amorphous: sexual arousal. She felt it clearly, was baffled, flustered by the degree. It left her without her usual solid footing, unable to function in the midst of a party, where she had always functioned so well.

Her hand went flat. It arched on its own, every finger stretched out. She tried to take it back.

He murmured, "Your mother is watching." They both knew that Isabel Vandermeer, his advocate, would not approve of the limiting attitude Louise took with her new husband.

More breath than voice, Louise said, "Wh—what?" Beyond mere discomposure, she felt faintly dizzy.

As if to ease this, Charles let go of her hand.

But it was more an even exchange: He didn't relent; he merely rotated around in front of Louise, wedging her into the corner of the balustrade while hiding all view of her from the terrace with his body. He put his hands down on the stone rail at either side of her waist.

Louise leaned back, out slightly into the void of a long drop.

"Careful," he said. He took hold of her back. He moved close to her physically, feeling close to her emotionally, closer than they had yet managed to this point. He felt good. He was taking her back to Grasse, getting her involved in his own preoccupation. He was king of this party, if ever there was a French king of an American queen of glamorous allure. He couldn't get over her, how fabulous, how silky rich her hair, her skin, her dress, her composure, the way she moved . . . God, he was a regular idiot for this young woman.

It seemed utterly natural: He went to kiss her.

She turned her face. His mouth brushed her ear, her usual duck and parry. He was becoming an expert, though, at savoring little things, nothing at all—the sensitive skin of his lips against the wisps of hair at her hairline, his nose dragged along the dewy softness of cheek. With the tip of his tongue, he traced the thin ridge of cartilage that curled in her ear.

She bent her neck, ear to shoulder, turned her face, looking at him. "People will see," she whispered.

"Good. I am married to the object of my affection, so it is a new wonder for me to be able to express myself openly"—he admitted—"without worrying that a husband is going to tan me alive." It *was* a great marvel. His. His Louise. Not another man's wife, but his own. His own to love and cherish and, if he could figure out how to get in under the barriers, his own with whom to begin a family.

She arched back, out further over a drop of sixty rocky feet. "Charles. This isn't the place."

"Where is the place then, Lulu-girl?"

She just shook her head, wonder and worry and disapproval on her face. She seemed slightly appalled by either him or the circumstance, probably both. "Not here," she reiterated.

In *her* mind, nowhere was the place.

Everywhere was becoming the place, in Charles's scheme of things.

He could hear his own blood in his ears. Louise looked divine, all ribbons and draped taffeta and piled curls. She smelled divine—she was wearing that jasmine perfume he remembered from the very first night, the one with light notes of clover and acacia. She felt like an armload of silk, unraveled bolts of it in his arms, soft and shushy and slightly unwieldy as she shifted, trying to make him back off.

He did, slightly, so as to take her hand again. She relaxed a little, giving it over, a compromise. Yet he could feel her light, ragged breath hit his thumb. He could see the rise and fall of her silver-blue breasts— as he rolled her gloved arm over again, cupping the top of her wrist in his hand, rubbing his thumb over the inside, the buttons of her gloves.

He lifted her wrist to his mouth, brushing his lips along the buttons, then pressed kisses onto the only skin available: into the spaces between the glove's closures. Looking as chaste and innocent as possible, he licked his tongue into the first of these openings, wetting the skin there. A man took what he got. He closed his eyes.

"Charles——" She tried to pull her hand away.

He wouldn't let go. "Take off your glove," he murmured.

"Charles." She couldn't catch her breath. He could hardly believe this. Louise, breathless for strange-looking him. "I— No one has ever— This—" She couldn't speak, either.

What he was doing to her felt so strange and new to Louise. So indirect. So unlike what she was familiar with. It hinted that there was more, a great deal more, with which she was sexually unacquainted . . . things Charles Harcourt knew all about, a man whose appearance in all likelihood required he make a special-ty of the circuitous, the suggestive, the slow, strong, inexorable build that insinuated itself into a woman's senses before she knew what was happening.

Not a monster—no vampires or incubi here—but a man, a husband in possession of a preternatural ability with an explainable origin, a faculty that was rather frightening in its strength.

"I can't have much of you." He entreated, "Let me have your hand." Adding, "Your bare hand."

She pulled her kissed hand away, rolling her fist, glove and all, into a curl against her chest.

He kept his palm out, asking. "Let me. It's just your hand."

"But the way you hold it—" She couldn't finish. She looked around, a quick glance that yielded noth-ing since he had her more or less backed out onto the cliff.

Yes, villain that he was, Charles thought. Her lovely

violet eyes looked at him, a sweep of long lashes and heavy lids—not exactly a maidenly glance. Then she looked down and, rather fetchingly, bit her bottom lip with the edge of her teeth.

Charles's scrotum tightened. His trousers lifted slightly into her skirts. God bless, he thought. He took her hand back and rolled it over again, the inside of her wrist up. He undid the buttons himself, then, starting at her elbow, began to work the glove down.

He didn't get far before she stopped him. Her other hand came up out of her skirts—a fist laid over the rumpling glove, a fist that contained something that rapped Charles across the hand: her fan. And here was something else that he remembered from that first night on the ship, the largish fan she had used like a cane, then a bayonet, as she'd disciplined a young lieutenant.

Charles saw it; he felt it, the little echoing knock of wood slats and stretched silk across the cuff of his shirt and the side of his thumb. Not much of a whack. But it made him see red—a quick flare of temper. No. Enough. Not from a young woman to whom he gave so much leeway. A wife whom he had only kissed once in all their short marriage; one kiss and one kiss only. It was insufficient suddenly, unbalanced. He deserved more.

Also, perhaps someone bumped him. He would never be sure. People were close, chatting away, moving around behind him. Charles stepped up against his wife partly of his own volition, though the last centimeter may have had help from the jostling of the crowd. He was suddenly body to body with her, pressing into her dress.

"Charles," she breathed. She tilted her head up, her eyes wide.

He tipped his head down, angled his face—she tried to duck again. "Come on, Lulu-girl," he said. "You're safe. There are a hundred witnesses behind

s. What can I do?" He put his hand to her cheek to old her face steady and kissed her full-mouthed.

And suddenly it was a really shame there were so many people, because his success was astounding. If one could call this success: Married almost two weeks, nd he at last kissed his wife for the second time in the way of a man and a woman. A deep, carnal kiss. And he kissed him back—withholding herself somehow et not quite able to withhold everything. As if she ked it, but wasn't comfortable with liking it. He ngled his head to get as deep a drink of her as he ould.

And, ooh, God, it was wonderful, whether she liked t or not. It was like leaping over the balustrade and alling the distance toward the rocks and trees below. His stomach lurched then was pulled home by the raining twist of his testes that seemed to draw every ast ounce of blood he possessed toward his lower arts. He tongued inside her mouth, pushing against he soft, glassy-wet lining of her cheek, engaging her ongue—it was small, very warm, lively. He stroked er tongue with his, wooing it. Charles instantly found imself erect, as stiff as the pine tree beside them, its op blocking the sun, its roots down on the ridge.

A voice said, "Excuse me."

Charles drew back, breathing like he'd landed from he fall as well. Kissing Louise knocked the breath out f him. Her eyes were half-closed, that look that could utright level him. He and she stood there, a few anting breaths apart from each other's face.

"Charles?" The voice spoke again.

He glanced over his shoulder. He'd be damned if he as going to turn further and let anyone see how loody far astray he was from social decorum.

"Charles? Louise?" It was Isabel Vandermeer tanding at his elbow and looking ever so disapprov-ng. "Would you like to go in for a while?" She made a weak smile. And a transparent offer: "I was thinking that Louise looks a little tired. Perhaps you should see her upstairs, Charles."

"Um, ah—" He smiled sheepishly and turned around as much as he dared, revealing Louise while being still in proprietary contact with her skirts, her shoulder. He squeezed her to him, a pull at her waist with his arm round her back.

Louise bent her head, looking down between their bodies, a crimson-deep flush all over her in the way only he seemed to produce. She said, "It's all right, Mother. We have to be going anyway. Thank you for such a nice afternoon. It was a lovely party."

What? Charles thought. He had just arrived. Oh, this was not going to make anyone happy. But him, of course. His spirits took wing. "Yes, we must be going." *Oh, yes, oh, yes,* Charles thought. After a kiss like this, he was going to consummate this absurd marriage in the coach on the way home.

Even more heady, as they walked through the crowd to say their good-byes, he realized he'd made a regular spectacle—and couldn't say that he was anything but elated by it. And, alas, not just because he adored the feeling of half-eating Louise's hand off her wrist then mopping his tongue around inside her mouth. Charles's ego reeled and staggered at the kiss at his wife's blushing exit as she picked up her shawl. He was instantly drunk on his own bravado, in front of half a dozen young fools who ogled her.

Poor insecure ape, he thought. Yet, joy of joys! To let them know (somewhat dishonestly for the moment) that she who walked in the ethers of the most ethereal beauty of all was his. All his. He walked to the carriage on air. Oh, things were going well. Better and better. He wanted to crow about the conquest of his own wife, imminent though it still was, shout it out to the world.

As they stepped into the carriage, however, Louise

said in a vehement whisper, "If you ever do that again in public, I will slap your cocky, one-eyed face. Do you understand me?" She prevented his sitting beside her by spreading herself, dress, pocket bag, shawl, and fan into the center of the seat.

After a pause, he sat down opposite her, twisting his "cocky, one-eyed face" into a grimace. "No, I will never understand you. You liked it."

"It embarrassed me. You may as well have lifted your leg like Virgule"—one of his dogs, a rude mastiff here in Nice—"and marked me like a tree: mine."

He crossed his arms. "You are mine."

She leaned toward him a degree, contradicting. "No, Charles. I belong to me."

He scowled. He couldn't even argue, for he understood too clearly what he had done.

They took off in silence.

Chapter 23

Ambergris is alchemy. It proves the earth is magic, that transmogrification exists: feces into something more wonderful than gold; treasure that drifts upon the sea till it finds a likely shore.

Charles Harcourt, Prince d'Harcourt
On the Nature and Uses of Ambergris

As they jostled along, sunlight flitted through the carriage window, mostly across Charles's chest and face, making him squint: a monstrous expression if ever there was one.

After watching this for a while, Louise felt vaguely penitent. Stiffly, she offered, "You shouldn't be jealous."

"Well, excuse me if I am."

"It would be better if you would control it."

He looked at her sullenly, then asked, "Has it ever occurred to you that, given my wife's amazing looks and mine, I will never be able to cope beyond this."

"You're a grown man—"

He threw something at her from the seat beside him. A wad hit her chest.

"Oh, that's quite mature." His handkerchief wrapped and knotted into a ball.

He snorted. "You don't outgrow frustration or confoundment or—"

"Behaving stupidly."

"Right." *Exact.* The word buzzed in French.

It reduced them to riding along in silence again. Fine, she thought. As the coach descended, Louise realized its interior smelled strange. The small space contained a faint but peculiar, really peculiar, odor, and the scent emanated from the balled handkerchief in her lap.

"What's this?" She picked it up.

He glanced, then looked back out the window. "A gift. I was bringing it to you."

"A gift?" she repeated.

He didn't explain. He didn't answer at all, but rather stared out moodily at the sky. From the evidence out his window, their carriage could have been aloft, flying. The earth was nonexistent but for treetops and the rocky joggles that creaked springs and axles. Noise.

Scent. Louise let the "gift" take her attention. It wasn't much of a gift. A simple handkerchief wrapped tightly around something small. The odor, sweet, strong, and mossy, grew heavier as she untied then unfolded the corners of linen. She unrolled the center from its edges—whatever was inside was well-wrapped. As she opened the last layer, she saw a small, unimpressive, waxy-gray nugget. Pellucid, marbled. And the smell, though strong, was not unpleasant, not at all.

Just powerful. Indeed, as pungent as excrement, only sweet, good, if that were possible. Cool, mellow, faintly seaweed-like, the odor was as fresh and clean as rain, almost loamy like earth from a damp woods.

The little gray bit contained fragments, debris—ground squid beaks, she decided—embedded, clouding it. Louise knew what this was, what it had to be. She let the small ball of ambergris roll from the handkerchief into her palm. It was soft. The warmth of her clenched hand melted it slightly, the texture of solid oils, waxy tallow. It was fascinating. On her hand, its odor changed. It smelled muskier. Faintly spicy, somehow almost oriental.

"This is fabulous stuff," she said aloud for the sake of the man who would not look her way.

This won her an irritable glance.

How was it that *he* had come to be the one irate here? she wondered. She was the one who had been made into a beet-red spectacle.

After a moment, she told him again, "You shouldn't be jealous. You should get hold of yourself."

He got hold of the hand strap instead, clutching it, white-knuckled. He said: "My God, I behave this way because I am so much in love with you."

Louise startled. Her mind went blank. All she could think to say was, "Why?" A sincere question. Less sincerely, snidely, in fact, she asked, "What do you *want* from me?"

Without so much as a pause to gather himself, he said: "I love you because of your drive, your honesty regarding yourself, your resolve, the amazing force of it—the way it propels you toward what you, and only you, chose. I love your choices themselves: I want to be one of them. What do I *want?*" he repeated. "I want you to choose me. Freely. I want you to come at me headlong with all the force of your steely will."

He sat back and folded his arms, not satisfied so much as finished. Too disturbed to continue. As if all this had come upon him with as much surprise as it had Louise.

He had spoken a mouthful. She couldn't look away, his words, his bizarre and beguiling declaration of love holding sway as they rocked down, then around a steep slope.

Till she consciously lowered her gaze.

In her cupped palm, she caught sight of the little

pebble of ambergris. Its looks so unimpressive, its
smell huge. An insistent, implacable attraction—
visceral, invisible. Its odor hung in the air; it insinuated itself into the pores of her hand. It was the
strongest scent she had ever come across that could
still be termed *pleasing*. Cool, fragrant. Like kneeling
in a spring rain, ripping the mossy mat up off the floor
of a forest, smelling this, pressing the soft, furry tufts,
the tender roots, the gritty soil to one's nose.

How little the sight of ambergris, she marveled, had
to do with its draw, its full nature. Or its origin:

How strange that such divine scent, such permeat-
ing tenacity, should get somehow into the uncouth
concretions of a whale.

At the house, Charles descended the carriage. When
he held his hand out to Louise, though, she paused in
the vehicle's doorway. Bent, she looked him levelly in
the eye, assessing him. He was still livid; he couldn't
hide it. As she put her hand into his, she said, "You
needn't feel so insecure, you know. You are not so
ugly as all that."

Oh, fine, he thought. At least though they weren't
going to discuss his absurd confession of love.

Then they were. Obliquely. She stepped down,
smiling faintly, and said, "My 'will'?" Half a question, half a mockery.

He didn't know how to answer. She was shaking her
head, no—though *no* to what, he couldn't decide.

Then she repaired his bewilderment and called back
any hurt with surprising effectiveness: She took hold of
his arm. "Charles," she said, "you have been saddled
with a difficult mate." She frowned, narrowing her
pretty eyes, a troubled visage. After which she offered,
"I know who I am. I'm selfish. And I can't be unselfish
except in the most insincere ways. I never *feel* generous. I've all but given up trying. My drive? Charles, I'm
willful. I'm vain. I haven't the least real interest in

wifely business. I am socially adept—I can be nice to anyone for two minutes—but only because I'm such an accomplished liar." When he opened his mouth, she waved away his objections. "Oh, I know I'm pretty— and it's a good thing you value this. I'm a lot of things. But I'm not nice. I wish I were. You are."

Without warning, her hand came up. He ducked at first, flinching his eye closed and turning his head. Her hand smelled powerfully of the ambergris he'd thought was going to be such a clever thing to bring her.

Then he grew still—her fingers settled against his cheek, the marred side, so gentle, just warm pressure that traced down his eyelid, down the numb scar. Louise studied his face in a way that made him inwardly cringe at what she must be seeing. Pity. Oh, no pity, please. Then she murmured in a perfectly acceptable tone, "No, not so ugly at all."

She lay her flat palm against his jaw, like a sorceress laying a spell upon him. He could not have moved if he'd tried. Her eyes boldly searched over his features, covering his face, studying it. Charles felt unsettled, unmanned to be so scrutinized. She continued, staring sincerely with interest and attention, then she took his breath by telling him, "Your face fascinates me, Charles. For what it is worth, I minded the kiss—and possibly even the way you made love to my hand— because I hate to reveal myself so wholly in public: Don't make me show everyone how strangely you affect me. If you need to show others that I am faithfully yours, then I shall attend to this for you. I shall make a point of it." She paused. "It is only fair. You make such a point of seeing to me."

Her hand dropped away. She picked up her skirts again and walked past him.

Charles couldn't move. He was left out there in the drive for a full five minutes, speechless, warmed from the base of his heels to the crown of his head, his scalp rippling. Waves of appreciative heat kept sweeping up over him, as he wondered just what this was, this amazing "seeing to him." What exactly was being offered? By this cool, cheeky girl of eighteen?

Chapter 24

In blending perfume, ambergris can be used to intensify a fragrance. Just a touch of it mellows and strengthens. It makes its surrounding scents glow, as from a soft warm light within, a radiance that cannot be duplicated by any other ingredient.

Charles Harcourt, Prince d'Harcourt
On the Nature and Uses of Ambergris

What Louise meant by "seeing to him" appeared to be this: At the baptism of his sister's new daughter that week—to which the twit on grand tour somehow wrangled an invitation—Louise took Charles's hand as they left the church. She held it the entire time as they greeted family and friends. Afterward, at the party that followed, when Charles restlessly followed the silly mummery of his own cousin, as the young man tried to impress her, she crossed the room to Charles. She acknowledged those with him, casually latching her arm into his, then stood up onto her toes, leaned, and kissed his cheek.

The sensation itself was astounding, her taffeta bosom pressed up against his coat sleeve and arm for an instant, her soft lips just forward of his ear, at his bad side, no less. But the emotion, the feeling of connection to her as she did this, was overwhelming. Louise matter-of-factly turned the jealous insecurity he felt—what could have been such a bone of contention between them—into an easy, pleasant release of a partner's angst.

Her attitude didn't eliminate his anxiety. Charles still could become fearful and unhappy that other men, handsomer than himself, wanted her attention. But somehow she wooed his edginess; it became tangible, like a sting they blew on together, a sting she preferred to encourage to heal rather than to chafe and aggravate out of careless disregard.

Charles had not asked for this understanding. He had not known to want it. Louise herself could still be quite distant. Her face could grow vacant. She was not promising love or undying passion, but this "selfish" girl gave Charles what he could never recall having: close, honest knowledge of him tempered with compassion. And he so loved her for it, he hardly knew what to think, where to look.

They returned to Nice again the first weekend in October. They had just entered the house. Charles was in the process of making himself comfortable, taking off his coat and vest, loosening his cravat, when he and Louise found a huge bouquet of roses in a box on the dining-room table.

Charles read the card enclosed, then said, "I hope you don't mind. I am going to have to wrap my cane about the throat of that young fellow on grand tour, then hang him out to dry."

Louise laughed and threw the roses into the trash.

Charles, not laughing, got them out again and wrote a scathing reply, after which he snapped the heads off each flower, then boxed the mess back up, note, headless stems, buds and all. By the time he had done this, however, Louise had disappeared.

He sighed. He could return the flowers, but what did it matter? For there was one fellow that neither he nor Louise could seem to send packing. Himself. His other self from the ship. He knew where Louise was and what she was doing, but had no idea how to intervene.

She had gone where she always went immediately upon returning to Nice. Charles followed after her, down onto the beach.

As recently as two weeks ago, Charles had thought, Louise will get over the man from the ship. Hers was a case of first love. A bad case, but still essentially a young woman's first experience with adult emotions, adult dealings; her first fully realized romance with life. It would fade with time, maturity. Meanwhile she would have Charles in the flesh before her, demonstrating daily all they had in common, all they didn't have in common that dovetailed so perfectly. A living, breathing man could outshine a memory any day.

Yet something out there, within the Charles he *had* been, drew her like unfinished business. He worried about the intensity of their shipboard relationship. He worried about the bewilderingly hurt young woman he had carried out of the bathtub at the end of their first day of marriage, then the woman who'd demanded to go to Nice after smelling perfume. The affair seemed to have ended with more pain for Louise than he would have imagined. He feared less obvious problems, things she wouldn't admit or he could only guess at. For one, he had encouraged her imagination. *I am whatever, whomever you want me to be.* He feared she had somehow made his other self into a paragon, filling in the blanks of the dark with all her young heart desired, to an extent that no real man could meet expectation—leaving her to be constant and faithful to an ideal.

On the beach, as he came up on her, she stood

facing seaward, watching out over the water, quite possibly facing the invisible shore of Tunisia. In love with a phantom. In love with disaster, if ever Charles saw it coming.

So, tell her, he thought. This was the time. Things were good between them. Now. Tell her. Yet he counseled himself with these words a hundred times daily, then he always opened his mouth and said things like, "So have you told this young scallywag he should damn well leave you alone?"

Louise startled. Her hair blew. The breeze had taken wisps of it out of its coil. One blew across her face as she turned toward him. This slightly disheveled creature blinked. She hadn't known he was here. She asked, "Told whom?"

"The British bloke who sends you flowers."

"Aah." She nodded and relaxed, looking back out to sea. The water was calm but for ripples of wind gusting the surface. The air was cool, overcast, brewing the first autumn rain. "Yes, Charles, I have told him. But sometimes fools take a while to understand."

Yes, he thought. He looked down, inadvertently chastised.

He could remember himself on the ship—oh, so cynical, so cleverly avoiding the word *love*. He had just petted Louise and listened to her and stroked her night after night, cooing at her pleasure, calling her in his mind his poor, misjudged darling, his sweet friend, his wife. Without ever saying the word, he had emotionally married Louise Vandermeer somewhere back on the ship during five days' acquaintance. He hadn't been the same since.

She touched his arm. He captured her hand, kissed her palm; this had become reflex. In private at least, he was allowed to touch and hold and kiss Louise's hands all he wished, and, heaven above, did he do it; he knew this woman's fingers and palms and knuckles

and the backs of her hands better than he had known
any part of any woman he'd possessed from any
which way or direction. Then Louise wrenched her
hand free. Unexpectedly she ran her fingers along his
neck, a touch inside the collar of his shirt, then out to
drift flat-palmed down the shirt's placket, his chest.
Charles tried, unsuccessfully, to suppress his jerking
spasm of pure, startled delight.

At the waistband of his trousers, her hand pulled
back, while her eyes, her extraordinary gaze—the
color of hyacinths—regarded him.

He had been about to say something, but now
forgot what it was. He'd lost his grip on any rational
reason for having come out here.

Except to be touched like that again.

Addled, he tried to remember the thread. He began,
"You know the fellow you've told me about, the one
whom you say is dead—"

"No." She interrupted. She compressed her lips,
shaking her head. "We needn't speak of it. Once, this
might have been the one place where you had reason
to be jealous, but not now."

Not now? Charles tried to decipher where this put
him, this no longer having to be jealous of himself. It
didn't matter. He was going to do what he'd set out to
do. "Louise," he said. "I want to tell you
something—"

And they both stopped. He'd said her name. The
name he called her in his mind had come out of his
mouth. She turned immediately.

Louise looked to see the face of this man. And there
it was, of course. His odd, appealing face. Yet for an
instant—

No. He had only said the name that she wished
sometimes to hear. Still, she couldn't help asking,
"Why did you call me that?"

He didn't say anything for a moment. "I don't
know. It just came out. It pleases me, I suppose, to

have all your names, every aspect of you." He said, "I want all of you, you see: the full and open you."

Full and open. The phrase reminded her of the day he had taken his clothes off in front of her bathtub. He was like that now, she sensed, ready to strip down again in front of her.

She became facetious. "I was open once—" She stopped herself with a short dry laugh. "But it didn't work out."

He stared at her till she turned away again, looking back out over the water. Then very quietly, his voice said, "Be that way now. With me." So painfully sincere.

She wanted to say something, but her throat was too tight.

When she didn't respond, he seemed to guess the reason. He began again, "This other fellow whom you say is dead—"

She interrupted. "Really, Charles, it's over. It's so, so over." Then she confessed, "And he's not dead. I only wish he were."

"Pardon?"

She kept her eyes straight, looking out to sea. She couldn't face her husband. But she was going to do this for him, force herself out into the open again. She began awkwardly, "We had an affair. You see, it was supposed to be safe. I thought I—that I would let him see—well, not see exactly—that I would be—" She sighed, frustrated with her inarticulateness. "With—"

Her throat tightened again, this time taking her voice. She forced the words out anyway, forming them with only lips and breath. She said, "With him, I became aloud the person I had always been silently inside myself."

This left a pause, which she quickly tried to fill, still whispering. "I thought I could let myself be . . . candid. That I could try candor out, because we were having an affair. It would end." Her voice cracked as it came back, vocal one moment, only air and insistence the next. "If I made a mess of all my private fears and hopes and opinions or hated the sound of them, I could go back, pretend they had never been uttered. Only this openness and the way he seemed to respond to it, to the secret me—"

She couldn't go on for a moment. Her throat closed completely, tight, painful. She swallowed, bit her lips together, then said with surprising vigor, "It made me feel closer to him than I'd realized it would. I liked it. I liked me. I liked the whole feeling.

"He didn't. He left me. Exactly as we'd planned, yet, well— I thought I had changed something, that I— Oh—" She shook her head. "It doesn't matter. He was handsome, dashing, a real Casanova, now that I think back. Very smooth. He'd done this before, I'm sure." She added, "And I hate him for the deception of it all, for the way he peeled me down to the quick, then left: making a joke of my trust."

She waited to hear what Charles would say, afraid to look at him for fear of seeing abhorrence on his face. When he said nothing, she added, "The reason I'm telling you is that you think it's your looks that make me distant. It's not. I have become quite fond of your appearance. It's not you.

"It's me. I have always felt—" So ungraceful, this, so halting. Ineloquent, blunt. But she continued, "I have always felt estranged from other people. And now I'm in a rage, to boot. Such a turmoil inside." She pressed her lips together. "I am so angry— At myself. At him, too, I suppose. A fury."

There was just the lap of waves for a full measure before his voice said, "You don't seem furious. Surely, you're not so angry that you—"

"Oh, I am, I assure you." She laughed at him, at his rancorless inability to know precisely what she meant. "I'm too well-taught to let it show. I rage quietly: I seethe." It felt really good to speak these things finally, to tell Charles in particular.

Louise said, softly, clearly, "It's a little like grief, loss. I keep remembering him. Even when I don't want to. And the fact of remembering enrages me. Everything makes me indignant. *He* makes me furious. I was open, nakedly so; while he was as closed as a locked, windowless room. And he had a knack for playing on this, actually making it appealing—to put yourself blindly in his power. Sometimes, I think, that if I could find him for just a minute, if I accidentally came across him, I'd, you know—" She risked a sideways glance.

Charles was staring at her, his face blank, a man without a clue. He murmured, "No, I don't. What would you do?"

She laughed, surprisingly: heartily. "Lay into him, at the very least, I'll tell you that. I would enjoy it." With good-natured vengefulness, she imagined out loud, "Oh, I could knock that stupid, game-playing Lothario down, shove him to the ground and stand on him. Unforgivable," she said. "Such a shallow, stupid way to entertain himself. The idiot."

After a moment, the voice beside her said, "Yes. I don't blame you a bit. He sounds like a damn stupid bugger to me."

Louise kept her head down, waiting for something more. She didn't realize Charles had turned away from her till she heard his footfalls treading, sinking in wet stones.

She jerked her head up, fretful for an instant. Had she hurt him telling him these things? That someone else used to be important, someone she was angry with now? That it was he, her husband, whom she trusted—so much in fact that she could speak to him of what had hurt her more than she could ever remember being hurt? This was good to tell him, wasn't it?

Good, bad, indifferent, the man who walked down
the beach did not seem to be sulking or particularly
injured. He looked merely introspective, a man with a
lot on his mind.

Cold water lapped suddenly over Louise's feet to
her ankles. She lifted her skirt automatically, watching the wind blow Charles's shirt against his torso.
The breeze flipped his dark hair out to the side.

Yes, she *was* fond of his appearance. He was a fine,
fine figure of a man. With a loping, even walk when
his knee wasn't stiff. With an intriguing sort of
rhythm, when he was riding too much—his knees and
thighs used overlong, overhard on horseback. He was
not willing to live as he should to keep himself free of
pain—an attitude that put a slight catch to his walk
now every two or three steps.

The wind flapped Charles's shirt against his back,
then wet it with the first spray of rain, making
cambric cling into the deep channel between muscles
that cut from between his shoulder blades down into
the waistband of his trousers.

Oh my. Oh, me, oh, my. Louise tented her hands up
over her nose and mouth, a gesture of discovery—
shock and wonder. Never mind her anger or the other
man or even why this one walked away. *This* man.

She wanted him.

And not just a kiss on the hand. She wanted the
whole of his body. When had this happened? When
had she started to want inside her the man with the
strange eye and scar and uneven gait . . . and beautiful back and strong shoulders. And sincere, gentle
concern for her.

Gracious heaven, she might even love him. Flaws
and all, in reality, not fantasy.

This prospect delighted her at first. It would work
out perfectly: They could love each other.

But on second consideration, Louise grew wary of
what her half of "loving each other" might mean, of

what she had to offer. Yes, her remarkable beauty; ho hum. Surely something more. What else had he told her? Her will. This made her smile. Her will? She didn't know about this.

But she knew she had a sharp mind. And, alas, sometimes a sharp tongue. To the good, she had also a vivid imagination. (She imagined for a moment, her husband walking away—something in his move-ment—looked like her shipboard Charles. Which was impossible, since she had never really seen him.) She had integrity, she hoped; she was working on it. She laughed again. *Flinging herself headlong toward it,* Charles would say. Her will. Yes. She had this quality. Something newly recognized. She had a will of iron, and this was a powerful thing, a good thing if she used it right.

Were these things, their combination, lovable?

Despite the love Charles claimed, she feared they weren't. She wished for sweetness, for compassion, for goodness and kindness. She reached for these, but any instant of any one of them was always hard gained. It wasn't that she didn't care for others. She cared for Charles, she was sure. She just held every-one, including herself, to a very high standard.

Then she wondered, did any of this matter? She wanted the man down the beach anyway; hang wheth-er or not she was worthy of him. Aah, she laughed to herself, the joys of true and utter selfishness: to have what one didn't deserve.

If he thought he loved her, why not test this out? Try it, sample it. See if what she and Charles Harcourt felt for one another were connected, even remotely, to this word. *Love.*

She surveyed her husband now openly as he tramped in the tide, one hand shoved deep in his pocket. She knew no one, had never known anyone else, like Charles Harcourt. He *was* a magician, a wizard in his own self-creation. He had taken what

fate had given him and made a masterpiece, a lovely,
velvety harmony of stylish taste, strength of character,
gentleness, generosity, intelligence, all of which had
been intensified or mellowed or strengthened or
something by his oddity of appearance: enhanced by
it into something far, far more appealing than the sum
of his parts without it.

The sea broke Louise's reverie by washing her bare
feet cold again. She missed her skirt this time. The
water receded, and the skirt clung to her ankles. The
water swayed toward her again. The gentle Mediterranean. She looked out across its blueness, heavily
rain-spattered at the distance, a staccato-blue that
appeared to run all the way to the opposite shore. Oh,
dear. Charles and Charles, only inverted. It was her
husband she wanted, the other that she wished would
leave. This ghost she couldn't exorcize, so alive and
viable sometimes—she had more imagination than
she liked. She looked at her husband again and
frowned. He so reminded her sometimes. . . .

Louise tried to act on her new thinking. That night,
she went into Charles's bedroom there in Nice, a huge
place with every modern amenity. He was brushing
his teeth at a plumbed sink.

He stopped when he saw her, his brush in his
mouth, his regard watching her over the brush handle.
She took the brush, set it down onto the porcelain,
then pulled his face to her. She kissed him. He was so
taken aback, he let her proceed with neither help nor
interference for easily ten seconds, just a low-throated
groan in response. He loved it, there was no doubt.
She did too. His teeth felt glassy, his mouth acrid
from the soda he used. The kiss was tasty, cool from
water, warm from the heat inside the mouth of a man.
Then the man part of it took hold of Louise with such
manly force, she went backward. Her shoulders hit

the wall—and the wall switch of their modern house—interrupting the circuit.

Instant dark.

Her husband halted a moment, seemingly bewildered. Almost as if he couldn't find her in the blackness. She halted, too. The two of them stood there, just the sound of their breathing.

The moment was somehow very puzzling. To both of them. Then it was broken. He flipped on the light. They stared at one another. As if someone, another man, had sneaked in between them. The other Charles. He seemed as present in that moment as if he stood there for them both to see.

It had happened again. One man. Two men. A relentless, unexplainable parallel. Louise could have made sense of it to herself if only her husband had been on the ship. Or been handsome and unhalting, obnoxiously confident. She now knew he walked sometimes without the limp by which she had thought at one time to rule him out—then she had to ask herself, *Rule him out for what?*

For nothing that made any sense.

Thus, Louise's small revelations of love and yearning came to little or nothing at first. No immediate change in the course of her life or in the trajectory of what seemed to be happening to her.

The sea became a kind of fixation. As if it were the source of her conflict. While in Nice, she walked across the street to it most everyday. When they returned to Grasse, she hardly missed an opportunity to catch sight of it between cliffs or trees or rooftops. She wanted to be where she was, beside Charles. Yet she daydreamed sometimes, thinking she could hire a boat for a day, for a week. She would understand everything if she could only sail out, float with the wind to Tangier or Marakesh or Casablanca . . . the names of these places sounding as fanciful to her mind's ear as Eden or Paradise or Valhalla. Or Hell.

She attempted to do more than ponder and fret. She tried to face the jasmine perfume Charles brought her, but in the end simply faced its closed bottle. She met with her tutor once, then forgot to do the reading for next time and canceled. Her appetite became picky. She lost weight. In Grasse, where Tino was so capable, she let herself fall into an unhealthy habit: She would get up, go out to her bedroom balcony, then sit in her nightgown and stare at the Mediterranean twenty kilometers off, all the while thinking she was about to go into town or study her lessons or write a thank-you for the last party or other.

A little despondent, nothing more. This was what she told herself. She was between successes, as it were, her life momentarily empty. She had accomplished all the goals set for her; she'd debuted, been wooed, then wed. Her girlish triumph was over. Beyond it, she hadn't found what she wanted to do in life yet; this was the reason she did nothing. She had looked for her raison d'être; she couldn't find it. So it was perfectly logical now that she wait for it to find *her,* right here in a nice cozy chair in the sun.

"May I come in?"

Louise jolted awake. "Wh—what?"

It was dusk. Charles's head peeked around the French doors that opened out onto her bedroom balcony. "I let myself in," he said. "May I join you?"

She sat up in her chair, disoriented. Join her? Where was she? Where was the sun? Where had the day gone? "I'll ah—" She uncurled her feet out from under her, then realized she wore the famous lavender dressing gown, the one he had made somewhat lighter in color. Underneath it, she wore nothing at all. It lay loosely open showing most of one breast. She drew the lapels up, clutching them, and said, "Give me a minute, Charles." She motioned him inside.

When he withdrew, she stood, tied herself in better,

combed her fingers once through her hair. It hung loose. She was a mess.

She walked into her bedroom on the defensive, embarrassed by her laziness and ennui with the faintly angry outlook of a drunk caught taking a swill. Drunk on disorder, she thought. "What do you want?" she asked none too kindly.

"I have something for you." He stood, a large, flat box tucked under his arm. "I know you have not been very happy. I was hoping to cheer you up."

"You don't have to cheer me up, Charles. I'm fine."

"No, you're not," her husband said. He was dressed nicely, a crisp shirt, silk cravat, dark trousers, a slightly florid vest of deep, vividly embroidered colors, one of his long, formal frock coats, one of his fancier canes.

He swiveled the broad box out from under his arm, with the sort of prestidigitatorial flourish of his wrist he could do so naturally. The box was dark velvet, square, the sort used for fine jewelry.

Oh, fine, she thought. More stones. Just what she needed. She was down to her last fifty or so tiaras and necklaces— Then she stopped herself.

She could see the box meant something to Charles. And that he had a speech prepared—she could see his struggle with it in a wincing awkwardness on his face.

He cleared his throat. "I went to Paris and bought this," he said, "before we were married, thinking I was about to become your lover, something I wanted very much. Something I still want—" He waved this away, not what he wished to speak of.

He said, "But I would like to give this to you now because I have become something else that I never imagined to become: your friend. We are real friends. Dear friends, I think. And so, because I have had a hundred lovers, yet seem to have acquired only one dearest friend, I would like to present you with"—he laughed a little bleakly—"a wedding gift." He offered

the box out with a huge exhalation of relief, ordeal
ended.

The box was covered in midnight blue velvet, silk
velvet, Louise realized, as she took it into her hands.
"Oh, Charles," she said. Jewelry or not, she felt
pleased by the gesture. "Charles, you don't need to do
this—"

"Open it." He smiled widely.

The hinge was sprung, the lid rimmed in etched
silver. The box opened easily with a twist of the
fingers. It contained—

Black pearls. Louise stared at them. They were
rather like her black pearls that lay broken. A string of
them having snapped then bounced all over a ship's
deck . . . one single pearl rolled on her cheek, eaten
off fingers . . . then looping and rolling across a tilting
floor. . . .

Indeed, the floor beneath Louise's feet seemed to
tip.

"Here. Let me put them on for you," he said.

"But— How— How could you know?" she asked.

"Know what?"

"That, that I love—oh, God—miss—"

"You wore black pearls in the photograph your
father sent me and in the painting they have of you at
their house in New York. I decided you would like
these. So I bought them."

Yes. Yes, this made sense. "No," she said, which did
not. She backed up.

Charles came forward, lifting the box away from
her. A moment later she felt the weight—not ounces,
more like pounds—of hundreds of black pearls hitting her chest. Multiple strands that started high at
her throat, looping down over the front of her dressing gown past her waist.

"Oh, Charles, this is so kind of you. They are so—"
Heavy. Cold. The higher strands at the base of her
throat fell down into the front of her gown. Then,

each time she moved, these pulled another strand in; the tiers were interconnected by tiny platinum bars. Meanwhile, Charles kept fastening, his arms blocking her vision, the smell of him up against her. A citrusy musk with—she recognized the scent now—rich amber notes. So unlike her husband, so like—God, was it possible that he had somehow bought, used her lover's soap or aftershave? She reached over her shoulders to grab round back of her neck, making the pearls down inside bobble and roll over the tops of her breasts. "I—" She couldn't speak.

He said, "I'm glad you like them. Here, let me. I'll do it; move your hands. You're just getting your hair tangled into the clasp." He pushed her hands out of the way, clicked three or four things down the back of her neck, then said, "There," and stood back.

More pearls fell into the front of the dressing gown, a bizarre and awful sensation. Louise raised her arms again. Behind her, she couldn't find the clasp immediately under her hair. She wasn't sure she wanted them off. She was trying to like them. Trying to.

Then suddenly, quite emphatically, she couldn't like them at all.

She found the clasp only to discover the fastenings to be multiple and unbelievably complicated. Frustration mounted. She gave a twist, elbows in the air. "Oh, Charles, help. Take them off." She shook them. More pearls fell down inside the gown, heavy, clacking.

Then with her next jerk, the last of them were drawn inside and, with a *click* and *tappety-clatter* all swung forward and out between the lapels, parting the dressing gown. This pulled the sash, which did a slow, drooping untie. It dropped down. The dressing gown opened completely.

With Louise wishing for nothing but the damnable black pearls off her body. They swung against her, rolling over her breasts as she wrestled with the clasp.

They caught on one nipple, then, when she shook herself to loosen the strand it swung wildly, banging then rolling across her chest to catch on the other. "Help me." She looked at Charles, pleading.

The necklace felt eerie, terrible. The embodiment of the obstacles—this other man, her own fears, her own uncontrolled, sometimes mean spirit. "Please," she said.

He just stood there. "Good God." His mouth hung open a moment. He closed it. He licked his lips. He stared. "You—your skin is the color of ivory— And—and—" His attention tried to avoid dropping downward, scanning for a safe spot to look, then gave up. He fixed his gaze on the last place he should. "And you're blond. The color of the sand at Antibes."

Damn him. "Charles, I can't undo it." Louise's fingers felt fat, stupid. "You put it on! Take it off!"

"Take it off?" he murmured, as if she were talking about something else.

The necklace's miserable clasp had eighty-seven pieces to it. It was hard and sharp-edged and tiny. Her blasted hair was everywhere, in the way, snarling through a pearl-strung nightmare. A heavy, slithering strand parted over one breast, a cord that swayed, as slick as glass, all but alive, licking, flicker-tongued, to her waist, looping.

Louise shuddered. Her whole body had begun to shake with an urgency. "Charles—" she begged. "Please." Tiers of miserable pearls attacked. Tiers—

Tears. Oh, no, not tears. Yet the more distraught she became, the more her throat tightened, her eyes stung.

While the wretched man stood there, immobile, staring her up then down, covering her body that stood exposed in the shadows of lavender flaps. His breathing became audible, while he kept his mouth clamped tightly as if by sheer will he might regulate what could not be controlled. "God's mercy," he let out in a breath, then couldn't seem to get air.

"Damn you, Charles. Here." She turned around, so he could see her problem. "Undo this."

Behind her, he said, "Louise, if I come near you, the only thing undone will be me. And you. I would—"

"Will you help me, please?" She rattled the clasp that wouldn't give, the heavy necklace *clack-clack-clacketing* as it beat between her breasts and whipped her stomach. She grabbed the thing in her fists. She would break it—

"Stop." Charles. He came up behind her. Warm, tall, solid Charles took hold of the clasp.

The desire to cry eased, though there was somewhere more anxiety. For what? She realized he was trying to help. While he was also drawing her backward into him, up against him. He batted her fingers out of the way, separating hair from pearls. In the midst of this, he bent his head and kissed the curve of her neck.

It was a strong, biting kiss, warm and sharp. It left her hands out, grasping nothing. Then he took hold of her with a force that drove her forward into the wall, her palms and cheek against the wallpaper. He wrapped himself around her, one hand pressing a breastful of pearls, flat-palmed, to rub them round and around as if slowly polishing her chest, the other descending boldly between her legs to mold and cup against her.

Like this, he pulled her into him, his hips from behind pushing against her. Pulled back. Pushed forward. Caught in a strong opposition he held taut. At her buttocks his movement was small, tight, a grind—as he let out a long, slow, satisfied groan, then more intelligibly, "Oh, Go-o-o-d" in a whisper near her ear. *Dieu-u-u-u. Mon Dieu-u-u.*

Oh, God was right. He clutched her and shoved her, holding himself to her, and the pleasure, oh, the pleasure of him. More than strong, more than eerie;

more than healthy, she was sure. A sweet suffocation. She slid an inch up the wall then back, chafing her cheek as his movement lifted her up onto her toes then let her down. His hand between her legs stroked, rocking, firm contact, while his hand above kept rolling what was strung round her neck, some of the beads smooth round pearls, some angularly cut, all balls rotating on string. *Yes. Oh, yes.* Her husband. She wanted this. She would not think. She would just let it happen. *Yes, Charles, hold me. Love me. Take me as close as you can to you.*

"Turn around," he murmured.

She didn't. She clung, hands flat. He remained behind, while she was hardly able to breathe from the sweet smothering closeness of him pressing her to wallpaper and wainscoting.

"Turn around, Louise."

Such a commotion rose up inside her. Something felt terribly wrong. "Take—" she said, then her voice caught. It had to do with the pearls. "Take the necklace off for me, please."

Charles kept her pinned against the wall, even as he reached up under her hair, nimble fingers that knew what the clasps were all about. She felt the pearls drop down between her and the wall, cupped heavily into the valley of her bosom pressed there.

"Let me up," she said.

She felt him ease back. The pearls fell, rolling over, between, and down the curves of her body—as he turned her by her shoulders.

He pinned her back again, shoulder blades to the wall, as he slipped his arms inside her dressing gown, his palms against the indention of her waist. Then these warm hands slid around to her back and down to her buttocks. He caught her there solidly, lifting. He bent, pulling her forward, naked, into him, pressing forward into her. Effectively sandwiching her between himself and the wall, he kissed her like this.

The kiss was something close to insanity. Hungry.
Unleashed. Unhinged. The power of it was knee-
bending one minute—a swift, ecstatic ascent straight
up into melting carnal sensation—then disturbing,
then slightly horrifying, then out and out terrible. The
sense of wrongness magnified. *His* mouth. *His* body.
While lust, longing, repugnance, attraction, pearls in
the dark . . . these mingled in Louise's mind and
body with spectral force. . . . He smelled of her other
Charles. He felt like her other Charles. He even kissed
like him, moved like him. If he put himself inside her,
he would feel exactly— Oh, dear Mother Mary—

No. Impossible. Her wonderful, loyal husband
would not do such a thing.

Yet when her husband delved his tongue deep into
her mouth, a voice said, *No, he is not similar: He is
identical, the lover on the ship. This* is *he.*

No— Why? To what purpose? No!

Louise began to struggle, a physical corollary to her
internal turmoil. "Charles, let go." She shoved and
floundered.

"What?" he murmured. A rude, blunt *Quoi?* "What
is it, Louise?" The low, deep voice of her Charleses—
both of them.

No. Her husband, she said quite firmly to herself.
And her own vivid imagination. "Get off me," she
said. "Please, Charles—" then for a confusing moment was unsure whom she was speaking to. It didn't
matter. "Please. Stop," she said. "Leave me alone. I
don't feel well."

An understatement. The walls wavered. The floor
seemed to gyrate. Her legs were shaking.

"Lulu?" she heard distantly. She felt cool air up the
front of her.

"Go," she commanded. She opened her eyes, slits.
Her husband backed away, strictly her husband. From
several feet, Charles Harcourt stared at her as if she

were certifiably insane. "Go!" she said more emphatically.

He backed toward the doorway, his odd gaze riveted to her. She pulled her gown around her, then crossed her arms over herself. When he stepped back once more, into the sitting room, she walked forward, full of slow, conscious dignity. She closed her bedroom door, closing out this alarming man.

She pressed the final click of the latch by leaning her shoulder against the dark panels.

And Louise couldn't explain what came next.

She began to slide down the length of the door—as a deep wave of despair rose up like a storm swell, then came down crashing on top of her. It beat her, dragging her down till she sat huddled at the foot of the door. There, ineffable misery found her. Unnameable, no clear cause. Or too many causes; too many dissatisfactions, too many significant failures, too much self-loathing. This feeling pulled her under, making her cry from its onslaught. She could find nothing to hang onto, no possible way to mitigate or pacify the effect. Louise sank deep into a dark pool of defeat and injustice, down, down to the bottom where she drowned for more than half an hour in diaphragm-deep, hiccuping sobs and tears.

This left Charles on the other side of the door, his forehead leaning against it while he witnessed the sounds of Louise's collapse. He felt bereft, appalled— appalled at himself. And guilty. Guilty above all else. She grieved for something, for him possibly, the other him. As if he really were dead.

Which, Charles thought, he may as well be.

This can't go on. Enough. It was time to sit her down and explain the whole dastardly business. No more hedging or protecting himself. He was making her sick with this game.

Chapter 25

❧❧❧

*In some oriental cultures, ambergris is
believed to increase fertility.*

Charles Harcourt, Prince d'Harcourt
On the Nature and Uses of Ambergris

What you have made her, Harcourt, is pregnant," said Doctor Olivier. Charles had
called him the next afternoon when Louise had slept
like the dead past midday. "Don't fret so," the doctor
told him. "Your wife is perfectly healthy. Robust, in
fact. She may have lost a little weight, but that
sometimes happens at the beginning. The new baby
affects the mother's appetite. Favorite foods don't sit
so well as they once did. And you mustn't take it to
heart if she cries over one thing or another. New
mothers can be a little emotional."

"Pregnant," Charles repeated stupidly. "Then—
Then what do I do?"

"Do?"

Charles didn't know what sort of advice he was
asking for. Pregnancy was the one thing that had not
occurred to him as a reason for Louise's listless
behavior. One didn't leap to the idea of a fruitful

womb when one hadn't planted, well, any fruit in a while. "Pregnant," he repeated again.

Olivier laughed. "Yes, and you do nothing. These things take care of themselves. Besides, she is only a little bit pregnant."

"A little bit pregnant?"

"The internal tissue has begun to darken, change color. The uterus is up, the tiniest bump rising up out of her pelvis, hardly anything. But I am fairly sure: She tells me her menses are two weeks late." He winked at him. "This is a very indicative sign when one has been married just over a month." He winked again, like a nervous twitch of the eye. "A honeymoon baby." He thumped Charles on the back, his *thwack, thwack, thwack* saying, *you potent dog, you.* "Congratulations." The doctor offered his hand. "With a beginning like this"—he pumped Charles's arm vigorously—"you will catch up to your uncle in no time: knee-deep in children."

The doctor left, and Charles just stood there in the foyer. Pregnant. His wife, whom he had never slept with as his wife, was pregnant. This could be a little delicate—

But, no. No more delicacy. Pregnancy might explain some of Louise's distress, but it didn't explain the degree of it. And Charles was fairly certain what did. He must be absolutely brave and forthright. He was going to march up to her room, tell her everything, and—he smiled at the thought—claim this child. A child. A family. Charles was astounded to think of himself as a father. A baby. His baby.

In a kind of delighted daze, he walked upstairs, steeling himself with explanations, admissions, apologies. Long, heartfelt apologies. Louise was about to have the object of her rage appear before her. And he had no illusions that he would get off easy, just because a baby was involved. He was prepared; she would be fuming-mad. But once she knew, once she forgave him—

He paused at Louise's bedroom door, then drew a deep breath and knocked.

"Come in," Louise's voice said.

Charles entered, nodding at Josette. To the maid, he said, "Would you leave us alone, please?"

The door closed as he walked to the foot of the bed. Louise looked quite a bit better than yesterday. Her eyes were slightly puffy, but her color was good. She lay flat out under the canopy, her head and shoulders propped up. As terrible as it was, he thought she looked fabulous, all tousled from a bad night's sleep, her hair unbraided, under and about her in tangles, lying there with his child inside her.

And she looked guilty. This realization—that she felt guilty of something—was surprising for an instant, then almost humorous. Louise had always spoken of her "affair" in phrases that sounded distant, in a previous time, a previous life, an eon ago—never so recent as to leave her present self pregnant.

She thought *she* had something to explain.

Charles would have laughed if he hadn't been so nervous himself. He put his hands in his pockets, glanced down a moment at her toes where they steepled the covers. "Are you all right?" he murmured.

She nodded in the affirmative, her gaze coming up only as far as his chin, then said, "Though still trying to find my dignity after a pretty embarrassing doctor's examination." She added, "Not half so embarrassing as his diagnosis, though." Meekly, she asked, "Did he tell you?"

"Yes."

The two of them stayed like this for a minute: Charles at the foot of the bed, praying for an easy time, a quick acceptance and forgiveness. Louise, her

face slightly lowered, her color high; pink cheeks. Her
eyes availed themselves of their long lashes, hiding.
Self-convicted and condemned.

"I lied to him," she said.

"Did you?"

"My menses are four weeks late. Almost. You see,
they were supposed to come right about the time
we were married, so I thought, what with all the excitement and what-not, that they were just late.
It's happened before. But—" She sighed. "I guess
not."

"No. I guess not." He didn't know what else to
say. She was upset. He was actually happy. A baby, he
kept thinking. The family he wanted. Charles smiled
at her then took hold of her toes under the covers,
jiggling them affectionately. "It will be all right,"
he said. He didn't know where to begin, so he just
blurted out the best part: "You see, it's mine. The
baby is mine."

Louise sluiced her eyes up to him immediately. She
pondered this a moment, frowning. She bit her lip.
"Oh, no, Charles, you mustn't—"

He said it more clearly: "I am the baby's father."

She looked confused a moment, then looked away.
"Charles." She pressed her lips. "I appreciate what
you are saying, what you are trying to do. You are the
most noble, upright, wonderful human being—"

He shifted. "Well, I'm not so—"

"No, no. You are such a good man." She meant it.
Her eyes raised up to him, full of belief. Or perhaps of
wanting to believe. "So, you see, I absolutely won't
have any more pretense between us. I want you to
know: The affair I've told you about. It was on the
ship." She put her hand over her mouth, bowing her
head. "Dear Lord, I am so embarrassed." Then, with
her head down, looking as demure and sweet as
possible, the lovely Louise murmured in English, "He

said something about protection, something: He did this on purpose, that son of a bitch."

Charles's brow rose up of its own accord. He felt his scalp slide back.

She continued. "As much as I love you—and I do, Charles—the memory of this other, oh, this scoundrel, won't let me be. I just want revenge— If I could just have revenge. And now there's a damn"—*sacre*, another surprise, she used the word correctly—"piece of him inside me. I'm so mad, I could spit."

"Don't you want the baby?"

She thought a moment. "Well, yes, I suppose I do. I like the idea of a baby. It's an exciting idea. But— Well, I hadn't planned on it happening exactly like this."

"No," he agreed. "But it really is mine, Louise. You see—"

"Charles," she interrupted. "If you want the rest of the world to think the baby is yours, if you want to stand by me, I will be only too grateful. I will tell everyone, of course, whatever you wish. But between us, no charades. Please. I am so glad that every last bit of this affair is out in the open. What a relief. I so hate deceit."

Charles watched and listened and chewed the inside of his cheek.

"And I think," she said, "it might be best if Tino and my parents knew the truth as well, because the baby is going to look like someone else. They will think the worse of me, but, believe me, they will think the better of you. And we will all talk about it and be open and get rid of my pasha, exorcize him with honesty."

"Your what?"

"My pasha." She smiled sheepishly. "That is what I called him to myself. He was Arab, I think. Oh, Charles, the baby is sure to have darkish skin and

very brown eyes. Oh, my. Oh, no—" She looked
contrite. Humble. All in all, not an unpleasant expression to see on this usually self-possessed young face.
"Charles, I'm so sorry. No one will believe it is yours,
no matter what you say: We both have blue eyes."

"Louise, what I am trying to tell you—"

She looked up. "Oh, Charles. You are so dear."

"No." He shook his head. "You see—"

She shook hers. She wasn't listening. She said, "I
wouldn't have expected anything less of you, I suppose. You are the most noble man I have ever met,
Charles Harcourt. The esteem in which I hold you,
my husband, is enormous." She fixed a look of utter
sincerity on him.

He stared at her for a long moment, then looked
away, embarrassed. Charles walked to the window
and looked out.

She said, "The man who sold you the jasmine was
Arab, wasn't he? What was his name?" She was going
to proceed point blank.

He snorted. "Who? Old Al Baghdad?"

"Who?" Her voice was understandably alarmed
after such a strange introduction. She said cautiously,
"I suppose." After a hesitation, she asked, "He is the
father. Do you know him well?"

"I used to think I did." He crossed his arms over his
chest. "And he's no Arab. He's French. A French ass,"
he said. "Who pretends to be Arab or whatever else
suits him, who's seduced half the women up and
down this coast like some idiotic Don Juan, just to
please his vanity. And who is a coward of the first
order." He threw a glance at her over his shoulder.
"And he has fair eyes, by the way."

She frowned. "I don't think so, Charles. He had
brown eyes."

He turned all the way around to look at her. "You
are actually going to argue about this, aren't you?"

Patiently, quietly, she said, "Well, they're brown, Charles."

"They are? You have looked? You have looked deeply into his eyes and found them to be brown?"

How annoying. She didn't believe him. More than annoying. Charles had actually told her he was her romantic interest on the ship, and the damn girl was so sure the fellow was otherwise, handsome and suave—with two fine brown eyes, for God's sake— she didn't believe him.

Louise herself sat, staring at the covers, not sure what she remembered. A quick glimpse of a darkish face behind dark glasses from within the folds of a flowing Middle Eastern headdress. A smooth— brown-eyed?—voice over the ship's telephone?

She asked, "How long have you known him?"

He shrugged.

"Is he so horrible as you say? I mean, I can get fairly indignant about him, but—"

Charles threw her a quick glare, his most fearsome expression.

She shut up. Though not out of fear.

How tormenting this must be for him, Louise thought. Here was a man, after all, who snapped the heads off flowers for no more reason than an amorous note. A man who now faced an amorous note of the largest order—one written on the inside of his wife's womb. It was ruthless to ask further about her lover. Nonetheless, she said, "Tell me about him."

Her husband didn't, of course. He merely shook his head and let out a long sigh—the exasperation of a man put out, not hurt. Not betrayed, just frustrated.

She would think later, here was where her questions ceased wanting information and began overtly testing her reaction.

He opened his mouth.

She spoke first. "Is he handsome?"

Charles's eyes narrowed into a squint. He said vehemently, "He is ugly."

The second the words were out, he blanched, then drew in a deep, violent breath, as if he could suck them back in.

He won her sympathy for a moment. "Oh Charles," she said. Louise became confused, unsure again.

Whomever, whatever they spoke of, the ugliness seemed somehow his *own* admission—a brave one she had never heard out his own lips. It cost him a piece of pride to say it. She told him, "There is nothing ugly about you, sir. You are the finest man I know." She meant it. She said from deep feeling, "From the moment I met you, you have been heroic in your consideration of me, in all you have done and continue to put up with. And I have not always appreciated it. But I want you to know I do now, and that I think you have a magnificent soul, the handsomest heart I know."

Yes. Her handsome, doting husband pleased her. She admired him. She loved him. He loved her. All was perfect.

The finest man she knew then looked at her, a long, fixed stare from across the room by the window. After which he sighed again and headed toward the door. Stopping by the foot of the bed again, he said, "Yes. Hero that I am." He cleared his throat. "If you don't need anything right now, Louise, I think I want to go downstairs for a drink. You know, a little celebration. Of sorts." He admitted, "I guess I am pretty befuddled." He asked again, "Are you all right then?"

"Certainly."

"Good." He ran his hand through his hair. Then he straightened his coat.

Vanity, she thought. Her husband was vain. In the nicest possible way, of course. But he had a discern-

le vanity, so robust and palpable one could have felt
t in the dark.

A palpable vanity in the dark. This thought made
er stop.

No, no. Of course not. Her husband was a good
nan trying to act nobly. Not a scoundrel playing a—
Vhat? A joke? She was a joke to him? No, no, her
usband loved her. Indulgently. To extreme. He did
verything she asked of him. He was loyal and forth-
ight.

The question became, though, how long could an
ntelligent woman lie to herself?

Louise knew as she lay there. She knew that the
uality that had confounded her for more than a
nonth had drawn into one clearly defined entity, and
he was staring right at it: her husband. No, no, she
hought again. She wouldn't admit it. Perhaps by
gnoring it, it wouldn't be true. She smiled at him.
Thank you, Charles. Thank you for so much. You are
o kind, so good to me."

She watched him leave, still not admitting to herself
vho exactly walked quietly past her bedpost and out
er door. Accepting it would mean, of course, that her
ear, loving husband was not so perfectly devoted
nd straightforward as she might like, that he was
erhaps a crafty old soul with a twist or two in his
ature. And, if so, well, then her chief weapon, her
efense against all comers, her perfect exterior, was
ot as all-powerful, as omnipotent and fearsomely
rotective, as she'd thought.

He'd laughed right past it within the first twenty-
our hours of knowing her.

Five minutes later, downstairs where he was pour-
ig his fourth shot of whiskey, Charles heard a loud
cream, a kind of feminine roar, then something—
vo somethings, one crash, two—hit what sounded
ke the wall in Louise's room.

Fine, he thought, as he emptied the shot glass. The
woman upstairs—the victim of a biological
comeuppance—was throwing things. In the interval
of silence that followed, however, Charles decided he
should make sure Louise was all right.

He made it up the stairs without mishap, reflecting
absently at the top that he was amazingly stable. He
could already feel some of the liquor in his blood, yet
it registered in that deceptive way whereby everything
seemed clearer. As he opened the door to Louise's
room, every detail stood out, sober, lucid.

Louise stood by her washstand in her nightgown—
the pretty lilac one he had only ever seen up till now
in bits of lace escaping the dread purple bathrobe. Her
eyes lifted to his from the sight of her washbasin and
pitcher that lay in pieces by the far wall, thrown a
good twenty feet. He watched emotions flit across her
features: anger, dismay, almost perplexity, as she
looked at the broken bits, then up at him, and her
frowning face crumpled.

"It's all right," Charles murmured. He stepped into
the room. She let him fold her into his arms. "It's
okay. You can break everything in the damn house."

He was about to say more, but she took his breath
away by leaning back then running her palms up his
chest. Two hands up the front of him, then out over
his shoulders and down his arms till she stopped
poised there, her hands on his wrists behind her as she
leaned out—the leverage pressing her hips with
alarming snugness to his. She stayed like this, elbows
back, her face frowning, scanning his features, looking for something, God knew what.

Her lips parted, as if she might say something. Yet
her soft, damp mouth remained speechless. Inside, he
could see the slick top edge of even, white teeth. And
something, maybe the liquor, made him a little dizzy
for a moment. Louise's hair was disheveled. His hand
supported her, her long, graceful back narrowing

beneath his palms into the small, his forearms resting on the curve where her hips flared, full and feminine. And there it was: unendurable. He would have kissed her.

Except, surprisingly, she kissed him first, pushing forward and standing on her toes. It was a hungry kiss, full, eager, welcoming, her mouth wet and hot as it should be. Yet as he took what she offered—the moment he twisted his head, tucked her up against him, and tongued her mouth the way he wanted to—her fists came up to pound two hard blows on his chest. Mystifying.

Charles knew, though, that something had changed. He picked her up and had them both on the bed with surprising alacrity for a man who was starting to feel the room sway.

Lord, she was soft and smooth. And he was greedy. He found her most tender, vulnerable place then loved the leap of her body, her crooning pleasure, as he slid his finger inside her. Oh, yes, he thought, she was slick, copiously wet. The room began to spin, maybe partly from the whiskey, but definitely mostly from Louise.

As he pulled at buttons along the fly of his trousers, she murmured, "Tell me."

So he did, as he kissed her neck, her cheek, her jaw. "I am mad for you. I want to touch you everywhere, love you with my body, weigh you down, feel you—"

"No," she said and shoved at him, then rotated in his arms. "Oh, Charles." Inconsolable again. She curled up.

No? He curved around her, pulling her into him, thinking to comfort her—whereby his very stiff erection, now free, ended up nudged into the valley between two smooth, warm moons of buttocks. He shuddered, trying to figure out why she'd turned and what *no* was all about when every other cue said *yes*. But poor man. So desperate. His hips moved forward, one stroke through the cleft and into the tight space between her thighs, and his body lit up like a sky at sunrise. His mind went blank, a hot, bright white from the feel of the intimate surround, the powdery-warm smoothness of her flesh along the shaft. Then—the real one-eyed monster—the tip of his penis, like the end of a divining rod, found her wetness. His hands seized her hips, and the head was in before he even knew what he'd done.

She resisted a moment, though it was hardly anything, for he had vigorous hold of her. Her flesh seemed to cling to him, slippery, grabbing, pulling, releasing then sliding and reaching again, complemented by this other long, blissful caress through her creamy-smooth haunches. She moaned—he couldn't tell if it was the sound of pain or pleasure, dispute or cooperation. He wrapped his hands, his arms about her and gripped her with all the strength in him, entering again.

And Louise, sweet Louise, angled her buttocks, cocked it back as she pushed into him and bent forward over her knees, an instinct so right, so blessedly right. He went so deep he bumped the neck of her womb. And exploded. That was it. Bursts. Bright cannonballs with a seeming weight and force that scattered him.

He came to a semblance of sanity with the bed's canopy doing a slow tilt and rotation that lifted his stomach. The whiskey was rampant at this point, chased into his veins by the pounding bliss of Louise. A few square inches of his body was full of gladness, but the rest of him was under siege. And Louise herself . . .

She did say something, but he only shook his head He should take his arm off his eyes, he thought; the room would move less if he kept his sight focused This advice to himself was the last thing he remem bered. Exhaustion, anxiety, unconsciousness, whatev er it was, it took him.

Chapter 26

A ritual exists among whalers: Immediately upon hefting a sperm whale onto the deck, harpoons are struck deep into the animal's hindgut. These harpoons' tips, withdrawn, are then smelled for the telltale odor of a quick fortune.

Charles Harcourt, Prince d'Harcourt
On the Nature and Uses of Ambergris

The legend had grown from this: an elopement after two weeks' acquaintance, public kisses— not just on the mouth, but on the knuckles and palms and at the wrists between buttons of gloves. These witnessed facts were embellished by rumors of a wedding night that could not outwait dinner, with wild, literally upturning results. From the serving classes came the additional gossip of a cavort through the house that left a trail of water and wet clothes from the bath down the hall, through a sitting room, and into the bedroom. Add to this a necklace of excessive and uxorious value which that very next night to the opening of a play, Louise was suddenly and appreciatively able to wear without tearing it from her neck) and, well—

There was not much Charles could have done about it. He found himself the idol and envy of every man, the amorous ideal of every woman, he met, with Louise his female counterpart. The Prince and Princess d'Harcourt were pronounced the most romantic couple up or down the Riviera—a title bestowed on them, no matter how modestly he had tried to redefine it, by family, friends, eventually mere acquaintances, strangers, finally reading it in the morning's newspaper two days after the mayhem of Louise's discovered pregnancy and what Charles now thought of as the worst sexual debacle of his life.

"Well, someone didn't waste time. Listen to this," he said to Louise over breakfast.

They sat in their formal dining room in Nice, the large space being required, since "breakfast" entailed a bewildering feast. Louise, who had arranged it, ate with appetite. Charles drank *café au lait* as he read from the morning paper. "'And guess who is expecting a little prince or princess of their own? None other than those two lovebirds that have us all swooning from heatstroke just watching them: the Prince and Princess d'Harcourt. Rumor has it that the next generation of old French "royalty" may even be just a teeny bit early. Wicked congratulations, Your Highnesses. Apparently even old royal blood can come to a boil a bit faster than strictly correct.'"

Louise laughed.

Charles looked up over the edge of newsprint at her. She sat cater-corner to him at their long dining-room table, where she scooped "American" scrambled eggs onto a fork. "Oh, that is vicious!" Her laughter became hearty. If she found the snipes in the society columns mean, they were apparently a brand of meanness that she could deeply appreciate. As tasty as the bacon she took to go with the bite of eggs.

He made a pull of his mouth. " 'Heatstroke'?"

"They're being silly," she said.

" 'Heatstroke'?" he repeated. "You cry in the bath or you threaten to slap my face, and they get heatstroke?" He couldn't even speak aloud of their one strangely at-odds sexual union night before last. It demoralized him. All he knew was that since then Louise was somehow edgy and angry with him. And that he didn't even want to consider what this might imply.

She grew quiet and buttered her toast.

Charles folded the paper, "So were your parents suspicious?"

"Regarding what?"

He nodded a glance toward her stomach, toward the baby that would arrive early.

"Aah," she said. "No, I don't think so. I'm glad we're not telling them who the real father is."

Charles had convinced her not to tell their families the "truth." He smiled, pleased that at least this complication, and humiliation, had been removed from his path.

Then he wasn't pleased at all to hear, "No, the only one we really need to be honest with is the father himself. How do we get in touch with, ah, who did you call him? Baghdad Al?"

"We don't." Charles set his coffee cup down stiffly.

"He has a right to know."

He frowned. "No, he doesn't."

"Wouldn't you want to know if you had a child on the way?"

"Absolutely not. I would definitely not wish to be told I had fathered a child on some woman during a brief affair on a ship."

She made a dubious face that sweetly called him a liar. "Yes, you would," she said. "Ask him to dinner."

"What?" Charles laughed at first.

"Invite him to dinner," she said.

"I most certainly will not." He pushed away from

the dining-room table and stood. "He wouldn't come anyway, Louise." A virtual certainty.

"Explain. You know him. Tell him—"

The walls of the room did an interesting thing, three of the four of them were covered in framed mirrors, every shape and size. It was a lifetime's collection, an interest of Charles's; his gallery of looking glasses. These reflected him in multiple incarnations now as he suggested, "I can inform him about the baby."

"I want to tell him myself. You convince him to come."

"I won't." More plausibly, he said, "I can't."

As if they had arrived somewhere in this conversation, Louise sat back and folded her arms. She asked, "All right, Charles: Why not?"

Why not, why not, why not? This phrase repeated like his image in the mirrors. Charles caught a look at his own face, a man confused, uncertain in every framed piece of glass. *Why not?*

Because, Charles thought, he had completely lost his way. Because his own machinations had become so convoluted, he had given up trying to find the path out of them. He just wanted to bury her pasha at this point. (Her *pasha,* for God's sake. Why did women think this way?) Louise was angry with this other Charles; she was fierce. She admired Charles Harcourt. So Charles Harcourt guiltily accepted her admiration. Her idealized impression of him seemed the only thing in his favor. A hero indeed. But heroes occasionally got to shag the rescued maiden, and he was fairly certain rotten bastards didn't.

He prayed for insight and a rematch.

Sexually, he feared that Charles Harcourt compared badly to her pasha, which especially worried him come to think of it, in light of her request—no, her demand—to see this other fellow.

Lost again, Charles thought. He couldn't figure out *what* Louise's relationship was to his other self. She hated the shallowness of their affair, the trickery, yet he feared that she had never completely let go of the fantasy man in the dark.

Louise seemed to care about both of him. (*Both of him.* The phrase itself made him dizzy.) So where did this leave him?

Nowhere. Blank for a moment.

Then, unbidden, an insane idea occurred to Charles. A kind of mad, torturous answer to his dilemma.

No. Not even worth thinking about.

Then, as he stood in their mirrored dining room, watching his multiple reflections—all of them looking faintly wild and needy—the unholy thought rose up, fully formed, into consciousness. He considered it, threw it out again, then the idea crept back into his mind and insisted upon serious consideration.

Her pasha could return and take his own measure. He could even *be* a miserable son of a bitch, make *her* give *him* the heave-ho, fix her wounded feelings and get rid of the fellow in one fell swoop.

While leaving Charles Harcourt the hero, standing alone center stage in Louise's life.

No. God, no, he told himself. What an idiotic notion.

The logistics themselves were impossible. He couldn't just walk in his own front door and pretend to be someone else. The idea was unworkable, not to mention devious—beyond the pale of any "heroic and handsome heart."

But what if . . . What if her pasha returned to behave more in keeping with his original purposes: like the game-playing, inconsiderate bastard Charles knew perfectly well how to be? Then a worse what-if appeared from nowhere, catching him off-guard.

What if Louise's demand to see her pasha meant

she was not finished with her affair after all? What if her pasha behaved like a bastard, and she liked it—just as she had before?

It was the original question that had started this mess in the first place. Would the highly desirable Louise Vandermeer Harcourt do what she could do so easily, at any moment she chose: make a cuckold of her ugly, lately-fumbling husband?

"Charles?" Louise's voice said. "What has gotten into you? Are you all right?"

He blinked, then set his folded newspaper down on the credenza. "Certainly," he told her. "I'm fine." He looked around for his coat. "I'm, ah—" He found it. "I'll just go into town and wire the fellow, shall I?"

"What?"

He glanced at her, at the strange choke in her voice. Louise was staring at him over a half-eaten apple held in her hand.

He smiled. "Old Al Baghdad," he explained. "I'll just wire him and see if he'll come, all right?"

Where was the man who wanted directness? Louise wanted to know. Who wanted her to *choose* him, come at him *headlong?* And how did one choose someone who made of himself a multiple, moving target? Where was her husband going in such a hurry? Not to the telegraph office, that much was for sure. Where was his crooked line of reasoning taking him now?

Were she and this circuitous man in love? Or were they merely entangled?

Louise would not have been able to imagine a snarl as large as Charles had woven for them, if she hadn't been an unknowing—then suddenly very knowing—party to it for the past six weeks. Impossible, yet here it was:

Her pasha's deep, rich voice, speaking perfect French, wondered where in the blazes he'd left his hat. Louise followed Charles through the house as he searched. He had no limp. None whatsoever. Or perhaps only the faintest one that he could control, she had realized, if he walked carefully—which he always did in front of her.

Be yourself, indeed. That's what he had told her in the dark, but apparently it was advice he didn't follow himself.

"The newel post," she said. "On the newel post."

Louise got there ahead of him and handed Charles his hat from off the fat knob where he'd set it on their way upstairs last night. Dear man, sweet man. He had been fairly shattered when he had come into her room, then been allowed to stay. He had had none of his normal composure or savoir faire. And it had been wonderful. Perhaps less thrilling in her body, but deeply, deeply pleasing in her heart. She might have been happy, if she weren't still waiting for him to tell her the full truth.

And now. What was this? He was going to send himself a telegram?

There had been much to forgive, but she had done it. No small feat for the cool and exacting Louise Harcourt.

All she needed now was for him to be honest. *Tell me, Charles. Reveal yourself. Put yourself in my power. Tell me. Tell me all about this stupid idiocy you have devised.*

But, no, he took the hat she offered. She frowned. She had been sure that, after last night and with a little bit of prodding today, he would spill everything.

He kissed her instead. A nice kiss. He pulled her up into his arms and pressed his mouth on hers, just like her pasha might have. A big, wet, suave kiss. To which her husband even managed a smooth end, then a neat, unlimping exit. With her pasha's poise.

Oh, there was no doubt. It was wonderful to look upon him at last; it was also vaguely horrid.

The wet taste of his mouth, left on hers, reminded her of earlier actions and motives. This man, without a doubt, had nurtured all the shallow designs on her that she had credited to his ocean self. He'd set her up as a dupe. He'd hurt her, though perhaps not so intentionally. And, worse, he knew everything. All the things she'd volunteered about herself, all that she and her parents had tried to keep from the prince, the prince had heard from her own mouth.

Naked. Naked twice. Once on the ship. And once here on the beach, telling her husband in odd reverse all her secrets about his *other* self.

"Oh, Charles," she murmured as she watched him leave. "You'd better not be setting up more of your plots and schemes. For, if you are . . ." If he was, well, it boded very badly for their present, their future.

Louise shook her head. "You must come clean," she murmured.

And she meant it. If that's what he was doing, if this "telegraphing" was yet another knot added, then his tangle was endless.

Everything condensed down to this: *If you can't stop yourself, if you can't get hold of yourself . . .* as she had told him to before, *If you can't speak your mind to me, if you can't show yourself, put yourself in my hands . . . Oh, Charles, then I will ever be able to get hold of the whole man?*

And she wouldn't even try.

Louise promised herself that if Charles went further into this charade, if all the prodding and waiting meant nothing, then she would take herself and this baby home. Life was strange enough, hard enough. She would return to where large breakfasts of bacon and eggs were easier to come by—and where she wouldn't be left standing naked alone.

Chapter 27

~~~oOo~~~

*Recipe for spirit of ambergris: 1.5 oz of
ambergris, 30 grains of musk, and 20
grains of civet to powder in sugar loaf, to
which add the juice of one lime. Pour into
3 pints of pure alcohol spirits and stopper
jar. Embed jar down into the constant
heat of horse manure for 21 days. The
liquid decanted will be clear: ambergris
tincture—the beginning of the best perfumes.*

Charles Harcourt, Prince d'Harcourt
On the Nature and Uses of Ambergris

Louise went to bed early that night. Like most
evenings, the baby made her so tired she could
barely stay awake through dinner. Thankful she knew
why at least she was so exhausted, she said good-night
to Charles. He kissed her lightly, preoccupiedly, and
promised to come along later, as was becoming his
practice. He simply didn't need to sleep as much as
she did.

So she was alone when she heard the noise outside,
only half awake. She could not identify the sound

367

exactly. When she got up to see what it was, *voilà*—
there was suddenly a man on her balcony. She leaped
back, exclaimed something, then was not allowed to
get a full scream out before she was pushed into her
room with force, a hand over her mouth, and a lot of
shushing.

"Sh-sh-sh-sh. He'll hear you." English. A British-
educated whisper with a slight foreign accent under
it—an undertone she knew immediately to be
French, not Arabic.

"Ch-Charles?" Even knowing whom she spoke to,
Louise could not quite believe it. The robe, the
headdress, the shadow in the dimness— Charles's
errand in town. And a suddenly familiar shadow in
the dark that made her giddy.

She wanted to laugh. She wanted to throw him back
over the balcony from whence he had come.

"How did you get up here?" she asked. A man with
one eye—no depth perception—and a bad leg had no
business climbing up trees or across vines or however
he'd gotten here. A sane man would have developed
by now a healthy fear of heights.

Which, come to think of it, he had. Louise blinked.
Her Charles of the ship wouldn't leap over railings
when other options were present. So stupid, Louise
thought. *I am so stupid.* How had she missed this?

"Charles," she said. As if repeating his name were
going to call him out into the open.

It didn't, of course, because she—*she*—had woven
this particular circle into their mess through *her*
devious thinking. More and more idiotic, she felt.

But she couldn't stop saying it. "Charles, it's you!"

"Of course, it is. Your half-blind husband said
that—"

"Oh, stop! Don't do this!"

He tried to take hold of her.

She took hold of him, two fistfuls of robe, one
containing a piece of shoulder, the other an upper

arm. She tried to shake a man as heavy and immovable as stone. She said, "Tell me."

"I am telling you." Additional stupidity—of a more dismaying nature—flew in her face. "You wanted an affair, because your husband was ugly. He's still ugly. Do you still want one?"

"Charles—"

"And my name in Alain—"

"Stop it, stop it, stop it!" She tried to pound, to shove, but he caught her arms. Almost pleading, she told him, "You have started to tell me a dozen times"—this was true, she realized—"do it now, without that little, dancing sidestep at the end, when my reactions aren't perfectly k-k—" *Kind,* she was trying to say.

And Louise let go and ran for the light across the room.

She hit it before he even knew what was happening.

Charles, all of him, his swirling, be-robed self burst into visibility, squinting at her with his one bad eye. "Louise," he said.

She turned away. "Oh." Unable to look. Louise yanked open the nearest drawer in her bureau. She began to throw things out onto the bed. Underdrawers, handkerchiefs.

"What are you doing?" he asked.

"I'm leaving. I can't do this, Charles."

All he said in return though was, "You knew. You knew since before tonight."

She turned on him, defensive. "Yes, and that wasn't the point. I knew two nights ago when you made love to me. What I wanted was for you to tell me. I wanted you to *choose* to tell me—"

"I tried—"

"You didn't. You were always waiting for the perfect moment. I wanted you to come at me headlong, like you talked about. I liked that idea. I wanted to try it."

He groaned slightly, then murmured, "I'm sorry."

But it was to her back. Louise yanked a bag from
the floor of her wardrobe, stuffed it full of undergarments,
then buckled the bag tight. Tucking it up under
her arm, dressed in her nightgown, she carried it and
herself out of the room.

"Where are you going?" he asked, following, sailing
behind her in his Arab dress. "Montreal?"

She walked faster, down the hallway. "No. I'm
going to my parents, then back home."

Charles thought, perhaps, if he tried now. He
switched to French, and apparently the sound of his
voice in this language was enough to give her pause.
She hesitated at the top of the stairs.

He said, "I didn't mean to hurt you. I often thought
that what I was doing was going to spare you."
Honestly, he added, "I mean, once my original idiocy
was a fait accompli and there was no turning back. To
keep it up, Louise, cost me, oh—" There weren't
words. Just the memory of so much frustration, he
couldn't express it.

She looked at him for a long moment, then simply
pointed out, "Twice, Charles? You felt so bad you did
it *twice?*" She began down the staircase.

"Now. Let me tell you now, Louise. Stop. I'll say
whatever you want me to say."

"It's too late."

Charles said, "No." He tried to keep up, but his
knee hurt from the climb up onto her balcony. He
couldn't do it. He called to her, "I am committed in a
way even I don't understand fully. I just know I won't
leave, and you shouldn't either: no sneaking off the
gangplank of this ship. We should sail through together.
You *can* trust me, Louise. Just forgive me and let it
go. And I'll forgive you."

She turned on the landing midway down to glance
at him, clutching her insane bag of packed lingerie.
"Forgive me? For what?"

"You made me do it," he tried.

"*I* made you do all these stupid things?" she demanded. "That is the most childish, irresponsible nonsense I have ever heard in my life. I'm leaving." She all but ran down the last steps.

To the floor below, there were two runs of them with a landing between. With his leg hurt, there was no way he could get down them fast enough to catch her. He realized she was outrunning him, heading toward the front door.

She was about to escape. With her cleverness intact. No, goddamn it. Charles hesitated. He had no clear idea how far it was down. A lot of steps if he did the two turns of stairs. Three or four meters, the drop of one story. It seemed possible. He put his hands on the railing, leaning up onto them, then leaped, drawing his legs up, swinging them out to the side, and over.

He fell. And fell and fell. No clear idea where he was for a few seconds. Up in the air. Down on the floor. He landed, in the process twisting his good knee. He sprawled out onto his back, cracking his head, seeing stars, though he stayed conscious enough to think, *Oh, this was smart.*

But not that stupid, either, perhaps. Louise halted, the doorknob in her hand. "What have you done?" she said tightly. She pursed her mouth, scowled. Then came over to him. She repeated, "What have you done?"

From the floor he looked up at her, her face bent over him. "I've been a little headlong, I think."

Her eyebrows went up, her tone slightly reprimanding. "Headlong?" she said.

"It seemed possible." He looked down at himself, perplexed, miffed. "I just didn't think the floor was coming up so quickly. A little miscalculation."

"Are you hurt?" She squatted down, still angry but not leaving.

Not that big a miscalculation either, he thought. He grinned, then groaned for the first time. "No-o-o. I am destroyed. Overwrought. Ruined." He made a face.

"My leg is probably broken. You have to be nice, Louise. You have to say everything is all right, forgive me, then move on."

"You are despicable."

"You are as guilty as I."

"I am not! I didn't start a mean, complicated charade on you before we had even been introduced—"

"No, you decided to have someone else. If you hadn't been fooling around on that ship—"

They both talked at once.

"I was fooling with you—"

"—with that bloody lieutenant—"

"I didn't know you. I was looking for you—"

"I was angry with you for standing with him in the dark. I wanted you to wait—"

"I didn't know to wait for you—"

"—to respect me and what I was offering you—"

"Respect is something you earn. I didn't know you deserved it."

"You insulted me—"

"I thought you were ugly." She took a breath. "And that I was—"

"I am." He stopped. "You? You think you're ugly?"

"Well, yes. Sometimes. In the way I behave—"

Louise stopped. She blinked then said, "My parents do this."

"Do what?"

"Talk at the same time, while no one else can make heads or tails of their conversation." She laughed. "I always thought it was—sweet. I was jealous." Louise fell over onto her bottom, then let herself fall straight back, sprawled out beside him. "It's awful!" Awful or not, she laughed.

Charles caught her humor, laughing at whatever she was laughing at; he wasn't sure. They both lay there, inexplicably cheerful on the entry room floor. Then she shrieked, "Sweet!" Her laughter became deep, a drum roll of mirth. Hardly able to contain it, she

turned her face toward him. "My God, I've been
sweet." Still laughing, "In a kind of backward way.
What do you think of that?"

He caught her hand. "I think this is the moment.
Run at me, Louise. I want to take a run at you." After
a pause he added very, very quietly, "You see, I love
you."

Silence.

Then he pulled her onto him, dug his fingers into
her hair against her skull and kissed her.

Louise kissed him back, catching and halting her
breath in a kind of leapfrog of pant-and-gasp down
her nose. He remembered. He smelled her—ah, the
coup de grace: her smell up close in the dark beyond
any perfume, beneath it, over it: wholesome, fresh,
sweet, green, like morning milk, fresh from the mead-
ow, warm in the bucket, rich, the cream so dense you
could scoop it off the top with a finger.

He caught her mouth in his, then followed her
mouth each time she turned, kissing and re-kissing
her. So eager. So genuinely happy to hold her. It
became difficult to get a word out. Though she still
seemed to be trying to say something. Something
about wanting the privacy of upstairs. With the lights
on.

Yes, indeed. With every light in the bedroom blaz-
ing: That's how he closed the door, in a kind of haze
of backward staggers, a dance against it as he pushed
on their modern lighting. Then a drop—he pushed
her straight back, off-balance onto the bed—she was
flat on her back. She groaned when he slid up beside
her.

She rolled toward him and touched his face with
spread fingers and curved palm, fitting these against
his cheek. Then both her hands, sliding over his eyes,
his nose, feeling him like she had wanted to on the
ship.

"Are you sure you are in one piece?" she asked.

"No." He rolled over on top of her, then rolled again, taking her with him till she was on top. He said, "How to you feel about this position?"

"Position for what?"

He said, "And the wall. I am really good at walls, did I ever mention? And chairs. You really ought to get to know me on chairs."

"Chairs?" Louise looked down narrowly into his face. "Oh," she said, then blushed. Deep, deep red, even as she pulled her mouth taut. "Walls I think I knew about. Now, listen to me, Charles—don't think, just because I didn't leave you downstairs on the floor, that everything is all right."

"Everything will never be all right, Louise." He mugged a face. "Like they say, it's always something. But, dear one, precious, sweetness, may I tell you: All my roads lead to you, no matter how crooked. And all your roads lead to me. Stay. Stop your traveling, Louise." He blew gently into her face, making her close her eyes, turn, arch slightly. He said, "Let me blow cool air on all the stings inside you." Then he pressed her head down, turning it to him, and blew into her mouth.

And there in her husband's feather bed, deep inside a nest of down, Louise took some initiative. She peeled off Charles's suspenders, then shirt. She rubbed her closed eyes then her cheek, her lips on the hair, the skin of his chest. She and Charles exchanged services. He undid the back of her dress and folded it off her shoulders. He looked at her, touching what he saw. Silly man, at one point he pressed his nose to her bare belly and sniffed her loudly in circles that tickled.

"Mmm," he said. He stood beside the bed to take off the last of his own clothes, then when his underdrawers dropped, he rose naked. A spectacle before her eyes.

"Oh," she murmured. "Oh, Charles, you are so fine. So divinely well-made and male." He was Hercules unchained. Priapus. She said what she told him once before: "You're beautiful."

He didn't seem to know what to say for a moment, but he knew what to do.

He climbed back into bed, finished the work of her clothes. Louise was faintly embarrassed at first, used to silks and feathers and fancy accessories to her appearance. He encouraged, "I've seen you already, remember? On the ship. Though you were blindfolded."

Yes, oh, yes. She put herself in his power. And ran at him headlong.

Author's Note

For years now, trade in ambergris has been banned worldwide by treaty and various national marine mammal protection acts. In the United States, it falls under the Marine Mammal Protection Act of 1972 and is illegal to import. The closest available scent today comes from the bee balm plant, which contains a large amount of the same chemical scent-substance, ambrein. The fragrance of ambergris is now more a matter of nostalgia which, for the sake of the sperm whale, certainly is best left to imagination and fiction.